Many, many thanks to my awesome critique partners, who are always quick to lend support and gently push me to be a better writer than I am. I'm so blessed to have these wonderful ladies. They welcomed me into their little family and made me feel that I truly have something to contribute. Our friendship and admiration for each other means the world to me. May each of us keep learning and growing and ever striving for the elusive golden ring as we travel this amazing path together. I love you all.

One

North Central Texas
Spring 1878

IT WAS STRANGE HOW A DAY COULD GO SOUTH quicker than a steam locomotive on a downhill slope.

Cooper Thorne drew his black hat farther down on his forehead and reflected on that fact as he rode across his ranch land, trying to recapture the good mood he'd enjoyed before his morning turned into an unholy mess.

He kneed Rebel into a trot and navigated a small rise before reining the powerful buckskin to a halt to take in the breathtaking sunrise. This was his favorite vantage point from which to gaze out over the gently rolling hills that comprised the Long Odds Ranch.

Tall cliffs bordered the six hundred and forty acres on three sides. The only way to enter his spread was from the east. He felt safe here.

It had taken blood and sweat and dogged determination to get where he was. Fair to say he'd been through hell and come out the other side to claim this life for his own.

He rested his elbow on the saddle horn and took in the view.

This wild Texas land was his home. For the first time in his almost thirty years, he'd truly found a place to belong. It felt right, and his soul was at peace at last.

Or as much as it ever would be.

The rich black soil that could raise fine crops or prime cattle was now in his blood. It had put back together his broken dreams.

He'd chomped at the bit to get out and put his hands to work…until he got to breakfast. Mack Malone, the cook he'd hired a month ago, had burned the biscuits, charred the eggs, and mangled the flapjacks. Then his horse threw a shoe and Cooper had to round up the ranch blacksmith to put a new one on. And to make matters worse, one of his ranch hands up and quit with branding about to start. All before dawn. He needed this moment of peace before heading back to work.

Because heaven only knew what awaited him next…

෴

His middle brother, Rand Sinclair, sat cooling his heels on the porch when Cooper finally made it back to the house sometime that afternoon.

Rand's ever-present grin widened as he unwound his tall frame and got slowly to his feet. "Thought I'd have to send up smoke signals or get Brett to track you down or something. Figured you'd be coming in to get some vittles sooner or later, but I'd about decided maybe you'd packed up and moved on without telling anyone."

Cooper dismounted. "I do run a ranch, you know. Out here we work from can to cain't, unlike you. All you do is pour whiskey down drunks and watch their wives have a conniption."

"There's a lot more to it than that, and you darn well know it. I work hard to make a living."

"Reckon so. You eaten?"

"This an invite?"

"All you'll get."

"In that case, I can always eat."

"Don't I know it." Cooper led the way to the kitchen table.

Over a plateful of beans with chunks of ham and fried potatoes that were thankfully almost edible, Cooper turned to Rand. "What brings you all the way out here? Shouldn't you be in town lubricating those drunks and taking their money?"

Rand owned the Lily of the West in the nearby town of Battle Creek. Their younger brother, Brett Liberty, had acquired the Wild Horse Ranch, five miles as the crow flies from the Long Odds Ranch, though it was more like seven or eight if you traveled by road.

"They don't need me for that. It'll happen whether I'm there or not." A big grin stretched from ear to ear and devilment twinkled in Rand's blue eyes. He leaned back as though very satisfied with himself.

"What's got you in such a good mood?" Cooper sensed a shoe was about to drop. He didn't like dropping shoes. Or grinning brothers who knew something he didn't. "You look like a cat that just caught himself a big fat mouse."

"A woman arrived on the stage today. A mail-order bride. Claims you agreed to marry her."

Cooper's fork clattered to the table. "Of all the…! Whose idea of a sick joke is this?"

"Can't understand why you didn't see fit to tell Brett and me that you'd changed your mind about taking a wife," Rand teased. "You being head honcho of the Battle Creek Bachelors' Club and all."

"You know better than that. Wipe that grin off your face before I knock it off," Cooper growled.

Rand shrugged but kept grinning anyway. "Fact is, she stepped off the stage and was mighty put out that you weren't there waitin' to welcome her. I did what I could to help."

"I'll just bet."

His brother put his hand over his heart in mock horror. "You wound me."

"Yeah, well, whoever is behind these rotten shenanigans had best take warning and find a rock to crawl under. When I catch him, there'll be hell to pay. For all I know, this could be one of your harebrained stunts. You seem to think it's so all-fired hilarious."

The grin faded from Rand's face. "I wouldn't joke about anything as serious as this, Coop. After all these years, surely you believe that."

"Yeah, I don't reckon you'd be mixed up in some-thing like this. But someone sure the hell brought her here and put her up to this." Either that, or the woman had hatched the scheme all by herself. Maybe she was looking for some easy money and thought Cooper would pay her off to leave.

Well, the joke would be on her. Cooper had little money, easy or otherwise. What he got he turned around and put right back into the ranch. All except for the nest egg he'd put aside to buy the Zachary place that neighbored his property. He almost had enough saved, and then the better portion of the valley would be his.

Rand laid a hand on Cooper's shoulder. "Reckon only one thing to do. Come into town and straighten her out. Name's Miss Delta Dandridge. Came all the way from Georgia. Says she's not leaving till she talks to you. She took a room at Mabel's Boardinghouse—you can find her there."

If that wasn't just dandy! The day that had begun with such promise had certainly gone to hell in a handbasket fifteen ways from Sunday.

And who in the hell had a name like Delta?

"You tell that little conniver I'll be in town first thing in the morning," Cooper snapped. "I'll send her packing."

❧

Delta tried to still the tremor in her hands as she stepped onto the porch of Mabel's Boardinghouse. She breathed the crisp morning air.

Rancher looking for a wife. Must be of sound mind, body, and moral character. That's what the notice in the *Matrimonial Harvest* catalog had said. She'd upheld her end of the bargain and could attest with certainty to her exemplary mind, body, and character.

But the gentleman?

That Mr. Thorne hadn't seen fit to meet her stage yesterday still smarted. Alone, with only a stranger to guide her, she'd taken a room here at the boardinghouse rather than the dark, dreary hotel that had sent a sense of foreboding shivering up her spine.

Now she wasn't sure she was quite ready to meet the man who'd agreed to be her husband.

Yet, here he was, a few feet away.

Fortunately, the tall rancher had his back to her, which gave her the advantage of seeing him first.

"Mr. Thorne? Cooper Thorne?"

He turned and Delta's breath caught in her throat. *My goodness, he was quite impressive.* Tall and lean, there was a rugged quality about him from his chiseled features down to boots that had many miles on them. And a good deal of cow manure, if she wasn't mistaken. His dark gray shirt stretched tight across his broad shoulders, and the black Stetson that shaded his eyes had seen better days.

Yet it was the deadly Colt on his hip that gave her pause. He appeared a man to be reckoned with. Everything about him was hard and unyielding and put her in mind of someone who'd never known any kind of softness. For a moment, it took her aback. She wondered if she could please him.

"Miss Dandridge, I suppose." The deep timbre of his voice seemed to vibrate the air between them.

"Yes. I'm so happy to finally meet you." She smiled, covering the few steps with her hand extended.

He touched her palm for the briefest of seconds and cleared his throat. "There's been a terrible misunderstanding."

The wild beating of Delta's heart suddenly stopped, and for a moment she feared it wouldn't start again. "What are you saying?"

"I don't know how to break this to you gently. I'm not looking for a wife, ma'am. Never was. I'm a bachelor and quite content to stay this way. I'm not sure how such a mix-up could happen."

"So you never intended to keep your promise? You dragged me here under false pretenses. Why would you do that, Mr. Thorne?"

From under the brim of his hat, she glimpsed surprise and something indiscernible in an honest gaze that was the color of gunmetal.

"What I'm saying is…well, I didn't send for you."

White-hot anger swept over Delta. It was one thing to spurn her, but calling her a liar made her mad enough to fight. Yanking the packet of letters from her pocket, she thrust them into his hands.

"Then would you mind explaining these? If you can."

Cooper didn't spare them a glance. "Look, lady. I didn't write them. And if I ever find out who did, I'll make him rue the day he took it into his head to claim to be me."

"If you'll just read the letters, you'll see the promises, the words of endearment that brought me here."

A muscle in his jaw worked as he shook his head. "Once and for all, I'm sorry. I truly am."

"Maybe if you just gave yourself a chance to get to know me."

"I can't offer hope where there is none. I'm sure you're a very fine woman who'll make someone an excellent wife." Finality echoed in his soft words. "I'm not on the market."

Delta went very still. Slowly, her situation began to sink in. There would be no marriage. She was stuck in Battle Creek, Texas, with an empty purse and no prospects. She blinked back the tears that threatened to spill and humiliate her even further.

He continued, "Seems we've both been played for fools. I'll be glad to pay your way to wherever you want to go."

The last thread of Delta's dignity held fast. Her voice was cold and brittle. "You can keep your money, Mr. Thorne. I won't take one cent from you."

With that, she jerked the letters from his hand and strode into the boardinghouse with her head held high.

Two

SAFELY UPSTAIRS IN HER ROOM, DELTA SAT NUMBLY ON the edge of a bed that sagged on one end and bowed in the middle and let the tears flow. What was she going to do now? She couldn't go back to Cedartown. She couldn't ever go back. That bridge had burned. Her mother had died three months ago, although in truth she'd been dead long before that. Delta had no family, no friends, no place to belong.

She allowed despair to grip her for only a moment. Crying wouldn't solve a blasted thing. What was done was done. She would survive this latest blow somehow.

Wiping her eyes, she opened her small, frayed reticule. There was fourteen cents inside, which was every penny to her name.

What was she going to do? Shaking, she clung to what strength she had.

Battle Creek was her home now. Here she would stay. No one was going to run her out. Surely there was a job of some sort for a woman with willing hands. She'd look until she found one, even if she had to beg.

By the time noon arrived, she'd washed her face and

straightened her best dress—the one she had intended
to wear to the marriage ceremony—carefully arrang-
ing the folds over the tear she'd mended. Inhaling a
calming breath, she went downstairs. Mabel King had
fixed a simple lunch. Delta took a place at the empty
table, wondering where the other boarders were.

"Are you all right, my dear?" Mrs. King passed her
a bowl of savory vegetable soup. "I thought I heard
you crying."

"Please, don't you fret about me, Mrs. King. I'll be
just fine." Delta accepted a chunk of bread to go with
her soup. "Where is everyone?"

Last night the table had been almost full.

"I'd like it if you'd call me Mabel. I packed their
lunches this morning. They eat where they work."

"Speaking of that, would you know of any jobs
around here for an enterprising woman who's down
on her luck?"

"Why, yes, maybe I do. Mr. John Abercrombie
mentioned that he's hard-pressed to handle the mercantile by himself. His wife died a few months ago.
She ran that business mostly by herself. John doesn't
know how to make a go of the store without Nell."

Flickers of hope rose. Delta wiped her mouth with
her napkin. "Then I intend to pay him a visit."

"One thing I should tell you. John…well, John is
a hard man to get to know. And since Nell died, he's
gotten worse. Just don't let him scare you."

Like old dogs, Delta supposed. If they sensed
fear, they went for the throat. What could very well
be the only job in town called for someone with
steely resolve.

Yet she doubted she had any choice. Besides, she could always throw John Abercrombie a bone. Or growl back.

Less than an hour later, she strolled toward the mercantile, her heels striking the sidewalk with determination. At the precise moment she passed the saloon, Cooper Thorne stepped out and into her path.

Surprise rippled across his face when he noticed her. It was obvious that he hadn't planned to run into her. But she had to give the man credit—instead of turning away, as she fully expected, he tapped the brim of his hat and gave her a half smile, though it appeared to be with considerable effort.

"Miss Dandridge." His voice was whiskey-roughened and unapologetic.

Delta raised her chin a trifle and glared. "Mr. Thorne."

Stepping smartly around him, she continued on her way with her head held high. She should probably thank her lucky stars that she hadn't wed him. It appeared the man had a drinking problem. Swilling whiskey in the middle of the day was a sign of a serious character deficiency.

Why, he'd likely beat a wife if he ever were to take one.

Putting him out of her mind, she entered the dim interior of a mercantile that was narrow across but extended a good ways back. It had only one window to the left of the doorway. As dim as the store was by the window, she could only imagine how dark it was at the rear.

Squaring her shoulders, she approached a thin man behind the counter whose skin was stretched tightly over the bones of his face. "I'm looking for Mr. Abercrombie."

"What for?"

If Mabel hadn't warned her of his surly nature, she'd have raced from the store. "Would you be Mr. John Abercrombie?"

"So what if I am?"

Taking a deep breath to steady her nerves, she prayed for patience. "Mrs. King over at the boarding-house told me about your predicament. My deepest sympathies for your loss. I think we might be useful to each other, sir."

"Whatever you're peddling, I don't need. Take it somewhere else. Just get on out of here and leave me be."

"I wish I could. I truly do," she said softly. "But the fact is, I desperately need a job. And it looks like you're in great need of someone to help you."

John Abercrombie braced his hands on a nicked and scarred wooden counter. "How would you know what I need? You ever work in a place like this?"

She glanced at the grimy window that barely allowed a sliver of light through and an overturned barrel with mice nibbling on the crackers inside. Everything was disheveled and dirty. And sad. If buildings had hearts, this one would surely be broken.

"No, sir. I never have."

"How do I know you can do the job, then?" he snapped.

"Hire me on a trial basis. If I haven't made a differ-ence and increased your sales in two weeks, I'll gladly go on my way. You won't even have to fire me."

"Can't pay you much," Abercrombie said stubbornly.

"All I ask is enough to pay Mrs. King for my room and board. Then as the store makes more money, we'll discuss the terms of my employment again."

"Don't expect any favors from me."

No, she wouldn't. She'd never expected favors from anyone. No need to start now.

⁂

Cooper's gaze narrowed as he stared at the mercantile. He wondered why Delta Dandridge would decide to go there when she should be buying a ticket for the next stage. Probably needed a button or some thread or whatnot. The things a woman could get in her head to do—a man never could figure them out.

Thank goodness he didn't even have to try. He'd set her straight, and that was the important thing.

He had to admit the lady sure was a looker, had curves in all the right places and the sort of walk that made single, bachelor-type men think of things that would land them in a heap of trouble. He'd nearly drowned in eyes that reminded him of moss at the bottom of a clear, gleaming pool. Instead of hair that glistened in the sun like a shiny gold piece, though, she should've been a redhead, with that hot temper of hers.

That Southern drawl as soft as melted butter did certain things to him.

Yes, her drawl and the dark beauty mark on the right side beneath her mouth had driven him to distraction.

Fair to say he hadn't been prepared for someone so pretty. He'd expected her to be…well, homely. And desperate.

Though she'd tried to hide the sudden tears from him, he'd seen the wet shimmer in her eyes. That part had nearly done him in. Women's tears never failed to turn his heart to mush. Not that she was the kind to give in to tears often, he suspected. The lady seemed to have more grit and steel than most men.

But he'd meant what he said. He was a bachelor and he'd stay a bachelor. The sooner she got that through her head, the better off they'd be. He supposed she'd leave town on tomorrow's stage and go back to Georgia. He doubted he'd ever see her again. No use getting maudlin over her. She'd be fine.

The fact that she'd been duped same as he had been was crystal clear. She'd believed every word in those letters someone sent her. If he ever found out who'd played the cruel trick, he'd pound them into the street and drive a wagon over them.

It occurred to him that whoever did it would want to see how the fruits of their labor played out. He scanned both sides of the street for someone who might show undue interest. But everyone seemed to be going about their business, not giving him a second glance.

But secrets didn't stay buried—he just had to be patient and keep his eyes and ears open.

At that moment a boy he'd befriended some years ago, Ben Barclay, skidded to a halt in front of him. "Hi, Mr. Cooper."

"Ben, how are you doing these days?"

"Lost another tooth." The boy's copper hair flamed under the sun's rays. Ben grinned and Cooper could see the gaping hole in the middle of his teeth.

"You sure did. Did you pull it yourself?"

"Nope. Mama did."

"How's your mama?"

Ben shrugged, staring up at him. "Fine, I reckon. Just wonderin' when I could come out to the ranch."

"Anytime would suit me. Gonna start roundup next week, though, and I'll be busier than a one-armed blacksmith. Might be better to wait until after that." Cooper fished in his vest pocket for a small sack of lemon drops he always carried. He took one out and handed the rest to the seven-year-old.

"Thanks, Mr. Cooper."

"Your father behaving himself?"

Ben's face darkened and he shrugged again. "Guess so."

Cooper popped the lemon drop in his mouth. The boy's answer fell short of being reassuring. Something was up. Hogue Barclay must be back in town. The man was as sorry as they come. Stuck around long enough to make misery for everyone, and then he was gone again. And to make matters worse, the man had a mean streak as wide as the floodwaters of the mighty Mississippi.

Cooper draped an arm around Ben's scrawny shoulders. "Just remember what I told you. Anytime you or your mama needs me, I'll be there."

The boy had been a babe in his mother's arms when Cooper rode into town with Rand and Brett. Right off, he'd recognized Jenny's look of pure desperation and decided then and there to watch over them. He could count on one hand the number of people he truly cared about. But for those he did, it went bone deep. Jenny and Ben stood next to his brothers in that way.

Every time Jenny's husband, Hogue Barclay, got a snoot full of liquor, he beat Jenny something fierce. Six months ago, Cooper had threatened Hogue with sure death if he ever did anything like that again. He might need to reinforce that threat soon.

"Ain't gonna forget, Mr. Cooper."

Ruffling the top of Ben's head, Cooper turned toward his horse. "It was real nice seeing you. Watch out that you don't get too snaggletoothed."

"Bye, Mr. Cooper."

He stuck a boot in the stirrup and slid into the saddle. Though the ranch lay in the opposite direction, he found himself heading to the mercantile. Dismounting in front of the establishment, he loosely wrapped the reins around the hitching post.

"Need to pick up a few things," he told his horse as if he owed the animal an explanation.

What things, he hadn't a clue, but he'd think of some.

Cooper sidled up next to the window and tried to peer inside. But seeing as how they could've added an extra street to the town with the dirt on the window, he couldn't make out a blessed thing.

Damn. All he needed was for Miss Dandridge to see his face pressed against the glass like some three-year-old.

Taking a deep breath, he strode to the door and turned the knob. Delta swung around when he pushed it open and stepped inside. Her eyes narrowed to slits and she pursed her lips.

"What do you need, Coop?" John Abercrombie came from around the counter.

The question caught him off guard. He'd figured to walk around the store and hopefully hear what the two were discussing. No such luck.

He quickly scanned the shelves behind the counter. "Bullets. Four boxes."

A man could never have too many bullets. But four boxes could start a war.

"You figuring on doing a lot of shootin'?"

"Never can tell on a ranch. Want to be prepared."

Abercrombie gave a quick nod. "That all?"

"And…some chewing tobacco." Of all the stupid things to say. Hell. He didn't even use the stuff. Coming into the mercantile had been one of the dumbest ideas he'd had.

"I never knew you to use tobacco, Coop."

"Getting it for one of my ranch hands." He avoided meeting Delta's gaze and paid for his purchases. Taking them, he got the hell out of there before he did anything else stupid.

Before he could unloop the reins from the hitching post, Delta Dandridge strode from the mercantile and marched right up to him.

"I do declare, Mr. Thorne," she said in that sweet Southern drawl that flowed out smoother than warmed molasses. "Not that it's a bit of your concern, but if you're curious about what I'm doing, just ask me."

"Lady, don't flatter yourself. I went in there because I needed to and for no other reason."

"Bullets and chewing tobacco? That was a pretty flimsy excuse."

A hot flush crept up the back of his neck. "Around

here, Miss Dandridge, we step pretty carefully over piles of manure or else we wind up facedown in them."

Delta sucked in a quick breath. "Are you threatening me, Mr. Thorne?"

"Nope. Just stating facts, ma'am." He mounted up and tipped his hat. "Have a pleasant trip back to Georgia, Miss Dandridge."

Three

Turmoil churned inside him, whipping the contents of Cooper's stomach into a froth as he headed for the Long Odds Ranch. The nerve of that husband-hungry woman. Why, she'd almost come right out and called him a liar to his face.

A darkening in the sky off to the west caught his attention. His eyes narrowed. A whole flock of buzzards circled above something on the ground.

Alarm rested low in his gut. *Maybe a dead coyote or wolf.*

Or at least he hoped it was.

The saddle leather creaked as he straightened. "Guess we'd best go see about it, Rebel."

The horse whinnied softly and nodded as though he'd understood every word and agreed.

When they reached the source of the feeding frenzy, the sight curdled his blood.

A cow lay on the ground. The degree of bloating told him it had been dead for a day or so. He couldn't see the brand to know if it was one of his or not, but he assumed it was. He threw a long leg over the saddle and dismounted for a closer look. Then his attention shifted to a half-dozen cows nearby. They swayed on their feet and had thick foaming saliva hanging from their mouths.

Those definitely wore his brand.

Cooper didn't know what it was, but something told him it was more serious than anything he'd ever dealt with.

There was precious little time to waste. He mounted Rebel and spurred him to a gallop. Gathering his three remaining ranch hands, he returned to face the unknown threat.

"What do you think it is?" he asked Zeke O'Grady. The grizzled old man had been the first hand Cooper had hired. Despite Zeke's advancing age, there wasn't anything about cattle ranching the man didn't know. And that made him invaluable.

"Deadly hoof-and-mouth disease. Ain't seen nothing like this for thirty-odd years." Zeke ran a hand across his bristly jaw. "Back in forty-four, to be exact. I rode for the Thornhill brand then. We lost half the herd before you could whistle 'Dixie.' Thornhill came near to losing his ranch. It was bad stuff."

Cooper sucked in a deep breath. To lose the Long Odds…well, they might as well dig a hole and shove him in. This ranch represented all that he was, all that he wanted to be. It was his one chance to come into his own and prove something to himself.

"What can we do?" He lifted his hat and shoved his fingers through his hair, trying to ignore the fear squeezing his heart.

"Gotta get the healthy livestock separated from the

sick ones, an' fast. It's a goldarned good thing you noticed this when you did, Coop."

"Is that all we can do?"

"Afraid so. Besides a powerful lot of prayin'."

After separating and driving the healthy cows into a pasture near the house where he and his men could keep a close watch on them for further signs of the disease, they returned and shot the sick ones and burned their carcasses. With luck, they wouldn't lose too many of the herd.

He wondered how in the hell they'd come in contact with the disease. He'd owned these cattle for five years and never had anything like this. Hoof-and-mouth disease didn't originate from the soil like other diseases. Other cattle brought it, and from what Zeke said, it was extremely contagious. That was the part that perplexed Cooper, because he hadn't bought any new cattle.

He'd had a plan from the first day of how best to grow his herd and stuck with it. He always kept his bloodline clean and only sold cows when he needed money to stay afloat or to prevent overgrazing. In five years, he'd doubled the number to over five hundred.

So why this disease and why now? If only he had checked the brand on the initial dead cow before he set it ablaze. Maybe it hadn't belonged to him. Maybe it had wandered onto his land.

Or maybe someone had deliberately run a sick cow onto the Long Odds. No, it couldn't be that. He didn't have any enemies.

Though didn't he, what with someone forging his name and writing letters to the lovely Delta

Dandridge? Maybe it was the same damn person. Awful strange that both things happened on the exact dadgum day.

He took off his hat and shoved a hand through his dark hair, racking his brain for the name of someone who might want to both embarrass and destroy him.

There had only been one man who fit the category, but Cooper had killed the sorry no-good jackal. Tolbert Early hadn't given him any choice.

The memory of that day still haunted Cooper. The night he shot Early he'd become his father's son, the thing he'd sworn he'd never be. Now the die was cast and he couldn't change it. He cursed and jammed his hat back on his head.

"We got a lot of work to do. Might as well get to it," he said to his faithful buckskin. "No use wastin' time."

Or fretting about the past.

The remainder of the day, the men feverishly worked to inspect as many of the herd as possible. Before Cooper knew it, the sun glowed a fiery red ball low on the horizon.

Thank God, they hadn't found any more sick cattle.

Cooper turned to his men. "Let's call it a day and head to the house."

"Now, that's a right good idea," Zeke agreed.

Again, Rand was waiting for them on the porch. It didn't take long to discover the reason—seemed he was busting a gut to find out what had happened between Cooper and the lady Dandridge. Snoop that his brother was.

"I've got far more serious worries than a woman who's trying to leg-shackle me." Cooper told him about the disease infecting his herd. "It'll be a miracle if I don't lose everything I've worked for."

"You think it's deliberate?"

"Not saying that. Not ruling anything out, though. But it had to either be a sick cow wandering onto Long Odds land or someone dumping it into the midst of my cattle."

"Pays to keep an open mind," Rand agreed. "Anyone have a grudge against you?"

"Only one."

Rand nodded. "Tolbert Early."

"Yep. And he's dead, so that leaves me at zero."

"I'll keep my ears open at the saloon. If I hear of anything, I'll holler."

"Appreciate it, Rand."

"One of us has trouble, we all have it." Rand laid a hand on Cooper's shoulder. "We'll figure this out. You're not in it alone. Brett and I have your back."

Cooper gazed at the distant horizon as though, if he tried hard enough, he could see the trouble that rode toward him. The only thing was, trouble usually snuck up on a man from behind when he least expected it.

A deep sigh filled the night air. "Have you taken to chewing tobacco, Rand?"

Four

DELTA ARRIVED AT ABERCROMBIE'S MERCANTILE EARLY
the next morning, ready to work.

John Abercrombie stared in icy silence as she set
down the lunch bucket Mrs. King had made for her
and briskly pulled an apron over her head. After several long seconds, he spoke. "Frankly, didn't expect to
see hide nor hair of you."

"One thing you should know about me, sir, is
I keep my word. We have a bargain. Now, where
would you like me to start?"

"Don't much matter, I reckon. Just know that I
expect a full day's work from you. No lollygagging
around. You won't find this an easy job, Miss…"

"Dandridge. Delta Dandridge." No, she was under
no pretense that it would be a picnic working for the
man. She already feared he could be a hard taskmaster.
But as long as he paid her the wages due, she could
ignore his sour disposition. Having lost her mother,
first to despair, then to death, she knew the power
grief had on a person. She would show Abercrombie
nothing but kindness.

The man's frown deepened. "That's a rather odd name."

"I suppose, sir. If you have no objections, then I'll start by cleaning the window." Then maybe she could get a better idea of what she was dealing with. She didn't work well in the dark.

Getting a bucket of soapy water and a rag, she set to work. It took repeated washings, inside and out, to remove the thick layers of grime. Having a clean window made all the difference in the world. Bright, glorious sunlight streamed in. It was then she saw exactly how much work lay ahead of her.

Delta had just put the cleaning supplies away when the first customer walked in, a good two hours since Abercrombie had opened the store. His business was not brisk, to say the least. But she meant to change all that.

The elderly woman hobbled in on a rickety cane. A large goiter hung from her throat. "Praise the Lord, I can see where I'm walking," she exclaimed. "The last time I was in here, I fell and came near to breaking my leg."

"I'm sorry to hear that, ma'am. May I help you?" Delta put on a bright, welcoming smile.

The patron dragged her attention from the clean window. She appeared dumbstruck at Delta standing there. "Oh, do you work here?"

"I do indeed. I just started this morning."

"Never thought John would hire anyone. A government mule doesn't have anything on that man. Never saw a more god-awful stubborn cuss." The woman leaned closer to Delta and whispered,

"Don't let him run you off. He just forgot how to smile."

The old lady spoke the truth on all counts.

"What can I assist you with, ma'am?"

But the woman was in no hurry. She took a pair of spectacles from her pocket and put them on. Her eyes looked huge through the thick lenses. She gave Delta a long stare. "You're a right pretty little thing. I 'spect you'll have all the single men in this town ogling you. All except Cooper Thorne and his brothers. Don't hold your breath there. They've got this crazy fool notion that they're happy being bachelors."

The old lady appeared to know the way they sat in their saddle, Delta thought wryly, recalling her almost-groom's firm avowal to never marry.

"Cooper and his brothers formed the Battle Creek Bachelors' Club, you know," the woman expounded.

A club? Of all the silly notions. Did they truly need to band together to keep some female from slipping a rope around one of them and dragging him kicking and screaming to the altar? Their efforts to cling to independence seemed a bit desperate.

Bachelors' club, indeed!

The woman leaned close and peered up into Delta's face as if she'd just noticed her. "I don't think I've met you. You're new here, aren't you?"

"Yes, ma'am. I'm Delta Dandridge."

"Pretty name. I'm Granny Ketchum, but everyone just calls me Granny. What brings you to Battle Creek, dear?"

Heat inched up Delta's neck. She wondered what would happen if word got out that she was a mail-order bride and the intended groom had spurned her before she even stepped off the stage. She'd die before she admitted any such thing.

"I'm just passing through. I like the town and decided to stay a while." Delta glanced up. John Abercrombie glared his disapproval. His stern, unyielding face became even harder. "Ma'am, what did you say you came in for? I'll be happy to help you find it."

"Oh, I clean forgot. I need a thimble. Someone came right into my house in broad daylight and stole mine. Can you believe anyone would be so bold? It's scandalous. Why, last week they came in and stole my poor cat."

"That's terrible. Did you tell the sheriff?"

Granny Ketchum drew herself up. "I certainly did. He didn't do a blooming thing about it, either."

Mr. Abercrombie came out from behind the counter. "Miss Dandridge, I don't pay you to air your lungs all day. You're here to work. If you can't do that, then you and I should part ways."

"Yes, sir."

"Oh, go blow a smoke ring, John. Leave the poor girl alone." Granny clutched Delta's arm to steady herself.

"Let's go find you that thimble, Granny." She led the old woman over to the display case and helped her select one.

A short while later, the woman hobbled out the door. Delta returned to her cleaning. She tackled the spilled cracker barrel next. Mice scurried into other parts of the store as she uprighted it and swept up the crackers.

"Mr. Abercrombie, would you by chance have any mousetraps?"

With his lips still set in a thin straight line, he showed her where they were. He put her in mind of a buzzard, with his piercing gaze and hooked nose. The long conversation with Granny hadn't helped her tenuous situation with him. So when the noon hour came, she never mentioned lunch, working right on through it.

The rest of the day went by in a blur, but by the time Mr. Abercrombie locked up and called it a day, she'd managed to neatly restack the pile of blankets, straighten up the yard goods, clean the countertops, and sweep the floor. In between all that, she'd waited on the customers who came in.

One was a woman who wore a heavy black veil over her face. She'd introduced herself as Widow Sharp and bought baking supplies.

By quitting time, Delta was exhausted but proud of her efforts. As she blew out the oil lamps, she vowed to tackle them the following day. The globes were so filthy, the lamps put off little light. When the women saw how clean and inviting the store was, they'd be more eager to spend time and money in there.

She made her way to Mabel's, trod wearily up the stairs to her room, and collapsed on the bed. She'd close her eyes for only a moment.

The next thing she knew, Mabel was calling her to supper. She'd never meant to fall asleep. She couldn't remember being so tired. She got up and washed her face.

"How was your first day, dear?" Mabel passed a plate of meat loaf to Delta when she got down to the table.

She told Mabel and the full table of boarders about meeting Granny Ketchum and her wild tales.

"We should've warned you about Granny," Mabel said. "No one is stealing from her. She misplaces things and can't find them, is all. So she's convinced thieves break into her house."

Delta could understand a thimble or a cup. But a cat? How on earth could anyone lose a cat?

"She seems like a sweet old lady." Delta took a bite of meat loaf. "I'm sure she's very lonely."

"Oh, she is," Mabel agreed. "Pa Ketchum passed over several years ago and that's when Granny's forgetfulness got decidedly worse."

"We could tell you stories that would make your head spin," a fellow boarder, Charlie Winters, added. A silver deputy sheriff's badge stood out against the young man's black shirt. "Granny puts Sheriff Strayhorn through the wringer. Her complaints never end. Someone's always stealing something."

It could be the woman simply wanted some attention, to know someone cared. Delta suspected the same thing held true for Mr. Abercrombie. She couldn't fault them for that. Knowing you mattered even to one person was important. Delta knew the special kind of heartbreak that came from being invisible.

"Granny never had any children, and I think that added to her loneliness and grief." The words came from Violet Finch, another boarder. Her small frame and fidgety movements reminded Delta of a little brown wren. Violet worked at the milliner's and wore big hats that dwarfed her head.

For several long minutes, they ate in silence. Then

another boarder—Mr. Nat Rollins, the clerk at the hotel—cleared his throat, his large Adam's apple bobbing up and down. "Miss Dandridge, since you're new to town, I reckon folks have yet to tell you about Battle Creek's fame."

Delta wiped the corners of her mouth with her napkin. "What's that, Mr. Rollins?"

"We're...the town that is...the proud possessor of a piece of the opera singer Abigail Winehouse's shoe. You see, when she passed through here three years ago on her way to Austin, the heel of her shoe broke off when she stepped from the coach." Nat Rollins leaned forward with his elbows propped on the table. "We got it in safekeeping over at the Lexington Arms Hotel. You can stop by and take a gander at it any time you want to. Be happy to show it to you."

"I'll remember that, Mr. Rollins. Thank you."

Deputy Winters put down his fork. She grew uncomfortable under his piercing gaze. "Where did you say you were from, Miss Dandridge?"

"Georgia," she mumbled.

"A real Southern peach," Mabel said.

"Georgia's a big state. Where exactly?"

"Charlie Winters! That's none of your business." Mabel shot him a disapproving glance. "I'll not tolerate rudeness in my house."

"I didn't mean nothing by it. I apologize, Miss Dandridge. Sometimes I forget my manners."

If he ever had any to begin with. She wondered if he'd asked because he was a lawman or out of idle curiosity. She couldn't take the chance.

"That's quite all right, Deputy." Delta had lost her

appetite. If he were to telegraph Cedartown… She pushed back her chair. "Excuse me, but I've had a long day."

"Don't you want pie? I made peach. Most folks don't know Cooper Thorne has a small orchard on his ranch. He brought two bushels of peaches by last July and I canned them. These are all I had left. Some of the sweetest you'll ever eat."

"It's very tempting, Mabel, but I think I'll skip dessert."

Upstairs, Delta gazed out over the town from the corner window in her tiny room. Twilight bathed the people walking below and every building in dusky purple hues.

Battle Creek, Texas, was a strange place. She'd never seen one quite like it. For starters, it only had one of everything. One mercantile, one saloon, one barbershop, one newspaper, one boardinghouse, one livery, and so on and so forth. It was as if they had a policy against having two of anything in the town. Maybe they feared competition. Or maybe they simply had no energy left to bring in more.

The only thing they seemed to have two of was cemeteries. Not that you could rightly call the one planted smack in the middle of Main Street a cemetery. The more accurate term would be burial plot, since it held only four graves. Someone, probably the blacksmith, had built an iron fence around the section to protect it from being trampled. Otherwise, she suspected folks might drive their rigs right on top of it instead of going around. Whoever kept the weeds out deserved a medal—burial plots needed to be tended.

Mabel King had whispered to her over breakfast that no one even knew the names of the people buried there, as though it was something scandalous she couldn't bear to speak aloud. She said folks had bickered for years over what to do with it. Some wanted to dig the bodies up and rebury them in the Battle Creek Cemetery, at the edge of town. Others fought to keep them right where they were.

If the citizens wanted to cast out the dead inhabitants, what would they do to living ones? Delta's stomach churned and she fought down nausea.

Then, there was the overwhelming shabbiness of the rickety buildings. Most were well on their way to collapsing in on themselves, held up by a few nails, peeling paint, and abundant prayers. The buildings reminded her of ugly stepsisters that'd been left behind and forgotten while everyone else went to the dance.

It saddened her that these people clutched that opera singer's broken heel as their only claim to fame, and yet it deeply touched something inside her. Like this town, she was searching for her own reason for being.

A sense of excitement suddenly swept over her.

No one knew her here. Her secret was safe. So far.

Besides, this place could be no worse than what she'd faced in Cedartown. Less-than-savory recollections came unbidden. She closed her eyes against searing pain. She could start fresh, her life a clean slate. She'd take special care to fit in and not draw undue attention.

Her thoughts drifted to Cooper Thorne. Everywhere she turned, his name came up. People sang his praises as if he were a founding father or something. Maybe his family had settled the town. He appeared pretty vital to Battle Creek. She wanted to find out more about the man who gave peaches to a friend but refused to offer kindness to a newcomer searching for a place to belong.

Battle Creek Bachelors' Club, indeed!

Five

COOPER WOKE IN THE DARKNESS TO UNBIDDEN memories of Tolbert Early and the Steamboat Bathhouse in Hannibal, Missouri, sixteen years earlier. He'd been a scared boy of fourteen.

So much blood on his hands and clothes. Smoke from the gun in his hand clouding his vision.

He didn't think he'd ever get the stench out of his nostrils or block out the screams of his younger brother Brett that still echoed in his head. He doubted he'd ever forget the sight of his little brother standing there in the clutches of Tolbert Early, with his shirt ripped half-off, eye swelled shut, and blood oozing from his mouth.

And then Isaac Daffern discovered them hiding in the back of his wagon the night the boys ran for their lives. Best thing that could've happened. The kind rancher took them under his wing. If not for him, Cooper would probably have been tried for murder and possibly hanged. But Daffern gave them food and shelter and taught them how to be men. And when the old man died, he left them each four hundred dollars in his will.

Cooper wiped the sweat from his forehead and assured himself again that Tolbert Early was dead. He tried to go back to sleep but found it impossible.

By the time the first slivers of dawn peeked over the horizon, he was atop his favorite lookout spot, hoping to find the peace he sought. He thought about the long list of things to do before Monday rolled around, one of which was going into town for supplies.

Thank goodness he didn't have to worry about the maddening Miss Dandridge, because she'd likely left by now.

The first order of business—right after a quick breakfast—was riding over to talk to Brett. Cooper wanted to tell him about the disease and maybe get his thoughts. Possibly his help if it came to that.

Back at the ranch house, he gave Zeke the orders for the day and asked him to hitch up the wagon. Then he strapped on his Colt. Climbing into the wagon box, he set out across country for Wild Horse Ranch. He was proud of his little brother. Brett had one of the best horse ranches in several counties. He rounded up wild mustangs and broke them before selling them to the U.S. Army. His spread only measured a couple hundred acres, but he made every inch count.

Passing under the crossbar proclaiming the land as Wild Horse Ranch, Cooper headed to the far eastern corral, where a fair amount of dust rose. Sure enough, Brett stood in the middle as if he had not a care in world while a wild mustang ran circles around him, kicking and pawing the ground.

Cooper held his breath, sure that the horse would plow Brett down and leave nothing but blood and bone and past glory. The animal was majestic, no doubt about that, but the stallion had the eyes of a man-killer. That, too, was a true fact.

Setting the brake on the wagon, Cooper jumped down and took a ringside seat on the top rung of the corral to watch, ready to charge in and rescue Brett if needed.

Brett had a knack for this line of work. He seemed to know before the horse what it was going to do next. And Brett showed no fear. He spoke to the mustang in a gentle calming voice, no matter how near the animal came to running over him.

Finally, the mighty beast got tired of fighting the inevitable and came to a sudden stop. He stood there with his powerful muscles quivering and let Brett put a blanket on him. Brett put it on and took it off, repeating the action several times. Brett showed uncommon patience in getting the animal accustomed to the feel of something on his back.

Brett finally walked over. "Hey, Coop. What brings you out this way?"

"Got something to talk to you about. Besides, I haven't seen you in a coon's age."

Brett wiped the sweat from his forehead. "I'll let this stallion into the pasture and meet you at the house."

Cooper nodded. Minutes later, he pulled up at the "house," which consisted of a canvas-covered wagon. Brett cooked over an open fire and took his baths in the nearby creek. From all appearances, his brother was content, though.

Brett Liberty was as wild as those mustangs he tamed. He hadn't had an easy life and had the scars on his back to prove it. Everyone had picked on him in the orphanage, mostly because of his Indian heritage. With a white father and Indian mother, he'd had to endure being called a half-breed…and worse.

It was in that orphanage that a bond stronger than steel formed between the boys. They'd each nicked their thumbs and swore they were brothers in every sense of the word. Nothing had come between them and nothing would. They were the only family each other had, and it was more than enough.

Cooper had built a fire and had the coffee makings out by the time Brett joined him. Standing a good six feet, with broad shoulders, Brett got no shortage of female attention on the rare occasion he went into town. Not that he sought a speck of it. Like him and Rand, Brett was a confirmed bachelor and liked it that way.

Though his baby brother was tall, Cooper still beat him by a few inches and never let him forget it. He knew the fact that Brett and Rand had to look up to him stuck in their craw. But that's the way it should be, seeing as how Cooper was the oldest of the three. It seemed reasonable he'd have the most height. Besides, he'd needed it for all the fighting he'd had to do to protect them.

Brett removed his hat—which had an eagle's feather sticking from the band—and shook his long hair back. "Glad you came. I have need of your help."

"Doing what?" If Brett was going to ask him to go toe to toe with that mustang, Cooper would have to give that some serious thought.

"Putting up my tepee."

"A tepee?"

A wide grin covered Brett's face. "Every self-respecting Indian needs a tepee."

"Yep, I reckon so. It's a damn sight better than living in a wagon." Cooper squinted into the distance, wondering when Brett would finally find the peace he yearned for. "Any other ideas about what you think an Indian needs?"

"Plenty of wide open spaces, sweet grass, and cool water."

"Well, you've got all that. Shoot, Brett, you'll be chewing peyote and doing a war dance before I know it."

"It's time I remembered my heritage," Brett said quietly.

Cooper considered the fact that Brett was lucky, though his life had been far from easy. At least his little brother *had* a heritage that he could be proud to claim. Cooper thought about the different types of cloth he, Rand, and Brett had been cut from while they got a decent pot of coffee made and sat cross-legged on the ground to drink it.

"What did you come to talk about?" Brett finally asked.

"We have trouble over at the Long Odds." He told Brett about the hoof-and-mouth disease.

"I've heard of it but don't know a lot about it. Tell me how I can help."

Cooper filled him in and ended by warning him to be careful if he saw signs of it.

"Any thoughts on how it got in your herd?"

"Have some theories, but nothing solid."

Silence stretched as both men got lost in their own

thoughts. Cooper wanted to tell Brett that Tolbert Early had been strong on his mind. But he didn't. That night they'd left Missouri in the back of Daffern's wagon, they swore to never talk about what had happened. A lot of water had washed under that bridge, but not near enough.

Instead, Cooper told Brett about Delta Dandridge and how someone had played a dirty trick on them.

Brett threw back his head with a hoot of laughter. "A mail-order bride? I would've given five of my best horses to have seen your face."

"It wasn't all that funny. You can bet I wasn't laughing. Neither was the lady."

"Who do you think did it?"

Cooper shrugged. "I only know thirty people. Been racking my brain but haven't come up with anything yet. Don't suppose you'd have any ideas who the guilty party is? I accused Rand, since he's the jokester, but he swore he didn't have a hand in it. He seemed to take a little too much fun in it to my liking, though."

"It wasn't us, but I sure wish I'd thought of it. You, married?" Coffee spewed from Brett's mouth as laughter bubbled up again.

"Just don't get carried away, little brother. This is serious. I swear the woman has pointy mule ears beneath that mass of golden hair."

Brett finally sobered and wiped his eyes. "I'd like to meet her. Sounds like she's more than up to going toe to toe with you. But for now, you ready to get to work, Coop?"

Setting his tin cup on a rock, Cooper stood. "Might as well. That tepee isn't going to put itself up."

A little while later, after lots of sweat and a good deal of cussing, they stood back and surveyed their work. A lump formed in Cooper's throat. The tepee stood as tall and proud as the twenty-four-year-old who'd just claimed a piece of his heritage.

"Anything else you want me to help you with?"

Brett shook his dark head. "Nope."

"Then I reckon I'd best get my carcass into town for supplies and back to the ranch pronto. Can't afford to be gone for too long." Cooper clasped hands with his brother. "Watch out for shadows in the night and rotten varmints."

"You too."

Climbing into the wagon, he filled his lungs with fresh Texas air and turned toward town. If he expected to get anything done, he'd best be moving. The sun was fast crossing the blue, expansive sky.

For some odd reason, Delta Dandridge suddenly filled his thoughts. It didn't sit well that she'd refused to let him help with expenses. Stubborn pride for you. Despite all that, he was certain she'd boarded the stage and was probably well on her way back to Georgia by now.

Thank God.

Six

COOPER WAS THE KIND OF RANCHER WHO DOVE IN
right alongside his men. No standing idle.

Isaac Daffern had taught him that was the mark of a
good cattleman and the way to gain his men's respect,
so he wasn't afraid to get calluses on his hands. Or on
his butt, either, from long hours in the saddle.

On the ride into town, he thought of the disease
that had struck his herd. The only positive was that
he hadn't found any more sick ones. But he wouldn't
truly know until they rounded up all the cattle that
had spread to the far corners of the ranch.

Hope lodged in his chest that the disease would
vanish as quickly as it had appeared.

Battle Creek looked sleepy when he rode in, and
for a second, he almost thought he'd gotten the day
wrong. It seemed like a Sunday. But Abercrombie
wouldn't be open on the Lord's day. No, this had to
be Friday. Pulling the wagon to a stop in front of the
mercantile, he set the brake and climbed down.

His leather chaps slapped against his legs and his
spurs jangled in the quiet as he entered. He stared at

the changes. Everything was neat and tidy, and for once, he could actually see what he was looking for. That's when he noticed the sparkling window and the clean lamp globes.

"May I help you with something, sir?" The voice definitely *wasn't* John Abercrombie's.

Cooper turned and found himself staring into Miss Delta Dandridge's pretty green eyes.

Damn it to hell.

What the heck had she done with Abercrombie? It occurred to him that since she came to town looking for marriage, maybe she'd taken advantage of John's loneliness. After all, he was recently widowed. Maybe one man was as good as another in her way of thinking. And maybe John's age of fifty-two years didn't matter to her.

"Where's John?" It was the first thing to pop out of his mouth. Immediately he wished he could take it back, especially when he saw how stiff and straight her spine got.

"Mr. Abercrombie is out of the store at the moment," she said through pursed lips. "If you need assistance, Mr. Thorne, you can either accept my help or return later when he's in."

Miss Delta made it amply clear that it was no skin off her nose if he left and never came back.

His raspy sigh ruffled the air. "I apologize, ma'am. I didn't mean that the way it came out. You caught me by surprise. Not sure what you're doing here."

"If it's any of your concern, Mr. Abercrombie hired me."

So that meant she hadn't roped the man into marriage.

"I thought…I was under the impression that you were going back to Georgia after our…" He let the sentence trail, not wanting to say the wrong thing again.

"Parting of ways," Delta supplied, giving a sarcastic snort. "The only thing we discussed was me not accepting your money. I never said I was leaving town."

"So you're staying?"

Her chin raised a trifle and her eyes narrowed to green slits as though she was readying for battle. "I most assuredly am. I like it here. It's a nice, quiet little town and *most* of the people are friendly."

If that wasn't a how-de-do. He wondered if she'd decided to stay to irritate him or if she didn't have the money to leave. He wasn't about to mention money again to her, though. That got her riled up quicker than a horse with a whole mess of cockleburs under its saddle.

"So, Mr. Thorne, get used to it. I'm here to stay."

"Well, I can see the difference you've made. The store didn't look this good when it was newly built."

He didn't just say that to mollycoddle her. He meant it.

"Thank you, I'm pleased you noticed." She dusted off the counter. "Now, if you don't want my help, I have work to do. Mr. Abercrombie doesn't pay me to stand around engaging in trivial conversation."

Cooper finally remembered what he came for. "I have a list here somewhere." He rifled through his vest pocket and produced a wrinkled piece of paper.

Delta took it. "This may take a while. If you have something else to do…"

"You just get it all ready. I'll be back in an hour."

The clink of his spurs echoed in the silence as he strode for the door. He could feel Delta's sharp gaze boring into him. She probably couldn't wait to get him out of there. When he moved onto the sidewalk, he saw her hurry to the window to watch. She seemed awfully curious to see where he went.

Moments later he stood with a hand on the batwing doors of the saloon. She'd have to wonder no more. Like most women, she likely believed whiskey was a man's ruination. He had to agree that some men fell under the spell of liquor, but that wasn't him. He never touched the stuff, afraid of what would happen if he did. He vowed to never be like his father, who'd lived in a drunken rage.

Cooper sauntered into the Lily of the West and up to the bar.

"Hey, Coop," Rand greeted him. "I swear! You must've smelled Widow Sharp's fresh hand pies."

"That black veil she wears gives me the creeps, but she sure can bake. What kind did she bring?" Cooper's mouth was already watering.

"Apple. Hey, aren't widows given a time limit to wear those contraptions?" Rand pulled a plate of the delicious treats from under the counter.

Everyone in town knew about Cooper's sweet tooth, especially for flaky, moon-shaped hand pies.

"I'm not the person to ask about such things. The only thing sure about women is that you never know what they're thinking." Much less doing. He still reeled from the shock of finding out Delta had decided to stick around.

"And the pies aren't all. She's always patting my

hand and asking me if I'm eating right. Does my laundry too. Won't take a cent for it, either."

"Better watch it, Rand. It may be you instead of me standing there at the altar. You know how lonely widows are."

"Take care of your own affairs, Coop, and leave mine alone. About the pies…just don't eat 'em all this time. My customers and I want some too. What are you gonna wash 'em down with?"

"Sarsaparilla will do," Cooper said around a mouthful of pie. Rand opened the bottle and slid it before him. "Where's your barkeep? Don't tell me you fired him."

"Nope. He took the day off on account of his wife being sick. What are you doing in town?"

"Came after supplies. Got quite a jolt to see Miss Dandridge working at Abercrombie's. You could've warned me."

"Yep, I could've, but it wouldn't have been as much fun. She's the talk of the town, the way she cleaned up the store and got it shipshape. Awful pretty too. And smart. She'd make some man a good wife."

"Long as it ain't me," Cooper growled, taking a swig of his sarsaparilla while reaching for another hand pie. "You seem to have taken quite an interest in her, Rand. How is that?"

His tall younger brother shrugged. "Just remarking on her attributes is all. No more. No less. You could be more charitable toward her, you know. Give her the benefit of the doubt. She's not the enemy."

"It wasn't you she came to town intending to set up house with and raise a mess of young'uns."

"All the same, wouldn't hurt you to be friendlier to her." Rand dried a beer mug and set it on the shelf underneath the mirror.

Tipping up the bottle of sarsaparilla, Cooper drained it in one long gulp. "Don't reckon you've heard anything about who might've lured her here."

"Nope. Nary a word. Whoever did it is keeping quiet."

"Had to be someone with money. It cost a pretty penny to pay her way from Georgia. He'll slip up one of these days and I'll catch him. You can bet on that," Cooper promised.

"I'll keep an eye out. How are things at the Long Odds?"

"Haven't found any more sick cows. Won't know until we get them all accounted for, though. We begin roundup on Monday."

A wistful look crossed Rand's angular face. He rubbed his dark stubble that he could never seem to keep off no matter how often he shaved. "One of these days I figure I'll sell the saloon and buy me a nice parcel of land. It'd be nice to own a ranch and a fair-to-middling herd."

"The saloon business losing its sparkle? If you hadn't tried to take the easy way out, you could've had your own spread. It was your choice, brother."

"Don't think I don't know that. Let's say I've grown up a lot in the last few years. Learned what was really important."

"Glad to see you're thinking about more than easy money."

"Just hope when I do get my ranch, I remember

all the stuff Isaac Daffern taught us. Guess I can always ask you or Brett about things I don't know, though."

"Of course. We're always here for you," Cooper said quietly. He'd do anything for his brothers and they for him. Seeing Rand wanting something so badly and not having it created an ache in his chest.

"Speaking of Brett, it's been a while since he's been to town. When've you seen him last, Coop?"

"Just came by his place. Needed to warn him about the hoof-and-mouth disease. Helped him put up a tepee."

"You don't say." Rand threw back his head and roared with laughter.

"Says he's embracing his heritage. I have to admit that tepee is a damn sight better than living out of a wagon."

"Before we know it, he'll be paintin' his face and doing a war dance around his campfire."

They both sobered, and Cooper knew Rand was remembering the raggedy little boy they'd taken under their wing and defended with everything they had. Both knew that without a doubt they'd paint their faces and do a war dance right alongside Brett if he asked them to.

The brothers discussed various and sundry other things, then Cooper reached for another fried pie and pushed back from the long oak bar. "Gotta collect my supplies from the mercantile and get back to the ranch."

"Don't let the lovely Miss Dandridge get the drop on you and drag you to the preacher," Rand warned.

"You seem to be worrying about that enough for both of us, little brother."

"Stranger things have happened. Say, I might ride out and watch the branding next week. Might learn a few things for when I have my own spread."

"You're welcome anytime. Heck, I'll even let you join in and help us." Cooper adjusted his hat, bringing it lower on his forehead. "I'm thinking we need to have another meeting of the bachelors' club as soon as I've finished with the roundup."

"Thinkin' of dissolving it? I mean, with you being tempted to get hitched and all."

"Drop it, Rand. Enough is enough."

⁓

Abercrombie was back in the store when Cooper returned. He didn't see Delta Dandridge anywhere, which was probably for the best.

"Hey, John, missed you earlier. I like what you've done with the place."

"Cain't take any credit for it. Miss Dandridge's idea."

"All the same, it's a welcome sight to behold."

Just then Delta emerged humming from the back room with an armful of boxes, looking happy and content. Their eyes met and held. A look of guarded caution quickly replaced her carefree demeanor. It bruised something deep in his heart to know he caused it.

Her lips tightened in a straight line. "Your order is ready, Mr. Thorne."

"Thank you, Miss Delta."

John Abercrombie looked surprised. "You two know each other?"

Cooper squirmed inside. "We met shortly after she got to town."

"Well, I'm right glad she needed a job. She's been a real keeper. Almost makes me feel like Nell is here." John's voice broke and he looked away.

Laying a hand on the man's shoulder, Cooper spoke low. "It's okay, John. I'm sure Nell's watching over you."

The dour man must've reached inside for the gruffness that hid all his feelings, for his next words were unkind. "Well, don't just stand there all day, Miss Dandridge," he snapped. "Take the man's money. He's got more things to do than wait for you."

"Certainly, Mr. Abercrombie." Delta reached for the tally of the purchases. "That comes to four dollars and thirty-two cents."

Cooper paid it and threw the sack of flour onto his shoulder. He put the bag in the wagon and turned to go back for the rest. He wasn't expecting Delta Dandridge to be behind him with a boxful of other supplies, and he nearly toppled her. Quickly, he grabbed her arm to steady her, but the box wasn't so lucky. It crashed to the ground with a loud thud.

"I'm sorry, ma'am. Didn't mean to plow over you. I wasn't expecting anyone to sneak up behind me. Bet you thought you could put one of those letters of yours in my pocket and I'd have to reconsider."

Twin spots stained her cheeks red. She was quite a sight, standing there all soft and pretty and full of an extra helping of spirit. For a moment, he had a devil of a time keeping his train of thought from jumping the tracks.

She drew herself up. "I wasn't sneaking. I was helping, you...you big..."

"Careful there, Miss Delta, before you say something you can't take back." Cooper's gaze swept to her moist rosy lips, and for a long moment, he wanted to kiss her. He didn't know what the hell came over him.

But the glare she shot him warned that she'd likely kill him if he tried. He could almost see the steam coming from her ears as she struggled to find a suitable reply. For a moment, he thought she might haul off and wallop him.

Instead, she smiled sweetly. "My dear Mr. Thorne, you're absolutely determined to think the worst of me. I assure you, I try to never say anything I must retract later."

"Look, Miss Dandridge, why don't we start over? We'll be running into each other on occasion. No reason why our hackles should rise every time we cross paths."

"Hackles! I do declare. Your neck may have hackles, but I guarantee that mine does not."

"No, ma'am. I can certainly see that." He was hard-pressed to keep from grinning. "I simply meant we should try to get along."

"I suppose," she murmured slowly. "Just so we can be civil to each other. I don't want you to get the idea that I harbor any untoward ideas about love and marriage, though."

He crooked an eyebrow. "What does that mean?"

"Just because you don't like women—"

"Hey, wait a cotton-pickin' minute. I never said I don't like women. I love 'em. For your information, I've kissed more than my share. Just don't intend to be married to one."

Delta put her hands on her hips. "Well, don't get any ideas about kissing me."

"You don't have to fret about that." He glared. "Is this your way of burying the hatchet?"

"No, it's yours. Hackles indeed. I'm not a dog."

Cooper would have to be as blind as a suck-egg mule not to see that. "It's plain this is a complete waste of time. I wish you a pleasant stay in Battle Creek… however long it is."

"Good-bye, Mr. Thorne."

He picked up the box that had fallen from her hands and finished loading the rest of the supplies, evading the green flames shooting from Delta's eyes. He was glad to get back on the road to the ranch, where it was more peaceful. The town was fast living up to its name.

Seven

NEWS OF THE CHANGES AT ABERCROMBIE'S MERCANTILE spread, and it seemed everyone in town came by to see for themselves. Delta didn't have a quiet moment after Cooper left.

Granny Ketchum hobbled in and said someone had stolen her glasses. She couldn't see a blessed thing. It took forever to get rid of the dear woman, and it was only after Delta's promise to have a cup of tea with Granny that she finally left.

Midafternoon, Mr. Abercrombie went home, leaving her to lock up. That he entrusted the store to Delta thrilled her heart. He truly wasn't as mean as he wanted her to believe, just terribly sad and lonely.

Purple shadows had settled over the store and it neared quitting time when a tall, handsome man with a smile that could melt a ruthless killer's heart sauntered in.

She ignored her aching feet and stepped forward. "May I assist you, sir?"

"I'm in need of a pound of coffee."

"Would you like me to grind it for you?"

"Please, if you don't mind."

Delta opened a bin and scooped out the appropriate amount of coffee beans and put them in the grinder. She turned the wheel and in minutes they were a fine grind.

"Anything else for you, sir?"

"Have supper with me tonight, Miss Dandridge."

The request took her aback. "I'm sorry, sir. I don't even know your name. And how do you know mine?"

His blue eyes twinkled as he took her palm in his hand and lifted it to his lips. "I'm Rand Sinclair. I own the Lily of the West Saloon. I believe you're acquainted with my brother, Cooper Thorne. You certainly put him in his place, by the way. And, besides, everyone in Battle Creek knows who you are by now. They're completely enamored with your grace and beauty."

The man certainly knew how to turn a lady's head, she'd give him that. Not that she believed him for a second. She had only to look in the mirror to see she was passable, at best.

"I do declare. You're Cooper's brother?" Her mind raced. This would give her an opportunity to ask some questions.

"I am indeed. Not in the normal way, though. It's a long story and best told over a mouthwatering steak shared with a beautiful lady."

The man was a silver-tongued devil, with his pretty compliments and winning smile. Still, it might be nice.

"You certainly have the market cornered on charm, Mr. Sinclair." She tugged her hand free.

"Rand. And I can be most persistent. Please say yes."

"I really shouldn't."

"Don't you ever do anything wild and crazy?"

Did answering an ad in the *Matrimonial Harvest* catalog count?

Delta chewed her lip. "I suppose it wouldn't hurt anything. Give me a minute to close up."

Rand helped her blow out the lamps, and after locking the door, they strolled toward the Three Roses Café.

Seated across from him, Delta studied his face. She couldn't see even a speck of resemblance between him and Cooper. Rand had blue eyes, where Cooper's were a haunting gunmetal gray. Rand's hair was light brown, whereas Cooper's was the color of midnight. But then, Rand had said they weren't brothers in the normal way. She was curious about what that meant.

"You've never had a steak until you've had Rose's," Rand said. "And you have to save room for her rhubarb pie. It's worth dying for."

Delta's stomach rumbled, proclaiming its emptiness. She prayed Rand hadn't heard it. She hadn't eaten all day. "That sounds heavenly. I'll have mine on the done side."

When the waitress came, Rand ordered for them, then he leaned forward, resting his elbows on the table. "I want to hear all about you. What's a pretty woman like you doing so far from home, and why did you want to marry Coop?"

Her guard went up faster than flood waters in the Mississippi delta. "There's nothing really to tell. I'd hoped it wouldn't get all over town. I feel very foolish."

"Don't worry on that count. Only three people know about that, and we're not saying a word."

Three people? Panic rose.

"I thought only you and Cooper knew. Who is the third person?" Gossip traveled, especially the kind that had the power to wound and destroy. She knew more than she wanted about that subject.

"Not to worry. Just my younger brother, Brett. Takes an act of God for him to talk to anyone, so you can relax. His horse ranch is not far from Cooper's. And I wouldn't say you're foolish. Something drives all of us to do the things we do." His words were quietly spoken, and she sensed he referred to himself more than her.

Delta tightly gripped her cloth napkin, praying she wouldn't tell too much or Rand wouldn't dig too deeply. "I needed a fresh start after my mother's death. So when I saw the advertisement, I believed it an answer to a prayer."

"You thought Cooper wrote the letters bringing you here."

"I had no way of knowing otherwise. I don't regret coming, but I do wish I'd known the facts before I arrived." She glanced around the small café. Nearly every table was filled. "This appears to be the place to gather."

"It's not as if we have anywhere else. It's Rose's or Rose's."

She laughed. "It's your turn now. You said Cooper was your brother, but not in the normal way."

"We're blood brothers." Rand explained how he, Cooper, and Brett had nicked their thumbs when they were boys and vowed nothing would ever separate them.

"And did it?"

"Nope. We wouldn't let anything come between us. It was us against the world, and we decided we were true brothers in every sense of the word. We face everything together."

"You must be very close."

"We're the only family each other have. Our bond is unshakable."

Delta wished she'd had someone to stand with her when her misfortunes came. It would've made so much difference. But she'd had no one. No one she could talk to. No one to wipe her tears when she cried.

"How come you're the only one who didn't go into the ranching business? Why a saloon?"

"I got it at a steal and it was the only thing I really knew much about." Rand's smile crinkled the corners of his eyes. "It's just temporary. I have a hankering to be a rancher like my brothers. Just waiting for the right opportunity."

"I think everyone should have a dream that they hold close and never let go." Only hers would never come to pass. It was far too late.

"Yes, ma'am. Sure makes the nights less long and dreary."

"Granny Ketchum told me about the Battle Creek Bachelors' Club that Cooper started. Are you a member also?"

"Yep. And Brett is too. We'll never settle down, and the only knot we'll tie is the one in a piece of rope. That's why Coop thought it so odd that you appeared out of the blue. It's as plain as day that someone played a cruel joke. Just wish we could figure out who."

"If you think it might be helpful, I could let you, or Cooper if he asks politely, read the letters. Maybe there's something in them that would shed light on the person who wrote them."

"That's a good idea, Miss Delta." Rand was silent for a moment. When he spoke, the words were quiet. "Don't mind Cooper's rough ways. He likes to pretend he's all horns and rattles, but truth be told, he's real soft underneath."

"I wouldn't know anything about that." The man had only shown her his grouchy side.

"Just don't be too quick to judge him."

It seemed a tad late for that request. Cooper Thorne was simply insufferable. To a fault. But he did have rather nice eyes, and lips that could probably make her tingle if he ever dared touch them to hers. Her face grew warm.

Goodness, what bold thoughts had popped in her head!

Their steaks arrived and they ate in silence. Rand hadn't exaggerated. The meal was the best she'd ever had.

Afterward, Rand escorted her to the boardinghouse like the true gentleman he was. She'd enjoyed both the food and the conversation. She'd made a friend and she'd learned a little more than she'd planned.

Upstairs in her room, she stared out into the darkness from her window, as had become her habit. A buggy appeared in her line of vision and came down the street. It was going a little too fast to negotiate around the burial plot and almost clipped the wrought iron fence that guarded the ghostly occupants. The middle of the street certainly wasn't a good place for the plot. But still, she would side with the folks who wanted to leave it where it was. There was something very wrong about disturbing the dead or creating misery for the living.

When the buggy faded from view, she turned her attention to Rand's saloon, the Lily of the West. The watering hole was brightly lit and doing a brisk business, judging from the number of horses tied to the hitching rail.

The building reminded her of an aging saloon girl whose dress was tattered and torn. In her mind, she saw a piece of lace dangling from the hem.

The small newspaper office sat next to it as though waiting for something to happen. A light burned faintly through the ink-smudged window. She wondered what the editor would find newsworthy in a town like this. It would be interesting to see.

Suddenly a thought sprang from the blue. Cooper Thorne hadn't smelled of whiskey when he returned for his supplies. If he'd had even one drink, she'd have smelled it on him when she fell into him. But she'd only caught the scent of saddle leather and fresh hay.

His reason for frequenting the saloon had to be to visit his brother Rand. The man with the steely gaze did not swill whiskey in broad daylight every chance he got.

She didn't know why, but that made her secretly happy.

❦

Miles away, on the Long Odds Ranch, Cooper unsaddled Rebel and brushed down the buckskin. It'd been a long day and his troubles had gotten worse.

When he rode back from town with the supplies, he'd found Zeke waiting by the barn. The look on the grizzled cowboy's face had told the story even before he opened his mouth.

Zeke had found another dead cow. Cooper quickly saddled Rebel, and Zeke took him out to where the steer was located. One thing immediately became clear—the animal didn't have the Long Odds brand. In fact, it didn't wear any brand. And there were hoofprints all around it from more than one horse.

This was deliberate.

Someone had a ruthless plan to ruin him.

"Ain't one for speaking my mind, son," Zeke had drawled. "But if it was me, I'd damn sure consider buying some of that newfangled barbed wire everyone is talkin' about and fencin' off the Long Odds."

"If I'm not mistaken, you said you were against that."

"Never thought I'd see the day when I said this. Fencin' goes against everything I know. I believe in the open range. But hell and be damned, a man has to use whatever tools he has to beat these yellow-livered varmints."

Cooper stared at the old man as if he'd suddenly sprouted horns and was covered in red paint. Zeke had told him straight out when he was hired that if Cooper intended to fence off the ranch, he wanted no part of it and would be moseying down the road.

Maybe it was the solution, though.

Cooper pondered that now as he marched toward the house and the cold supper that awaited him. The muscles worked in his jaw. If someone wanted a war, they'd get one. He wasn't going anywhere. This land was his, bought and paid for in blood, sweat, and tears.

They just better heed a warning. He didn't intend to lose. He'd fight with every bit of strength and determination and grit he had in his body. Brett and Rand would stand with him.

Three against whoever was doing this were pretty good odds.

Eight

DELTA WOKE IN A GOOD MOOD. WORK AT THE MERcantile agreed with her, and she found a deep satisfaction at the close of each day knowing that she was good at what she did. Despite the pain of Cooper's spurning that still brought an ache to her heart, she brimmed with optimism.

Business boomed at the store of late, people had accepted her, and she'd helped improve the town by making at least one establishment look less run-down.

Mr. Abercrombie was even beginning to grow on her, despite his gruffness.

The man was tallying some figures when she strolled in humming a tune. He looked up with his ever-present frown and growled like an old bear with a toothache.

"Good morning, Mr. Abercrombie. It's a glorious day."

"Cain't you see I'm busy?" he snapped.

Paying him no mind, she drew her apron over her head and tied it. Today nothing would spoil her happiness. She had just gotten a clean rag, all set to tidy up the mess under some shelves behind the counter, when Granny Ketchum wobbled in.

"Good morning, Miss Dandridge."

"Granny, how wonderful to see you." Delta came out from behind the counter. "What can I help you with today?"

The old woman leaned heavily on her cane, making it bow out in the middle. "Someone stole my snuff can. Can you believe that? If they'd wanted some, all they had to do was ask. They didn't have to take it." Granny gave a long-suffering sigh. "But they brought my cat back, so I can't complain too much."

"That's good news." Delta hid a grin. "So you came in to buy more snuff?"

"Nope. I'm giving up the habit. It's a sign from God. My Elmer, God rest his soul, always yapped about it being an unfit vice for a delicate woman like me. And I reckon he was right. 'Course, I wouldn't have told him so when he was alive. Wouldn't have been any livin' with the old coot."

"No, ma'am. What can I help you with?"

"I want to buy a bell."

"What kind of bell?"

"Oh, a small one."

That didn't tell Delta anything. She had no earthly idea what kind of bell the woman was talking about. She tried another tack. "What are you going to do with this bell?"

"Why, put it around my cat's neck, of course, so he won't sneak up on me and scare me half out of my"—she looked around, then lowered her voice— "bloomers. I swear, I believe he does it on purpose just to see me jump."

"I see. I think I have just what you want. You wait

right here and I'll get it." Delta walked to a shelf and took down a box of small bells. Surely one of these would satisfy.

"Do you have a place for me to sit?"

"Yes, ma'am." Delta brought a chair from the back room. "Now you sit right here and take your time looking at these bells. Find the perfect one."

Granny proceeded to ring each bell. She went through the whole box, then started over. "I just can't decide."

In the midst of all the tinkling bells, the door opened and Cooper Thorne sauntered in. Delta's heart beat a little faster at the sight of the tall cowboy. Raw masculine heat as wild as the vast Texas land that she was coming to embrace radiated from him.

"Mr. Thorne, what do you need today?"

"Miss Delta." His gray eyes held no warmth and the deep lines around his mouth were set. "Came to order some barbed wire. That is, if it can be ordered."

"I don't know. I'll have to ask Mr. Abercrombie." She looked around the store, but her boss had disappeared. She guessed all the racket had gotten on his nerves. "Is everything all right?"

"Things could be better. Would you mind just getting John?"

His curt tone set her back on her heels. The irritating rancher's lack of civility brought a quick reply to the tip of her tongue. But thankfully, she kept the words she itched to say to herself.

"I'll look in the back. Excuse me." Though her words came out through clenched teeth, she kept her dignity.

Delta found Mr. Abercrombie and relayed Cooper's request.

"Dadblast it, I can't hear myself think with all this infernal bell ringing. Can you just hurry Granny out of here?"

"I'll do what I can, sir."

Abercrombie and Cooper huddled together, then her boss got out a book and they pored over it. She assumed there was trouble of some kind on the ranch.

She turned her attention to the bell ringer. "Have you found the one you want, Granny?"

"I just don't know. They sound so much alike."

If that was the case, then it didn't make much difference which one she chose. Delta picked up one that had a red ribbon tied to it. "I'm partial to this one. It has a real jingle."

"I suppose so."

"It's only a nickel. Can't beat that."

"Yes, it'll do, I reckon." Granny handed her the box of bells. After paying, the woman left and blessed quiet settled over the store. She just prayed Granny would get home with it before someone ambushed her and ripped it out of her hand. The poor lady was a dear, but she could get on a person's nerves.

"When can I expect it to arrive?" she heard Cooper ask Abercrombie.

"Two weeks, if I lay my hands on some down in San Antonio."

"Fine. Go ahead and order it. Let me know the minute it comes in."

Cooper's spurs jingled when he straightened, but instead of heading to the door, he moved toward Delta.

"Did you find what you wanted?" she asked.

"Yep. Just wish it didn't take so long to get here." He took off his hat and held it between his hands. "Miss Dandridge, I apologize for being so short with you."

"No need. We simply don't see eye to eye."

"All the same, I would still like for us to be friends."

"What kind of friends?"

"The sort that don't want to kill each other."

She had to admit he'd sorely tried her patience, but the thoughts that invariably kept her awake at night were of kissing, not killing.

Sudden laughter bubbled up. "My dear Mr. Thorne, I'd never do anything involving blood loss."

"I feel so much better now." His mouth quirked up at one corner as if he wanted to smile but wouldn't let himself.

"You're very welcome."

"So, this friends business…how about it?"

"For now, we'll see how it goes."

Cooper nodded, adjusting his worn Stetson back on his head. "Guess I'll pay a visit to the saloon before I head back."

"Speaking of that, I met your brother Rand. He's quite the charmer. Has lovely manners and is a perfect gentleman. He invited me to take supper with him last evening. We had an interesting conversation." Let the man chew on that.

His face darkened. "I'll just bet."

From the corner of her eye, Delta saw Mr. Abercrombie watching. His face got tighter and more furious with each passing second.

"Well, as absolutely fascinating as this conversation has been, I have work to do, Mr. Thorne."

"Then I bid you good day." He tipped the brim of his hat to her. The bell over the door tinkled when he left.

Despite the fact that she should count her blessings every day that she hadn't married him, she couldn't stop herself from hurrying to the window to watch him walk down the street. That loose-jointed saunter of his...*oh my*, it made her pulse race. It was a lot like watching a lazy river meander along its course as if it was in no hurry at all to get there.

Part of her would give anything—

Stop it right there. If wishes were horses, beggars would ride. No use thinking of things beyond her reach.

Snatching up her cleaning rag, she turned her attention to the unruly shelf. In removing every scrap of paper, every receipt, and every bit of clutter, she knocked a book to the floor. Something flew out.

Delta bent and picked up a small envelope. On the outside in flowing penmanship were the words *To my darling John*.

Unsure what to do with it, yet sensing it was something important, she took the envelope to Mr. Abercrombie. "Sir, this fell out of a book when I was cleaning just now."

"Well, what is it?" he snapped.

"It looks like a letter or something. Might be important."

"Did you read it?"

"Of course not! I would never do that."

The man jerked it from her. "I don't have time for

such nonsense. You're always messing with my things, and I'll thank you to leave 'em alone."

Anger rose. "Sir, you can be angry with yourself, or life, or your circumstances, but I've given you no cause to treat me worse than a guttersnipe. Whatever is inside that envelope is probably from your wife. The least you can do is look at it."

Delta turned away, blinking back sudden tears. She didn't know why people, men especially, were so quick to criticize or sling blame. She'd faced more than one such man in her life. Langston Graham had been worst of all. She could say nothing to excuse the man who'd fathered her. He'd passed her on the street every day in Cedartown with no word, not a speck of kindness, not even so much as a smile. She'd been invisible to him.

A child he'd never wanted, much less acknowledged.

His utter scorn had turned her heart to stone.

Shaking herself, she forced her thoughts back to the present. She'd wasted enough tears on that matter. She put Langston Graham out of her mind and returned to her shelf.

When she next cast a glance at Mr. Abercrombie, it broke her heart. He stood clutching a paper valentine to his chest. Tears streamed down his gaunt cheeks. Her hunch had been right. He'd never seen it before.

She stood, undecided what to do. Though she longed to comfort the shopkeeper, she didn't want to intrude on his privacy, or worse, wound his pride.

All of a sudden, he crumpled to the floor, heaving great sobs. She quickly went and put an arm around his shoulders.

"I'm so sorry, sir. I shouldn't have—"

John Abercrombie's watery eyes met hers. "It's from Nell. A decorated valentine. This was probably one of the last things she did before she died the morning of February 15. Which book did you find it in?"

"Charlotte Brontë's *Jane Eyre*."

"That was her favorite book. She kept it in the store and read every spare minute. She must've stuck the valentine in there, intending to give it to me, but she passed too quickly. This means more to me than anything on earth. I'll always treasure this. Thank you for finding and insisting I open the envelope."

"You're very welcome, sir."

"You must think I'm a foolish old man."

"Quite the contrary. I think you're still very much in love with your wife," she said softly.

"Sometimes the yearning for her smile, the sound of her laughter, eats inside me with such a fierceness that I can barely stand it."

"I feel the same about my mother." Even though Phoebe Dandridge had never shown a lighter side.

"When did she pass over, if I'm not too bold?"

"Christmas Day."

"Then your grief is as fresh as my own." He clutched her arm. "Will you help me up?" Then he added, "Please. Before a customer comes in?"

"Yes, sir."

"Stop with this 'sir' business. I'm John. Plain and simple."

Letting him rest his weight on her, she helped him to his feet.

What a surprising day. First Cooper had tried to

mend burned bridges, and now Mr. Abercrombie was allowing deep emotion to show through his stern facade.

Delta had a feeling she may have reached a turning point with both men.

Nine

COOPER RESTED HIS LONG FRAME AGAINST THE OAK BAR at the Lily of the West. Rand stood beside him, idly fingering a brass ring with over two dozen keys on it. Cooper had never known why his brother carried so many keys. He just knew Rand had started collecting them as a boy, snatching up every one he ran across.

"Might as well spit it out, Coop. What's stuck in your craw?"

"Did I say something was?"

"Didn't have to. I can recognize when you're looking for someone to whip. I ain't blind, you know."

Cooper shot his brother a glare. "Delta Dandridge told me she took supper with you last evening. I think you owe me an explanation."

Rand straightened to his full height. His words came out smooth as velvet but left in no doubt the layer of steel underneath. "I don't owe you a damn thing. Reckon my dealings with Miss Dandridge are a private matter. I didn't do anything wrong. Just because you've had your nose out of joint since she arrived doesn't mean mine has to be."

"I want you to leave her the hell alone." Cooper knew full well Rand's reputation where lovely females were concerned. He could list a whole slew of them who'd had their hearts broken by his lothario middle brother. Delta Dandridge would end up just another conquest. That fact sat like soured milk in Cooper's stomach.

"I don't exactly care what you want, brother. She's beautiful, charming, and has a sharp mind. I intend to see her whenever I take a notion, whether it rubs you the wrong way or not."

Tension so thick Cooper could cut it with a knife lay between them. Finally, he allowed a tight smile. "If that's the way you feel."

Rand's glare could've melted snow off a mountaintop. "It is."

"Then all I have to say is watch out. The lady has quite a temper. Don't come running to me when she gives you a piece of her mind. I warned you. And you'd better not show her anything but respect either."

While he still thought Rand should abide by his wishes, Cooper recognized that his brother had a right to his own opinion. Rand was always the one who had to figure things out for himself and dared anyone to interfere.

Now that the set-to had passed, Rand put down his keys, lifted his beer, and took a gulp. "How are things at the ranch?"

"I just came from ordering enough barbed wire to fence off the Long Odds." Cooper told him about the newest dead cow and how it didn't wear any kind of brand.

"And you now believe someone is deliberately trying to spread this disease?"

"Sure looks that way." And if he didn't catch the culprits soon, he'd lose every single thing he had in this world that meant anything.

By the time Cooper left the saloon, it was nearing noon. He swung into the saddle and meandered toward the ranch. He went around the burial plot that sat dead center in the middle of Main Street and as usual wondered who lay beneath the soil. Folks had told him how Indians massacred a group of government surveyors here in October 1838. Only seven out of twenty-four survived. More than likely these four graves held the bones of some of those men.

The small section of hallowed ground had created lots of arguments over the years. But to him, the townsfolk of Battle Creek had a sacred duty to protect those buried there. You could tell a lot about a town by how its citizens treated the dead. He liked that they hadn't moved them when Battle Creek was settled.

Cooper paused near the edge of the community at a run-down shack adjacent to Mabel's Boardinghouse when an animal's frantic yelps split the air. A burly man with a head full of wild red hair, Cyrus Tull, was chaining a young dog to a tree. The poor animal's ribs and hip bones protruded—the result of being starved for most of its young life, by the looks of things. The pooch's pitiful cries cut Cooper to the quick. It was so weak it could barely stand.

Anger stewed inside Cooper. He never mistreated

an animal and couldn't abide anyone else doing so. He dismounted.

"Mind me asking what you're doing, Cyrus?"

"Ain't no concern o' yours," the man snarled.

The hell it wasn't. "Well, I'm making it my business. Unchain that dog, if you know what's good for you."

"And if'n I don't?"

"You won't like that option much. Trust me." Though Cooper spoke softly, he could tell by the flicker in Tull's eyes that he'd gotten the man's attention. But would the drunk heed the warning?

On her way to the boardinghouse for a quick bowl of soup, Delta Dandridge stopped, transfixed by the scene playing out before her. She'd seen the poor dog and had watched in horror as it became weaker from lack of food and water, its situation ever more desperate. Several times under the cover of darkness she'd slipped over there and had shared with the pitiful animal what little morsels she could sneak from supper.

Before becoming a bag of skin and bones, it must've been a pretty dog, all white except for a black ear on the right and a circle around the left eye. It reminded her of an eye-patch-wearing pirate.

Now she watched Cooper Thorne try to save the animal.

"This is my dog, an' I'll do as I damn well please with the stupid mutt." The man Cooper had called Cyrus remained defiant.

"Not today. Today you're going to unchain it and let me take it."

"You gotta be smokin' locoweed," the ill-tempered

fellow snorted, pulling a revolver from the waist of his pants.

Cooper's long legs covered the space and he knocked the gun from the dog owner's hand. His powerful arm shot out, his fist connecting with muscle and bone. The blow sent his adversary tumbling to the dirt.

But Cooper wasn't finished. He grabbed Cyrus's shirt. Hauling him to his feet, he hit him again. Blood spurted from the mean good-for-nothing's nose and mouth.

Delta bit her lip, praying Cooper wouldn't kill him, even though she was glad to see the miserable excuse for a human get what was coming to him.

At last the horrible man lay in a heap in the dirt. Cooper stepped over him and undid the chain, then gently lifted the shivering dog, tucking him close to his side beneath one arm.

"What are you going to do with the little thing?" Delta hurried toward Cooper.

She realized she'd made a mistake when he spun around with a doubled fist and murder on his face, ready to take on another foe. It took a few seconds for him to grasp that she posed no threat. Her heart resumed its normal beat when he relaxed.

"I'm taking him to the ranch." The words rumbled in Cooper's throat before finding their way out. "With luck, I can nurse him back to health. It'll take time to undo the damage."

The dog gazed up at Cooper with its big brown eyes and licked the rancher's hand, his tail feebly wagging.

"It might mean trouble for you." She glanced at the

bloody man who was slowly coming around. "He'll come after you."

"Let him. I've got a bullet waiting for him if he sets foot on my land. I don't tolerate anyone who mistreats animals. I'd like to chain him up and starve *him*. See how he likes it." Cooper smoothed the dog's short fur, which was bare in spots. "What brought you here, Miss Delta?"

When his gray gaze swung to her, she forgot everything except how much she wished things could've been different between them.

Finally, she managed to say, "Lunch. Mr. Abercrombie relieved me so I can eat."

John Abercrombie had been quite different since he read the valentine that his wife had left in the book. Never before had he allowed her time to eat a bite of anything, not even an apple. She burned to know what the card said, but he hadn't offered that information. Whatever it was, he seemed more at peace now.

Cooper gave her a crooked smile that made her stomach dip and her pulse race like a herd of runaway wild horses.

"Well, I'd best let you get to it. Don't want to put you on the wrong side of John again."

"Thank you for rescuing the dog. I had wondered if anyone even cared. It broke my heart to see him so mistreated." Delta held the dog while Cooper mounted, then handed the animal up to him.

"Good day, Miss Dandridge."

"Mr. Thorne."

For a moment, she stood watching him ride toward

his ranch. He sat tall and straight in the saddle, his body as one with the handsome buckskin.

It appeared no one sat a horse quite like this big Texan. Cooper Thorne was indeed a man to be reckoned with.

Her estimation of him had risen considerably after witnessing him with the unfortunate animal. The belligerent, bloody man in the yard began to stir. She turned and hurried inside the boardinghouse before he caught her gawking.

∽∾

Zeke ambled from the barn as Cooper rode up. "Where'd you find this little fellow, boss?"

"In town." He passed the dog to Zeke and dismounted. "He's had a hard life so far."

"Yep, ain't disputin' that. Poor thing."

"This place needs a dog after Rowdy died last year. See if you can round him up some food while I find him a place to sleep." He took the animal from Zeke and walked toward the barn.

It didn't take long to make a warm bed on a mound of fresh hay. He added an old blanket and gently lowered the dog. Then he got a pan of water. The dog drank thirstily.

"You look like a bandit." Cooper examined the critter and didn't find any broken bones. He got some salve and rubbed it on the raw place around the dog's neck where the chain had been. "Yep, Bandit will be a fitting name for you."

The dog gave a sharp bark and licked Cooper's hand as though in agreement.

Zeke entered just then with some food. "I like that.

Bandit's a mighty good name. How old you reckon he is?"

"I'd say about six months old." Cooper put down a piece of salt pork left from breakfast. For a while they were going to have to go slow, feeding Bandit four or five small meals a day. Too much too quickly would make the dog throw up.

"Mack had a fit when I asked him what he had to feed a starved dog." Zeke laughed. "The fool man started gettin' out his pots and pans and doodads, all set to whip up a meal for the little feller. I 'spect Bandit will be fat and happy before you can hum 'The Battle Hymn of the Republic.'"

Cooper sat with the dog for a while, thinking of all the ways he'd like to kill the animal's previous owner. If the heartless man hadn't wanted the dog, he should've set it free so it could scrounge for food. Didn't make sense to watch an animal, or a person either, for that matter, waste away, knowing you could do something.

"Rest easy, boy, I'll watch over you." Cooper patted Bandit's head.

The dog whimpered, then sighed and closed his eyes.

Other images from the day crowded into Cooper's mind. Delta Dandridge in particular. The lady had a way of barging into his thoughts, not to mention his life. She'd been equally concerned about Bandit's welfare.

She seemed to have a heart as big as the brilliant smile that snuck past all his defenses and filled the ache in his chest with a strange longing.

He fished in his pocket for the lemon drops and popped one in his mouth.

All he knew was that Rand had best not break her heart, or he'd answer to him.

Ten

OVER THE NEXT WEEK, DELTA FOUND BEING AROUND
John Abercrombie almost pleasant. He'd been less
grouchy and more obliging. He'd insisted that she take
lunch every day, and lo and behold had even given her
a five-cent raise. The world must surely be coming to
an end.

And yet it thrilled her to have won the man over.
This town might be a wonderful place to settle down.

She was in the midst of restocking the ladies'
notions one day when a woman came in who, judging
from her low-cut bodice and painted face, was clearly
a working girl. Her listless gaze hurt a place in Delta
deep inside. But for the pure grace of God, this could
be her life.

Delta put on a bright smile and hurried forward.
"May I help you, miss?"

The young girl stared at her feet and mumbled low,
"I need a pair of black cotton stockings, please."

"Of course, right this way." Delta led her to the
selection of women's unmentionables.

The bell over the door jingled and another customer

walked in. The minute the woman spotted the lady of the evening Delta was helping, she sniffed loudly, turned on her heel and stomped back out.

The rude behavior stung and sent Delta's thoughts scurrying back to Cedartown. People there had treated her the same way, and in her case, for circumstances totally beyond her control. Her heart went out to those who lived on the fringes of society. She knew what it felt like.

"I'm sorry," the stricken girl whispered.

"You have nothing to apologize for, miss. You have every right to shop in here. People are always going to find a way to treat others poorly."

"Thank you for being so nice."

"My name is Delta Dandridge." Delta stuck out her hand.

"I'm Emmylou." The beginnings of a tiny smile brightened the girl's face, replacing the dull, listless gaze.

"It's a pleasure to know you, Emmylou." Delta longed to ask if the girl was in Rand's employ but she didn't really want to know the answer. She preferred to think that Rand only sold beer and whiskey, not operated a flesh business. Surely he didn't. Surely.

Emmylou paid for her purchase and left. A few minutes later, the customer who'd been so disdainful returned.

"Afternoon, ma'am. What can I help you with?"

"You can keep the likes of her out of here," the sour woman snapped. "This is where decent people shop. John runs a clean store. He doesn't allow that kind of riffraff in here."

"I'm sorry you feel that way, ma'am, but everyone is welcome here."

"Where is John? We'll just see about that."

Suddenly Mr. Abercrombie spoke from behind them. "Miss Dandridge said it pretty plain, Mrs. Hatfield. If you don't like it, you can trot on over to Corsicana."

Mrs. Hatfield gasped. "Why, that's over twenty miles."

"Yes, ma'am, it still was the last time I checked."

"Well, I never!"

"No, ma'am, I don't suppose you ever have." John calmly chewed on the end of a cigar.

"If Nell was alive, she wouldn't put up with this nonsense," the woman huffed.

A sorrowful look settled in John's eyes. "Good day, Martha. And don't let the door hit you on the way out."

She shot them both a glare and, with her nose high in the air, marched for the exit.

"She may cause you trouble, John," Delta said.

"Oh, that old biddy? No big loss. Martha Hatfield's always been more trouble than she's worth. Ain't anyone with half sense ever spared her a passing thought."

With that, Delta dove into a job she'd dreaded but couldn't put off any longer—sorting a drawer full of screws and bolts according to size. She needed something to take her mind off persnickety women who sought to make others feel as worthless as a sack of wormy corncobs.

Deep in thought, she glanced up in time to see Widow Sharp enter the store. Delta put her task aside and went to assist the veiled woman.

"I would like you to fill this order please." The

widow's beautiful, cultured voice appeared a bit strange in an out-of-the-way town like Battle Creek.

"You must do a lot of baking," Delta said as she gathered sacks of flour and sugar plus various other cooking supplies.

"I guess you haven't heard. I furnish the saloon and café with pastries. My specialty is fried hand pies."

"I'm sure they're very delicious."

Widow Sharp laughed. "You should try them. I think I can make a convert out of you."

The widow intrigued her. What was her story? Had she known a great love? She'd evidently suffered much heartache.

Then it dawned on her. Mrs. Sharp knew what the inside of the saloon looked like. Few women went inside those dark, sinful male domains. Delta had always speculated about what went on inside there. If she and Mrs. Sharp became friends, she could find out.

After the widow left, Delta put her musings aside and returned to sorting the screws. She was making progress when Rand Sinclair sauntered in as if he were out for a Sunday stroll. The man was a nice diversion and she welcomed his friendship, but he didn't make her heart race and her palms turn sweaty the way Cooper Thorne did. Every time the bell jangled over the door, she half expected to see the tall rancher standing there. Many times she'd wanted to ride out to the Long Odds Ranch. She needed to check on the dog. Just to see how the animal fared, she told herself. Nothing more.

But unsure how Cooper would take her visit, she'd talked herself out of renting a buggy and going to check on things.

"Afternoon, Miss Dandridge," Rand greeted her.

"Mr. Sinclair. What brings you in?"

"I was thinking of buying my brother, Brett, a pair of moccasins. Would you happen to carry such a thing?"

"I do believe I saw some the other day stuck at the back under a pile of horse blankets." She rummaged around and pulled out a pair of buttery soft leather footwear with long leggings. "Here they are."

"I can't believe it." Rand grinned. "I always heard this mercantile had everything, and now I see it for myself. Bless you, Miss Dandridge."

"Delta. I insist."

Rand leaned against a rack of bedding. "Miss Delta, would you do me the honor of taking another supper with me?"

"I don't think that's wise, Mr. Sinclair."

"Rand. My friends call me Rand. Give me one good reason why you shouldn't, and I promise to go on my way."

He seemed bent on pestering her until she gave in. She had no idea why Rand had taken such an interest in her. No one ever had, and she'd long despaired of ever catching a gentleman's attention. She chewed her lip. If only she knew his motives.

"I don't exactly…" She quickly swallowed the *trust you* part of that sentence.

"Know what to say," he finished for her. "Say yes. It didn't kill you before. I'll be on my best behavior." He winked and crossed his heart. "I promise."

The saloon owner could be quite persuasive when it came to getting his way, and he most assuredly knew it. Still, it was only a meal, not an invitation to sleep in his bed. And she did enjoy his company.

Delta laughed. "Then, yes, I'll dine with you."

"Excellent."

It bothered Delta that she didn't yet know what Rand Sinclair was up to. A niggling in her brain whispered it was far more than an innocent meal. But she guessed until she found out, it was all right to enjoy the pleasure of his company. After all, she didn't struggle under the enormous weight of other invitations of any sort.

By the time the orange sun dipped below the horizon, Delta was seated with Rand in the Three Roses Café. She couldn't help but smile at the charming blue-eyed saloon owner across from her who certainly portrayed the perfect gentleman.

So far.

"I met a young lady today by the name of Emmylou. Would you perhaps know of her?"

"Matter of fact, I do. She's one of Miss Sybil's girls out at the edge of town. Stay away from there. Why do you ask?"

Relieved that Rand didn't have such women working out of the saloon, Delta relaxed. "She came in the store today. I felt sorry for her. She seemed very sad."

"Emmylou's had her share of hard times. You can't help everyone, Miss Delta," he said softly.

"Maybe not." Didn't mean she couldn't try.

"And just to clear up any misconceptions you may have, I only employ two saloon girls and I have strict rules. The main one is that no customers are allowed upstairs no matter what. I catch 'em, they're gone."

"Thank you, Rand." She told him about Cooper rescuing the poor little dog. "I feared he would kill that man. I've never seen anyone so angry."

"Coop can keep a lid on his temper for a while, but when it blows off, you'd best duck behind something. One thing about my brother is he never leaves anything half-done. Sounds like the man deserved everything he got and then some," Rand said quietly.

"You're exactly right."

"Where did you say the man lives?"

Delta told him. "Do you know him?"

"Afraid so. Cyrus Tull is a mean drunk. I've thrown him out of the saloon more times than I can count. Always causing a ruckus." Rand reached across the table for her hand. "Now let's talk about more pleasant things. Would you like to ride out to the Long Odds with me? You could check on the dog and I could watch the branding. I told Cooper I'd come out while the roundup is in full swing. What do you say?"

The warmth of his hand was nice but nothing exciting. "I'd have to ask Mr. Abercrombie for some time off. Not sure I should, though, in light of how busy we've been. And I wouldn't leave him in the lurch."

"We could go on Sunday, when the store is closed."

"Before I answer, please tell me one thing—what do you hope to gain by seeking out my company?" The question was blunt, but she needed to know. Better to lay all the cards on the table so to speak. It saved time.

Rand chuckled and released her hand. "I see you like things straight and to the point. My kind of lady. You're safe. I want your friendship. I think you're an exciting woman and a breath of fresh air. Frankly, I enjoy being with you. You remind me of someone who was once very dear."

Pain flashed in his eyes and Delta had to look away.

"Whoever she was, you must've thought a lot of her."

He cleared his throat. "Enough about that. Please say you'll ride out to the ranch with me on Sunday."

The offer proved too tempting. Just the chance to see Cooper Thorne in his element enticed her.

"How can I refuse? All right." Delta prayed she wouldn't regret the decision.

❧

Cooper stood on his porch early Sunday morning inhaling the fresh air that held just a hint of moisture and taking a moment to reflect. Though he'd just risen, he was already bone weary. Most days he climbed into the saddle at daybreak and didn't fall out until it got too dark to see.

Roundup always took a lot out of him. Luckily it only came once a year. He was anxious to see how much of his herd the hoof-and-mouth disease had wiped out.

It still continued to sweep through his cattle. He'd had to shoot at least a dozen more and burn them to try to stop the onslaught. There seemed to be no end. More unbranded cows were showing up among his adult population.

It was amply clear that someone had it in for Cooper. But who?

What had he done that someone would seek his destruction?

He'd done his best not to rile anyone and thought he'd managed just fine, except for last week, when he'd whipped Cyrus for abusing his dog. Cooper couldn't, wouldn't, ever turn a blind eye to cruelty, whether it be man or animal. But other than Cyrus, he couldn't think of anyone else who'd have so much hate for him.

Bandit scampered from the barn, apparently eager to see Cooper and get a belly rub.

Or maybe the dog smelled the bacon frying.

"Hey, boy. How are you?" Cooper knelt and accepted the wet kisses Bandit plastered on his face. "You're really feeling your oats these days, aren't you, fellow? Miss Delta will hardly know you."

Now where had that come from? Delta Dandridge snuck into his thoughts in the oddest moments lately. But she *was* there when he'd rescued Bandit, so it was logical her name would cross his lips. Wasn't it? Not that thinking of Miss Georgia Peach was such a bad thing.

A grin insisted on covering his face. Thank goodness no one was watching him make a fool out of himself.

He quickly roped his thoughts and dragged them back to the dog. Though the mutt's bones were still clearly visible, he was beginning to fill out.

How could he not, with Mack around? The cook had taken to fixing special meals for the dog. Shoot, Bandit ate better than Cooper's ranch hands. And when Mack wasn't putting out a plate for the animal, Zeke was. Cooper was surprised they didn't include silverware and napkins.

"You're gonna be spoiled for sure." Cooper rubbed the dog's belly. "Not gonna be fit for crow bait."

Bandit's tail wagged in excitement as if the mutt thought crow was something tasty to eat.

Zeke O'Grady sauntered from the bunkhouse and joined Cooper on the porch. "Morning, boss. Smelled the coffee all the way out here."

"Got some with your name on it inside."

Zeke disappeared and emerged a minute later with a steaming cup of dark brew. "Reckon me and the boys'll finish up the north pasture today."

"That's my plan." Cooper stood. "Damn if I can figure out the rhyme or reason for this disease. I won't rest until we round up every last cow and see where we stand."

"While we've been out beatin' the brush, I've kept an eye open for signs of trespassers. Yesterday I found some places that looked like someone had dragged something heavy across the south pasture. There were three dead cows. None of 'em had our brand."

"Hell and damnation! You didn't see fit to tell me?"

"Tellin' you now. Couldn't find you yesterday, and it was late when me and the boys came in. We was so beat, we fell into bed."

"Take me out there. I want to see for myself."

"Sure thing, boss."

Right after breakfast, Cooper, Zeke, and five cowboys rode out for the south pasture. While the cowboys went to work rounding up strays and getting them in a bunch to drive to the corrals, Zeke showed Cooper the drag marks.

Cooper slid off his buckskin and knelt to eyeball them. Looked to be six horses involved.

A round piece of metal half-buried in the soft ground caught his attention. He picked it up and ice formed in his veins. It was a brass token for the Steamboat Bathhouse in Hannibal, Missouri—the same bathhouse in which he'd shot Tolbert Early.

A coincidence? He didn't believe in that nonsense.

Could Early somehow be alive? Was that even possible, given his horrific wound? Wild tales of ranchers cutting off the head of a snake that still tried to inject its venom crossed his mind.

No, Tolbert Early was dead. Only one thing made sense—this was simply a friend of Early's, someone familiar with the story and out to exact revenge.

His breakfast churned in his stomach, threatening to spew.

The barbed wire would fix them from bringing the sick cows onto his land. But the wire wouldn't arrive for two weeks.

In the meantime, he'd get some men to stand guard at night across the two-and-a-half-mile section that was the only way in and out of the ranch.

His hands clenched tightly.

He *would* catch these culprits. And then he'd get his answers one way or another.

Eleven

Delta met Rand at the livery Sunday afternoon. Excitement and anticipation hovered in the air as though the world had thrown a party and invited her. For once in her life she was accepted. The realization made her heady.

Rand hitched his horse, a black-and-white piebald, to a buggy he insisted on renting. Said it was more fitting for a lady than the buckboard he hauled whiskey in. She cringed at the thought of seeing a few turned heads when they set off, but no one paid them any mind. She relaxed, determined to enjoy the day.

Mother Nature had put on her most glorious smile and decked out the countryside in a profusion of dazzling color. Spring flowers of every kind carpeted the hills and valleys. Their wonderful fragrance wafted in the slight breeze.

An hour and a half later they drove under the huge crossbars that proclaimed the ranch as the Long Odds.

Following the cloud of dust and the sound of bawling cattle, they found Cooper. He was astride his buckskin, going after a calf. When he got alongside the animal, he leaped off the horse and tackled the calf. He quickly tied its legs and dragged the unfortunate thing to a fire where a branding iron waited. Delta's heart went out to the poor frightened calf. It seemed horribly cruel, but Rand had explained everything on the ride out. He assured her the animals didn't feel a thing. It appeared they had tough hides. At least she prayed they did.

Cooper spied Delta and Rand. He said something to one of his men and led his big buckskin over to them.

When he got closer, she noticed the layers of dirt and the perspiration soaking his underarms. Probably a normal state from working with cattle. From the whisker growth, she could tell he hadn't bothered to shave in a few days. But it lent a dark ruggedness to him that made her pulse beat a little faster.

From beneath the brim of his hat, his stormy gray eyes found her, and she squirmed under his piercing stare. She reconsidered the wisdom of coming.

"Miss Delta. Rand. What brings you here?" His deep voice sent tingles dancing up her spine.

"I wanted to check on the dog," Delta explained. "Rand was kind enough to offer to bring me."

"I'll just bet." Cooper's curt tone cemented the fact that he didn't want her or Rand there.

"Now, brother, don't get your tail feathers on fire," Rand said. "I told you I'd be out to watch some of the branding."

"I remember. I'm still in control of my faculties. Just didn't know you planned to bring an audience. This is no place for a lady on a Sunday stroll."

"Well, you know how things are. It was such a

nice day, and Miss Delta needed some fresh air." Rand boldly winked at her.

"And you can't resist a pretty female. I know. I've heard it all before."

Heat flooded Delta's cheeks. "I'm sorry, Mr. Thorne. I wouldn't have come if I'd known I'd be unwelcome. Rand, take me back to town please." Her stiff words mirrored her spine. She shouldn't have come.

"Now, just hold on a minute." Rand leaped from the buggy and jabbed Cooper's chest with a finger. They stepped out of Delta's hearing, and from the looks of things were about to come to blows. Angry words flew, judging by the hand gestures, and though their voices were low, she had no doubt about the subject of their "discussion."

Well, they didn't have to worry. She knew when she wasn't wanted. She'd learned that lesson a long time ago.

Without a word or a backward glance, Delta climbed from the buggy and stalked toward the road back to town. Cooper could go jump in a lake, preferably a deep one. She wouldn't bother him anymore. In fact, both brothers could go straight to perdition. She'd walk to the boardinghouse on her own two feet.

The devil take them both.

She managed to get several yards before Cooper caught her arm. She whirled and her angry gaze slammed into his stormy grays. "I don't need this, Mr. Thorne. Let me go, please."

His right eyebrow arched as he released her. "I apologize for being a donkey's smelly behind. You're welcome at the Long Odds. Me and Rand just had a

little disagreement, an old argument between brothers. I promise I'll mind my p's and q's. Besides, you
haven't seen Bandit. I think you'll like his progress."

Delta hesitated. Cooper, a gentleman? She'd have
to see that. "Fair warning. If I continue to feel out of
place, I'm leaving."

Cooper nodded. "Anytime you want to leave, just
say the word and I'll take you back to town myself."

"So you named the dog Bandit?"

Cooper gave her a crooked smile. "Kinda fitting,
don't you think?"

"It's perfect."

"Rand is going to pitch in with the branding for a
bit. Why don't you let me take you to see the pup?
That is, if it's to your liking."

"I'd like that just fine, Mr. Thorne."

"Now, why is it that you can refer to my brother as
Rand yet you call me Mr. Thorne?"

"You and I are still trying out this friendship thing."

"And?"

Delta couldn't help smiling. She liked keeping the
man who seemed so sure of everything off-kilter. It
was probably a place he hadn't been very often.

"Haven't decided. After all, you wanted to run the
other way when we first met, if I recall."

"Like I said, I'm a donkey's rear end."

"Your words, Mr. Thorne, not mine."

"Can't you consider calling me Cooper? Mr.
Thorne sounds like a doddering old fool with half his
teeth missing."

"I'll give it some thought." Didn't mean she'd
honor his request.

She watched Rand mount Cooper's buckskin and take off after a runaway calf. He wore a big goofy grin. Rand reminded her of a kid just getting his first pair of long pants.

On the other hand, Cooper seemed never to have worn anything but long pants. She'd always heard the expression that still waters ran deep. That described this man perfectly.

She admired the corded muscles in his arms, the firm jaw and sensual mouth, from under the shadow of her lashes. Where had all the air gone? The rugged rancher who rescued mistreated dogs and gave peaches to his friends seemed to have stolen it.

In an effort to cover the effect he had on her, she glanced around for the small orchard Mabel spoke about and located it not far from the whitewashed two-story house. He'd built a fence around the little grove or else the cattle would've tromped down the trees.

A strand of silence spun between them.

"Please, take me to see Bandit. I'm anxious to see the change." The words came out breathless and quite unlike her.

Cooper offered his arm and they strolled back to the buggy. For all his confidence and surety about every-thing, his touch seemed more than a little hesitant as he helped her up. Bandit must've been keeping a sharp eye out, because he shot from the barn like a bullet before Cooper could get the buggy stopped. The dog was like a whirling dervish, dancing around the horse and yipping, evidently excited to see Cooper. The listless look in Bandit's eyes was gone.

Delta expected Cooper would politely offer her a

hand down, but she wasn't prepared when he placed his hands around her waist and swung her easily to the ground. The movement brought her against his hard body, and he held her for a long moment.

It seemed as though the world had suddenly shifted. The ground had become sky and the clouds were beneath her feet. To cover her startlement, she knelt and buried her hot face in the dog's fur. When she glanced up, Cooper was staring as though seeing her for the first time, amusement twinkling in eyes that had darkened to a deep, strange hue.

Delta quickly looked down at the dog, unsure of what Cooper's strange expression meant. Maybe he was laughing at her for being such a ninny. "He's changed so much. I can't believe he's the same dog you rescued."

"About to eat me out of house and home," Cooper growled. "Can't get a blooming day's work out of my men either. Seems all they can think about is feeding the mutt."

The complaint carried no weight. He didn't fool her. She knew Bandit's recovery meant everything to him.

The door to the house opened and a tall, skinny man stepped out. Luckily, he wore wide suspenders, or else his pants would've fallen around his ankles. A big grin covered his face as he ambled toward them.

"Boss, I wonder if the lady would like some refreshment? I got some lemonade and a batch of fresh cookies that I made for Bandit. Ain't often we get someone as pretty as her out here, beggin' your pardon, ma'am."

She smiled and nodded to him.

"Miss Delta, meet my cook, Mack Malone."

"I'm right proud to meet you, Miss Delta." The man's slick, bald head glistened in the sunlight. "Come inside an' take some lemonade with the boss an' me."

"Thank you, Mr. Malone. I'd be delighted."

"Shoot, ma'am. I'm just plain ol' Mack."

And that's how she came to be sitting in Cooper's small parlor with Bandit lying with his head on her feet. For the last two hours she'd sipped on lemonade and eaten cookies while Mack told stories of times past when he cooked for General Lee during the war.

Rand entered the house a while later, bringing pure bedlam in with him. "Well, damn! Here I was busting my rear tackling ornery calves, up to my boot tops in cow patties and horse apples, and you're in here being treated like a queen." Rand's grin still hadn't slipped but he was a sight. His shirt was torn half-off, his arm was bleeding, and he walked with a limp.

"Rand, are you all right?" Delta leaped to her feet.

"Never better. Whooee, that was fun!"

"My brother had his brains scrambled sometime back, Miss Delta." Cooper stretched his long legs out in front of him. "Hasn't been the same since. I learned a long time ago to just accept his shortcomings and try to make the best of it."

Rand snorted and turned to her. "I hope Coop hasn't been too prickly and gave you a true Long Odds welcome. Hopefully he didn't bore the socks off you."

"I've enjoyed myself." She didn't know what to make of Cooper and Rand's exchange. Were they being sarcastic or merely teasing? Hard to tell. But one thing was clear—they cared about each other more than any brothers she'd ever seen.

"I'll wash up and take you back to town. Didn't mean to keep you out here so long," Rand said.

"I'm fine. Truly."

"Glad to hear it." Rand glared at Cooper.

Cooper brushed back a lock of hair that had fallen onto his forehead, untangled his long legs, and got to his feet. "It's not every day I get to spend time with something that doesn't snort and bellow."

Rand left the room. But when Mack followed him, Delta fidgeted under Cooper's stare. The silence became uncomfortable. She leaned to pet Bandit.

At last, Cooper spoke. "I'm glad we have this chance to speak in private."

"Why's that?" If she'd had those hackles Cooper spoke about, they'd have been standing on end.

"Wanted to warn you about Rand. You'll get your heart broken if you get too close. He likes all women... for a while. But like me, he'll never find the altar."

Delta covered the space between them so quickly Bandit scurried for safer territory. She glared up into eyes that reminded her of a cold winter's day. "I can't believe this. You have a lot of gall, Mr. Thorne. The way I see it, you gave up your right to meddle in my affairs when you told me in no uncertain terms that you weren't looking for a wife. Therefore, what I do is none of your concern. If I want to—"

"Do what? Live in sin with Rand?" Cooper brushed her cheek with a fingertip. "You won't. Women like you won't throw your reputation to the wind. You want it all or nothing."

She glared. "You're awfully sure of yourself."

"I know more than you think." His words were soft. "I see the yearning for permanence in your eyes. Dear God, you're a difficult woman to forget."

Cooper tugged her against his lean body, lowered his head, and pressed his sensual lips firmly on hers. The long kiss held passion and promise and warmth. Delta's breath got caught somewhere between the need for more and wishing she'd stayed in town, far away from men who indulged in contradictory behavior.

Her knees grew weak and she clutched the shirt covering his broad chest to keep from falling as the world tilted on its axis.

As the kiss deepened, their breaths mingled in a heated flurry while blood pounded in her ears. She heard a low moan and realized it came from her. Strange how it sounded so very far away.

Her stomach whirled and dipped as though she'd fallen from a great height. Tingles raced up her spine in some kind of mindless confusion. The anger that had propelled her into dangerous territory melted away and left a strange desire in its wake. She shouldn't have let this happen. Before she could unclench her hands from his shirt to take a step back, he released her.

The kiss ended suddenly, leaving her wanting more.

Cooper's sinful half smile turned her knees to jelly. "And that, Miss Delta, is how we do things here in Texas."

Twelve

IN A DAZE, DELTA TURNED TO ESCAPE OUTDOORS. SHE noticed Rand standing in the doorway and her face flamed even more. Fury hardened his blue gaze and she knew he took offense to Cooper kissing her. At the moment, she wanted nothing to do with either brother. She pushed past Rand and raced into the fresh spring air.

She was mortified. What had she done that made either of them think that she welcomed their attention? Or vied for any man's affection, for that matter? She'd done nothing except tend to her own affairs.

Burying her face in her hands, she wondered how she could ever look either of them in the eye again. Gathering her skirts, she climbed into the buggy and fumbled with the reins. All she could think to do was get back to the boardinghouse.

And yet, the lingering taste of Cooper on her tongue, the memory of his firm mouth on hers, sent waves of pleasure washing over her.

Maybe this was just another kind of torture for someone like her.

Maybe Cooper hadn't meant to kiss her.

Or maybe he was used to taking liberties with women. After all, he'd spoken plainly about the many women he'd kissed. Had even bragged about it. It could be he collected kisses like old men collect lint in their pockets.

All she knew was that she had to leave as soon as possible. She was in the process of turning the buggy around when Rand charged from the house.

"Wait," he hollered.

Delta pulled back on the reins and Rand got into the buggy. When she glanced up, Cooper stood in the doorway of the house, his face bathed in shadows. She wondered what had happened between him and Rand.

Or more importantly, between her and Cooper.

Dear God, help her. The man bewildered her and complicated her orderly life.

❧

Cooper watched the buggy until it vanished from sight. He called himself every name he could think of. He had no idea what had come over him. The fresh fragrance of her, that damn beauty mark beneath her mouth, had driven him crazy. When she'd sprung to her feet, her temper flaring, all he could think about was kissing her senseless.

Hell would likely freeze over before he ever got another chance to taste her lips.

Miss Delta Dandridge was the most maddening woman he'd ever met. Most of the time he didn't know if he was up or down. She had no idea what she did to a man. How she tied him in knots and made him forget his good sense. Hell!

Quite possibly after today, she'd never speak to him again.

The one thing he regretted was Rand. Cooper had never meant for the kiss to happen, but that his middle brother witnessed the act was unfortunate. They'd had words, had both said things they shouldn't. Never had they let a woman come between them.

Until now. He winced.

He'd have to apologize the next time he went into town. But first, he'd give Rand time to cool off. Then he'd do his sorry-saying and everything would be all right again. They wouldn't stay mad long. After all, their bond was strong.

Exactly why seeing her with Rand had burrowed deep under his skin he didn't know. But it had. He wasn't up to examining the reasons.

Not yet, anyway.

With regret weighing heavy on his chest, Cooper turned his attention to the branding. He'd best get on with it. He had lots to do before dark.

He meant to take the first shift of guard duty for the section farthest from the main gate when night fell. If anyone crossed onto his land, they'd probably do it there. Swinging into the saddle, he pointed Rebel toward the corral and the branding that couldn't wait.

Then the day was gone before he could blink. The hot supper filled him, even if the fried potatoes were black underneath. At least the beans were good and the corn bread hit the spot. He looked longingly toward the bedroom and his soft bed before grabbing his rifle and trudging out to saddle Rebel.

It was going to be a long night.

A short while later, he pulled up the collar of his jacket against the chill and settled under a big tree, with the rifle lying across his stomach. The buckskin nibbled on some rye grass nearby. A quarter moon dimly lit the countryside.

He'd stationed three more men at intervals up and down the mile-long stretch of land. Cooper was grateful that steep cliffs guarded most of the Long Odds. Sure made his task a lot easier. He'd told his men to fire three shots in the air if they saw intruders.

Somewhere in the distance, coyotes howled. The night predators had come out, it appeared. Sudden rustling of the brush made the hair on his neck stand on end.

Pointing the rifle in the direction of the sound, he slowly stood. Surprise and relief came in equal measures when Bandit bounded out.

The way the scamp's tongue lolled to one side, it looked like he was grinning to beat all. The dog jumped up on Cooper's leg.

"Hey, boy." Cooper knelt to take the animal in his arms. "Don't know what you're doing out here, but I'm happy to see you. Long as you're here, you might as well learn how to guard. You appear to be a natural at tracking already."

Resuming his place under the tree, he reflected on how blessed he was. A man couldn't hope for more than a good horse and a faithful dog. Sure helped ease life's trials.

It neared midnight when strange sounds reached his ears. Hooves struck the ground and brush snapped under the weight of something. Bandit's ears perked up.

Cooper quietly stood, his finger resting on the trigger of the old Winchester. He crept forward on the balls of his feet as the moist night air swirled about him.

All of a sudden a horse came into view, pulling an oxcart that had a steer in it.

"That's far enough," Cooper warned.

In the next instant, another horse and rider came at Cooper from behind at a full gallop.

He aimed the rifle, but before he could get a shot off, he had to leap out of the way to avoid being trampled.

Hell and be damned!

Rolling out from under the horse's hooves, he jumped to his feet. The rider pulled hard on the reins and the horse turned. Back they came even faster. Cooper grabbed Bandit and scrambled behind the tree. He'd lost his Winchester during the fall. The moon's rays glinted off of the rifle where it lay several yards away.

Jerking his pistol from the holster, he squeezed off three shots. The rider yelled and grabbed his arm. The man driving the cart returned fire, all the while trying to get his cart turned around.

Evidently seeing it was useless, the obscured trespasser scrambled onto the back of the horse that carried the lone rider and they galloped off into the blackness.

Reinforcements arrived about five minutes later. Cooper and the men inspected the abandoned cart and the steer inside. The poor beast had thick mucus hanging from its mouth and could barely stand, leaving no doubt about its purpose.

"Did you see the varmints, Coop?" Zeke asked.

"Just barely. Both men had their hats pulled down low, and I was too busy trying to stay alive to try to get a better glimpse of them. This is the last button on Mabel's drawers. You can bet I'll pay a visit to the few neighbors around here bright and early tomorrow. Should've long before this."

"An' I'll go with you," Zeke declared.

"What're we gonna do with this poor critter?" another cowboy asked.

"If we can get it out of the cart, I'll shoot it and we'll set it ablaze." Cooper stalked to the conveyance and pulled the wooden pins to release the back. He tied a rope around the sickly beast's neck and urged it to the ground.

Zeke moved the horses far away from it.

One well-aimed shot put the steer out of its misery. Zeke and the other cowboys set it on fire.

"What're we gonna do with the horse that's pullin' the cart?" Zeke wanted to know.

"Someone'll have to drive the horse and cart up to the barn for now. Keep the horse away from the others just in case he's carrying the disease. I'll decide what to do tomorrow." Cooper looked around for Bandit. He'd lost track of the dog during the excitement.

But Bandit wasn't anywhere to be seen. Cooper whistled and called. He searched the brush and came up empty. He'd about given up when the canine scampered into view. The dog had a black felt hat clenched in his teeth. He laid it at Cooper's feet, then sat back and looked up expectantly.

"Good boy!" Cooper ruffled Bandit's ears and

picked up the hat. "This must've fallen off one of the trespassers. You're gonna make an excellent tracker."

Zeke grinned from ear to ear like a proud parent. "He must've chased after 'em, all right. I think he's earned his keep. Maybe you can get some inkling about who the owner might be from the hat."

"Reckon so," Cooper agreed. He'd need more light to inspect it though. "Let's head for the house. It's time for the second shift. I doubt they'll be back tonight, but we should still keep watch just in case."

❧

Miles away in Battle Creek, Delta Dandridge threw back the covers and swung her legs over the side of the bed. She couldn't sleep. Thoughts churned inside her head. She couldn't get the kiss out of her mind.

A woman's first kiss, she learned, wasn't something she could easily forget. So many emotions swirled inside her. One minute she wanted to laugh and the next to cry.

A silent tear slipped down her cheek. Her fingers stole to her lips. She savored the remembrance and couldn't stifle the fervent wish for more. Not that it would ever happen again. By now, Cooper Thorne had likely come to his senses and realized his mistake.

She kept hearing that deep voice of Cooper's that rumbled like distant thunder and turned her insides to jelly.

Wanted to warn you about Rand, he'd said. *You'll get your heart broken if you get too close. He likes all women… for a while. But like me, he'll never find the altar.*

Was the warning not so much about Rand, but himself?

Again. How many times did he think he had to remind her? She *could* understand English.

Delta walked to the window that overlooked Battle Creek. Darkness bathed the town, softening the sad, shabby buildings. It would be hours before daylight. The town hadn't changed, but she sure had. She wasn't the same woman who'd set out for Cooper's ranch with such high anticipation.

She should probably be angry. Most women would. But she wasn't.

Though the kiss had come so suddenly, like a summer rainstorm sweeping across the hills and valleys, Cooper's touch had been gentle. He hadn't kissed her out of anger. And she supposed it surprised him as much as it did her. At least that's what she'd seen in his honest gray stare.

The memory of the firm pressure of his lips on hers persisted despite her efforts to put it in perspective. She'd come to Texas to find a new start and had not been disappointed.

This was a place in which to mend broken dreams and find true worth. Opportunity abounded. It was all around her, and all she had to do was reach out and grab it.

No one taunted and jeered at her here.

Leaning her forehead against the windowpane, she sighed. Whatever hardship she'd gone through to get here, it'd been worth it a hundred times over. The memory of selling the only thing she had of value in order to bury her mother brought pain. The gold locket had been given to Phoebe Dandridge by her grand-mother, who'd emigrated from Ireland. That woman too had been looking for a fresh start and found it along with the love of a lifetime. Phoebe had only found a rotten, no-good weasel who'd refused to marry her after she found herself in trouble. Her poor mother had been beneath the wealthy Langston Graham.

Delta's thoughts rambled on until she arrived back where she started.

The kiss.

Rand hadn't said much during the drive back to town. He'd apologized for talking her into going out to the ranch, and that was the extent of it. Delta had tried to assure him that everything was fine, but she knew he'd not bought her fib. She wondered if he sensed the change in her, wondered if it was that apparent.

Not that it would lead anywhere.

It couldn't. Cooper Thorne had made that crystal clear.

But, Lord, why did he have to have his heart set on being a bachelor?

Thirteen

THANKFULLY, DELTA HAD HER JOB TO OCCUPY HER wayward thoughts. Dwelling on Cooper and the way she'd felt all warm and melty when his lips touched hers would gain her nothing.

She reported for work on Monday morning and immediately grabbed a broom and went out to sweep the sidewalk in front of the general store. Loud sobs drew her attention. A young, copper-haired boy who likely hadn't seen too many birthdays ran up the street as if the devil bit at his heels.

Delta put down her broom and walked toward him. Her heart skittered when she saw the blood and dark bruises on his face. "Do you need help, young man?"

The youngster seemed in a daze. He swiped at the tears on his cheeks with his torn shirt sleeve. She recognized him from seeing him talk to Cooper and the few times he'd come into the store. She didn't know his name, though. He never bought anything—just stood silently in front of the candy jar and stared.

The boy jerked and glanced up when she laid a

gentle hand on his arm. "Where's Mr. Cooper? He said to come find him."

"I haven't seen him." She led him out of the street. "Can I help?"

"My mama. She ain't moving. I cain't wake her up." His voice lowered to a whisper. "I'm scared."

Delta untied her apron and tossed it near the broom. "Show me where she is. I'll see what I can do. What is your name?"

"Ben. Ben Barclay." His chin quivered when he spoke.

"Okay, Ben. Let's get your mama some help." She took his hand.

"Pa got likkered up and he took his fists to her." The boy bravely tried to swallow his sobs, but one made it past his bloodied lip. "Mr. Cooper always knows what to do. He's my friend and I need him."

"Take me to your mama." Hot anger rose. One thing she couldn't abide was a man who beat his family. She didn't know what she'd do if she ran into Ben's pa, but she wouldn't back down from him. That much she knew. She glanced toward the saloon. Maybe she should get Rand. But she didn't get a chance before Ben was dragging her down the street in his hurry to get back to his mother.

Little more than a lean-to, the hovel where the youngster and his mother lived was surrounded by thick brush with only a trail of sorts leading to the front door. Ben held back, clearly terrified. She could tell he wanted to be brave, but fear was winning out.

"You wait outside until I call you. Hide in the brush where you won't be seen." When the boy hesitated, she added, "I'll be fine. Go on now."

Delta made sure he was safely out of sight before she stepped to the door and rapped smartly. No answer. She turned the knob and entered. Her eyes had trouble adjusting to the dark interior. It appeared the only light came from cracks between the boards. The floor was dirt.

"Hello?" She waited for a response. Ben's father was either gone or passed out. She didn't see him anywhere.

Stumbling toward a dark figure lying on the floor, her foot met with an empty liquor bottle; it went skittering across the floor before hitting the leg of the table.

"Ma'am, I'm Delta Dandridge." She bent over Ben's mother.

She didn't move. Delta desperately needed some light. She spied a lamp on the rickety table and lit it, then carried it over to the woman.

A nasty gash sliced her head. Bruises, old on top of new, colored her face. Delta needed some water to wash off the blood, but she didn't see any so she lifted her skirt and tore a strip from her petticoat. Using that, she wrapped it around the woman's head to stanch the wound.

Low moans coming from Mrs. Barclay gave Delta hope. She needed to move her to a safe place where she could doctor her.

"Ma'am, can you hear me?"

Feebly lifting her arm, the woman muttered, "Help."

"Yes, ma'am. That's why I'm here."

"Cooper?"

"I'm sorry, ma'am, but he's out at the ranch. I'm Delta Dandridge. Do you think you can stand if I help you?"

"Gotta see to my boy."

"Ben's fine. He's safe."

Clearly her patient wouldn't be able to walk under her own power. Delta stepped to the door. "Ben, can you run and get the sheriff or Mr. Sinclair at the saloon? Do you think you can do that?"

The brush rustled as the boy came out. He gave her a nod.

"If you see your pa, run for help."

The lad whimpered and raced down the street. While she waited for reinforcements, she made Mrs. Barclay as comfortable as she could. Looking around, she found a pillow of sorts and put it under the woman's head. A pitcher had a few drops of water in it, so she tore off another section of her petticoat and wiped away a little of the blood. Then she located a length of wood from a smashed chair. If Mr. Barclay returned, she'd crack it over his head as hard as she could. All the while, she kept an ear open for the sound of footsteps.

Before long she heard the sound of Rand's voice. She breathed a sigh of relief and put down her weapon. He and a man he called Pettibone wasted no time.

Rand gently lifted the limp, broken woman in his arms. "Where do you want me to take her?"

Delta hadn't given any thought to that. She searched her mind for a suitable place and only one popped into her head. "The boardinghouse."

Mrs. Barclay moaned a few times, then went limp in Rand's arms as he wended his way toward the establishment. Since Delta couldn't assist with the carrying, she hurried ahead to explain the situation to Mabel. When Rand arrived, Delta held the door for him, then followed him up the stairs to the room Mabel indicated.

"Land's sakes, that rotten man nearly killed Jenny this time," Mabel exclaimed after Rand laid their patient on a bed.

"Yes, ma'am, he did." Delta turned to Ben. "Can you go get the doc?"

The boy nodded again and scampered loudly down the stairs.

Delta touched Rand's arm. "Thank you."

"Glad to help." He and Pettibone looked mighty uncomfortable. At last Rand said, "If you have everything under control here, we have some business to take care of."

"We can manage this part."

The two men left, and while they waited for the doctor, Mabel King bustled downstairs to heat some water. She returned with it, along with an armful of clean cloths.

Pushing aside Jenny's blood-soaked hair, Delta examined the wounds. A cut next to her right eye looked troublesome, as did a large protrusion on her jaw. But a great deal of blood still flowed from the wound on the side of her head. "I didn't know where else to take her. I hope you don't mind."

"I'm glad you brought her here. Jenny's my baby sister." Tears filled Mabel's eyes. "I always knew that husband of hers was a sorry, low-down excuse for a man. I tried to warn her he'd hurt her real bad. She just brushed my fears aside and said she knew how to handle Hogue Barclay."

Just then Ben returned with Doc Yates. Delta

hadn't had the opportunity to make his acquaintance but she instantly liked him. The short, stooped man had wise eyes and a shock of snow-white hair that hadn't been combed in Lord knew how long.

Ben pressed close to the bed. "Is Mama gonna wake up?"

Mabel's arm stole around her nephew. "She sure is. Don't you worry none. Sometimes it takes a while for the brain to remember to tell the eyes to open." She cleared the hoarseness from her throat. "How about we go down to the kitchen and see what's in my cookie jar?"

"But Mama…"

Doc Yates patted Ben's head. "Go with your aunt, son. I'll take real good care of your mama."

Delta dipped the blood-soaked cloth she'd used to clean Jenny's wound into the basin. "Ben, let Doc work. We'll put her in a nightgown and make her comfortable. Then you can sit with her all you want. How about that?"

Ben's bottom lip quivered as he nodded. "I reckon."

To Delta's relief, he went with his aunt, although reluctantly.

When the door closed behind them, Doc Yates examined every inch of his patient. Suddenly, he turned. "She's pregnant."

Shock rippled through Delta. "Is the baby all right?"

"Near as I can tell. Has a good heartbeat."

"How far along is she?"

"I'd estimate about five months. 'Course, she's so thin, it's hard to tell."

The poor thing. Her heart broke for Jenny. To be

in such a bad marriage and now in the family way on top of it compounded everything. Maybe her husband had tried to make his wife miscarry. Maybe that was why he'd been so angry.

After Doc bandaged Jenny's head, Delta got her into a nightgown. Now that she could see Jenny Barclay's face, the deep bruises and cuts made Delta's heart ache. She had probably been a pretty woman once, but the years and the mistreatment had taken a toll. How on earth could she have kept her son in that environment? It was bad enough she chose that for herself, but for her son too?

Or maybe Jenny had taken the beatings so Ben would get fewer? Possible. Delta shouldn't judge.

One thing she knew—she wouldn't rest until she persuaded the sheriff to put Hogue Barclay in jail and throw away the key. He wouldn't get a chance to do this again, if she had any say-so in the matter. She'd tar and feather him herself and run him to the far ends of the earth, where pestilence and disease and deadly vipers would make his life unbearable.

"Well, I think this is all I can do." The doc sighed, peering over his spectacles. "The rest is up to the good Lord and Jenny. I'll check on her tomorrow. If you need me, you know where I'll be."

"Thank you, Doctor."

As soon as Mabel and Ben returned to sit with the patient, Delta marched straight to the sheriff's office. "I demand to have Hogue Barclay arrested," she said without preamble.

Sheriff Strayhorn glanced at her with bleary eyes over a handbill he'd been studying. It appeared he hadn't had much sleep. She didn't know crime was so rampant in Battle Creek. "Miss Dandridge, is it?"

"That's right." She ignored his gesture for her to take the chair in front of his desk. She was far too mad to sit and pretend the world was all rosy. "I want the man arrested."

The heavy sigh told her this wasn't the first time the sheriff had dealt with Hogue. "May I ask what he did?"

"Beat his wife and son within an inch of their lives. Jenny's over at the boardinghouse unconscious, and Ben's black and blue with bruises."

Strayhorn smoothed his bushy mustache that almost completely hid his mouth and laid down the handbill. "I warned him about this. Frankly, I didn't know he was back in town. Never stays too long when he does show up. A shiftless sort. A mystery to me what Jenny sees in him. Reckon I'll know where to look."

"So you'll lock him up?" Delta pressed.

"I'll have a talk with him, Miss Dandridge, and get to the bottom of this," the middle-aged sheriff ground out. "And I mean to check on Jenny. I'll decide for myself if the facts warrant an arrest."

Delta felt like grabbing the lawman and shaking him. Could he not see the gravity of the situation? "Is that the best you can do?"

"Afraid so, ma'am." Sheriff Strayhorn stood and jerked his hat on. His imposing height coupled with the gun belt around his waist told her the barrel-chested lawman could handle whatever arose.

If only he took the matter seriously.

Perhaps the fact she was new in town had some

bearing on things, she supposed. No one knew anything about her. The sheriff probably took her for a
troublemaker. Well, she'd have to convince folks of
her good character, but that took time, time she didn't
have at the moment.

Outside the jail, they parted company. The lawman
ambled toward the saloon and Delta stomped up the
street to the mercantile.

Once she told John Abercrombie the circumstances
of why she'd abandoned the store, he insisted she take
the rest of the day off.

By the time she returned to Mabel's, Jenny Barclay
still had yet to open her eyes. Not uncommon, though.
A deep head wound could leave a body unconscious
for days. To find the sheriff there surprised her. The
deep lines of his face had hardened into a mask. He
was clearly affected by what he saw.

Strayhorn grimly rose from a chair beside the bed.
"I'll have Hogue in jail within the hour."

"Thank you, Sheriff." Relief flooded over her.

"No man is gonna do this in my town and get away
with it." His voice turned to hard granite. "Don't
know how long I can keep him locked up, though.
If she dies, I'll charge him with murder. If she lives,
he'll go free. No law on the books against a husband
correcting his wife and kids however he sees fit. Not
yet anyway, though there definitely should be."

The inequality made her furious. She wrestled
to keep her tongue. After a few moments, she said
tightly, "We'll deal with that when the time comes,
I suppose."

Ben tiptoed into the room after the sheriff left.

Mabel had cleaned the blood from his lip and tended myriad other cuts. He sat in the chair and took his mother's limp hand in his. "I wish she'd wake up."

"She will," Delta assured him. "She's going to be fine."

Her heart went out to the boy. He'd been through so much for someone so young. She made herself a vow—not only would he have Cooper as a guardian angel, but he'd have her also.

A person couldn't have too many guardian angels.

Fourteen

NOON NEARED BUT DELTA HAD MORE IMPORTANT things to do than eat. She'd just stepped out of the boardinghouse when her attention shifted to a fight in the middle of the street. Two men. One was Rand; she didn't recognize the other.

"Cooper and I told you to leave Jenny alone," Rand yelled, jamming his fist into the man's face and knocking him backward. This must be Hogue. Delta joined the crowd that had gathered around. Her heart rejoiced that Jenny's husband was getting his just deserts. She wished she could get in a few licks herself.

"She's my wife," snarled Hogue through a cut lip.

"Not for much longer, if we have our way about it," Rand shot back.

Just then Sheriff Strayhorn barged through the flock of onlookers. "Break it up. I'll handle this, Rand. Let him go."

Rand Sinclair shoved Hogue to the packed street, where the man landed with a hard jolt. "Good thing you came along, Sheriff, because I meant to kill him. His brutality has gone on far too long."

"Reckon I know that, Rand. But if you kill him, I'd just have to arrest you."

"It'd be worth it." Rand picked up his hat and slapped it against his leg, then he wiped a trickle of blood from his lip.

"Hogue, you messed up real good this time." Strayhorn jerked his prisoner to his feet and shoved him toward the jail.

Delta hurried over to Rand. "Are you all right?"

"It'll take a sight more than Hogue Barclay to whip me."

"I was thrilled to see him get what was coming to him. Thank you."

About that time, Pettibone came from the saloon. "Boss, got trouble inside. Better come. George just busted a bottle over Hank's head. Blood's spurtin' everywhere."

Rand went with Pettibone, and Delta turned in the direction of the livery. Minutes later, she'd rented a horse and buggy. She hated to have to use what little money she'd stashed away from her job at the mercantile, but with Rand tied up with business affairs, she had no choice. Little Ben had said Cooper was his friend and he needed him. She imagined Jenny would also say that if she could speak.

Besides, she suspected Cooper would want to know what happened. Thank goodness she remembered the way to the Long Odds. Soon she passed under the high crossbar. A quick scan told her he'd probably be in the thick of the branding. She was right. He stalked toward her with his leather chaps slapping against his trousers. He wore a deep scowl and Delta wasn't sure that coming was such a good idea. She trembled a little as she climbed from the buggy.

"It's really not wise for you to be here—"

"Save it. I came to tell you about Jenny. And Ben."

Instantly his expression changed to one of concern. "What happened?"

Cooper's big hands clenched and unclenched as she told him everything. He called a young cowboy over. "Saddle a fresh horse and make it quick."

The cowboy nodded and sprinted for the barn.

"Did you tell the sheriff?"

"I did. At first he didn't seem that enthused to do anything, but seeing Jenny changed his mind."

Jerking his hat off, he slammed it to the ground. "I should've been there. They depend on me."

She wanted to comfort him in some way but wasn't sure how he'd take it. She finally brushed his arm with a light touch. "You have a ranch to run. They understand. I don't know much about Ben or Jenny, but no one wants to be a burden."

"I suspected Hogue was slapping them around. But I did nothing. I should've—"

"Cooper, you can only do so much. Stop torturing yourself."

He shoved a hand through his hair, picked up his hat, and jammed it back on his head. "I promised I'd be there if they needed me. But I wasn't."

"There's something else you probably need to know. Jenny's in the family way."

Shock rippled across his face and deepened the lines around his mouth. She could tell he wanted to say something, but he didn't get a chance, for at that moment the young cowboy galloped from the barn. He jumped off when he reached them and handed his boss the reins.

Cooper tied the horse to the back of the buggy and helped Delta up onto the seat. He quickly followed and yelled to her to hold on. Delta fell against him as the buggy jerked forward at a high rate of speed.

He put an arm around her and pulled her tightly to his side. Seconds later, the buggy careened around a curve on two wheels.

Even if she'd wanted to, she had no time to protest the fact she was in his lap.

Holding on occupied every thought as they flew down the road as though Lucifer's hounds were chasing them.

≈

The boardinghouse was tomb-like when Cooper raced through the door. Ben stumbled from the small parlor.

Searing anger burned a path through him at sight of the battered face. He'd walked in Ben's shoes and knew what it was like to have fists pounding him and watching a father beat his mother to death.

"You got my blood in you, boy, an' don't you forget it," his father, Otto, had snarled at him from the time he could remember. The man beat Cooper down until he'd rather be dead than live with the torment.

No, forgetting he had Otto's killer blood inside him was impossible. It was burned into his brain. It was why he would never marry, why he'd never have children. He wouldn't pass along his bad blood to anyone. The violence would stop with him.

He'd been no older than Ben when they hanged his father. Strangers came after that and hauled Cooper to the orphanage.

Shaking his head to clear the memories, he returned to the present.

The thing about Hogue Barclay was that he was fine until he took to the bottle—then he went plumb crazy. Cooper didn't know what made a man crave alcohol when he had so much to live for.

The boy stared at the floor. "Pa done it, Mr. Cooper. He beat Mama real bad this time. I done thought he'd kilt her. I looked for you ever'place, but Miss Delta said you weren't in town. She came and got Mama and brought us here."

Cooper pulled the scared youngster to him in a fierce hug. "I know. I'm so sorry."

He ground his back teeth. He'd warned Hogue of what would happen if he continued to take his anger out on his family. The man hadn't listened. This time there'd be hell to pay. And this time he'd make certain that the man would never again get within a hundred miles of Jenny and Ben and live to tell it.

"Miss Delta had the sheriff put him in jail." Suddenly Ben slowly smiled. "Pa cain't get us now. He cain't hurt us."

"Nope, he sure can't." Cooper was going to make sure of that. He was done with Hogue Barclay. No more. The sooner he made a believer out of the man, the better it would be for everyone.

Ben was an old soul who'd lived many lifetimes. He'd

dealt with things a young boy his age shouldn't have had to. Cooper saw a lot of himself in Ben, so he knew what the youngster thought before he even said the words.

Delta stepped through the door just then. Their eyes met and held for a long second. His tongue seemed glued to the roof of his mouth. Frankly, he didn't know what to say. Other than when she came to the ranch to get him a little while ago, they hadn't spoken since *the kiss*. She'd most likely nail his hide to the wall if he so much as tried to explain. That is, if he *could* offer a reason that made sense, but he had yet to figure out what happened that day, why he'd grabbed her like that. All he could say was that his brain went haywire whenever she was around.

Ben wiggled away from Cooper and wasted no time in throwing his skinny arms around her waist.

They looked a pair standing there, Delta with her proper manners and ready smile that hid the sadness in her eyes and Ben with his dark bruises and battered self-esteem.

It got under Cooper's skin more than a little that the boy had turned to someone else. In fact, it appeared they'd grown awfully close in one day's time. Thank goodness he hadn't dillydallied coming into town, or Ben would've forgotten all about him. All the same, he was glad Delta had stepped up and filled in when he couldn't be there.

At the first opportunity, he'd damn well let her know he could handle things from this point forward.

Cooper stood there with his hat in his hands and a big helping of regret lodged in his chest. "Well, I'll just…I'll go look in on Jenny."

"I'm sure she'd like that." Delta gave a half smile and smoothed Ben's obstinate cowlick. "Even if she's still sleeping, she'll know you're there."

With a nod, he went up the stairs. Mabel directed him to Jenny's room. He wasn't prepared for what he saw. Jenny's hair was caked with dried blood, but it was her face, all swelled and bruised, that made him suck in a wobbly breath. Her eyes were closed and she didn't stir when he came in.

Though Jenny was just a young woman on the shy side of twenty-four, she looked at least forty years old.

Taking a chair beside the bed, he held Jenny's hand. He glanced at her belly, where a new life grew. "I promise you I'll make this right. You won't have to go through this ever again."

Of course, she couldn't reply, but it felt good just saying the words. He sat there silently, breathing with her and praying she'd be all right. A short while later, he kissed her hand and told her he'd be back.

❧

White-hot fury settled in every bone, every muscle, every ounce of blood coursing through Cooper's body. People scattered as he took long strides toward the jail. He didn't pay them any mind. Justice for Jenny was the only thing he cared about. And by God, he'd have it.

Sheriff Strayhorn glanced over the rim of his coffee cup when Cooper shoved the door open. "Want some coffee, Coop?"

"Nope. You have Hogue in one of your cells?"

"I do."

When Cooper marched to the door separating the sheriff's office from the jail, Strayhorn yelled, "Hey, you can't go back there."

The sheriff's chair clattered to the floor in his hurry to plant himself between Cooper and the door.

"The hell I can't." Cooper's hard glare might've given some men pause, but not Strayhorn.

"Take a seat, Coop. I'm not letting you back there all worked up like you are, and that's that. I couldn't care less what you do to that drunk, but I'm not in the mood to clean up a bunch of blood today."

Though sitting was the last thing on Cooper's mind, he obliged the tall, barrel-chested sheriff. "You saw what he did. He deserves like treatment, not a dry roof over his head, a soft mattress to sleep on, and meals handed to him like royalty."

Righting his chair, Strayhorn sat down and leaned back. "Don't you think I know that? Hell, I'd just as soon turn you loose on him and sit back and watch. But it's my job to uphold the law and that's what I aim to do."

"How long you planning to keep him?"

"Cain't hold him but a couple of weeks, I reckon."

"You know that's not long enough. He'll kill Jenny when he gets out."

"What do you want me to do? I can talk to him until I turn blue in the face, but if the man ain't of a mind to listen, I might as well save my breath for breathing."

"Do me a favor. Let me know when you're set to release him. It's the least you can do for Jenny and Ben."

"Okay, Coop. I hope you have a plan to protect those two."

Not yet, but he was working on it. One thing he was sure of, he wouldn't let Hogue near enough to Jenny and Ben to do any more damage. No matter what steps he had to take. Even if he had to break the law, even kill the low-down skunk, he'd keep them safe.

"You can bet on it."

Now that he had the matter of Hogue Barclay out of the way, Cooper told the sheriff about the raiders who'd ridden onto the ranch big as life the previous night.

"And you didn't see their faces?"

"I wouldn't be sitting here talking to you if I had," Cooper snapped. "I'd have delivered their bodies to you in the back of a wagon."

"What about the brand on the horse they left behind?"

"Didn't wear one."

"That's pretty strange."

"Yep." Cooper rubbed eyes that felt as though they had sand in them. He'd only gotten a couple of hours sleep. "I have a hat that belonged to one of them."

"Anything distinguishing about it?"

"Not much. It was just a black felt one that had a bullet hole in the crown and a narrow strip of a red bandanna for a band."

"Not much to go on. I'll ride out to the ranch if you want and take a look around."

"Appreciate it, Sheriff." With his stomach feeling like he'd just taken a big gulp of sour milk, Cooper rose and strode out the door, wishing he could put off this next piece of business.

❧

Rand occupied a corner table, shuffling a deck of cards, when Cooper strolled into the Lily of the West. He took a chair across from him.

"I can tell by the set of your jaw that you're not here on a social call," Rand drawled.

"Looks like you tangled with a mountain lion."

The middle brother touched his lip. "Not much of a fight, really. Got a piece of Hogue is all. Would've mopped up the street with his damn carcass if Strayhorn hadn't stopped me."

"More than I got. Guess we have to be satisfied with that. Just came from the jail, but Strayhorn threatened to shoot me when I tried to go back to the cells."

"Guess you came into town to see Jenny."

Cooper nodded. "Delta came to get me."

"I haven't seen Jenny since I carried her to the boardinghouse," Rand said quietly. "She's in a bad way."

"Reckon it's a little hard to justify." Cooper's words came out sarcastic and hard as a chunk of granite.

A dark flush crept up Rand's neck. "Just what are you saying?"

"I'm merely curious why you sold Hogue a snootful of whiskey when you know how mean he gets. Surely you knew what he'd do to Jenny and Ben. Or didn't you care?"

"Believe it or not, Coop, I don't have time to write down how much each man drinks. I was in my office working on the books. For your information, I fired my barkeep. Told him to draw his wages and clear out. He should've seen how drunk Hogue was getting and refused to sell him any more. I run a reputable place. Hell, you know that."

Even though Cooper was still mad enough to drive his fist into Hogue's face and come out the back side of the man's skull, he knew Rand wouldn't lie to save his own skin. "I apologize. Seems that's all I do anymore. I should've known you didn't have anything to do with it. Friends?"

Rand grinned. "Always. Gonna take a sight more than Hogue Barclay to come between us, big brother. You're gonna have to realize though that Jenny is a grown woman. She makes her own choices."

"You know why I have to watch out for her," Cooper snapped.

"I do, but at some point it's gotta sink into your thick skull that you can't save the world."

No, but he could try, especially when he owed a debt.

"Want something to drink?" Rand asked after moments ticked by.

"Coffee, if you've got it." Though he doubted it, maybe a cup of strong brew would get rid of some of the hate bubbling in his gut.

Within a few minutes, Rand slid a cup in front of him, along with a hot fried pie. "How are things at the ranch?"

Cooper's mood improved a tad as he took a big bite of the pie and licked his lips. Blueberry, one of his favorites. Between bites he told Rand about the raiders who'd brought another sick cow onto the Long Odds the previous night and the shots they'd exchanged.

"You're lucky they didn't kill you, Coop. But at least now you know this is deliberate. It's clear you're in a war with someone. Wish we knew who. Have you posted guards at night?"

"Yep. I just wish I could've seen the polecats' faces."

"They weren't wearing masks?"

"Nope. Had their hats pulled down low onto their foreheads, though, and the quarter moon only gave out a thimbleful of light. Zeke and I visited every ranch in a ten-mile radius just after daybreak to see if any had hoof-and-mouth amongst their herd."

"I take it they didn't."

"You would be right. According to them, they have no sign of the disease on their land."

"But you think they might be speaking with a forked tongue, as the Indians say?"

"Can't say, but men have lied about less. No rancher likes word to get out that he has disease spreading through his herd. That's one secret that's been known to start a mess of trouble." Cooper fumbled in his pocket, removing the brass token he'd discovered the morning Rand and Delta had come to the ranch. "I found this near a dead steer. Been meaning to show it to you."

Rand took the coin and examined it. Shock rippled across his face. "The only Steamboat Bathhouse I've heard of was in Hannibal. How did it wind up on the Long Odds?"

"Asking myself the same question. Since Tolbert Early lies in a grave, it has to be some friend of his who's out for revenge."

"Or a brother maybe?" Rand handed back the coin.

"I never considered the fact he might have kin. How many more Earlys do we have to kill?"

"However many it takes. We have plenty of bullets."

"That we do." Cooper's thoughts flew to the four boxes he'd bought the day he told Delta he couldn't marry her. He hadn't known then how badly he'd need them.

"Let me know how I can help. Say the word and I'll be there."

"Appreciate that, Rand. Oh, one of the trespassers last night lost his hat. Black with a red bandanna strip for a band. Have you seen anyone wearing something like it?"

"As a matter of fact, a man came in several days ago wearing that hat. His shifty eyes and surly attitude drew my attention. Felt in my bones he was trouble."

"If he comes in again, keep him and get word to me. I'd like to have a little chat about his criminal activities." Cooper gulped the last of his coffee and stood. "Can't be gone from the ranch long, and I want to check back in on Jenny."

"I'll keep an eye on her." Rand clapped him on the back. "You keep dodging those bullets out there, big brother."

∽

The boardinghouse was deathly silent when Cooper entered. He climbed the stairs and went into Jenny's room. Delta sat in the chair with Ben on her lap. She looked tired.

"Any change?" he asked.

"Not yet."

Jenny lay unmoving. Cooper couldn't ignore the

ache squeezing his heart until he couldn't breathe. He'd failed.

Fighting his guilt and anger, he touched her limp hand. "Reckon I'll head back to the ranch."

Delta walked him down to the door. The faintest scent of lilacs drifted around him. "I'll let you know when she's out of the woods."

"I'd be obliged if you'd send someone with word."

A tired smile tilted the corners of her mouth. "I'll do better than that. I'll ride out to the ranch myself."

It took considerable effort but he managed to drag his attention from that dark beauty mark sitting beneath her mouth. "Delta, when all of this is over, we have things to talk about, you and I."

"About that kiss…"

He brushed his thumb across her lips. "This is not the time or place. What we have to talk about is best done over a nice juicy steak and a long walk beneath a full moon."

"But—"

"There's too much risk of being overheard. It can wait until we're alone."

Her moist, supple lips parted slightly in protest. He recalled they were even more so when he'd boldly pressed his mouth to hers.

Damn, he wished he could yank her against his chest and kiss the daylights out of her again. But he'd found out the hard way, one kiss was too many and a thousand would never be enough.

Delta Dandridge was like the promise of a brilliant golden sunrise after a long, cold night, and he'd just begun discovering the things she didn't want people to see.

Even as he denied the attraction he had for her, he had to admit she'd shaken him to the core. It hadn't been just his mouth pressed so firmly to hers—it had been far, far more than that.

Stepping back, he put on his hat. He had to put some distance between them before he did something he'd regret.

Laying a hand on his arm, she spoke low, "Be safe, Cooper. I do look forward to having my say. It's time we come to an understanding."

He nodded and opened the door. Sounded like she meant to lay down the rules of battle. He was positive that did not bode well for him.

Fifteen

DELTA SAT BY JENNY'S BEDSIDE THE WHOLE NIGHT. She wanted to be close in case the woman woke. But it wasn't until after they'd eaten breakfast that Jenny opened her eyes. She came awake by degrees, looking around the unfamiliar room, appearing confused.

"Where am I?" Jenny croaked, licking her swollen mouth.

"Your sister's boardinghouse," Delta said gently. "I'm Delta Dandridge. Ben came and asked me to help. I found you and brought you here."

The horror in the woman's eyes told Delta that everything had come back to her in a rush. She tried to sit up.

"Please, you have to stay in bed." Delta laid a calming hand on Jenny's shoulder. "You're safe here."

"But H-Hogue…"

"The sheriff locked him in jail. He can't hurt you."

"He'll k-kill me for this."

"No, he won't. We're going to protect you."

"You don't know him. He has a mean temper."

Delta stared into Jenny's badly swollen eyes. "I can see that. But he can't get to you. I promise."

"Ben? Where's my boy?" Jenny tried to get up again, only to be restrained by Delta.

"Shhh. Ben is fine. He's downstairs with Mabel."

"Hogue was so mad. Ben tried to stop him, tried to protect me. I watched in horror when Hogue threw him into a wall."

"Ben's resilient and he worships his mother, that's plain to see." Delta plumped up the pillows. "He's a fine boy. You have every right to be proud of him."

"My baby?" Jenny whispered, as though afraid to speak the words aloud.

"Doc says it's fine."

"Thank the Lord. I can just imagine what my sister will say." Jenny's voice sounded weak and far away. "Mabel always warned me this would happen. She'll tell me in no uncertain terms how right she was."

"Oh, I don't think Mabel is like that. She was so scared she'd lose you. And she's been wonderful with Ben. She's teaching him to cook and he's enjoying every minute."

"I'm glad. Hogue laid down the law, forbade me from seeing my sister. But Mabel is Ben's aunt."

"Could you handle a bite of breakfast, Mrs. Barclay?"

"I'd like it if you would call me Jenny. And some milk toast might be nice, if it's no bother."

Delta rose but Jenny's feeble hand reached out. "Could you tell Ben I'd like to see him?"

"Absolutely. He'll be thrilled."

The boy's face lit up when Delta told him his

mother was awake and wanting to see him. He gave a whoop and bounded up the stairs.

Delta found Mabel in the kitchen kneading enough dough to make her daily loaves of bread. She quickly told her about Jenny and her wish for some milk toast.

"Hallelujah! This is great news. I'll get it whipped up before she gets out of the notion of eating. I'm not surprised she wants it, though. Our mama always made it for us when we were little."

Leaving Jenny in Mabel's capable hands, Delta went to work. John Abercrombie was trying to assist Granny Ketchum, but he clearly was making no progress. Delta couldn't describe the look of relief on his face when she walked through the door.

"At last someone who knows what they're doing," declared Granny. Her thick glasses had slipped onto the tip of her nose.

"What do you need?" Delta put on her apron and tied it.

"Well, like I was telling John, I need some thingamajigs that you use to keep your stockings up. He don't know beans from turnips about women's things."

"Oh, you mean garters."

"Yes, didn't I just say that?"

Granny was fast losing what little mind she had. Delta reached and adjusted the old woman's glasses, replying softly, "Yes, you did. I'm sure we have exactly what you're looking for. Did someone come into your house and steal yours?" She led Granny to the women's section of the store.

"How did you know? I ain't breathed a word of this to anyone 'cepting you. A delicate woman like me can't bear to talk to Sheriff Strayhorn about such things."

Delta couldn't hold back the smile. She leaned over and kissed Granny Ketchum's wrinkled cheek. "I love you. You're the grandmother I never had."

Tears misted in the lady's rheumy eyes. "No one ever said anything that nice to me before."

"Would you consider adopting me?"

Granny patted her hand. "I already have, dear. Out here in Texas we don't need scribblin' on a piece of paper to take people into our hearts. You're in a special place."

Words clogged in Delta's throat, and if she ever had any doubt that she belonged in Battle Creek before, she certainly didn't now.

This was her town as much as if she'd been born here.

⤜⤛

When noontime came, she told Mr. Abercrombie that she might be a little late getting back. She had to let Cooper know that Jenny had regained consciousness. She'd promised.

The short stable owner grinned when she requested a horse and buggy a few minutes later. "I reckon at this point you own them more than I do, seeing how often you're in here. I seem to just be keeping them for you."

"I can't help it, Mr. Ferris," she said, returning his grin. "It's too far to walk where I'm going."

"Well, mind that you be careful. A woman alone shouldn't be running all over the countryside."

Delta waved and was soon out of town. At the ranch, she again headed toward the cloud of dirt and bawling cattle. Bandit's legs got tangled up as he ran to meet her. She hurriedly got from the buggy and took the wriggling ball of fur in her arms.

"The rascal is happy to see you," a voice growled.

Glancing up at Cooper, she found humor and something she couldn't describe in his gray stare. She wondered if perhaps he knew the turmoil he unleashed inside her and how deeply their kiss had affected her.

"He's a sweet dog," she murmured.

"Well, he won't be worth a plug nickel if you don't stop coddling him. I'm trying to teach him how to track and herd cows and guard the place. When you come around, all his lessons go out the window. What brings you out? Is Jenny…?"

Delta straightened. "I promised I'd tell you when she woke up."

His crooked grin did things to her that she wouldn't admit to anyone. "That's the best news I've had."

"I sat by her bed all night, and then this morning she opened her eyes and wanted a little something to eat. She asked where she was and where Ben was. She breathed easier when I told her Ben hadn't suffered too much from the ordeal."

"Thank you for riding out to tell me. I'll come into town to see her in a bit."

"She'd like that."

The deep relationship between Cooper and Jenny puzzled Delta. It seemed more than mere friendship. There was something a little odd about it. Maybe Ben held the key. But that would mean… She pushed that thought aside. Ben was Hogue Barclay's son, she told herself firmly.

Now that she'd delivered the news she came to give him, she didn't know what to do next. "About that kiss the other day, don't think you can—"

But again he quickly silenced her. "Have supper with me and we'll talk about it to your heart's content."

A supper invitation? She never expected that so soon. In fact, she thought he'd forget all about it.

"I suppose I can do that." They needed to get this kiss out in the open so it would stop haunting her every waking moment. She had a few things to get off her chest, and the sooner she did, the better. "When?"

"How about tonight?"

"Tonight it is." Thank goodness. Now she could get a few things straight.

Putting a booted foot on the metal step, she climbed into the buggy. She glanced back when she got to the road. Cooper was still standing there so tall and handsome, even with a thick layer of dirt on his clothes. He looked like a warrior king about to set out to conquer new worlds to add to his kingdom.

A dizzying current raced through her. How easy it would be to imagine herself in his arms for more than a few fleeting seconds.

～⌘～

Cooper rapped lightly on Jenny's door and entered. He was happy to find her sitting up with her back propped against the pillows, but sharp pain shot through his heart at the sight of her swollen face and black eyes. He should've been there to protect her.

He'd made a solemn promise he wouldn't leave her to Hogue's mercy. And yet he had.

"I knew you'd come," she said with a tentative smile.

"I was here yesterday, but of course, you were unconscious." Cooper dropped into the chair beside her bed and laid his hat on the floor. "Jenny, I'm sorry I wasn't here when you needed me."

"Running a ranch takes a lot of focus and staying on top of things. I don't expect you to drop everything in your life to make sure that I'm…that I'm…" The rest of the sentence was lost in heartrending sobs.

Cooper moved to sit on the bed. He put his arms around her and pulled her close. He didn't know what else to do. Crying females always threw him for a loop. Somehow patting her back and letting her cry her heart out didn't seem to be enough. If he could've gotten to Hogue at that moment, he'd have beaten the man to within an inch of his life. That was, if he'd be able to stop once he started. From the anger boiling inside him, Cooper knew he wouldn't be satisfied until he whipped every last bit of rottenness out of Hogue.

"There, there. Go ahead and have a good cry. It'll help to let all those feelings out," he murmured.

Jenny Barclay had always had a special place in his heart. There were things that bound them, things no one knew about.

For the thousandth time, he wished Hogue Barclay hadn't ridden into town full of sweet talk and promises. Mabel had told Cooper how the man had swept Jenny off her feet and put stars in her eyes.

It didn't take long for Cooper to see that Hogue

got meaner than a hot-blooded bull with no heifer in sight when he drank. He'd tried to warn Jenny, but she'd stood up for Hogue. Said the man just needed a chance and that she loved him. But Hogue only got more bad-tempered and more determined to keep Jenny firmly under his thumb.

"I'm sorry." Jenny accepted the handkerchief Cooper handed her and blew her nose. "I didn't mean to carry on so."

Gently, Cooper smoothed the hair away from her eyes. "You don't have one single thing to apologize for. Don't you know that by now?" he ended softly.

"I wish I'd have listened to Mabel. She tried to tell me."

"You loved him. Nothing she or I said could change that."

"I don't feel anything now but contempt and sorrow. Ben deserves a better father. I have to think of that. I've been so stupid and a horrible mother."

"Hush, no more talk like that. That boy loves you. One thing I learned a long time ago is you can't go back. The only direction from here is forward."

Jenny lay back against the pillows. "I don't know what I'm going to do. How…?"

"Your sole focus right now is getting well, letting yourself heal. Then we'll figure it out. You and me."

Her watery smile wobbled and faded. "All right."

"I'm just glad Delta Dandridge helped you when I wasn't here."

"I like her. She's a determined woman."

That was putting it mildly. Delta was flat-out

mulish. Might as well call it for what it was. "She certainly has a way about her," Cooper agreed.

"I don't know what might've happened to me if she hadn't come along. Most likely I'd have laid right there on that floor until Hogue came back and finished the job."

"You can thank Ben for going for help." The bed shifted when Cooper reached for his hat. "I'd best be going. Don't want to tire you out." He leaned to kiss her forehead. "If you need anything, anything at all, you know where to find me. Just send word. I mean it."

"You're a good man, Cooper Thorne."

He flashed a grin. "Just don't let too many people in on that secret. Wouldn't want it getting around."

❧

Off work after a trying day, Delta heard voices coming from Jenny's room. She rapped lightly on the door and entered. It took her aback to see Cooper sitting on Jenny's bed with her hand in his.

His words came unbidden into her memory. *I never said I don't like women. I love 'em. For your information, I've kissed more than my share.*

It certainly appeared to her that Jenny had been one of his conquests, and he still seemed to have feelings for the woman. "Oh, I didn't mean to interrupt. I can come back another time."

Cooper stood. "No, stay. Jenny would love to see you. I need to find Ben anyway. Don't forget, you promised to have supper with me."

"About that. I really don't think I should." Being anywhere in the same vicinity as Cooper was definitely not a good idea. He made her forget that he was a dyed-in-the-wool bachelor who would freely offer his affections but not his heart. Everything except the sound of his voice and the memory of his mouth on hers fled her brain when he came near.

"You changing your mind?"

"Cooper," Jenny exclaimed. "It's a woman's prerogative to change her mind."

"Says who?" His voice was rough and gravelly.

"Says the lady," Jenny retorted.

"Whose side you on here?"

"We women have to stick together, don't we, Delta?"

Delta squared her jaw. "I wholeheartedly agree."

Without any more argument, Cooper shut the door softly behind him. She moved to fluff Jenny's pillow. That's when she noticed tears lingering on the tips of Jenny's long lashes. It bothered her that Cooper had made the woman cry. Just wait until she got him alone.

But then the thought of being alone with him made her palms sweat.

After chatting a bit and helping the woman take care of some personal needs, Delta went downstairs. She found Cooper in the parlor talking to Ben.

What got her attention was the way Ben gazed at Cooper. The boy's eyes reflected so much love and a good helping of hero worship. Ben had a bad case of it if she ever saw one. He looked up when he spied her in the doorway.

"Miss Delta, I'm eating supper with you at the café. Mr. Cooper said I could."

Her first inclination was to set the boy straight right

then and there and tell him she had no intention of sharing a meal or anything but a piece of her mind with Cooper Thorne. But she hadn't the heart to do that to Ben. He'd had so little happiness.

No telling when he'd had such a treat, if ever. She couldn't see his good-for-nothing father taking him for a nice meal at a café.

Cooper rose. "I hope you don't mind that I took the liberty."

The man was a master manipulator. He knew good and well that it was the only way to get her to eat with him. At least with an audience he wouldn't be tempted to talk about kissing and long walks in the moonlight.

When Ben scampered across the room and threw his skinny arms around her, she could no more refuse than stop breathing.

"Thank you, Miss Delta. Oh boy, this is the best day of my life."

She smoothed the boy's hair. Ben Barclay had had a hard row to hoe in his short life.

And no one was more versed in hard rows than Delta.

Sixteen

A PRETTY WAITRESS APPEARED AT COOPER'S ELBOW before they even got settled into chairs at a corner table. Delta took in her dimples and big bosom.

The woman leveled a wide smile at the tall rancher. "Hi, sugar. What'll it be?"

Delta and Ben might as well have been a piece of the faded wallpaper for all the notice the trollop took of them.

"Whoa there, darlin', give us just a minute."

In spite of Delta's resolve to not let Cooper affect her, his deep voice sent tingles sashaying up her spine and he wasn't even speaking to her. But then, the vexatious man exuded more magnetism and charisma than anyone she'd ever met. Shoot, if he took a notion, he could easily charm the gold right out of a rich matron's mouth without half trying.

"Well, just give a shout when you're ready, Coop." The brazen hussy disappeared.

"I realize you're much more versed in the art of conversation, but is it wise to speak so familiarly?" Delta picked up her napkin and put it in her lap.

"Laurie knows I don't mean a thing by it."

"I wouldn't be too sure about that."

"You sound a little jealous there, Miss Delta."

"Good heavens, Mr. Thorne," she drawled. "I'm not some schoolgirl easily smitten by a handsome rogue."

"More's the pity." His eyes darkened.

Heat rose to her cheeks. She shouldn't have gotten so worked up. *Delta Rose Dandridge, get ahold of yourself,* she scolded. If she had the sense God gave a turnip, she'd get up and leave and take what pride she could muster with her.

"What strikes your fancy, Ben?" Cooper tucked the boy's napkin into the neck of his shirt.

"I ain't never been here. What do they have?"

Grateful to have something to do, Delta read the chalkboard on the wall to him, then announced that her choice was the ham, green beans, and carrots.

"Can I have the fried chicken, Miss Delta?"

"You can have whatever your heart desires," answered Cooper firmly. "Fried chicken it is."

As though on cue, Laurie reappeared, again at Cooper's elbow. "Did you decide, sugar?"

Cooper ordered for Delta and Ben, then told her he'd have the steak, red beans, and coffee. "And bring hot apple pie for everyone."

The silly woman trailed her fingertips across Cooper's shoulder as she left. She probably would personally cook his meal, cut it up, and feed it to him, if he made his wishes known. Some people were so transparent.

Men! They were as dumb as posts sometimes.

"Jenny has a high opinion of you, Miss Delta,"

Cooper said. "I'd say you're well on the way to becoming fast friends. Thank you for all you've done."

"No thanks are needed. I have a soft spot for Jenny and Ben. She'd have done the same for me." She grew silent when Laurie returned with Cooper's coffee, then left presumably to get her tea and Ben's milk. "I guess you've known Jenny for quite a while?"

"Yep."

"Must seem like family to you."

"For a fact. Ben too. Why all the questions?"

"No reason."

He took a sip of coffee as his left eyebrow rose in challenge. "Look, something needs to be said, so I'm just going to let it fly. I appreciate you looking after Jenny and Ben when I wasn't around, but I can handle things now."

In other words, fry your own kettle of fish and leave mine alone. Heated words rose, but being mindful of Ben, she swallowed them. A strained silence fell around them.

Finally she spoke, but the words came out stiff. "How is Bandit?"

"Who's Bandit?" Ben asked.

They told the youngster about the little dog, and Cooper promised to take him to see it soon.

"Oh boy! I can't wait." Ben's enthusiasm quickly died. "I asked Pa for a dog, but he said dogs don't earn their keep. He told me I'd have to start earning my keep or he'd take me to the orphanage. He can't do that, can he? I don't want to leave Mama and you."

The boy's quivering chin relayed the fact he was holding back tears. It brought a lump the size of a peach pit to Delta's throat. She got out of her chair and, kneeling down beside Ben, drew him to her in a fierce hug.

"You leave your pa to me," Cooper declared in a tight voice. "He isn't going to take you anywhere, son. You can bank on that."

The rest of the meal went well. Delta was careful to keep it light and happy even though she seethed inside. The nerve of Hogue Barclay and what he'd done to his son. Then she took into account their most delightful waitress, Miss Darlin'. She longed to tell Cooper that she was *not* jealous of that woman or anyone else for that matter. All the women in Battle Creek could take him, and good riddance.

It was all for the best that she hadn't gotten to address the kiss. With the mood she was in, she probably would've told him in no uncertain terms to go kiss a warty old toad next time he got the urge to pucker up.

The utter gall of the man, to tell her that he could handle Jenny and Ben from here and to mind her own business!

An hour later, she was still fuming as she looked out over the town from her room. It had become a custom, and she wasn't quite sure why she felt compelled to bid the town good night before she went to bed. She'd never had a town belong to her before, and it took away a few of the stings.

A moon bathed the buildings in silvery rays. The pale glow showed her what the establishments could look like in broad daylight with a little work and a willing spirit.

An idea took root in her mind. She would have to do a little more thinking on it, though. She didn't want to do anything to jeopardize her presence.

Just then, movement below captured her attention. Someone, a woman from the looks of it, was on her hands and knees in the small burial plot. Who on earth?

As she pondered the identity of the person, she looked up and the moonlight shone on her face.

Granny Ketchum!

The old woman appeared to be pulling weeds. Now Delta knew why the graves were so well tended. She had to go help. She quickly threw on her clothes and laced up her shoes.

Granny looked up when the creaking gate gave Delta away. Kneeling down beside the woman, Delta began yanking up weeds as fast as she could.

"Why are you cleaning up here in the dark, Granny?"

Pausing in her task, the woman answered, "Weren't anyone's business, I suppose. Didn't want 'em yammering about it and tryin' to make more of this than it is."

"But why do you do it?"

"Well, sweet girl, I'll tell you." Tears swam in Granny's eyes. "My brother disappeared along about the time this battle happened that killed these men. He was one of them surveyors, you know. I think one of these graves holds his bones."

Delta's arm slid across Granny's shoulders. "I'm sorry."

"Oh, it ain't so bad most times. After the sun goes down, though, I get to missing my loved ones something fierce. In the daylight I can piddle in my garden an' whatnot. But at night I cain't do a blooming thing to get away from the ghosts."

Ghosts were pesky that way.

"Let's finish up here so I can get you home," Delta said, yanking another weed.

"I'd be obliged if you'd take a cup of chamomile tea with me, girl. It helps me sleep."

"Thank you. I'd love to."

She'd do anything for the old woman who'd taken Delta into her heart. And if she got a chance, she might just ask Granny about Cooper's relationship with Jenny. She was sure Granny had an opinion or two about that.

Once they got the plot de-weeded, she sat with Granny in her kitchen, sipping a cup of hot tea. To her dismay, the old woman didn't provide any answers.

"No, siree. That's always puzzled me. I remember when Cooper and his brothers came to town. I believe it was about seven years ago. I recollect that the snow was coming down, an' it was colder than the dickens. Always thought that man is the handsomest cowboy that ever put on boots an' a hat."

So much for wondering if the man's family founded Battle Creek. The ticking clock was loud in the room as Granny sat lost in thought.

"What else do you remember, Granny?"

"Well, they dove right in and worked at whatever job they could find. Those boys weren't slackers. Why, they mucked out stalls at the livery, rode shotgun on the stage, or whatever else they took a notion to do." Granny's voice lowered to a whisper. "But I knew they had a powerful secret. I could especially see it deep down in Cooper's gray eyes."

Delta wondered what had happened to them. From appearances they seemed to have landed on their feet all right.

"What were we talking about?" Granny asked.

"Cooper and Jenny."

"Oh, were we? What were we saying?"

Delta stood and put her teacup in an empty dishpan. "I think I should probably go. Can I help you to bed?"

"That would be so nice, dear."

With a steadying arm around the stooped woman, Delta helped her to a small bed that was surrounded by so much clutter it barely left room to walk. In fact, the whole house seemed to be one large trash pile. No wonder Granny kept losing things. The poor dear desperately needed help.

And Delta made up her mind that Granny would get it.

Somehow or another things were going to change, even if she had to move a mountain or two.

Seventeen

AFTER WORK THE FOLLOWING DAY, DELTA, ARMED with a broom and mop, headed toward Granny Ketchum's. Beside her marched a small galvanized army that consisted of Mabel King and Violet Finch, who wore her most conservative hat—one that sported a real live bird's nest amid lavender and orange netting. Perhaps it was appropriate—after all, they might very well find bird's nests amongst the huge piles of collected stuff.

She rapped on the door of Granny's shack.

The old woman looked puzzled to see them standing on her stoop. "What are you doing here, dear? Did we make plans?"

"Remember that I promised last night I'd clean your house?" It was possible Granny had forgotten. She'd been very sleepy when Delta had told her.

"If you say so, but I don't have any money to pay you."

"We don't expect payment. Wouldn't take it if you were to offer. It's friends helping friends. I enlisted Mabel and Violet."

"Then I reckon you'd best come on inside."
Granny held the door open wide. "Just don't bother
my important papers."

"We're not going to throw anything away until you
say it's okay. Deal?" Delta couldn't imagine Granny
Ketchum having anything of too much importance.
Maybe her mind had taken to wandering again as it
seemed to do on an hourly basis.

Granny nodded. "I'll hold you to that."

It didn't take Delta and her two helpers any time to
set to work. Piles of newspapers, probably every edition
since the settling of the frontier, were everywhere.
They waded through a collection of empty boxes of
every shape, size, and color. They found spoons all
over the house, under the bed, under the rocking chair,
hanging over the doors, and even in Granny's knitting
basket. And everywhere they went, Granny was right
behind them, snatching things out of their hands.

Turning to the old woman, Delta asked about the
meaning of the spoons.

"My grandpappy—he was a Gypsy, you know—
told me they bring good fortune. The more you have
out, the better luck you'll have. Or maybe it was to
ward off evil spirits. I cain't rightly recall." Granny
grinned. "I put out a few extra for good measure."

"Yes, you did for sure. I'll return them all to their
places. Wouldn't want you to fall trying to get them
back up."

"I 'spect you think I'm a foolish old woman."

"No, not at all. You're wonderful and loving and
you're my adopted grandmother. I count myself very
fortunate."

They'd barely begun to make a dent before they had to quit and get back to the boardinghouse for supper.

"We'll return tomorrow." Delta kissed Granny's cheek. Thank goodness it was Saturday and John Abercrombie had already given her the afternoon off. "We'll have your house straightened up in no time."

Tears clouded Granny's pale blue eyes. "You're too kind to a poor old woman. You should be out sparkin' with Cooper…er, a man, dear, instead of cleaning my house."

"Don't you worry, Granny, I'll see that Delta doesn't spend *all* her time working," said Mabel. "But it won't take more than a couple of days to get your place in order. We've already started, and we're not quitting until we sweep out the last speck of dirt."

Delta hid her embarrassment. The last thing she wanted to do was spark with a man. Especially Cooper Thorne. Let him go spark that trollop who'd called him sugar. Delta didn't have time to waste on the man.

Still, he had a way about him that left an indelible mark. The wild ride in the buggy when he'd been worried about Jenny and the way he'd protectively anchored her to his side to keep her from falling out sprang from the recesses of her mind.

Friends? They seemed more than that in a way. Or maybe it was because she'd never had a friend before she came here.

Vowing to give him the benefit of the doubt, Delta reached to shut the door. The sight inside broke her heart. Granny Ketchum was dragging stuff out of the pile of things she'd agreed they could throw away. She fiercely clutched her belongings to her, unable to lose yet another thing in her life, no matter how small or insignificant it appeared.

Joining Mabel and Violet, they moved down the street.

A man with a long snowy beard that came within an inch or two of his waist sat on a bench in front of the saloon. He called out, "You ladies marchin' off to war?"

"Not exactly." Mabel stopped to chat. "How are you doing, Abner?"

"Cain't complain. At least not too loud. Wouldn't have a leg to stand on." The old man threw back his head and roared, revealing his toothless gums. Delta noted the crude crutch propped beside him and the empty left pant leg.

"At least you can still laugh, and that's something." Mabel patted his bone-thin arm.

"Reckon so, Miss Mabel. Who's that there with you besides Miss Violet? Ain't seen her around these parts before."

Delta approached the bearded man with her hand outstretched. "I'm Delta Dandridge. I'm new in town."

Abner spit on his palm and wiped it on his shirt before shaking her hand. "Whoo-ee! You're a purty thing. Name's Abner Winchell, ma'am."

"It's a pleasure to meet you, Mr. Winchell."

"Bless you, girl. Ain't no one called me mister in a coon's age. I'd get up from here an' join you but cain't do more than hop around like a wounded sparrow. Lost my leg in the big war. Reckon I know more'n most about pain an' misery. Now I just sit an' wait for Gabriel to blow his trumpet."

"I'm sure it gets hard," Delta agreed. "I'm really glad I made your acquaintance. Always nice to meet a new friend."

"We gotta be going, Abner," Mabel said. "Gotta feed my boarders. You look after yourself now."

"Watch out, an' don't take any wooden nickels." Abner cackled as the women continued on their way.

Delta's heart went out to the man who, like Granny Ketchum, had so little to live for. All they needed was someone to care, someone to take an interest in them. She didn't know what it was like to lose a leg, but she did know a little something about people passing her on the street without so much as a smile or a kind word.

∾

At the Long Odds, Cooper stood with his legs spread and his rifle resting in the crook of his arm. It neared midnight but he'd yet to find his bed. He sighed. Probably wouldn't get a wink of sleep anyway. Thoughts of Delta Dandridge kept him awake more often than not. He couldn't seem to get her out of his head. At odd times he found himself wondering what it would be like to run his hands over her satiny skin, imagining what she would look like wearing nothing but a smile, with her hair all mussed.

She'd looked a sight sitting in the café, getting her dander up good and proper over Laurie's familiarity. He probably should've told her that he'd known Laurie for years and their flirting was nothing more than a game they played. But he'd been having way too much fun putting that high color in her cheeks.

It felt real nice knowing Delta suffered from jealousy. Almost as nice as kissing her.

Maybe he'd steal another kiss next time he got a chance.

Dragging his thoughts back to the task at hand, he made sure his rifle was loaded. It wasn't a time for dreaming.

He'd positioned all eight of his men across the east side of the ranch, the only way to get onto his land. That left one man to guard over five hundred yards in the pitch-black. They were stretched thin.

Still, he dared the raiders to come back. If they did, they'd have a wad of double-aught buckshot waiting for them.

The moon cast nothing but a thin ribbon of light over the valley. It was a good night for righting wrongs and evening scores.

A little while past midnight, he heard them.

Trouble rode at a full gallop. Pounding hooves struck the hard ground as they came closer and closer. When they rounded a stand of oak trees, he counted at least a dozen riders. Hell was coming straight at him. It would either swallow him up whole or, if he was lucky, he'd run it back into the bowels of the earth from where it came.

Cooper tightened his grip on the rifle and clenched his jaw. Only cowards rode at night. The black hoods they wore over their heads indicated these cowards were even more spineless and lily-livered. He could see nothing but round eye sockets where their eyes should be.

He let loose a volley of gunfire. But the raiders quickly formed a circle around him, making it difficult to hit a moving target. They returned his fire.

Horses screamed.

Men cursed.

Bullets flew.

The quiet night became a chaotic bedlam.

"Get the hell off my land," he yelled.

Firing again, he hit two of them. Shouting curses, the hooded cowards retreated to a safe distance, where they watched.

Just then Cooper's men rode up and rained hell down as they emptied their rifles. Evidently seeing they wouldn't win on this particular night, the mysterious raiders lit out in the direction they came.

All except one.

That lone man whipped his horse around and galloped straight for Cooper. One of the ranch hands fired, striking the man's chest. The bullet seemed to hit metal and bounced off. That told Cooper the rider wore a piece of armor of some sort beneath his shirt.

A dozen more shots hit the armor.

Cooper took aim at the spot on the hood between the eye sockets, but a second before he squeezed the trigger, the rider's horse reared into the air.

As the animal landed back on its feet, another cowboy got luckier and put a piece of hot lead into the man's thigh.

Still he came. The attacker seemed to have a death wish.

Cooper braced himself, ready to leap out of the way if he needed to.

When the rider got within a few feet of Cooper, he suddenly whirled. As he did, the hood came off.

Staring into the raider's face, Cooper sucked in a quick breath.

What he saw was impossible. A ghost sneered down at him.

The ghost of the man he'd personally sent to hell.

Eighteen

RAND RUBBED THE SLEEP OUT OF HIS EYES AND SANK into a chair in the saloon's office as though his legs would no longer bear his weight. "Are you sure?"

Cooper wished he hadn't had to break the news so early in the morning, wished he could go back to that night so long ago and do it all over again, and he wished to damn hell that they didn't have to tell Brett.

"As certain as I'm standing here," he answered quietly. "I'd never forget that birthmark that covers the whole side of his rotten face."

"But you said you killed Tolbert Early."

Cooper was most thankful that he'd kept Rand out of the confrontation with Early that night. Rand had gotten Brett and helped him straighten his clothes. Cooper had no regrets for shielding them. This shooting was all on him, on his shoulders alone.

"There was so much blood. I would've bet my life on it." And almost had, thinking back to the grisly scene in that bathhouse. Furious that Cooper had barged in to save his little brother, Early had grabbed a knife and slashed Cooper's chest and belly before he could reach the gun lying on the floor beside the tub. He still bore the scars to prove it.

Rand's voice lowered to a raspy whisper. "We were scared out of our minds that night. Just three frightened boys."

Pounding his fist on the desk, Cooper spoke in a tight voice, "One thing about it, we're not boys now and we don't scare all that easy. Early had best get ready for a fight, because we aren't backing down from the no-good spawn of the devil."

"Did he say anything to you?" Rand idly picked up the ring of keys he kept close by.

"Nope. Too busy dodging hot lead." Cooper allowed himself a smile at the memory.

"And you're *positive* it was him?" Rand asked again. "After all, it was dark and the moon wasn't that bright."

"It doesn't help to keep circling the same damn bush, Rand. How much clearer do I need to be?" If Cooper was a drinking man, now would be the time for a stiff shot of whiskey. "What we've gotta do now is think of a plan of action. But warning Brett of course has to come first."

Rand opened a drawer, took out a bottle of whiskey, and poured a hefty portion into a coffee cup. "Damn. Just curious, how did Early get away, with his men running off and leaving him like that?"

"I swear, it was like trying to shoot a raindrop in a stiff gale. On top of wearing some kind of armor, he was twisting and whirling and his mount was rearing up. One of my men finally managed to shoot him in the leg. Wounded, he turned and raced into the blackness of the woods."

"At least you got some satisfaction. I wish we could keep Brett out of it."

"I don't like it any better than you. We've got no choice in the matter. If Early goes after him…" Cooper's stomach turned over at the thought of Brett in Tolbert's clutches again.

The only comfort was that Brett had grown into quite a man. At twenty-four now he'd become exceedingly proficient with both a knife and a gun. But their little brother would also need to have eyes in the back of his head. Besides, Cooper didn't know if Brett had killing in him if it came down to it.

One thing for sure, Cooper knew he himself did, and would without losing a wink of sleep over it.

"Early'll have to go through all of us to get to one."

"My feelings exactly. No matter which one Early is gunning for, he'll find a mess of trouble. Still, Brett needs to know about the situation." Cooper rose. "Strap on your gun. I say we ride out there together now."

Just when life had gotten halfway comfortable, up popped the devil with a pitchfork.

⤨

Delta pushed aside the torn lace curtain and looked out her bedroom window to catch the sunrise breaking over the town. Her eyes widened. Cooper and Rand strode from the Lily of the West.

Cooper untied his horse from the hitching rail and the pair proceeded toward the livery. Something had changed in the way Cooper walked. His movement wasn't as fluid, and there was a hardness, as unyielding as a piece of granite, that hadn't been there before.

Overnight, he'd changed into something to be feared. She wondered if anything could ever soften him now.

Both grim-faced men wore holsters strapped around their hips, and Cooper had his tied down to his muscular thigh. She was used to seeing Cooper wearing a gun—he was rarely without his Colt—but she'd never seen Rand sporting one. Judging by their expressions, they appeared to be on their way to a gunfight...or their own lynching.

At the exact moment when Cooper passed by, he glanced up and saw her. Their eyes met and held. He stopped as though he wanted to come in. Or wanted to say something.

A glimmer of yearning, and something she couldn't quite decipher, turned his charcoal stare into dark, brooding shadows.

She tried to step back, or at the least let the filmy curtain block his view, but the strong pull of his gaze rooted her in place. Unsure what to do, she lifted her hand and gave a tiny wave along with a hesitant smile.

That small action broke the spell binding them.

Cooper returned her smile, the kind that flashed his white teeth for merely an instant before it was gone. He raised two fingers to the brim of his hat in a salute...and winked.

Or maybe he'd done nothing more than react to the sun in his eyes and she was a ninny. She couldn't be sure of anything where Cooper Thorne was concerned.

Still, she chose to believe that he'd winked. It made her feel special somehow.

When the wink faded, the hardness returned to the lines of his face.

Rand said something to him, and without anything more, they continued down the street. She stood there a good minute watching the tall, lean rancher. With each purposeful stride he made, she could almost hear the jangle of his spurs in the quiet morning.

Wherever he was headed, whatever business he and Rand had, she got the distinct impression that he didn't want to go.

No amount of speculating would get answers, though. She'd just have to put away her curiosity and get her day started. Being nosy could buy a lot of trouble, and she and trouble had parted company when she came to town.

Dressing quickly, she looked in on Jenny. Sure enough, the woman was awake, so she aided with her morning ablutions and brushed her hair until it shone.

"Mabel tells me she's been helping you and Violet clean up Granny Ketchum's house," Jenny said, leaning back on her pillow, exhausted from moving about.

"That's right."

"I wish I could help. I feel so useless."

"Don't rush things. You will soon enough." Delta moved the porcelain bowl of water back to the wash stand. "I've been meaning to talk to you about something."

"I'm all ears."

"What do you think about forming a women's garden club?"

"In Battle Creek?"

"Yes. If Cooper and his brothers can have a bachelors' club, then we women can sure have a garden club."

"But I don't know much about growing things."

"You misunderstand. A garden club is just for women to band together and do different things to better the community. What I have in mind is cleaning up the town, painting and fixing up whatever needs done. This town is very special to me and I hate its run-down appearance. If it looked nicer, it might lure new people and businesses."

Towns were like people. They both needed a direction. From Delta's point of view, Battle Creek had no clear purpose—it simply moved from one day to the next, dying a little more with each sunset. It broke her heart.

"I see. I think you have a brilliant plan."

"We need a school and a library. We could form a committee and bring in a teacher." A memory from her childhood surfaced without warning. In Cedartown, the teacher had urged the children to bring an egg every morning so that she could sell them to help buy books and other things. They could do the same here. Everyone would benefit.

Jenny's face glowed. "I want my Ben to know how to read and write and learn interesting things. I've long despaired of him getting much of a chance."

"Then, what do you say?"

"Let's do it." Jenny threw back the covers as though ready to get up right then and start.

"Wait a minute. You're not well enough yet." Delta quickly drew the sheet and quilt back over the woman.

"I'm so excited. You've given me hope, given this town hope. Oh, I'm so very glad you found us."

As though the people of Battle Creek had been lost. Delta smiled, knowing it was she who'd been wandering around waiting for someone to actually see her. No longer was she unseen and unheard, and that brought her such overwhelming joy.

"I don't know anything about forming a women's club, Delta."

"I've never done it before either." When she'd tried to join the club in Cedartown, the members had blocked her, said she wasn't good enough to associate with them. That had stung her to the quick. Even now she wondered what it would take to be good enough for some people. "I know we have to get the word out, though, and see if other women would want to join. I'll visit the newspaper office and place an ad. And I'll put a notice in the mercantile window."

"I'll try to think of a name for us to call ourselves."

"Very good. Something catchy." Delta's mind whirled. Maybe she could get the mayor to pass an ordinance, fining people who let their property fall into disrepair. However, that would rile everyone. She didn't want that. Not when they'd started to accept her.

"Just one word of caution," Jenny warned. "Battle Creek has been this way as long as I can remember. Folks around here balk at making changes."

"If they want the town to grow and prosper, they need to make certain improvements. I think they just need someone to show them that this can be a place brimming with all kinds of exciting possibilities."

Once she got the town on a new path, then maybe she could start to work on fixing the part of her that was broken, the part that harbored her secret shame. Maybe with enough practice she could feel whole again. Yet a part of her wondered if that would ever truly be possible. A warped board that someone had left in the sun and wind and rain could never be straight again. Maybe people were like that sometimes.

All she knew was that she'd try her best. She had to believe that would be enough.

"Let's set a date for the first meeting." The words had burst from Delta's mouth without any warning and she wondered what she was getting herself into.

"How about a week from today?" Jenny suggested.

"I agree."

This would show Cooper Thorne that he wasn't the only one who could form a club. Only theirs would do worthwhile things for the betterment of everyone in addition to giving women a voice. Everyone needed a voice, especially those who were weak and downtrodden. If she could give them that, then she'd consider everything worth it.

Later that afternoon, she broke the news to her work detail and Granny Ketchum.

"Hee-hee! You're gonna make this town sit up and take notice of you, girl. Count me in." Granny clapped her hands.

"Me too," said Mabel and Violet at once.

"Thank you." Delta glanced from one to the other. These women were dear friends, the best kind to have. "I'll visit the newspaper office on Monday and get it all started. Tell everyone you know."

With that, they set about cleaning Granny's house. The old dear followed them from room to room, fiercely clutching an old cigar box under her arm. Did Granny smoke? Somehow that seemed unlikely. She never smelled tobacco when she hugged the woman. Then it dawned on her—the box probably held the important papers Granny spoke about. Delta finally urged the woman to sit down and let them do what they came for.

It made her heart ache to see a lot of the things Granny had initially said she would part with yesterday back where they'd been. But it had driven home an important lesson. She couldn't make Granny bend to her will. The caring woman had to want it for herself.

After explaining that to Mabel and Violet, they stopped throwing away and instead straightened everything into neat, organized piles.

Hours later, the trio finished the cleaning and gathered their brooms and mops.

Softly closing the door of Granny's house, her sweeping glance up and down the street took in the peeling paint, dilapidated structures, the burial plot in the center of the street, and the broken planks in the wooden sidewalks.

It would be just a matter of time until she and the rest of the ladies fixed it all up. She'd show Cooper what a few women could do when they put their minds to it.

Even a hardheaded bachelor needed convincing.

Again she thought about the bold wink and decided that he'd only had something in his eye. The man who'd refused to marry her would never give her a wink.

∽

That afternoon, Cooper, with Sheriff Strayhorn's help, put the finishing touches to his hasty defense plan.

They'd rolled out every wagon they could find and spaced them at intervals across the eastern portion of the ranch, including the opening to the Long Odds. Brett and Rand had brought others and added them to the line. It would make it a lot harder for the raiders to come onto his property now.

Brett wiped his forehead and put his hat back on. "We're ready for 'em. I think this'll make 'em think twice."

"I hope so. Thank you for coming to help, little brother."

"Wouldn't be anywhere else—you know that."

Cooper took in the slender man clad in knee-high moccasins laced over his trousers. He'd heard that Rand gave Brett the soft leathery footwear and that had brought a lump to his throat. Rand had always been the least sentimental of the bunch, and for him to give Brett something that was evidently so treasured made Cooper's heart smile.

"Things are looking good," Rand said, joining them. "We'll run those yahoos back to Missouri so fast, their heads'll have the dickens keeping up with their feet. I already have my name on the section I want to guard tonight."

Clapping his middle brother on the back, Cooper had a hard time trusting himself to speak. After several tries, he managed, "You have everything worked out at the saloon?"

"Yep. Even if I didn't, though, you can bet all the tea in China I'd be right here beside you."

"I know. And that means more than you'll ever guess."

Sheriff Strayhorn ambled over to join them. "I hope all this pays off. Coop, you never told me exactly why this bunch of riffraff wants to kill you."

Here was the question Cooper feared. To come clean about everything now was impossible. He ducked his head and mumbled, "A long-standing grudge. Happened a while back before Rand, Brett, and I came to Battle Creek."

"Well, if they show up tonight, they'll find themselves locked in my jail."

One of the ranch hands strolled over to speak to Strayhorn. Cooper breathed a sigh of relief when the sheriff moved off.

Along about five thirty, Mack Malone came, toting all kinds of large pots full of food on a wooden contraption he pulled with ropes. Bandit trotted happily beside him. "Thought you fellows would want to fill your bellies before the shootin' starts."

The cook had barely taken the lids off before he had a flock of hungry men swarming him.

Bandit lay down beside Cooper and promptly rolled over to get his belly scratched.

"Hey, boy, glad to see you." Cooper rubbed the dog's soft underside. "I still say you're not fit for crow bait." He laughed when Bandit squirmed and flailed his legs. One thing was clear—he loved the mutt. The hound carried on like the world was ending and looked downright pitiful when Cooper told him he had to go back with Mack. He almost relented when Brett picked him up and stroked the pointed ears. He didn't know who was grinning bigger, the dog or Brett.

"What are you doing, little brother? Don't be spoiling my dog," Cooper growled, knowing full well that it was Bandit who was doing the spoiling.

Brett's easy smile lacked the usual warmth. "Anytime you want to get rid of him, he has a home with me at the Wild Horse."

"He has a home right here on the Long Odds, and don't forget it. Find your own dog."

By the time darkness fell, they had silenced their growling stomachs and settled in for the long, uncertain night. Bracing himself against the chilly night breeze, Cooper pulled the collar of his jacket around his neck.

From out of nowhere, Delta's face crossed his mind. The last thing he'd expected to see that morning was her, framed in that second-story window. He'd been startled at first and wondered if he'd simply conjured up her image because he thought of her so often lately. She looked quite a sight, standing there bathed in golden light from the early sunrise. Her lips were parted as though eagerly awaiting a lover's kiss, and those sparkling green eyes made something turn over inside him.

Even now the image clung to him like sweet nectar to a honeysuckle vine.

The urge to change the direction of his feet had almost won out. But he'd had a serious task to tackle, so he'd given her a smile and a wink and went on his way.

One of these days he'd do more than that. Much

more. He'd show her what she did to him. Then she'd know without a doubt that he wanted her.

However, would she want him? He wouldn't blame her for running the other way. Lord knew, he was no prize.

Shaking his head to clear it, he checked his rifle and pistol one more time to make sure they were loaded, then propped himself against a tree trunk to wait. He prayed the raiders would return. He had a bullet with Tolbert Early's name on it and he itched to use it. Nothing would bring more satisfaction than finishing the job he'd started when he was just a boy. This time he'd do it right. They hadn't started this fight, but they'd damn sure finish it.

The thing that had him puzzled was why hunt them down now after all this time? Unless it had taken the man this long to find him. Possible. Tolbert must have a powerful lot of hate inside.

But why couldn't he let sleeping dogs lie? Why jab them with a sharp stick and dare them to do anything about it?

He took comfort in the fact that Brett had faced the news calmly and directly when they'd told him about Tolbert. Wasn't any emotion, just a flicker of pain in his eyes and then it was gone. His baby brother wore courage and honor like the colorful headdresses of his ancestors.

At least Cooper knew beyond a doubt that Tolbert Early had taken a bullet in the leg. Too bad it hadn't been between his eyes.

Justice would come. He didn't know how or when, but it would come as surely as the sun rose each morning.

When it did, God willing, he'd be there.

Nineteen

DELTA HELPED JENNY GET READY FOR BED THAT NIGHT after supper. She shared that she, Mabel, and Violet had finished up at Granny Ketchum's house. She told Jenny how grateful and touched Granny had been. They'd found all manner of items that she had accused some unnamed person of stealing.

"As everyone suspected, they were in her house all this time," Delta said.

"She's a mite on the cantankerous side but has always been very good to me and Ben." Jenny pulled her nightgown over her head and gave a growl of frustration. "If I have to be cooped up in this house, in this bedroom, for one more day, I'm going to scream. I feel so useless. I want to be out doing things, breathing some fresh air for a change."

"I'm sure it's very difficult for you."

"You don't know the half of it."

"If you feel up to it, we could take a short ride tomorrow. I don't know where we'd go, though."

"Oh, I would dearly love it. Would you take Ben and me out to Cooper's ranch?"

"I'm not—"

"He told me we were welcome anytime."

What could she say? That Cooper would probably be less than thrilled to have Delta show up
unannounced? She recalled when Rand had taken
her out there. Lord, Cooper was fit to be tied.
"I'm sure you are. It's just that they're in the midst
of branding."

"We won't get in the way. And if he's too busy,
we'll drive back to town. At least I can look at the sky
and breathe the fresh air. Please?"

Delta couldn't bear to disappoint the woman who'd
become a dear friend. "All right. I'll rent a buggy in
the morning and take you out there."

Jenny squealed and threw her arms around Delta.
"Thank you. It means the world to me."

What exactly did it mean to Jenny? Or to Cooper?
Delta wondered as she crawled into bed. Again, she
let the question of Ben's true father cross her mind.
Could Ben be Cooper's child? If so, why didn't he
claim the boy? Ben had a right to know. It was clear
that Cooper loved Ben, and the youngster him. It was
all so perplexing.

She snuggled deep under the covers, remembering
Cooper's lips on hers. The thought of seeing him
again stirred the embers that smoldered just beneath
the surface. Her last conscious memory was of the
bold wink in broad daylight. She fell asleep imagining
herself in his arms, inhaling his scent, which was as
wild and open as this Texas land.

◦◦◦

The next morning, Jenny was already dressed and had her hair combed and neatly braided when Delta knocked on her door. Ben had his hair slicked down and wore a goofy grin.

"I'm ready to go," he announced. "Mama is too. How soon can we leave?"

She put her arm around his skinny shoulders. "Hold your horses, young man. We're not leaving until we've had some breakfast."

"Do we hafta? I'm not even hungry."

"Your mother and I are, though."

"Can you eat really fast?"

Jenny stepped forward. "That ranch and Mr. Cooper aren't going anywhere. We have all day."

"But—"

"No buts, young man. Now, march downstairs."

They set out for the Long Odds an hour later. The day seemed perfect as far as weather went. The closer they got to the ranch, the more the shivers of anticipation built. Delta set her jaw, determined that she wouldn't let him ruin their outing, no matter what kind of mood he was in this time. Lord only knew.

About a mile away, a sign on a post got her attention. She stopped the buggy and stared.

For Sale: 120 acres. See Banker in Town.

Her mind raced. If only she had the money. She could own something lasting, something that would stand long after she left this earth.

"Jenny, would you mind if I look at this property?"

"I'm in no hurry."

Ben's huge sigh of frustration erupted as Delta

pulled onto the narrow trail that led to a large stand of trees. A white frame house stood in the midst of all that lush greenery. She could see herself living there, learning how to survive off the land. It was a piece of heaven if she ever saw one.

Only one teensy problem—she didn't have ten cents to rub together and wasn't likely to have it anytime soon either.

"Do you know who used to live here?"

Jenny replied, "The Zacharys. I heard they left everything and moved back East because of poor health."

"That's too bad."

"Mr. Jenkins at the bank would be the one to talk to."

Disheartened, Delta returned to the road. Still, she couldn't get that property out of her head.

When they arrived at the crossbars of the Long Odds, they received a shock. Someone had put wagons end to end across the entrance, blocking it.

"Oh my goodness, what on earth is going on?" Jenny sat up straighter, gripping the side of the buggy.

A young cowboy galloped toward them.

"I don't know, but we're about to find out," Delta murmured.

"Howdy, ma'am." The lanky ranch hand gave them a wary smile.

"We've come to visit Cooper Thorne," Delta explained.

"Sure thing. Let me move these wagons."

"Thank you, sir."

"What do you suppose happened?" Jenny wrung her hands.

"He mentioned to Mr. Abercrombie that he's having

some sort of trouble out here. I didn't know it had gotten this bad, though."

They waited patiently for the path to clear and soon drove under the huge crossbar. From out of nowhere appeared several riders. Cooper sat astride his magnificent buckskin. The lines of his face had settled into a dark scowl.

"It's dangerous for you out here." His voice had a cold edge to it.

Ben scampered out of the buggy before his mother or Delta could stop him. "Hi, Mr. Cooper. You said I could come out anytime. So we picked today."

The stiff contours of Cooper's face relaxed. "Well, son, you're a welcome sight." He pushed back his Stetson. "Hello, Jenny. Glad you're feeling well enough to ride out. I wasn't expecting you. Thought you'd still be laid up."

Jenny smiled. "Me and that bed have had enough of each other. I couldn't take another minute, so I twisted Delta's arm and persuaded her to drive us out. Please don't be angry."

"Simply worried about your safety." Finally, he spoke to her. "Hello, Miss Delta."

"Cooper." Delta met his unnerving stare. She refused to let him see her apprehension. "I see this is not a good time. If you'd prefer we leave…"

"No, you're already here, so you might as well stay." He reached down and lifted Ben into the saddle.

Delta followed behind in the buggy. At the house, she set the brake and climbed down, intending to help Jenny. Cooper beat her to it. Delta watched him gently lift the battered woman to the ground. She couldn't say that she could read anything into his care other than that he was solicitous of her condition. Yet she remained convinced that there was more to it than mere friendship.

Bandit scampered from the side of the house and stole the attention. Ben scooped up the excited dog and let the wriggling ball of fur cover his bruised face in dog kisses. Delta swallowed the lump in her throat. He deserved to laugh and play and do all the things little boys his age did. He'd missed out on so much.

"Mr. Cooper, he likes me."

"Of course, son. He's been dying to meet you. Gotta make up for lost time." Cooper had a thick huskiness in his voice that brought an ache to Delta's chest. He might be big and tough as shoe leather, but he seemed to melt when Ben was near.

"Can I ride a horse?"

"Yep, but first let's get your mama inside so she can rest. Looks like she's about to keel over."

Leaning heavily on Cooper, Jenny made her way inside to the parlor. Memories swarmed as Delta followed them into the room. She wondered if Cooper had forgotten the kiss. Most likely he had. The rancher probably had more things crowding his mind than an event that was best erased from memory. After all, he didn't even want to discuss it.

Yet when his gunmetal eyes met hers as he lowered Jenny into a comfortable chair, she had her doubts.

A second later, his lips twitched and he gave her a full-out sinful grin, the kind that crinkled the corners of his eyes. She knew the scamp recalled that kiss with perfect clarity.

Her face burned as she took a seat on a worn leather settee while Ben plopped down on the floor with the pup. The two began rolling, and laughter filled the small room.

"Can I get you ladies something to drink?" Cooper seemed to be playing host to the hilt. "Mack makes the best lemonade."

"That sounds heavenly," Jenny said.

"Miss Delta?"

"Yes, I'd love some, thank you."

He left the room and returned a few minutes later with two glasses of the sweet liquid.

Jenny took a sip. "That's so good. Now, tell me why you have the entrance to the ranch blocked. I want to know what's going on, and don't skimp on the details."

"Having trouble keeping trespassers out." He told them about the raiders and the flying bullets that led up to the decision to block the road.

Delta suspected he left out a lot. It was likely ten times more dangerous than he admitted. Even so, why would those men do such a thing? Why didn't people mind their own business and let others do the same?

Ben hadn't seemed to pay them any mind. All of a sudden he glanced up with big tears in his eyes. "But they can't hurt you, can they, Mr. Cooper?"

Until that moment, the thought never hit her that Cooper could be injured...or killed. Her breath hitched painfully. She couldn't imagine life without the man who could arouse a whole slew of tingles with nothing but a glance. He made her mad enough to spit sometimes, but he could kiss like a saint.

On second thought, better make that like a sinner, because his warm mouth on hers was quite sinful.

"Don't you worry, Ben. It'll take a sight more than a bunch of cowards to get me." He ruffled the back of Ben's head.

"Did they come back last night?" Delta set her glass down.

"Nope, and we were ready for 'em. Maybe they moved on, now that we made it harder for 'em." Cooper stood. "That's enough about that. Who wants to go riding?"

"Me!" Ben scrambled to his feet. "Oh boy."

"Young man, pay attention to Mr. Cooper and do what he says," Jenny said sternly.

"I will, Mama."

"Cooper, you won't let—"

"No, Jenny, I won't let anything happen to your boy." His quiet promise seemed to ease Jenny's fears. He lifted Ben onto his broad shoulders and they marched out into the brilliant sunshine.

He returned a little while later, saying Zeke had taken Ben out to see the creek that ran through the ranch. "Took a couple of poles along in case they wanted to drown a worm or two." He must've seen Jenny's concern because he added, "Ben is fine. Having a good time, so relax. Tell me what's happening in town." He settled his long frame in a chair and propped his legs out in front of him.

"Delta and I are organizing a women's club," Jenny announced proudly.

Cooper lifted an eyebrow. "That so? A club to do what, pray tell?"

Delta met his piercing charcoal stare, aware that her chin raised a notch. "We're going to improve Battle Creek, bring in a schoolteacher, and maybe start a seed library. You know. Things that women are interested in."

"If you men can have an old bachelors' club, then we can have a garden club," Jenny said.

"So you'll be gardening?"

"No. Our first order of business is to clean up the town. Paint, fix up buildings that need it, and make it where new businesses will want to come in," Delta explained.

Cooper's face darkened. "Folks won't take kindly to change. They like things the way they are. And frankly, I agree with them. I hear it's pretty much been this way in Battle Creek since the first settlers."

"All the more reason to do something. Progress stops in its tracks when towns grow stagnant," Delta argued. "A rosebush withers and dies when it doesn't get proper care. A town needs tending to in order to thrive and be vital."

"And you think you can accomplish that."

Delta glared. "It's worth a try."

"You're just opening up a can of worms and meddling in something you know nothing about." He glared back.

"We're going to try to get the mayor on our side. Maybe talk to him about passing an ordinance and fining those who let their establishments run down," Jenny said, breaking into the heated discussion.

That just added fuel to the fire.

"We?" he snorted. "This sounds like Delta's doing."

"And what's wrong with that?" Delta huffed. "Someone has to step up. I care too much for Battle Creek to let it die. Besides, what does it matter to you anyway? You don't even live in town."

"That's beside the point. You're gonna start a war, is what's fixing to happen."

"They might not like it much at first, but they'll warm to our plan when they see how much better it looks."

"Why do you want to change things?"

"Why do you want to keep everything the same?"

"Hey," Jenny said. "This isn't a war, where only one side is right. Cooper, Delta loves Battle Creek and wants to deck it out in its best clothes. And, Delta, Cooper doesn't mean that he's against change. He's just concerned that you and I will get our noses bloodied."

When both glared at Jenny, she ordered, "Now hug and make up. We're all friends here. I've had enough angry words and squabbling to last a lifetime. Do it for me if not for yourselves. I've learned life is too short to harbor grudges."

Hug? Get up close and let him put his arms around her? She'd never had a hug from a man before and found the idea of sharing one with Cooper enticing, but scary. He didn't much seem to be in the mood for such things. What if he pushed her away? His rejection would hurt too much.

"Come on, now. It's just one little hug," Jenny persisted. "For goodness' sake, it won't kill you."

"I don't have time for such foolishness," Cooper growled.

"It won't take but a minute. What are you so afraid of? Delta won't bite you."

"I just don't think this is a good idea."

Not only had he spurned Delta when she first arrived in town, he was spurning her again. Pain spread like long, gnarly fingers through her chest.

Jenny glared. "You're not leaving this room, buster, until you hug and make up."

Delta rose at the same time he did and slowly moved toward him. When she stood in front of him, he reached over and gave her shoulder a couple of pats.

"There. You happy?" He scowled at Jenny.

"That's the most pitiful thing I've ever seen. Ben could do better." With a strange gleam in her eye, Jenny shook her finger. "Now do it right."

Just when Delta was ready to give up and sprint for the outdoors, he opened up his arms and she walked into them. At first he seemed hesitant. However, the minute their bodies touched, he drew her tightly against him. She felt far from threatened by his fierce need, knowing he wouldn't hesitate to release her if she wanted free. However, she couldn't have moved if her life depended on it.

Tears stung her eyes as she breathed in the pleasant scent of him. The strong beat of his heart was strangely satisfying. Being so close to him, feeling the power of his body around her, gave her a sense of warmth and safety for the first time in her life.

Then his lips brushed her ear and sent a whole slew of tingles dancing up her spine.

"I don't know if I'm in heaven or hell," he whispered.

Heat flooded her face. The hug had meant nothing to him. He wanted nothing to do with her. This was only a game to him, something to mollify Jenny. Maybe he wanted to see just how big a fool she was. And like a fisherman who reeled in a big dumb catfish on the line, he'd hooked her, and now he was making a game out of the whole thing.

How many times would he reel her in, only to throw her back so he could do it all over again?

Twenty

DELTA'S EYES FELT AS THOUGH THEY HAD SAND IN them when she crawled out of bed in a Monday morning dawn. She'd tossed and turned all night, kept awake by memories of Cooper.

After they had hugged at Jenny's insistence, he'd pretty much kept her at arm's length. But all afternoon she caught him giving her strange stares, as if he was trying to decide whether to throw her back in or keep her.

He didn't touch her again until it came time to leave. His sooty gaze darkened when he helped her into the buggy, and he'd held her hand for several long beats of her heart.

Of course, she didn't know what it all meant, if anything. Maybe he treated all women like that. Trying to figure out Cooper Thorne was an exhausting job.

She'd best keep her thoughts on things she could understand.

On her way to work, Delta stopped in the *Battle Creek Gazette* office.

The editor, Jacob Quigley, as the lettering on the door proclaimed, glanced up when she entered. Wearing a green visor, he was hunched over a printing press and appeared to be typesetting. Some years older than she, he had a very fair complexion, so the slash of ink on his cheek stood out like black blood.

She quickly told him what she wanted. Between the two of them, they wrote the advertisement and she paid him.

He shook her hand. "It's a pleasure doing business with you, ma'am. You're lucky to have gotten this in on time, this being a weekly periodical and all. Next edition comes out bright and early tomorrow. Your ad will be in it. Let me just say, I think it's a wonderful idea to have a women's club."

"Thank you, Mr. Quigley."

"Looks like you've settled in just fine. At least that's the report I got from Granny Ketchum."

"Yes, I do believe Battle Creek agrees with me. I guess Granny reports, as you said, quite often then?" She offered it in a teasing manner but was puzzled when his face turned bright crimson. "I'm sorry. I didn't mean that the way it came out. Please forgive me."

"Don't give it another thought. I could never be upset with someone so beautiful and intelligent."

Delta thanked him again and emerged from the office wearing a satisfied smile. Quigley was most helpful. In fact, he seemed pleased that she'd placed the ad with his newspaper. As though she had any other choice. She thought it a bit odd that the town only had one of everything and again wondered why.

Had they tarred and feathered any rivals and run them out of town?

However, she was glad for only one of Cooper. Handling two of him would severely stress her abilities. Without a doubt, Cooper would take great satisfaction in sending her on her way. Hopefully without the tarring. Nothing was a sure thing where he was concerned, though. His comment about not knowing if he was in heaven or hell as he'd hugged her hammered in her ears. It had been a rather odd thing to say, and she still wasn't sure what to make of it.

One thing she did know—Cooper Thorne's touch had deeply affected her. She'd wanted to stay against his broad chest forever. His arms were so strong, and when he wrapped them around her, she'd felt safe and cherished. Yet despite his amazing strength, he was extremely gentle. Still, she harbored no illusions that if Jenny hadn't forced him, he never would've allowed it.

That brought her thoughts to Jenny. What must she have thought when Cooper hugged Delta as he did? Even though Jenny had instigated it, the embrace was far more than a polite show of friendship. And then he'd kissed her ear and murmured that odd statement. Jenny must've been deeply hurt. Odd that she hadn't seemed to pay it any mind.

Immersed in her thoughts, Delta failed to see Rand step into her path until she plowed into him. He quickly steadied her.

"Whoa there, pretty lady," he said, grinning.

Righting her bonnet, which had angled over one eye, Delta grimaced inwardly. "I'm so embarrassed. I wasn't paying attention. Forgive me, Rand."

"You were sure deep in thought."

"Just woolgathering. Nothing very interesting, I'm afraid." She wasn't about to confess the truth. No, he'd tell her she was a foolish woman. In fact, she didn't want to share her growing feelings about Cooper with anyone.

"There is nothing boring about you, Miss Delta. I'm glad we ran into each other. I was hoping to see you."

"Why's that, Rand?"

"I'd like permission to call on you at Mabel's this evening."

Oh, dear. Despite Rand's vow that she was safe, did he pin his hopes on the fact that they could be more than friends? It wasn't going to happen, though, and the sooner she straightened him out, the better for everyone.

"That would be nice. I need to talk to you about something."

"Until tonight then." He tipped his hat and she went on her way.

A surprise came a few hours later when Mabel delivered a letter that was addressed to Delta. "This just arrived on the stage and I brought it right over."

"Surely there's some mistake." Delta scanned the flowing handwriting on the envelope. It had her name on it, all right.

"Open it. Might be important."

"I doubt that."

She glanced at the smudged left corner where the return address was. When she finally made out the word *Cedartown*, an icy panic swept through her. It could only be from Langston Graham. Well, she wanted nothing to do with her gutless father.

"Aren't you gonna read it, dear?"

"Thank you for bringing this to me, Mabel." She jammed it into her pocket and hugged her friend. "I'll see you at supper."

The mercantile kept her busy, and that was good. She didn't have time to sort through her feelings about the mysterious letter or Cooper or Rand.

While her ability to straighten out the kinks in her life seemed near impossible, at least she had no trouble fixing one thing. When John Abercrombie fired up the potbellied stove midafternoon to make coffee, she threw the unread letter into the flames. Watching it curl up then turn to ash restored some semblance of peace.

The remainder of the day crawled. At last she locked up and headed to Mabel's. Jenny and Ben joined the boarders in the dining room that night, so it was a joyous occasion. Everyone had heard the reason for Jenny's dark bruises, so their presence didn't cause any awkward moments.

"How was your day, dear?" Mabel asked Delta as she passed her the plate of fried chicken.

Delta selected the wishbone part of the breast and handed the plate to Jenny. "Business kept me hopping. Seems everyone in town came in."

"I'm not surprised," Violet said. "You've made the store a very inviting place, especially for the women."

"And for the men too," Nat Rollins threw in. "By the way, you haven't been by the hotel yet to get a gander at that heel that came off of Abigail Winehouse's shoe."

"I do apologize, Mr. Rollins. I mean to rectify that. How about I come in during my lunch hour tomorrow?"

Nat Rollins beamed. "That would be just fine, Miss Dandridge."

"Give us an update on the women's garden club," Mabel requested.

"I put an ad in the *Battle Creek Gazette* this morning, and it'll come out in tomorrow's edition."

Violet clapped. "This is so exciting."

"What's this about?" Deputy Charlie Winters frowned.

Jenny related all the details, or as many as any of the women knew at this stage, and a discussion ensued.

"I think it's a crazy idea," the deputy blurted. "Gonna rile up a whole passel of folks. Sheriff Strayhorn ain't gonna like it one bit."

"Be that as it may, it's something this town has needed for a long time," Mabel argued. "Just took Delta moving here to set things in motion. People will change their tune soon enough. And our kids need a teacher."

"I've long bemoaned the fact that we desperately need a school but couldn't get anyone interested," Jenny declared. "The children's education has been sorely lacking. I'd like to see Ben learn things that I can't teach him."

Nat raised his hand. "I second that. Our kids will be nothing but ruffians if we don't do something."

Mabel stood and raised her glass. "Three cheers for Miss Dandridge."

Delta's face grew warm. "Thank you. It means a lot to have your support."

Upstairs, after she'd helped Mabel with the dishes, Delta paced and fretted, hoping she'd say the right thing when Rand arrived. Her thoughts flew back to what Cooper had said right before he kissed her that day in his parlor. *You'll do what? Live in sin with Rand? You won't. Women like you won't throw your reputation to the wind. You want it all or nothing.* How right he'd been.

She nearly jumped out of her skin when a light tap came at her door.

"Dear, you have a visitor," Mabel announced.

"Be right down." She smoothed her hair and went downstairs.

Rand sat in the tiny parlor with his dove-gray Stetson in his hands. He rose when she entered. "Miss Delta, you're a lovely rare rose."

A blush heated her cheeks. "Thank you." She started to take a seat when Rand put a hand on her arm.

"Please, I was hoping you'd take a walk with me."

Dreading where this might lead, the last thing Delta wanted was to be alone with him. Still, she didn't need an audience for what she had to do.

"I'll get my shawl from my room."

When she returned, he opened the door for her and they walked into the night air. She drew her wrap closer and lightly accepted the elbow he offered. He directed her to a spot away from the lighted house behind them. Their shoes crunched on the pebbly path.

"Rand, I don't think I should go very far."

"Scared I'll scoop you up and carry you off, like a pirate with his treasure?"

Delta chewed her bottom lip. "Not exactly."

Truth was, she wasn't sure what he intended, and that put her at a disadvantage. One thing for sure, she wasn't afraid of him. She knew he'd never hurt her. She considered him a friend, but that's all he'd ever be. Could he accept that?

"Relax. I'm only kidding." He bent down. Picking a wildflower, he stuck it in the hair at her temple.

"It's a nice night."

"That it is. Springtime is my favorite season of the year. It's about renewal and rebirth. I'm glad winter is over."

"Do the winters get bad here?"

"Sometimes. For brief spells. What were they like in Georgia?"

"Pleasant for the most part. I only recall it snowing once during my life, and that lasted for just a few hours. Sure was pretty, though. It put a thin coating of white on everything, then the sun came out and melted it all away. Almost made me think I dreamed the whole thing."

"Thank you for this." Rand's lips brushed her ear, his words soft.

This was quickly turning into something she didn't welcome. She looked around for a distraction. Nothing safe came to mind. "Rand, you know how much I think of you, how much—"

"I'm very fond of you also."

"No, please let me finish."

"What's wrong? You seem nervous."

"I'm just not sure why you brought me out here. What are we doing?"

"You once asked me what I hoped to gain by seeking your company." The stars seemed so close, like apples on a tree she could reach up and pluck. But the apple Rand appeared to be dangling wasn't one she wanted to pick.

She took a tremulous breath and pulled her shawl tighter against the night breeze. "I recall. And?"

He looked up and remarked, "Look, a shooting star."

Following the white trail across the inky blackness, she thought about the trail this conversation was leaving. A flash of light, but where would it end? "It's breathtaking."

"Almost as lovely as you. Nature's wonders always fill me with awe. But back to your question—here's the thing. From the first moment we met, you intrigued me. You have a great mind, one of the brightest I've seen. The thing is, I'm a bachelor and have no plans to change that. You're looking for permanence that I can never offer and I respect you too much to suggest anything less, although I sincerely regret that." *Rand loves all women for a time, but he'll never find the altar,* Cooper had said.

The brothers did, in fact, know each other well. But she was still confused. "Then you were what? Trying to seduce me?"

"Sounds rather shocking, but perhaps that was in the back of my mind. I quickly saw you would never settle for that kind of thing, though, and I respected you too much to ask. That's the crux of it. You deserve honesty."

"Thank you, Rand, I'm grateful to you for your frankness and I do value your friendship. But why are you telling me this?"

"I knew you wondered why I got so angry when I saw Cooper kissing you, and I want to clear up any confusion. I was furious because I had my doubts about the purity of his motives. I didn't want him to take you lightly, to kiss you, give you hope when he had no intention of offering more. I want more for you, pretty lady. I won't let him hurt you."

His admission deeply touched something inside her. She laid her palm on his jaw. "Oh, Rand, you're the kind of man who will find a special lady someday, and when you do, you'll forget all about this crazy notion of being a bachelor."

"I doubt that."

Delta met his blue gaze, shadowed by the starlight. "Never underestimate matters of the heart."

"Which brings me to the rest of my reason for asking you to enjoy my charming company." He flashed a grin. "Cooper has a lot to offer the right kind of woman, but it'll require god-awful patience."

"First you want to knock him sideways and now you're his advocate? My head is spinning."

"These last few days, I've come to view him differently. You really affect him. In fact, I've never seen him like this. Don't let him slip away. He can be roped, and you're just the one to do it."

Delta shook her head. "He has his life to live and I have mine. Marriage used to mean everything to me, but coming here opened my eyes. There's so much more awaiting me. The opportunities are boundless. I'll always count you as a dear friend." A woman like her could never have too many of those.

"Just try getting rid of me."

"I'd never do that."

"My brother's nine kinds of a fool." The words

came out gruff and she suspected his male ego had taken a beating this night, with all he'd admitted.

Egos were such fragile things and men set great store by them.

"Who was she?" Delta asked softly.

"Who?"

"The woman you said I reminded you of when I first arrived in Battle Creek."

"Rachel." He uttered the name with reverence.

"Tell me about her."

Rand picked up a small rock and sailed it into the darkness. "She came. She died. End of story."

"What happened? I'd really like to know."

"She rode into town with her father in a traveling medicine show. I helped them set up. Like you, she was beautiful, with her golden hair and sweet smile. They weren't here long before she took ill. Doc Yates didn't know much about scarlet fever, but he did the best he could. He couldn't save her. Nobody could. People were terrified of getting the disease, so they burned her body and everything she touched. Didn't even give her a proper good-bye."

"I'm sorry." She laid a hand on his arm.

It seemed everyone knew their own special kind of hell. Hers had been Cedartown. Rand's was losing Rachel. Jenny's was Hogue Barclay.

What was Cooper's?

Did he pine for a lost love? For Jenny perhaps?

Twenty-one

COOPER SADDLED REBEL RIGHT AFTER BREAKFAST. HE had business in Battle Creek. More than likely, Tolbert Early wouldn't try to come around in broad daylight, so Cooper wasn't afraid to leave for a bit. Snake that the man was, he preferred the cover of night in which to do his dirty work.

Bandit quit eating long enough to glance up and whine.

"You can't go with me, boy. Need you to guard the place." He placed his boot in the stirrup and swung his leg over.

The ride into town allowed him to let his thoughts drift toward Delta Dandridge. He could still feel her breasts pressed so firmly to his chest when he'd hugged her. He hadn't needed Jenny to prod him into it. He'd been more than agreeable to getting Delta in his arms again—he just hadn't wanted to appear too eager.

For a fact, the lady was growing on him. She'd turned out far different from his first impression of her that morning on the porch at Mabel's Boardinghouse. He'd been unprepared for the effect she was to have on him.

Gut instinct told him Delta Dandridge had seen her share of hard times. Every so often, pain flashed in those green eyes. One of these days, maybe he'd discover her secret.

It still puzzled him who'd forged his name and sent for her. His anger had long since faded, though, and he was rather glad she'd come.

Not that he wanted to marry her or anything.

He was quite content for the most part. He would be a lot happier when he'd taken care of Tolbert Early once and for all. The old enemy clearly posed a great danger.

The streets of Battle Creek were quiet. The town was still waking up when he rode down the main street and dismounted in front of the café. But as quiet as the town appeared outside, the eating establishment was not. The clamor of voices from inside hit him like thousands of angry bees when he opened the door. Rand sat at a table and hollered for Cooper to join him.

"What's going on?" Cooper asked as he slid into the chair.

"Read for yourself." Rand pushed the latest copy of the *Battle Creek Gazette* across the table.

The headline read "Women to Clean Up the Town."

Miss Delta Dandridge, a newcomer to these parts, is seeking to form a women's club to address several important issues. Miss Dandridge is convinced that the unkempt, dilapidated (her words, not this editor's) buildings are preventing the advancement of progress. The women's Battle Creek Garden Club will also tackle the issue of no school and no schoolteacher. They believe crime will see an upsurge if children are not properly schooled. Yes, folks, change is in the wind. It behooves this editor to climb aboard this progressive train before I get left behind at the station.

Cooper snorted. Progressive train his eye! No wonder folks were fit to be tied. While some change might be a good thing—in small doses, that is—they didn't want it shoved down their throats. Especially not by someone new to town who didn't understand their ways. And not by some Southern belle who had a penchant for meddling in matters that didn't concern her.

"It looks like she's done it this time," Rand said.

"Appears so. Wonder how she'll get out of this?"

"Why is it you aren't more riled up, Coop?"

"Already knew about it." Cooper picked up a cup of coffee the waitress set down in front of him. He never had to order. He'd been coming so long, they knew what he wanted before he even knew himself. "Jenny spilled the beans when she and Delta rode out to the ranch Sunday. I told both of them there'd be hell to pay."

"You ain't just whistling 'Dixie.' Rumor has it she's even gotten the mayor on her side, and pretty soon we'll have to pay a fine if we don't keep our property up."

"I wouldn't put a whole lot of stock into rumor and gossip." Cooper reached for a hot biscuit from the plate the waitress set in the middle of the table.

"Easy for you to say. You don't live in town."

"So everyone is fond of telling me." Cooper glanced out the window at the row of buildings across the street. When had they gotten so run-down? Maybe Miss Georgia Peach was on to something after all. "It wouldn't hurt to spruce the town up a bit. Bet some of these buildings haven't ever had a coat of paint."

"Whose side are you on, anyway?"

"Both of you are right." He took a big bite out of the biscuit and washed it down with a swig of coffee. "Look out there. The Lily's sign is all gotch-eyed and dangerous. The next big wind and it'll fall plumb down."

Rand sighed in defeat. "You've probably got something there."

A flash of petticoat out the window snagged Cooper's attention. Delta fought to keep her skirt from blowing up in the stiff breeze as she hurried toward the mercantile. The flash of stocking-clad leg stuck in his head like a mess of stubborn cockleburs. She looked mighty pretty with the sunlight caressing her hair and the rosy bloom in her cheeks. Yep, she was a mighty fine-looking woman, if he did say so. And she could kiss like the dickens. He just wondered if she knew the turmoil she'd caused in the town.

One thing about it, if she needs someone to stand beside her, I'm her man.

Long as she doesn't entertain notions of love and marriage, he quickly amended.

"I'm thinking it's time we called a meeting of the bachelors' club," he said to no one in particular.

"Past time, if you ask me," Rand grumbled.

"We'll have to do it early. I won't be gone from the Long Odds after dark."

"Any more signs of Tolbert?"

"Nope, and that worries me. Don't know what kind of game that polecat's playing."

"Just trying to keep you off balance, Coop. The man seems to be a master at that. You can bet he won't leave until he finishes what he came for."

That's the part that kept Cooper awake at night. He'd never been a very patient man. This waiting for the other shoe to drop was getting on his nerves. He wished he could find the no-good cayuse's hideout. He needed to end this and end it for good.

Rand put his hand on top of his cup when the waitress came by to let her know he'd had enough. "How long you gonna be in town?"

"Not sure. Why?"

"I'll ride out to get Brett so we can have our meeting. Won't take long, if you'll wait."

"Reckon I can. Have a few things to do anyway."

Both men stood. Once outside the café, they went their separate ways—Rand toward the livery and Cooper in the direction of the boardinghouse.

Jenny sat alone in the dining room. She looked up in surprise. "How nice to see you. Join me, Cooper."

"I'm full up with coffee. Just came from Rose's." He pulled out a chair beside her and dropped into it. "I need to talk to you."

She slowly put down her fork. "What's this about?"

"I want you and Ben to move out to the ranch so I can keep an eye on you."

"Why?"

Cooper paused a minute, unsure of how to go

about this. Finally he dropped his voice and spoke in a low tone. "I know about the baby."

Spots of red stained her cheeks. "I'd hoped to keep that a secret a while longer. How long have you known?"

"That's not important. What I want to know is why you didn't tell me, why I had to find out through someone else."

Jenny's chin rose a trifle, letting him know Hogue hadn't beaten all the spunk out of her. "Because it wasn't any concern of yours. You're not in control of my life, and why you seem to think so is something I'd like to know. Why did you take on the role of protector and savior in the first place?"

"I promised." Cooper didn't want to have this conversation. He'd never planned to tell her. And now he didn't see any way around it. He'd said too much.

"Promised who? Mabel?"

Cooper gazed out the window beyond the frayed lace curtains, beyond the rolling hills that had become a carpet of brightly colored wildflowers seemingly overnight, to a different time. "Your father."

"My father is dead. You didn't know him."

"Not the one you grew up with. The one you didn't."

Below the bandage that covered her head wound, deep lines in her forehead reflected her confusion. "You're not making any sense. My father was Frank Wylie."

"Forget it. I've said too much."

Her fingers dug into his arm. "You're not leaving here until you tell me. Whatever it is, I have a right to know."

"It'll serve no purpose. My lips are sealed." He

leaned to kiss her cheek. "Now, Mrs. Barclay, how about it? Come out to the ranch and stay awhile. Take pity on me. Please. I need someone to show Mack how to cook. He only knows two ways—charred and tasteless. And I'd be forever in your debt if you teach the man how to make apple hand pies."

The woman who'd seen a fist doubled in anger too often deserved some peace and calm in her life for once. He wanted to give her that.

"Don't change the subject, Cooper Thorne. You can't just drop something like that on me, then tell me to forget it. What do you know? Who did you make your vow to?"

"When you're ready to hear about it, I'll tell you. But not now."

"Why?"

"Because you're not ready. You're recovering from horrific injuries. Nope."

"I can see a team of oxen won't drag it out of you. You're the most obstinate man on the face of the earth." A look of defeat crossed Jenny's eyes. She sighed. "Ben would love to spend a few days at the ranch. I think that boy has ranching in his blood. But, Cooper, I've never found much of a purpose in life until now, until Delta came. I can help make a differ- ence in this town. I want to be a part of this women's club. I've been content to simply exist and stay in my rut. But no more. For the first time I want to really live. I want to experience all the things I've missed. Does this make any sense?"

"Yep, it does. You're blossoming before my very eyes. I'm really proud of you."

"To tell you the truth, I'm pretty proud of myself."

Jenny's smile was brighter than he'd seen it in a long while. "Then, how about this? How about if you come to the ranch for just a few days until this club thing gets off to a start? When you want to come back into town, I'll bring you. It'll make Ben happy, and I can teach him how to rope and ride. Bandit will think he's died and gone to heaven to have a boy to play fetch with. Whatcha say?"

"You drive a hard bargain. But it'll just be a few days. I want to attend the first meeting of the women's club."

"Let Mabel help you pack a few things and I'll be back to get you and Ben in a little while." He'd be glad when they were close, so he could keep an eye on them.

By the time he left, his heart was much lighter. He was a little put out with himself, though, for blabbing too much. Good grief. He'd acted like some gossiping old woman with too much time on her hands. He growled low and vowed to keep a padlock on his tongue.

⁓

Minutes later, he strode into the packed mercantile. He spied Delta helping a woman with some sewing notions. Her eyes met his and his heart skipped a beat when she let a smile flirt with the corners of her mouth. He wondered what she'd do if he were to cross the room and kiss her. He seemed to spend an awful lot of time thinking about things like that and he didn't know why. The only thing he knew was that Delta Dandridge was in his blood and he didn't know how to get her out.

John Abercrombie hurried from behind the counter. "Your barbed wire came in, Coop."

"Just what I wanted to find out."

Once he got the devil's teeth strung up, those faceless sons of Satan would have another think coming next time they tried to ride onto his ranch.

Delta finished waiting on her customer and joined Cooper while Abercrombie went to talk to someone else. He didn't know exactly what to say, but he knew he had to say something. "Saw the newspaper this morning. You've sure upset the apple cart in this town, lady."

"That wasn't my intention." Her green eyes darkened. "I look around and see so much need. I only want to help."

"Stop trying so hard. Folks will accept you better if you don't push yourself on them." Cooper's gently spoken words were not meant to criticize. It surprised him to see the quick flash of tears.

"What do you know about fitting in? You've never had to. Things are different for a man."

Clearly, she'd suffered something unspeakable. Whatever it was had created the woman she'd become. Seemed everyone had secrets they kept. Some were deadly.

And sometimes those things you'd carefully hidden away wiggled out in the light of day.

Jenny would surely ask more questions. He should have his butt kicked for opening that particular can of night crawlers.

Cooper wondered what Delta would do if she knew he'd murdered a man only to find the man was bound and determined not to stay dead. Her disappointment would kill him. He didn't ever want to have to face that.

"I'm no different than you. I was new in Battle Creek once," he said softly. "I laid low until I learned their ways. You've already completely besotted the men. Lord knows you have Rand and Abercrombie wrapped around your little finger, not to mention, a lot of the women have become good friends. Just go slow."

Delta chewed her lip. "I only know one speed. My heart breaks when I look at these establishments. I see what they can be, what this town could be. I have so much to give. All I need is for someone to let me give it. I'll be fine."

"Don't say I didn't warn you."

"Did John tell you the wire arrived?"

"Yep. I'm mighty glad too."

"More trouble at the ranch?"

"Though it was quiet enough the last two nights, I know more trouble is coming." In fact, it rode toward him on a swift dark horse, and he didn't know when it would next appear. "Glad I could see you. Jenny and Ben are coming to the ranch for a few days. Now don't get your back up, Miss Worrywart. I've fortified the ranch. It's more secure than an army fort. I promise. She wants to go, but she also doesn't want to miss the first meeting of the women's club. I told her you'd let her know and I'll bring her back."

"Yes, I will. I'm glad you talked her into going out there. She needs fresh air and sunshine and to be free of all the bad memories here. It'll do them both a world of good."

A man entered the mercantile and walked up to Cooper. "Hear you're having a meeting of the bachelors' club later. That true?"

"Don't believe I know you, mister. Are you a single man?"

"Does a skunk stink? I wanna join your cause."

"Well, be at the Lily in an hour."

The man moseyed out of the store. When Cooper turned back to Delta, she raised a sarcastic eyebrow. "What?" he asked.

"Isn't this the pot calling the kettle black? You're raising Cain for me starting a garden club that will greatly benefit this town, yet you insist on having one for you men who only want to plot against women. I can't believe this."

Warmth crept up Cooper's neck. When she put it that way, he could see her point. Except his club hadn't gotten the citizens up in arms and ready to shoot first and ask questions later.

"Delta, you're right. I'm all about fairness. I won't say another word about this garden club. Just don't come crying to me when you realize you've bitten off more than you can chew."

"Don't worry," she snapped. "I learned a long time ago that tears don't accomplish a blooming thing."

She spun on her heels and marched off to wait on another customer. Cooper followed the gentle sway of her softly rounded hips. He truly admired a woman with sass. In fact, he admired everything about Miss Delta Dandridge. But why in blue blazes did he pick a fight every time she came near, when all he most wanted to do was kiss the fire out of her? He'd like to wrap her in his arms and never let her go.

"I'm an utter fool," he muttered sourly.

The quiet hum below the surface, down where all the nerve endings were, reminded him that it had been too long since he'd been with a woman. But just any woman would no longer do.

Delta Dandridge had spoiled him. He wanted her and only her.

She'd burrowed under his skin, and one of these days, he'd have to scratch that particular itch or he'd go stark raving mad.

Twenty-two

THE NOISE IN THE BACK ROOM OF THE SALOON WAS deafening. Cooper pounded a gavel that the last circuit judge had left behind. "I call this meeting of the Battle Creek Bachelors' Club to order."

His brothers Brett and Rand were in attendance, as well as a half-dozen others.

When the men paid Cooper no mind, Brett shouted, "Quiet!"

At last the talking ceased.

"Abner, what the hell are you doing here?" Cooper peered at the one-legged man who sat outside the hotel every day and watched the comings and goings and reported everything to the sheriff. Some of it was accurate, but the biggest portion was nothing but figments of Abner's imagination. Lord knew the man wasn't in danger of anyone seeking to marry him. Besides, he smelled.

Abner puffed up. "Just 'cause I ain't got two legs, you think I don't belong here? We men gotta stick together. Why, just today I saw a group of those women attackin' George Lexington an' threatening to close down the hotel if'n he don't shape up."

"You've been seeing things, Abner." Cooper knew for certain that no one had attacked Lexington.

And there sat Old Hickory, the town drunk, as big as you please. "Hickory, what in God's name are you thinking? You can't stay sober long enough to join anything."

Old Hickory hiccuped. "Beggars cain't…cain't be choosers."

Chuckles went around the table. Rand stood. "Coop, I make a motion to change our name. Seems to me we have a bigger reason to band together these days."

"Just what are you proposing?"

"I reckon 'the Gentlemen's Society' would about cover it."

"I second the motion," Brett spoke up.

Every hand raised when Cooper called for the vote. "Then it's agreed the Bachelors' Club has become the Gentlemen's Society." He grinned. "I reckon it's a good thing, in light of the fact that I see three married men here."

"We gotta do something or these women will be telling us what clothes we can wear and how we can walk down the street," the barber said. "This is war."

A murmur of agreement filled the small, airless room.

Old Hickory raised his hand. "When do you serve refr-refreshments?" The man grabbed on to the table to keep from falling out of his seat.

"Any refreshments you want you're gonna pay for yourself," Rand declared. "Besides, you've had enough."

"The h-hell you say!" Hickory frowned and hiccuped again.

"What we need to do is figure out how we're going to deal with this," Cooper said, bringing them back to the subject. "Any ideas?"

"We could tie Miss Dandridge up and put her on the next stage back to Georgia," the barber suggested.

One of the married men stood. "I ain't been gettin' nothing but grief at home from the missus. We need to make a believer out of the woman."

"Now, hold on." Cooper slammed the gavel onto the table to be heard over the roar. He didn't like the direction this had taken. He was going to have to do something fast or Delta would be in a lot of danger. "I said quiet!"

Finally the men got the message.

"Go ahead, Coop," Rand said.

"There's been enough violence in this town. The women haven't done anything yet except take out an ad in the newspaper. I say we give them a chance. Let's see what they aim to do." Cooper met each man's eyes. "Anyone who harms Miss Dandridge or any of the other women will answer to me personally. Is that clear?"

The barber spoke up. "What's plain as the nose on my face is you've gotten sweet on little Miss Georgia. You gonna let her drag you to the altar, Coop, huh?"

"Nobody's dragging anyone to the altar. This has nothing to do with marriage."

"You wouldn't say that if you were married to my wife," hollered one of the new members, and he was rewarded with hoots of laughter.

Cooper tried one more time to reason with them. "Be that as it may, for now we're watching and waiting."

"Yeah, waitin' for that skirted army to tell you how the cow ate the cabbage," a voice from the back yelled. "We want our town to stay the same as it's always been. If we wanted things all whitewashed and frilly, we'd have moved to where they allow such things. This is a man's town."

"There's nothing wrong with a little fixing up." Cooper raised his voice. "This town belongs to everyone, the women as well as the men. Maybe we got the name of this club wrong. It's not a gentlemen's club at all, because you're acting like a flock of old pecking roosters. I'm ashamed of you."

The silence was broken only by loud snoring. Seemed Old Hickory had passed out.

"I stand with you, Coop," Brett said quietly. "The town can use a little elbow grease or it's going to completely die. I vote that if we can't help, we should stand out of the way."

"Amen, brother." Rand slapped Brett on the back.

"Oh, all right." The disgruntled barber took out a white handkerchief from his pocket and waved it.

Old Hickory came awake as the men filed from the room. "I'll...I'll take a wh-iskey."

"Go back to sleep, Hickory," Cooper flung over his shoulder on the way out the door.

He rented a wagon from the livery, then returned to the mercantile to load the rolls of barbed wire.

"You take good care of Jenny," Delta ordered. "And don't let her overdo. Change her bandage every day. And wash behind Ben's ears when you give him a bath."

"Yes, mother." Cooper grinned. He'd wished

many days and nights that his mother had lived to tell him these things. It felt nice to have a woman boss him around, especially one as pretty as Delta. She'd wiggled past all his defenses and barricades and settled herself in his heart.

Maybe one day when he got enough nerve, he'd tell her that.

Feeling lighter than a man with his problems had a right to, he lightly tweaked her nose. "Don't get into too much trouble."

"I don't plan on it. I'll see you in a few days. I'll need to ride out and give Jenny an update on things."

His smile slid off. "Have Rand drive you out. It's too dangerous for a woman alone. You might run into those men who've been attacking the ranch."

"I will." A deep wrinkle marred her smooth brow. "Cooper, are you absolutely positive it's a good idea to take Jenny and Ben out there?"

"I'm sure. I wouldn't jeopardize their safety for anything. I'd give my life for those two and my brothers. No one, absolutely no one, is getting past the main gate. The Long Odds is well guarded, and I intend to keep it that way."

"I hope you're right."

"Guess I'd better be. I'll never hear the end of it if I'm not."

By the time he returned to Mabel's, Jenny and Ben were waiting on the porch with their bags at their feet. Ben's grin stretched from ear to ear. The boy stumbled over his feet in his hurry to meet him.

"Mama and me are going to the ranch. This is my best day ever," Ben said, hugging him.

"Do tell." Cooper's chest tightened. It meant more than anyone knew to feel the boy's arms clinging to him. He wished Ben's grandfather could know how special his grandson was.

Mabel wiped away a tear and kissed her little sister. "It's gonna be lonely around here without you and Ben."

"It's only for a few days. And I'm not going far."

"I know. You get some rest now and don't fret about anything." Mabel stood back and let Cooper help Jenny onto the wagon seat. She waved until they moved down the street.

Once out of town, Cooper breathed easier. Towns stifled the air and closed in around a man. He took a sack of lemon drops out of his pocket, got one out, and handed the rest to Ben.

Scanning the brush lining both sides of the road, he kept one palm on his Colt.

If trouble called, he'd leave it his card.

❧

Delta was within minutes of locking the mercantile doors when a tall Indian dressed in leather trousers and wearing moccasins strolled in. She didn't know why, but she wasn't afraid, even though she was alone. His brown eyes reminded her of a wounded animal who had to learn to trust or it'd perish. A wildness about him told her that being made to fit a mold would destroy his soul. She suspected that someone had attempted to do that and now maybe he was trying to make himself whole again.

"May I help you?"

"I hope so. Cooper mentioned that you have

needles of all sizes. Would you happen to have one that sews leather?"

"You must be Cooper's and Rand's brother."

"That's right. I'm Brett Liberty."

"I've heard a lot about you. I'm Delta Dandridge." She stuck out her hand and found it engulfed by Brett's large paw.

"You can't believe everything they say." He gave her a teasing smile that nearly took her breath away.

Cooper and his brothers were definitely no slouches in the looks department. Each was handsome in his own right. No wonder they had to fend the women off with a stick.

But Cooper was the one who had her heart and always would, whatever happened. "If there's anything bad, they certainly failed to mention it. I'm glad to finally meet you."

"I'll admit I've been curious about the woman who turned this town upside down. You don't have pointy mule ears at all."

Delta laughed. "I keep those hidden from most people."

He followed her to the leatherworking supplies, where he selected a needle. After he paid and left, Delta locked up. She took a detour on the way to the boardinghouse by way of the hotel. She'd promised Nat Rollins she'd stop in. She hoped she'd relay the appropriate response that was worthy of the honor. Already she doubted she could keep a straight face.

The Lexington Arms Hotel stood tall across the street from the Lily of the West. Like most everything else in Battle Creek, the two-story structure had seen better days. She opened the door and strode up to the desk. The interior reflected the outside appearance. The lopsided sofa was missing a leg on one end, and the upholstered chairs were mismatched and different colors. None were without holes. In fact, one had a metal spring sticking out of the seat. The peeling wallpaper and warped wooden floor only added to the shabby condition.

It broke her heart. The place had lots of potential, if only someone would take an interest.

Nat Rollins came from a small room behind the desk. His face lit up when he saw her. "I'm glad you stopped by."

"I told you I would. I'm just sorry it took me so long."

He patted a steel box on the counter. "Well, this is it. Ain't she a beaut?"

With metal bars all the way around and a top that was secured with a padlock, the box resembled a small jail cell. Cradled inside the box was the broken heel of a woman's shoe.

Battle Creek's claim to fame.

"She certainly is." Delta took great pains to examine it thoroughly.

"This heel belonged to Miss Abigail Winehouse, the renowned singer and actress from Boston. Broke right off her shoe when her stagecoach lost a wheel and she ended up flat on her rear in the dirt." Nat colored when he realized what had just come out of his mouth. "Uh, I'm sorry, Miss Dandridge. I didn't mean to say rear. A lady…uh, a lady wouldn't…"

"Don't get in a dither, Mr. Rollins. I didn't think anything about it. We all have them."

His Adam's apple bobbed up and down like a cork on a fishing line. "Thank you for not taking offense."

"You're welcome." She ran her fingers across the cool steel of the box. You'd think the thing was made of solid gold the way the town protected it. According to Mabel, there had been some fighting over who would get to claim ownership. George Lexington won out. At least so far. But the fight was far from over, she suspected.

"I'd open it and let you touch it, but I'd get in big trouble."

"We wouldn't want that." She let her gaze drift to the hotel furnishings. "I'm curious. How long has the hotel been in business?"

The man rubbed a pointed chin that had a few sprigs of hair on it—he'd probably missed them when he shaved that morning. "Well, ma'am, I do believe Mr. Lexington built it fifteen years ago, thereabouts. It was the tallest structure around until Mr. Fletcher built the Flying Dutchman windmill on his property at the edge of town. Have you seen it?"

"Yes, I have, and I was quite impressed." She prayed Nat wouldn't see the grin that she tried desperately to hide.

"Me too. Fletcher's real smart."

"It's been nice chatting, Mr. Rollins. I promised Mabel I'd help with supper. I deeply appreciate you letting me look at your treasure."

"Yes, ma'am. Thanks for coming in."

Delta gave the hotel lobby one last glance and vowed to do something about the state of disrepair. Perhaps if she spoke to Mr. Lexington, she could persuade him to make some repairs. Surely he was a reasonable man.

She could do so much good, if only everyone would let her.

Twenty-three

THE WEEK PASSED QUICKLY. ON SUNDAY, DELTA AND
Rand rented a buggy and drove out to the Long Odds
Ranch. She missed Jenny something awful. Besides,
she had lots to tell her friend.

The previous day, Delta had received another mysterious letter. Like the others, it had been addressed
to her in the same flowing handwriting. As with the
first, she hadn't bowed to temptation to read it. Also,
like the first, she hadn't hesitated in throwing it into
the fire. Only one person could be responsible, and his
motives boded ill for her.

She turned her attention to the beautiful scenery.
Nearing the Long Odds, she noticed that in addition
to the wagons Cooper had placed end to end to seal
off his land, a barbed-wire fence now reinforced the
blockade. The ranch had indeed become a fortress.
In fact, they'd also stretched wire across the entrance
and had a stern-faced cowboy standing guard. In brisk
tones, he asked them to state their business.

Rand answered, "You must be new. I'm Cooper's
brother, Rand Sinclair."

Without a word, the guard nodded and removed the wire. Rand drove the buggy through and up to the house.

Jenny flew from the porch with a big smile on her face. Her bruises had turned yellow and green and the bandage that had covered her head was gone. "Oh, I'm so glad to see you."

Delta climbed from the buggy before Rand could help her down and wrapped her friend in a hug. "I thought Sunday would never get here. How are you doing? You look wonderful."

"So do you. Come in the house and tell me all the news from town."

Rand waved them on. "You ladies run ahead. I'm going to find Coop."

"He's down by the corral," Jenny volunteered. The woman linked her arm around Delta's and they went into the house and straight to the small parlor. "Can I get you something to drink or eat?"

"No, thanks." Delta settled herself on the worn settee, remembering the last time she was there and how Jenny had made Cooper hug her to end their arguing. Seated across from her, Jenny grinned as though she knew Delta's thoughts. But of course, she couldn't. "Now, young lady, tell me where the bandage that was on your head went."

"Doc Yates rode out yesterday and said I didn't have to wear it anymore," Jenny explained.

"That's wonderful! I take it you're healing nicely, then."

"I am indeed. Almost good as new. What's happening in town?"

"We have ten members of the garden club. The women are so excited and want to get started on our projects. The first meeting is scheduled for Tuesday evening."

Jenny clasped her hands. "I can't wait. I'll be there. I'll have Cooper bring me in."

"So it's been good being here?"

"I can't tell you how much. Ben is the happiest I've seen him in a very long time."

"And you?" Delta asked quietly.

"There's freedom here and oodles of fresh air and sunshine. I'm safe and out of Hogue's reach. Is…is he still in jail?"

"Yes. You don't have to fret about him."

Worry clouded Jenny's eyes. "But I do. He'll get out one of these days, and when he does, he'll look to get even."

"I know it's none of my business, but why did you stay with him?"

"At first I didn't think I had a choice. He told me that over and over. Said he'd kill me if I ever tried to leave." Tears spilled down Jenny's cheeks. "I was terrified of him. But I'm not scared anymore. He will not lay another hand on Ben as long as I draw breath. And he'll never see this child growing inside me." She laid a hand on her gently rounded stomach. "I think it's a girl this time. I'd like to have a cute little girl."

"She'll be beautiful and take after her mother." Delta took a deep breath, and before she could stop the words, they tumbled from her mouth. "What does Cooper think of you having a wee one?"

"That man is so protective. And sweet."

"He's that, all right," Delta said dryly to hide her

aching heart. It was clear from Jenny's blissful smile that Cooper meant something very special to the woman, just as she'd suspected all along. Delta had best get over any feelings she had for the tall rancher and fast, before she got hurt.

Deep in thought, she didn't hear anyone enter. She glanced toward the doorway and fell headlong into Cooper's gray stare. His crooked smile made her stomach lurch as though she were plummeting off a high cliff.

"Miss Delta, is Jenny making you feel at home?" His low rumble vibrated the air.

"Yes, we're enjoying catching up. I see you worked feverishly in implementing the barbed wire."

"One thing you should know about me is that I waste no time once I make up my mind about something." Though he'd stated it as simple fact, she heard a subtle warning rippling beneath the surface.

"That's good to know."

Worry suddenly crossed Jenny's face. "Is Ben all right? Is he getting under your feet out there?"

Cooper came into the room and stood beside the woman's high-backed chair. Delta noticed the gentle way he laid a hand on her shoulder. "Quit fretting, Jenny. The boy's just fine. I'm watching out for him. If he so much as pulls a hangnail, I'll fix it."

Jenny gave a troubled sigh. "I'm sorry. Hogue—"

"I'm not Hogue Barclay," he said softly. "I don't lose my temper and start whaling on those who cross me. And I have all the patience in the world with children, especially Ben. Now, relax and let me do the worrying for a change."

Delta observed the exchange and couldn't help wondering what would have happened between the two if she hadn't been in the room. Even as it was, she might as well have been a stick of furniture for all the attention they paid her. Finally, she stood. "Let me help with lunch, and then Rand and I have to get back to town."

Cooper pinned her with his gray stare. "I have a cook for that. You're company."

"There's no reason why I can't help," she replied stiffly. "One thing you should know about *me*, Mr. Thorne, is that I always earn my keep."

His gaze tangled with hers and she suddenly wished to be anywhere but in Cooper's small parlor. "All I want you to do is sit here and keep Jenny occupied. She needs a woman to talk to about womanly things. Lord knows she gets little of that out here, with a bunch of menfolk underfoot."

"He does speak the truth," Jenny said. "And, besides, I learned the hard way that Mack has a conniption fit when anyone invades his kitchen."

At that, Delta sank back onto the settee. Cooper left and soon she and Jenny were discussing various and sundry topics, including Granny Ketchum.

"The dear woman hasn't been in the mercantile once since we cleaned her house and found all her missing belongings," Delta said. "I do miss seeing her. I haven't mentioned this to anyone, but did you know she adopted me?"

"I'm not surprised." Jenny picked up a ball of yarn and her knitting needles from a basket. "You do have that effect on people."

Before Delta could think of an appropriate reply, a gunshot rang out. Both women jumped to their feet. They didn't know which direction to head, whether to stay in the front of the house or run for the back.

Beyond the door, men's voices shouted and boot heels struck the hard ground. The place had erupted into sheer bedlam.

"Ben! I have to see about Ben!" Jenny screeched.

"We have to get down on the floor. Now." When Jenny didn't move, Delta grabbed her arm and pulled her out of the line of fire.

"But Ben's out there."

"Cooper and Rand will make sure he's okay. You'll only distract them if you go running out. The best thing you can do for your son and your unborn baby is to stay indoors where it's safe."

"How do you stay so calm?"

"Practice." And knowing how to stay out of the way of a father who hated her very existence.

❧

When the rifle blast from a nearby group of trees came near to parting his hair, Cooper drew his Colt and darted for cover. After quickly making sure that Ben was all right, he shouted orders to his men and ran toward the location of the burst of orange flame. Rand came from out of nowhere and joined him.

Whoever had fired the shot tore through the thick undergrowth, leaving broken limbs in his wake.

Cooper itched to get his hands on the culprit who'd dared to try to kill him on his own damn property—and in broad daylight, no less. That smarted. Tolbert Early had them chasing their tails.

They had to make some changes. It was time Cooper ran Early and his men out of the county—shoot, out of the whole darn state—and put them back under the rock they'd crawled from.

Finally, he glimpsed the shooter through the trees. He ran faster, determined to capture the trespasser.

But just as he raced into a clearing, the man climbed onto a horse.

Cooper made a flying leap and grabbed a piece of his clothing, but it wasn't enough to prevent escape. He stood there clutching a scrap of fabric while the horse bolted and they went galloping down the road.

"Did you get a good look at him?" Rand asked, breathing hard.

"Nope. Damn! This bunch is like ghosts. They come and go at will and I can't seem to touch them."

Rand clasped his shoulder. "They'll have to come up for air eventually. When they do, we'll nab 'em."

They holstered their weapons and walked slowly back. Cooper's men hollered and told him they'd found the spot where the shooter had hidden.

From the small pile of smoked cigarettes on the ground, the man had lain in wait for some time before he'd fired. Cooper knelt to examine the ground closely.

"Rand, you and Brett would be walking up Boot Hill to say howdy to me from now on if I hadn't bent over to rub Bandit's head." That bullet had come way too close for comfort.

Just then, the women ran from the house. Delta spoke first. "Are you all right?"

His eyes met hers. "Fine."

Jenny spied Ben and hurried over to him. Like a mama cow concerned about her calf after being branded, she inspected him from head to toe and finally pulled him close for a tight hug.

"Mama, I'm okay." He squirmed out of her arms, looking around to see who'd witnessed his embarrassment.

Cooper sighed and shook his head. He sympathized with the youngster. Midway between a boy and a man, Ben had been coddled far too much. Cooper would have to see what he could do to even things out.

But first, he had more pressing issues. He gathered his men. "Search this entire ranch. I mean every nook and cranny. If you find any trespassers, bring 'em to me. And I want the fence checked out. I suspect the interloper cut the wire to get in. That'll have to be fixed, and fast."

"You heard the boss," Zeke O'Grady barked. "Now get to it."

After the men saddled up and rode out, Cooper pulled Rand aside. "Better go get Brett. And Sheriff Strayhorn. Something's brewing and it'll take all the help I can get to fight it."

"I agree. Figure they'll hit again along about dark."

When they did, Cooper would be ready for them. He'd fight to the last breath to protect his land and those he loved.

His searching gaze located Delta. She stood apart from the others, watching him. Her mysterious green eyes had turned a dark shade of emerald.

He covered the ground between them with long

strides. "Might as well get comfortable. I'm afraid you're stuck out here. It's too dangerous to let you leave."

"How long do you think it'll be before I can go back to town?"

"It's anyone's guess. Maybe morning, maybe longer."

"I have a job. John depends on me to be there. And I have other obligations." She waved an arm helplessly toward town.

"None of that is important if you're dead," he said softly.

Fear rippled across her face, then was gone. He liked that about her. She didn't indulge in tears and hysterics. Delta Dandridge calmly accepted things and tried to make the best of each situation. His thoughts went back to the day he first saw her and told her he couldn't marry her. She'd refused to let on how deeply it hurt her. She'd marched herself down to the mercantile and asked John Abercrombie for a job. And just like that, she began a whole new life for herself.

However, she couldn't make it more plain that she'd rather be anywhere than his ranch.

That was fine with him, because having her so near tempted him to forget all the reasons why no woman would ever hold his heart.

Twenty-four

DARKNESS FELL OVER THE LONG ODDS AND WITH IT came an eerie quiet that had their nerves wound tighter than a fifty-cent watch. Shadows whispered, flitting among the trees and over the gently rolling hills.

Cooper had concentrated most of his men, along with Brett, Rand, and Sheriff Strayhorn, across the most vulnerable area—the front section of his property. He alone guarded the house.

Trouble hit about an hour after dark.

A barrage of gunfire erupted. Hooded riders came from every direction at once. Dozens of thundering hooves shook the ground, reverberating in his heart. Bloodthirsty yells split the air.

But it was the screams of the horses that most unsettled him.

He was glad he'd already gotten the women and Ben in the house with orders not to come out no matter what. He posted himself near the front door and answered the gunfire with some of his own. He set his jaw, tightening his grip on the rifle. The riders would have to go through him to get inside.

And to do that, they'd have to kill him first. What they didn't know was that he didn't kill easy. Just ask the no-good son of a bottom-feeder who'd fathered him.

After thirty minutes or so, the enemy found no access to the ranch and pulled back, probably to regroup. Cooper's gut told him they hadn't given up and ridden off with their tails tucked between their legs. They would be back.

Now that the turmoil had passed, the deafening silence settled over the ranch like a wet wool blanket. He stood in the deep shadows of the porch and waited, watching, feeling the night pressing around, clawing at him like some kind of crazed animal.

Busy filling the empty chamber of his Winchester, he jumped when a hand reached out to brush his shoulder.

Cooper whirled, ready to fight.

Delta stood there shivering in nothing but one of his shirts, which almost reached her knees. His gaze swept the length of her shapely legs, then down to her bare feet.

Lord help him. Waves of desire rolled through him, making his trousers more than a mite uncomfortable.

If she knew she exposed so much of herself and had him in such a state of arousal, she'd die of embarrassment.

The inky blackness might hide some things, but not Delta. He could find her even if he lost sight in both eyes and she didn't utter a sound. "What are you doing out here? I told you to stay inside."

A wry smile flirted with her mouth. "I've never been real good at following orders. I wanted to see what was happening. Is it over?"

"Not by a long shot. Unless I miss my guess, we'll

see them again tonight." He moved from the shadows and took her arm. "Go back in the house, Delta."

A sliver of light from the window illuminated her face and revealed a throbbing pulse in the hollow of her throat. That familiar heat he felt whenever she was anywhere near rose from deep inside, pooling in his belly.

She was too close.

He was only a man.

The aching need for her was so intense, so powerful, he had trouble drawing air into his lungs.

Reaching out, he brushed her cheek with his fingertips.

As though in some kind of trance, he propped his rifle against the side of the house. He pulled her against his chest with a fiery need and buried his hands in her mass of golden curls.

When he thought he'd explode, he lowered his head and crushed his lips to hers. Deep hunger and smoldering desire melded together and rose up like the billowing steam of a mighty locomotive. Delta tasted of wild honey, sweet longing, and innocence.

"You make a man crazy with want," he murmured against her ear when the kiss ended after long seconds. "Do I frighten you?"

"No," she answered softly, her face uplifted.

"I'm glad." Cooper trailed feathery kisses down her slender neck and finally returned to her luscious mouth. He couldn't get enough. This mulish woman who challenged him at every turn did things to him that no other woman had.

Tracing the seam of her mouth with his tongue, he cajoled it open. When her lips parted, he dipped his tongue inside.

Still, he wanted more. He slipped his hand into the space between them and unbuttoned the shirt she wore. Once inside, he followed her curves, caressing, savoring. Her velvety skin was even softer than he'd imagined.

She was much more endowed than he'd thought, and he reveled in the knowledge.

The glorious weight of a breast filled his hand.

His fingers brushed the sensitive raised tips.

A little moan rose from her throat. When she leaned into him, her breath ragged, he knew she wanted him as much as he needed her.

She slid her hand across the muscles of his chest, then wrapped her arms around his neck. He lost all sanity. Every thought, every bit of sense he had, fled.

Nothing mattered except Delta and what she was doing to him. This night was made for feeling, for loving, for grasping the kind of pleasure that only came once in a blue moon. But the stark reality that this moon might be their last made the moment more urgent.

A low curse squeezed from his mouth. He forced himself to go slow when all he wanted to do was touch every inch of her bare skin as quickly as possible. Tenderly, his hand dropped lower to her flat belly.

"So beautiful. You make it impossible to think." He again pulled her against him and found her slightly open mouth. "You don't know how long I've wanted to do this."

When he let her up for air, she whispered as though she couldn't trust her voice, "Is this another Texas custom, pray tell?"

"Absolutely," he growled. "Welcome to Texas."

Delta grinned. "I like it here. I think maybe I'll stay."

"Mr. Cooper, I'm scared," Ben called from the doorway.

Cooper froze, then pushed Delta into the shadows so she could button up. "I'll be there in a minute, Ben."

Seconds ticked by and Delta nodded to let him know that she was again covered. "Stay here," he whispered. "I'll get him back to bed."

She nodded again.

Fifteen minutes later, he returned to the dark porch. He didn't see her. Just as he decided she'd slipped back into the house, he saw her huddling in the corner. "There you are. Wasn't sure you were still out here. What are you doing?"

"Calling myself a fool."

"Don't ever do that. You're no fool."

"What am I doing? What would Jenny say?"

"Jenny? What are you talking about?"

"I've seen the way it is between you and her. You're in love with her. You can't hide it."

A soft chuckle filled the dark space. "You don't know as much as you think you do. Sure, I love Jenny. But as a sister. I'm not *in love* with her."

"Then what is your relationship, if I dare ask?"

"I knew her father, Isaac Daffern. I didn't know Jenny existed until after Daffern died. He left me a letter among his things, begging me to find her and make sure she was all right. That's why Rand, Brett, and I ended up here in Battle Creek."

"Why didn't Jenny live with him? Why was she here?"

"I don't know all the facts, but Daffern explained in the letter that Jenny's mother died giving birth to her. Must've been before Rand, Brett, and I landed at his door. He didn't know anything about caring for an infant, so he sent Jenny to a couple here, an old friend and his wife."

"Mabel's parents?"

"Yes. They never told Jenny that she wasn't their child. To this day, she still doesn't know." Although she surely suspected something after the fiasco at the boardinghouse the day he brought Jenny and Ben here to the ranch. He kicked himself to the Rio Grande and back for his loose lips.

"How did you happen to be with Jenny's father?"

Without mentioning Tolbert Early, he told her about coming West on the orphan train, the escape, and how Daffern had taken them in and protected them.

"I don't know how we'd have turned out if not for his steadying influence. We loved that man like a father. We'd probably still be with him if he hadn't died."

"Will you tell Jenny about him one day?"

"Yes. She deserves to know who fathered and loved her."

"I'm glad you found someone like him to care about you." She spoke the words quietly. "We all need someone."

"What about you, Delta? Who cares for you?"

"No one," she whispered.

The deep sadness beneath the statement brought a tight ache to his chest. Cooper moved closer and let her fragrance wash over him. He caressed the delicate line of her jaw with the backs of his fingers. The prim and proper outer shell hid a warm-blooded tigress underneath.

She was a glorious woman of contradictions, and he wanted her more than air, or food…or maybe even his land.

God, he never thought he'd say that.

Yet that's what it had come to. Delta Dandridge had burrowed deep inside where his hopes and dreams lived. But a man like him had nothing to offer except a life full of regret…and a past he couldn't outrun.

He was damaged beyond any hope of redemption.

Was his punishment to live alone, always seeking, never finding? Was that to be the sum total of his remaining days?

"You're wrong. I care," Cooper said softly.

Tears glistened in her eyes when she met his stare. He touched her hair at the temple, then let his hand slide down to the curve of her jaw and farther, to the column of her throat.

He sucked in a ragged breath. "Would you mind if I kiss you again?"

Instead of a reply, she rose on tiptoe and pressed her mouth boldly to his lips. A groan rumbled in his chest as he wrapped her in his arms.

Loud gunfire erupted, abruptly ending the kiss.

Dragging her into the shadows, he ordered, "Get in the house. Stay away from the windows."

Without answering, she whirled and raced inside.

The second blistering attack came with all the noise and fury of a great whirlwind.

The number of hooded men had grown. The line

across the front that included Rand and Brett fell back as the fighting intensified. Cooper left his post at the house and joined them. This called for a desperate stand or the attackers would overrun them.

He took cover behind some of the wagons and aimed at the closest invader. One more down. But where that one used to be, five more popped up.

Bullets flew around him, and one grazed his upper arm, stinging like fire. He didn't stop to look. He kept firing at one dark target after another. They would not take his ranch or harm the womenfolk. He wasn't about to let that happen.

Rand raced from the shadows at one of the enemy who had jumped one of the wagons with his horse. Cooper watched him raise his weapon to fire, saw the panic on his brother's face when he realized the gun was empty.

The assailant lifted his pistol and aimed.

Without a moment's hesitation, Cooper turned and fired, dropping the man to the dirt.

"Thanks, brother," Rand yelled over the noise. "Thought he had me."

Cooper handed him a box of ammunition. "We'll keep firing until we run out of bullets, and then we'll use our fists."

"Damn right."

The sound of gunfire resonated in the air as the battle intensified. Cooper took shot after shot, sometimes missing but oftentimes hitting the mark. Bodies lay scattered as others limped off into the surrounding woods.

Just when the tide began to turn, the raiders drove

a herd of bawling, angry, snot-snorting cows past the barbed wire fence and onto his land.

In the chaos, the outlaws disappeared. Panic gripped him.

Fearing some would slip past and get into the house, Cooper retreated to plant himself in front of the door. He barely reached the shadowed porch when one galloped up and prepared to launch himself off the horse.

Cooper didn't give him a chance. He reached up and dragged the enemy to the ground.

Delta crouched below the window in the dark house. She raised her head and peered out into the darkness and the billowing clouds of dirt the cattle had stirred up. Her heart pounded in her throat as she watched Cooper fight with one of the hooded attackers.

What if he couldn't best the man? What if the intruder got inside? She had to protect Jenny and Ben.

Looking around the room for a weapon, she spied a thick piece of wood beside the fireplace. She crawled over to it, then returned to her vantage point.

Cooper drove his fist into the man's stomach. Delta thought that might end things. But it didn't. The hooded attacker fought back, slamming Cooper against the side of the house so hard it shook the walls. She didn't know how Cooper could take so much punishment and still come up swinging. But he did, time and time again.

Clapping her hand over her mouth so as not to

scream, Delta held back tears and prayed that Cooper wouldn't be hurt too badly. He had to win.

She recalled the moments earlier on the porch.

The way he'd kissed her.

Touched her bare skin.

And made her feel every inch a desirable woman.

A yearning for more consumed her. It seemed he'd awakened a part of her that she hadn't known was dead and buried.

And now he was locked in the fight of his life.

A tear slid down her cheek. She brushed it away. The man who could be so tender and rough at the same time, who loved his brothers with all his heart, and who could be so infuriating, would not lose. Too many people depended on him.

She depended on him. Only in that moment did she truly know how very important he'd become.

The chaotic scene taking place beyond the door struck fear in her heart. Cooper, Rand, and Brett, in addition to the ranch cowboys, were engaged in hand-to-hand combat. The ranch, so peaceful and serene a short time ago, had now become a battlefield. She even saw the cook out there in the mix.

Time was measured in frantic heartbeats.

Delta felt movement behind her and turned, ready to do her own fighting. When she saw Jenny and Ben, she relaxed and put down the wood. Keeping low, mother and son stole quietly across the floor.

"I can't stand it," Jenny murmured. "What's happening?"

"It's hard to tell, but I think we're winning."

"Mr. Cooper will whup 'em," Ben said confidently,

bumping her elbow as he crowded close to look out. "He will. You'll see."

"I'm praying for that," Delta said. "Keep your head below the window in case of shooting."

"This is too dangerous, son." Jenny took his arm. "We'd better go back upstairs."

"Aw, Mama. Why do you always treat me like a baby?"

"I don't mean to, Ben. I just want to keep you safe."

Then a gunshot rang out and Jenny didn't have to prod Ben toward the stairs. Delta watched them both disappear from view. She turned back toward the window, praying she wouldn't see Cooper lying in a pool of blood.

Thankfully, he was on his feet and tying up the attacker he'd fought with. The man's black hood lay on the ground like a dead vulture. She had to get to Cooper. She had to hug him and feel his rippling muscles beneath her fingers. But she stopped short when she remembered how little she wore. Besides, he'd only get mad if she didn't stay put as he'd ordered.

Worried about Rand and Brett, she didn't rest until her searching gaze located them. They both appeared to be uninjured. Relief made her knees weak. The fight seemed to be over. At least for now.

Maybe the hooded attackers had decided they couldn't win this war they'd brought to Cooper's doorstep.

But why had they come? Why single out Cooper? She wished she knew the answers.

Closing her eyes, she put her fingers to her lips, remembering the firmness of his mouth. Her hand moved down to her breasts, feeling, savoring. Delta didn't know why her skin tingled so, why his touch left her craving more.

What was this maddening attraction between Cooper and her? The sweet agony flowing beneath her skin was foreign to her. She only knew she had to have more or surely die from want.

A delicious yearning for something she couldn't define swept through her. She only knew when she found it, she'd then be complete.

Twenty-five

COOPER GRABBED HIS CAPTIVE AND SHOVED HIM ONTO
the porch steps. "I want some answers."

"There's a mighty big difference between wantin'
and gettin'," the man sneered.

"Oh, you'll tell me what I want to know, all right.
The only thing left to determine is how many strips
of your hide I'll have to yank off before your tongue
starts working." He picked up the black hood and the
interloper's rifle. "What's your name?"

"Pete. Turn me over to the sheriff."

"In case you haven't noticed, you're in no position
to give orders." Cooper pitched Pete's rifle out of
reach and drew out a long knife from a leather sheath
at his waist. "Now, where would you like me start?
The chest or the back?"

Pete's eyes widened and he swallowed hard.

"Since you don't seem to care, I think I'll take the
first strip off your chest. My brother Brett is an Indian
and he taught me how. The trick is to get the tip of
the knife just under the skin right above the muscle."
Cooper grabbed Pete's shirt. "You might want to

close your eyes and grit your teeth. It's a little messy. Want to bite down on something?"

"Ain't no call to do this. What'dya want to know?"

"You work for Tolbert Early?"

"Yep, and he's gonna kill you, Thorne."

"Maybe so. Then again, maybe I'll send him to hell first. Where is he holed up?" Cooper growled.

"He don't stay nowhere more than a night. Likes to keep movin'."

"Where did you sleep last?" When Pete hesitated, Cooper laid the knife on the man's cheek.

"All right. Don't cut me. Bedded down in an abandoned house over Spring Hill way." Before Pete finished spilling his guts, he told how Early had hired him and the others to bring sick cows from a ranch farther down the valley and put them on Cooper's land. Seemed Early wanted to deal utter devastation before the man killed him. At least one mystery solved.

"Where were you supposed to meet up after the raid tonight? Think about your answer very carefully."

"Early said to meet him at Fire Creek."

Just a mile away. With luck, they might catch them there.

"Here's what you're going to do. You're gonna draw me a map of every one of the places you holed up."

"And then you'll let me go?" Pete looked up hopefully.

"Nope. But I will let you live."

Rand, Brett, and Zeke O'Grady rode up with Sheriff Strayhorn. Blood soaked Zeke's shoulder.

"Looks like you caught one of 'em," Rand said, dismounting.

"Got lucky," Cooper answered. "Take charge of Pete here."

Satisfied that Rand wouldn't let the prisoner escape, Cooper returned his knife to its sheath and hurried to help Zeke from the saddle. "How bad you hurt?"

"Aw, ain't nothin' to make a fuss over. Just a little blood is all. I've seen a lot worse pain getting a bee sting." Zeke tried to shoo him away as though Cooper were a pesky fly.

Delta stepped out onto the porch. She'd exchanged his shirt for her prim and proper dress. His breath caught at the sight of her, and memories of their kisses in the moonlight flooded back. A lady like her deserved more than a few stolen moments. He owed her far more than what he could ever give her. That stark reality didn't do anything to stop the wanting that wound around his heart like a determined trumpet vine.

"What can I do to help?" she asked. "I see you're bleeding, Mr. O'Grady. Come into the house and I'll tend your wound."

"That's awful kind, little missy. But I don't wanna be no trouble. Ain't nothin' but a scratch."

"Get on in the house and let her fix you up, you old cantankerous mule," Cooper said. "Rand and Brett will help me decide what to do with this weasel."

"You too, Cooper Thorne," Delta insisted. "Don't think I can't see you're bleeding."

"Don't have time for that right now. Besides, it's nothing."

The pretty lady gave a soft huff of frustration. When she and her patient disappeared inside, Cooper asked

Brett to get paper and pencil from the house. "Pete here is about to draw us a map of where we might find the den of snakes."

"What are we gonna do with him?" Brett asked.

"I'll take custody of the prisoner," Sheriff Strayhorn spoke up gruffly. "Mind if I put him in your smoke-house for the remainder of the night? It's the most secure place for now."

"It's yours for the using."

Brett went inside the house for the paper and pencil, returning a few minutes later.

After Pete, much against his will, drew them a map, Cooper jerked him to his feet. "Once we get him settled, we'll see if we can find and root out Tolbert and his gang."

"I do like your thinking," Sheriff Strayhorn said.

"Take the war to Early instead of waiting around for him to come back," Rand threw in.

"If he's anywhere around here, we'll find him." Brett's words were softly spoken, but left no doubt that they would succeed before it was all over and done with.

Cooper nodded. There'd be no hiding and waiting. From now on, they'd comb every last inch of Navarro County. Evil would not win over three brothers who were united and an aging sheriff who was as tough as an iron jenny.

Stepping inside the house, Cooper looked for Delta. He found her bandaging Zeke's shoulder. Though she'd not gotten any sleep, she gave him a smile.

"The bullet passed through without causing much damage. He'll be fine," she announced.

"That's good."

Zeke jerked his shirt back on. "Could've told you so. But you wouldn't take my word for it. I got sense enough to know when I need fussing over." The old ranch hand definitely had his nose out of joint.

Cooper sighed. "There's no harm in getting looked after."

"Jus' don't need mollycoddling." He squinted up at Cooper. "Where you boys headed? What's blowing in the wind?"

"The guy I caught said he was supposed to meet up with Early at Fire Creek. He also drew us a map of all the places they'd hidden out. We're going to try to find the gang."

Zeke grabbed his hat. "I'm coming."

"Now, Zeke, I need someone to guard the prisoner and protect the women. I'd take it as a big favor if you'd do that for me."

"I ain't liking it, but I'll do it." Zeke jammed his hat on and stomped outside.

Cooper took Delta's hand. "I only have a minute, but I wanted to thank you for those moments on the porch. When I rid this country of Early, you and me have things to talk about."

"Please don't say you regret—"

"Shhh." He laid his fingers on her lips. "I regret many things, but kissing you is not one of them. My life is uncertain and...complicated. I can't offer you the things you want."

Removing his fingers from her lips, he kissed her. This time it was hard and full of need. God help him, he couldn't get enough of her. He buried his hands in her glorious silky hair.

Finally letting her go, he silently cursed himself for always taking but never giving.

He wished…

"Stay away from the smokehouse. Zeke and the boys will keep you safe. I don't know when I'll be back."

"When you return, I'll be here. I'll wait however long it takes," Delta whispered.

The quiet promise unraveled what was left of his tightly wound composure. She meant a lot more than this present situation, and he cursed himself.

Rising on tiptoe, she placed her lips on his. "Be careful."

Unable to answer, Cooper nodded and went to join Brett and Rand without looking back. For if he did, he'd never leave her.

❧

Delta put her hands over her swollen lips to stifle a sob. Paralyzing fear at the thought of losing him spread through her chest. It didn't help any to realize he was the kind of man who would always ride headlong into danger with no fear for his own mortality. She'd simply have to get used to it if he was to be in her life.

Turning, she saw Jenny standing at the foot of the stairs. She'd apparently seen everything. Jenny crossed the room and put her arms around Delta. "It helps to cry," she said softly.

"I'm so frightened for him. What if this Tolbert Early kills him?"

Jenny smoothed Delta's hair. "Get that thought out

of your head right now. Cooper is too smart and too tough to let that happen. Besides, he has Rand and Brett to help him. They're pretty amazing men. And there's none better than Strayhorn."

"Why does this man want to harm Cooper? If you know, I'd sure like for you to tell me."

"I'm not sure. Although, I gather from tidbits here and there that it's something that occurred a long time ago, before they came to Battle Creek. Those brothers don't talk about their past much."

She and Cooper had that much in common, it appeared. The only thing a past seemed to be good for was dragging a person down, threatening to destroy whatever scrap of happiness they found. Often, in the dead of night, Delta was jarred from a deep sleep struggling to breathe. It felt as though hands squeezed tightly around her throat, holding her underwater. She wondered if Cooper ever experienced that. Maybe one day she'd ask him—that is, if she ever felt comfortable enough to discuss such things. However, it was about as likely as roping the moon, seeing as how tight-lipped he was talking about his feelings.

"I wonder what happened to them."

"Only they and the dear Lord know." Jenny pulled Delta toward the stairs. "Let's get some sleep, now that the excitement is over. It's still a while before dawn."

Delta followed her but not to bed. She gazed out over the ranch from the window in the bedroom. Cooper had insisted she sleep in his room. It had felt strange at first. Now it was the only place she wanted to be.

She turned away from the window to take in Cooper's furnishings. The huge four-poster bed swallowed her. It had surely been built for a man of his size. The old quilt covering it gave the room a homey feel. A large braided rug covered the wood floor. A tall chest that had seen better days, a bedside table, and a washstand completed her inventory. She could see Cooper here. It fit him.

Keeping her dress on in case of trouble, she lay down on top of the quilt. Cooper's shirt that she'd worn until the raiders came caught her attention. Grabbing it, she inhaled his fragrance, which still clung to the fabric.

The heat of a thousand fires burned inside, threatening to consume her mind, body, and soul.

Closing her eyes, she remembered every detail of their time together on the porch. The stubble on his jaw. The rumble in his throat and chest right before he kissed her. And the way he'd boldly touched her bare skin had seemed the most natural thing in the world.

Maybe that was the way it should be between two people who needed each other more than they needed to breathe.

Delta suspected what he wanted to discuss with her. He'd most likely warn her again that he wasn't the marrying kind and that he'd dedicated his life to remaining single.

But that didn't matter to her. God help her, she'd take him any way she could get him.

Even if he wasn't perfect.

Even if he made her mad enough to spit sometimes.

Even if he never married her.

Cooper Thorne could be the most maddening, most stubborn, most kissable man who ever lived.

And he'd turned her world upside down.

God help her, she loved him, and that was a fact.

Twenty-six

COOPER AND HIS THREE-MAN POSSE RODE HELL-FOR-
leather through the darkness of a heavy downpour. He
prayed they'd catch Early at Fire Creek.

But if they missed him?

Even though Texas was large, it wasn't big enough
to hide his mangy rear.

Somehow, someway, good would triumph over
evil. It had to.

But when they arrived at the creek, they found
nothing but a smoldering campfire and a chorus of
frogs and katydids.

Brett dismounted for a closer look. "They haven't
been gone long. Maybe ten minutes. Near as I can
tell, it looks like about eight or nine of them. Rain has
washed away a lot of tracks, though. Be hard to pick
up a trail. Where to next?"

"We'll check out every place Pete marked on the
map," Cooper said, unfolding the paper. "Maybe
they'll go back to one of their old hideouts. Anyone
who needs to head back to town, go ahead. Sheriff?"

"I'm in this thing for the duration," Strayhorn

growled. "Time to rid ourselves of this riffraff. No one's safe."

Rand straightened in the saddle. "Count me in."

"And me," Brett said, mounting up.

"Then let's ride."

❧

High on the bluff that overlooked Fire Creek, Tolbert Early hunched in the cold rain, watching the scene below through narrowed eyes. Misery went all the way to the bone, making him more determined than ever.

His leg throbbed where they'd shot him. He glanced down at the bandanna tied to stanch the flow of blood. He'd dug the bullet out but had left a bloody mess. The makeshift bandage was now grimy and soaked.

Leading his horse to an overhang out of the downpour, he removed the saddle and dried the faithful animal as best he could. He'd have given anything for a sack of grain. But at least there was plenty of grass. With the horse cared for, he turned his attention to the men in his crosshairs.

How he itched to show them that they wouldn't get away with what they'd done. It might take a while, but he'd hunt each of them down and he would find revenge.

He'd show Cooper Thorne what it felt like to be shot and lose the ability to perform.

He'd make Cooper know the living hell of being unable to find pleasure even though desire coursed through his body every waking minute and kept him awake at night.

He'd get satisfaction each time he pulled the trigger. This living hell would belong to the three brothers.

Soon Cooper Thorne and Rand Sinclair would know what it was like to yearn for release and never find it.

This would be their punishment.

An eye for an eye.

How he'd laugh when they begged. But he had something else in mind for Brett Liberty. That one would be the best of all. The boy had stolen his prized gold watch. No one stole from Tolbert Early. Laughter rose from the depths of despair. A bunch of scraggly orphans would finally get what was coming to them.

Seeing that Pete hadn't returned and the fact Thorne and the rest had ridden to Fire Creek meant they'd captured his recruit. Pete always did have loose lips. Good riddance. It was better this way.

Now, he could work without nagging worry.

And when he was done, he'd be able to sleep again.

❦

Riding hard and fast, Cooper, his brothers, and the sheriff covered a lot of ground. They'd checked out all the places Pete had marked on the hastily drawn map and came up short.

Where had Early gone? Some new hideout?

Cooper took comfort in knowing that his old adversary evidently didn't work for any of his neighbors. That would've made the job harder.

Rand leaned on his saddle horn. "What now?"

The position of the sun poking through the rain clouds told Cooper that it was early morning, around eight or so. His stomach growled and he knew his wasn't the only one. "Head back to the ranch to get food and fresh horses."

"I want to ask Pete more questions," the sheriff said.

"In my opinion, I really don't think he knows much," Brett said quietly.

"All the same, it doesn't hurt to find out. His dumb act might be a ruse."

Cooper met Strayhorn's eyes. "It wouldn't hurt to make sure, all right."

The foursome set out for the Long Odds, where they could regroup. Getting a bit of nourishment would definitely improve things.

Delta jumped from a chair on the porch and ran to meet them as soon as he came into view from the house. Cooper swallowed hard. The pleasant feeling of someone waiting for him at the end of a long ride curled inside his chest as though it belonged there.

But it didn't belong.

He was a loner. He couldn't afford to give her the wrong impression.

He could never take a wife.

Yet the memory of her gentle touch and the way her soft curves fit against him refused to leave his head. The recollections had taken up residence and staked their claim on his heart.

"You're back." Delta glowed with happiness. "I was so worried."

Cooper waited until Rand, Brett, and Strayhorn moved toward the barn before he dismounted. He struggled with the need to pull her into his arms.

To kiss her. To touch her silky skin.

This strong-minded, sassy woman who'd appeared out of the blue shouldn't have caused such an upheaval in his life.

But she had, and Lord knew he'd never be the same.

Clearing his throat, he forced out the words that he had to say. "I don't want you fretting about me. Understand? Whatever we have here can never lead to anything."

The gruff words erased her smile. Angrily she lifted her chin. "I guess this is the talk you said we'd have. Well, you can take your words and your kisses and…"

Quick tears filled her eyes, but it was her quivering lips that undid him. He called himself every name he could think of. Now what? He'd made a real mess of things. He'd taken liberties, given her false hope that she fit in his plans somewhere.

How could he tell her that having his father's rotten blood coursing through his veins made it impossible to claim her?

How could he explain the murderous thoughts that filled his head? He was a dangerous man, and she needed to run as far as she could away from him.

And how in God's name could he keep from destroying her?

"Look, what I'm trying to say—and doing a rotten job of it—is that I can't live with myself if I keep letting you think that I have anything to give you," he said quietly. "I wish things could be different. I really do. In another lifetime I'd scoop you up and never let you go."

Through narrowed eyes, he watched her stiffen. Without a word, she strode toward the house.

He was nothing but a bastard. He'd hurt the only

woman whose light could remove the darkness inside him. But even now, even knowing all the reasons why he couldn't give in to his desires, intense craving for her buckled his knees.

Sighing heavily, he led the tired buckskin toward the barn and the sack of oats that waited, wishing that life came with a set of instructions.

Hell and damnation, he could even use a torn, beat-up map.

Clearly, it was a mistake to come here.

Shaking, Delta gathered her thoughts. She had to get back to town and she didn't care what she had to do to get there. She'd walk, if she must.

Cooper had just thrown her back into the creek again. Only this time, she was too tired to fight the current.

There had to be a limit to how many times a person could reject another, didn't there? She told Jenny she'd be leaving.

"I could see something's troubling you." Jenny laid a hand on her shoulder. "Oh, dear. Cooper's messed up again. Want to talk about it?"

"No, I'd rather not."

"I'd go with you, only I can't do that to Ben. He sets such store by this ranch, and the fresh air does us both good."

"You should stay a little while longer. At least until I get this garden club up and going."

"Promise to let me know how the first meeting goes. I so wanted to be there."

"There'll be others. The main thing right now is to do what's right for your son and gain more of your strength."

"Be sure and save some work for me to do."

Delta hugged Jenny. "I will. Thank you for understanding."

As much as it killed her, she avoided Cooper the rest of the time. When he rode back out with the others, she sought out Zeke O'Grady. "Would you please show me a horse that I can hitch to the buggy?"

Zeke scratched his head. "Ma'am, it ain't a good idea to leave, especially alone. Did Coop say you could?"

Delta drew herself up straight. "I'm not a prisoner here and I certainly don't need his permission to leave. All I want you to do is show me a horse that I can use. I'll see that it gets back to the ranch."

"Here's what I'll do, Miss Dandridge. I'll take you back to town myself, if'n you got your mind made up that's what you wanna do."

A kiss on his wrinkled cheek brought a wide smile and a twinkle to his eye. She liked Zeke. "Thank you."

"Don't rightly know what all this is about, an' I'm sure I'll catch hell for it, but I cain't stand to see a pretty woman all down in the mouth."

One thing was certain: Delta learned from her mistakes, and this latest one was a whopper. From now on she meant to protect her heart more and avoid those sharp hooks that had nice juicy worms dangling from them.

"I don't want to get you in trouble with your boss, Zeke."

"Aw, I've been in hot water before, an' I doubt this'll be the last time." He patted her arm. "You just leave it to old Zeke. Cooper would be angrier if I let you go back to town alone, with this hooded bunch runnin' around. Sometimes you jus' have to pick your poison an' down it real fast before your nose can smell it."

"You're a saint if I ever saw one."

"Just give me a minute to tell the men to watch over Miss Jenny and Ben until I get back. The hands are trustworthy. They won't let anything happen to those two."

A little over an hour later, Zeke pulled in front of Abercrombie's Mercantile in Battle Creek. He helped Delta from the buggy.

"You don't know how much I appreciate this, Zeke."

"Now, don't you worry none. It'll all come out in the wash. Whatever's got Cooper by the short hairs won't stay that way. An' I'll take the buggy back to the livery."

"You're too, too kind." Delta watched him move down the street, then she opened the door of the mercantile and stepped inside.

John glanced up and relief spread across his face. "I heard there was some shooting out at the Long Odds. I'd hoped you didn't get caught in it, but since you weren't at work this morning, I assume you were."

"Yes, it was a frightful night. It scared Jenny and me out of our wits." She told him about the mounted attack.

"The good thing is you're all right. Do they know who this hooded gang is or what they want?"

"If Cooper knows, he didn't share that with us." She didn't add that she strongly suspected there was more to it than anyone was saying. Grabbing her apron from the nail behind the counter, she put it on. "Now, what do I need to do?"

"Just handle the customers while I unload a wagon of merchandise that arrived."

"John, I'm really sorry I wasn't here first thing this morning. I would've been if I was able."

He walked over and put an arm around her shoulders. "Don't give it another thought. We can't always do what we want."

"All the same, I'll try not to let it happen again." In fact, it wouldn't happen again because she wasn't going anywhere near the Long Odds Ranch. The devil could take Cooper Thorne.

Delta watched John Abercrombie head toward the back door. The change in the man continually amazed her. She recalled the first day she'd walked in and asked for a job. John had nearly run her out of the store. If Mabel King hadn't warned her of his surly attitude and the reason behind it, she'd have scurried into the nearest hole. Now, she gladly counted him a good friend.

The rest of the day she waited on customers, and in between she unpacked some of the boxes John unloaded off the wagon. His new order would stock the shelves quite nicely. With business picking up, it was more of a struggle to keep the shelves full.

Darkness fell and quitting time arrived before she knew it. She was getting ready to close up when the bell over the door jangled. Dressed all in black from his head down to his boots, a stranger stood there.

His stringy, long gray hair fell onto his face, hiding his features.

The hairs on the back of her neck rose. Icy fear swept the length of her. She clutched on to a counter for support. If only John hadn't already left.

"May I help you?" She projected politeness she didn't feel.

"I don't know, can you?" he answered in a surly tone.

"I'm in no mood to play games, mister." Though the words seemed to get stuck in her throat, Delta forced a measure of firmness into her voice. "If you need something, I'll be glad to assist you. Otherwise, I must lock up."

The stranger moved on inside, turned the lock on the door, and flipped the sign to Closed. Trembling, Delta glanced around for a weapon. The ax handles were too far away. She'd never reach them in time. A pair of scissors lay on the counter. She snatched them up. At least they would offer some protection.

Go for the eyes, came a voice in her head. Failing that, she'd plunge them into his throat.

"I know who you are, girlie." His gravelly voice gave her chills. "You cain't get away."

"Are you new to town?" she forced out. "I don't think I've seen you around. What's your name?"

The wooden floor creaked when he slowly moved forward, walking with a noticeable limp. Since he stood between her and the street, the only way to freedom was out the back. Keeping an eye on him, she inched toward it, praying that John had left it unlocked.

"Name's not important," he said.

"How do you know me?" She took two more steps backward.

"I seen you around. I see ever'thing, even things nobody wants me to see."

Great shuddering fear enveloped Delta. She gripped the scissors tighter. This was no time to be fainthearted. To survive, she'd fight with all the strength she had.

"Ain't nowhere to run, girlie," he said quietly.

And then she saw what he held in his hand and froze.

Twenty-seven

THE BLACK-CLOTHED STRANGER RAISED A LONG bowie knife.

Stark terror plunged Delta into a dark pit. The hope she had faded. Her scissors would be no match for that deadly blade. She didn't know what he planned to do, but it couldn't be good.

Thoughts of all the things she had envisioned for this town she loved and never would get a chance to implement filled her head. She'd only wanted to make a difference. To matter in someone's life.

"There's no way out," he said.

Would anyone hear if she screamed?

She gripped the scissors and took two steps back when he came closer. "What do you want, mister?"

"You."

"Why? What have I done? I don't even know you."

"No more stalling, girlie. I got plans for you."

Two more steps closer to the back door.

If she lunged for it, could she make it before he plunged the knife into her?

"Ain't nobody gonna come to save you."

That certainly appeared true, she thought, as despair took hold. But as long as she had breath in her body, she had hope. Maybe someone walking past would look in the window, see this hideous stranger, and stop him before he snuffed out her life.

"I can help you if you'll just tell me what you need," she bargained. "This store is full of anything you might want."

"Except something to make a man whole. Ain't nothing can do that but one thing."

"Did something bad happen to you?"

He stood so close, his putrid breath gagged her. "Ask Cooper Thorne."

Cooper? Her heart pounded. He was in serious danger and she couldn't warn him. This man clearly meant to kill them both.

She grasped for a bit of reason amid the madness that had her in its clutches. "Since he's not here, I can't very well do that."

"Don't matter. Doubt he'd tell you the truth." He reached out to lift a strand of her hair between his dirty fingers. "You an' me got business now."

The time had come to make her move. Just as she prepared to lunge with the scissors and blindly stab until she ended this man's miserable life, the back door flew open.

She gave a cry and whirled. Cooper's big frame filled the doorway. His cold gray eyes and chiseled jaw were enough to strike fear in anyone's heart. Her savior held a deadly Colt in each hand.

"Tolbert Early, you've reached the end. I'm going to make sure you stay dead this time." Cooper bit out the hard, brittle words.

Delta realized she stood between the two men and Cooper couldn't fire. Before she could step out of the way, Tolbert Early ran to the front and launched himself through the glass window into the street.

Pushing past her, Cooper released a volley of gunfire as he gave chase.

Numb with disbelief, Delta hurried to the shattered window. The night had swallowed up both Cooper and his prey.

What if this Tolbert Early doubled back and returned?

She shivered, recalling the words that had struck such terror. *Ain't nobody gonna come to save you.*

Only this time, Cooper had. He'd appeared when everything seemed lost, when her very life had hung in the balance. Of course, it couldn't mean anything. No. She refused to let hope back into her heart. It hurt too much when he tossed her back into the cold, swirling current with the hook still in her mouth.

Most likely Cooper took pity on her the way he did Bandit and Ben and Jenny. He probably considered her no different than one of his cows that got mired down in some thick mud and was in need of a hand.

But how had he known she was in trouble?

People began to gather to see what had caused the ruckus. Delta took comfort in having friends around her. Tolbert Early couldn't get her now.

In the midst of explaining what happened, John Abercrombie pushed through the crowd. "I came as soon as I heard. Are you hurt?"

"Just shaken up."

John patted her shoulder. "With good cause, I'd say. From now on, I won't leave you to close up alone."

Tears pricked behind her eyes, blurring his worried face. Thank goodness she had him and the many others in Battle Creek. She could lean on them for strength when she grew weary and disheartened.

Everyone pitched in to clean up the broken glass. Abercrombie and the men were nailing a piece of wood over the window when Cooper returned.

He drew Delta aside. "Did Early hurt you?"

Avoiding his gaze, she shook her head. "Frightened me, mostly. I didn't know what he wanted. Did you catch him?"

"No, he got away." Cooper laid a hand on her arm and sent a current spiraling the length of her body. "I will find him, though, and when I do, I'll make sure he doesn't bother you ever again. I'm thankful I found you in time. Early is a rotten, venomous snake."

"Why me?" She finally stared into his eyes and instantly knew her mistake. They were like twin magnets, luring her into their depths. "What did he hope to gain by harming me?"

His low growl sent sparks of heat to her belly.

"My guess is that he intended to use you to draw me out into the open."

God, how she hated that he could turn her into a smoldering pile of embers with nothing but his low, rumbling voice. She struggled to keep her thoughts away from passion and desire and moonlit kisses. Time to stick to the straight and narrow.

"Thank you for rescuing me. I was certain no one would come. By the way, how did you know he was in the mercantile?"

"After looking all day, Brett and I finally picked

up his trail leading into town about sundown. Caught sight of him near the saloon. Lost him, though, when he ducked into an alley. Luckily, I was passing by the back door and heard his voice."

"This may be none of my business, but since it affected me, I kind of have a right to know... Why do you want to kill each other? He said I should ask you."

Wearily, he ran a hand across his dark stubble. It had evidently been days since he shaved. "I don't... I can't talk about it. For now, let's just say that the world will be a safer place without the likes of him in it."

"And you think it's your job to rid us of him, right? Not the sheriff or anyone. It has to be you. Only you." Delta flung the words at him like so many stones.

"I set this in motion. It falls to me to finish it."

"And nothing I can say will change it."

Cooper looked away into the gloom. He was already miles away from her, on the trail of a madman. "Nope."

"You needn't concern yourself with my welfare from now on. You just go your merry way and I'll go mine." Seething with anger, she blindly whirled away. If only he would trust her. Fear that Cooper wouldn't win petrified her to the depths of her soul. Early could kill him and she would crawl into the grave with him if that happened.

"I wish..." he muttered softly before she got out of earshot.

That did it. The anguish in his tone buckled her knees. Delta almost turned around. She wanted to with every inch of her body.

Luckily, Granny Ketchum appeared from the throng of people and took her arm. "You look like you could use a nice cup of tea."

"That would be wonderful. Thank you."

Deputy Charlie Winters escorted them to Granny's rambling shack. "I'll wait for you, Miss Dandridge," he said.

"You needn't do that," she protested. "I'm sure that horrible man is miles away by now."

"I have strict orders, ma'am."

"All right, then." Delta followed Granny inside. Insisting the old woman sit down, she set some water on to boil.

"You were awful upset after talking to Cooper," Granny said, pulling her threadbare shawl closer around her. "That man can sure unravel a person."

As if she were nothing but a shawl with a loose thread. The image made her smile. "For a fact. He makes me so angry I could chew nails sometimes and not even know that I was doing it."

"Looked like he was mighty worried about you."

"I wouldn't know anything about that. I tried not to look at him much. Every time I do, I get this crazy feeling inside like I'm drowning or something."

"It's called love, my dear." Granny smoothed back her hair. "He sure has nice eyes. Oughta be a law against havin' eyes like those."

"My thoughts exactly," Delta murmured. She wondered if she could talk the sheriff into throwing him in the calaboose.

"Had a feller come courtin' back when I was young and foolish. He had pretty eyes. One was green and

the other was blue. If'n I'd have married him, we'd
had children with blue-green eyes. I sure did fancy
that man."

"What happened to him?"

"My papa shook his rifle at him. Never saw hide
nor hair of him again. Then Elmer Ketchum came
blustering into my life and I forgot all about everyone
else. Reckon it worked out the way it was supposed to.
Elmer captured my heart just like Cooper has yours."

Delta shook her finger. "That subject is closed.
You're trying to get a confession out of me. I'm wise
to your ways."

Granny shrugged. "Guess you're the only one that
doesn't know beans from squash."

The teakettle whistled, saving Delta from thinking
of a reply. In truth, she wasn't ready to discuss her
relationship with Cooper Thorne with anyone yet. She
poured water over the tea leaves and set the cups aside
to steep. They talked about Jenny and the attack on the
Long Odds, then moved on to various other subjects.

Granny peered at her over her spectacles. "Don't
get your dander up too much at Cooper, dear. He's
the perfect match for you, whether you know it or
not. I made sure—"

When the old woman clapped her hand over her
mouth to keep the rest of her sentence from springing
forth, Delta had a sneaking suspicion she'd stumbled
onto a secret. They'd never known who had signed
Cooper's name to the letters Delta got. Could Granny
Ketchum be the culprit?

"What were you going to say, Granny? What did
you make sure of?"

"What were we talking about, dear?"

The blank stare over the rim of the cup puzzled Delta. She peered into the rheumy eyes of the woman she'd come to love. Could Granny's forgetfulness be an act, or was it real? "You were telling me Cooper is the perfect match for me and that you made sure of something."

Tea sloshed out of the cup as Granny set it down. "The thought is gone now. I have no idea what I was gonna say. I swear the thoughts scurrying around inside my head are like a bunch of scared little mice running willy-nilly."

Still, Delta had her doubts. She might as well get everything out in the open. "Did you write those letters to me pretending to be Cooper?"

"Now why on earth would I do a crazy thing like that?"

"Maybe because you think he'd be better off with a wife and needed a nudge in the right direction?"

"Well, he would, but I never wrote no letters," Granny insisted. "I'm gettin' tired."

"Then I'd best get over to the boardinghouse." Delta rose and washed their cups. Then she kissed Granny's cheek. "It doesn't make any difference if you did write the letters. I still love you. Nothing will ever change that."

She helped Granny into bed. As she left the room, she happened to spy the cigar box on the floor that Granny had taken great pains to protect when they'd cleaned her house. Important papers, Granny had said. If she had written the letters to Delta, her responses back would most likely be in that box. One peek inside would either confirm or dispel her suspicions. But she couldn't bring herself to do that. She had no right to pry.

Pulling the front door shut, Delta took Deputy Winters's arm and let him escort her home.

The night seemed thick and heavy. She couldn't help casting anxious glances into the shadows, expecting Tolbert Early to spring out. For once, she was grateful for the company.

Surely he wouldn't try anything else. All the same, she'd exercise plenty of caution.

At the door of the boardinghouse, Delta thanked the deputy for walking her home and went inside.

Up in her bedroom, she hurriedly pulled down the window shade and drew the curtains tight. Tonight there would be no gazing out over the town and telling it good night as was her custom.

She got into her gown, blew out the lamp, and burrowed deep into her bedcovers. But sleep refused to come. Every time she closed her eyes, she saw Early's face. His gravelly voice echoed in her ears. He'd struck sheer terror into her heart. Never had she been that frightened of anyone.

The man's evilness still spread over her skin like a coating of kerosene—one spark and she'd go up in flames. Whatever lay between him and Cooper was something that could only end with the death of one.

Dear God, please don't let it be Cooper.

Saying prayers didn't help. Neither did thoughts of Granny Ketchum and their odd conversation. She tossed and turned.

The only thing that brought comfort was

remembering what a welcome sight Cooper was when he'd suddenly filled the back door of the mercantile. She wouldn't soon forget that.

Every hard muscle and tendon.

The rumble in his chest when he spoke.

The softening in his gray eyes when he looked at her.

And the tingles his touch elicited.

God in heaven, why did she have to love such a complicated, exasperating man?

Twenty-eight

COOPER PULLED THE COLLAR OF HIS JACKET UP AROUND his ears and settled himself into the shadows of a huge oak tree across from the boardinghouse. He fastened his gaze on the corner bedroom that had gone dark. Delta must've climbed into bed.

It promised to be a long night. He might not be able to give Delta what she wanted, but he wouldn't leave her unprotected and vulnerable to Tolbert Early's perverted, evil ways.

He owed Delta Dandridge that much.

Fury had consumed him when he saw Early in that mercantile a few feet from her. If he'd gotten there a minute later, no telling what he'd have found.

Bloody images of her body lying on the floor all lifeless and still filled his head. He would not let that happen. No matter what. So help him God, she would not pay for what he'd done.

Closing his eyes for a moment, he recalled the warmth of her satiny skin, the fragrance of her hair, and the sweet kisses under the moonlight. Those were what made living worthwhile.

But the lady was a spitfire, no doubt about that. Flames had shot from her green eyes when he refused to tell her what had happened between him and Early.

You needn't concern yourself with my welfare, she'd said.

Cooper smiled at the memory and murmured low, "Better get used to it, darlin', because your welfare means everything to me."

Staring at her window, Cooper noticed a light suddenly appear. Had she gotten up? Was she sick? Or had Early found a way to get inside? His heart pounded.

He checked the doors of the boardinghouse and found them locked; the same was true of the windows on the bottom floor.

A trellis on the side of the house almost reached her window. Maybe he could get close enough to peek inside. Being as quiet as he could, he scaled the trellis. When he got to the top, he noticed a narrow ledge going around to her window. He carefully managed to climb onto it.

Minutes later, he was at her window. She'd pulled the shade down but accidentally left a slight gap. He could see her sitting on the bed with a pile of letters in her lap. She read one letter, then frowned and put it down. Picking up another, she did the same thing. He thought it a bit strange that she'd read letters in the middle of the night. Still, Delta was an unusual woman. He'd calmed his fear that Early had her in his clutches. She was safe and sound.

In an effort to backtrack to the trellis, Cooper's boot slipped and he fought for purchase. He ended up hanging from the ledge by his fingertips. His efforts in avoiding a nasty spill to the ground below created a good bit of noise.

Delta spoke from the other side of the window. "Who's there? Speak up now."

"It's me," Cooper whispered. "Can you let me in?"

"Who's me?" she furiously whispered back.

"Cooper."

Within seconds, she raised the window. "Oh my goodness!" Using all her strength, she hauled him inside.

Breathing hard, he chanced a glance at her. "Thank you."

Her eyes narrowed to dark green slits. "You shouldn't be here. What were you doing at my window, pray tell?"

"I know how this looks. It's not appropriate and I apologize. But I can explain." He moved back a few steps before she could haul off and kick the daylights out of him.

"That would be best." She crossed her arms and beat out a nice tempo with her foot.

He wasn't about to point out the fact that her crossed arms had pulled the nightgown tight against her. She'd be mortified if she knew he could see the outline of her bosom and the puckering of her nipples through the thin fabric.

"If you dare."

"Darlin', I dare a great many things," he said softly.

"I'll just bet." The tempo of her foot increased.

"Did anyone ever tell you how beautiful you are when you're angry?" He stood with both legs spread apart. Better to brace himself for when the blows came.

"Don't treat me as though I have no more sense than a…a rutabaga. You didn't appear at my window to tell me that."

Cooper sighed and took off his hat. "I was across the street and noticed that you lit your lamp. I feared that Early might've gotten in here. Since the doors were locked, I climbed the trellis so I could look inside." In hindsight, he could see how foolish he was. Though he wouldn't admit it to her, he'd deluded himself. He *wanted* to be in her room, see where she dreamed, spend a few quiet moments alone with her. That was the God's honest truth.

She sucked in a quick intake of breath. "You were spying on me?"

"Not exactly. Just keeping watch." Because he wouldn't put anything past Tolbert Early. And no matter what she thought about him, he'd protect her with his life. His gaze swung to the letters spread out on the bed. "What was so intriguing that you'd climb from bed at this hour?"

Much to his dismay, she jerked up a wrapper and slipped it on, hiding those luscious breasts.

"Something Granny Ketchum said tonight got me thinking." Delta told him about the partial sentence before Granny had caught herself. "So I took the letters out to reread them, hoping I'd find something in them that would point to the author."

"Did you discover anything useful?"

"It's very clear that you didn't write them. For instance, you'd die before you used the words *dexterously* and *adroitly* in relation to working your cattle and managing your ranch. But Granny Ketchum wouldn't use those either. She's a mostly uneducated, simple woman."

"So if she is guilty, she had help."

"Exactly. But who?"

Watching her mind work was like viewing a breathtaking sunrise. Cooper never tired of either. "The only one who uses language like that in this town is Jacob Quigley at the newspaper."

"Yes! Why didn't I think of that? It makes perfect sense. When I took out the advertisement for the women's club, he said that Granny had *reported* to him that I was settling in very well. At the time I didn't think anything about it. But he got red-faced when he realized what he said."

Cooper unglued his tongue. "Quigley and Granny. An unlikely pair. I never would've guessed."

"I think Granny talked him into putting the ad in the *Matrimonial Harvest* catalog in addition to newspapers back East because she was concerned about your lack of marital ambition." Delta chewed her lip. "I saw his ad and answered it. They must've done some investigation into my background and character and thought we'd make a good match, and from there the exchanging of letters began."

"We would, you know," he said quietly.

❧

"Would what?" She gathered the stack of letters and put them away in a drawer.

"Have made a good match." He took two steps and caressed her hair. "If only I'd met you in another lifetime…before I sold my soul to the devil."

Too weary to resist, Delta rested her head against his broad chest. "Cooper, we can't keep doing this."

The words were meant as admonishment. This back and forth stuff wasn't fair. It was time he either let her go for good or accepted what she yearned to give.

"What do you mean? Am I forcing you into anything?"

She felt him stiffen. Leaning back, she stared into his gray eyes. "No. But I can't take this hot and cold. You kiss the daylights out of me and touch me all over, then you push me away and pretend I don't exist. It makes a girl dizzy. How do you really feel about me?"

A smile flickered, lighting his eyes briefly, then vanished. "You're the best, most decent thing to ever come along in my life."

"But?"

He laid his hat on the bed and dropped down beside it. "There are things you don't know about me. I've done things. Bad things."

"Cooper, it's time I knew," she said softly. "I'll never judge, and whatever you tell me will never leave this room. Besides, I have my secrets too."

"Mine are…unforgivable."

"Let me be the judge of that. All right? Just trust me. For once in your life, trust someone."

"It's hard to do that. Some of this no one knows about, not even Rand and Brett. I've buried it so deep, I'm not sure I can get it out. I wouldn't even know where to start."

"At the beginning."

Delta's heart ached as Cooper told her what it was

like growing up. It was easy to see the hurt little boy inside the man.

"My father would get drunk and disappear for weeks at a time. To buy food, my mother washed clothes on a rub board until her fingers bled. One night we were walking by the alley next to the saloon on our way home. A man grabbed my mother and pulled her into the alley. Kicking and clawing, I fought as hard as I could to get him off her. Somehow I managed to get his gun out of the holster. I killed the piece of filth. Shot him in the heart. I was Ben's age."

The pure hatred in his voice chilled her. When he met her gaze, his cold gray stare frightened her.

"Is this what you wanted to know? Happy now?"

Tears trickled down Delta's face. She knelt and took his hands in hers. "You only did what anyone would've done. You were a little boy protecting his mother. You have nothing to be ashamed of."

"Didn't you hear me? I'm a murderer. My father taught me to kill. He always told me that I have his blood in my veins. It's true. I watched him beat my mother to death a few months later. I'm just like him."

"No, you're not. Don't ever say that. You're a kind, decent man. You care about people. What you've done for Jenny and Ben proves it. You didn't have to see to their needs. But you did. And there are countless others. That alone sets you apart from your father."

"Didn't you just hear anything I said?"

"I heard every word. But I still don't see why you believe you have to stay single."

"I'll not pass on these murdering tendencies to innocent children. It stops with me."

"That's crazy." Delta cupped his stubbled jaw. He had more to give than he knew. Cooper had more honor and more heart than anyone. If only she could find the words to convince him.

"It's what I know. That man I just told you about wasn't the only one I killed. It just got easier to pull the trigger after that." He rubbed his eyes as though to rid them of images.

"Who else?" she whispered, afraid to hear the answer.

"Tolbert Early."

"But he's not dead."

"By all rights he should be. I meant for it. He just won't stay dead is the trouble."

"What do you mean?"

"I've told you this much, so I might as well finish. Then you'll see what a real prize I am." He rose and stood looking out the window into the blackness that he probably thought resembled his soul.

She listened to his tale about the escape from the orphan train, the bathhouse in Missouri, and how when he was fourteen he shot Early in cold blood for what he did to Brett. By the time Cooper finished, she hated Early every bit as much as he did. The man deserved fire and brimstone, for he was surely Satan.

Cooper turned to her. "Now do you understand why this…we…can never be? I'm sure you're counting yourself lucky that I didn't uphold the marriage agreement, even though I didn't make it."

"I see a great many things. One is that you are not your father. No one could be more different. You have a caring, loving heart and a soft spot for abused women, little boys, and mistreated animals." Delta moved to stand in front of him and laid her hand on his chest. "I wish I'd have known all this before now."

"Then you agree that we dodged a bullet?"

"Never. I don't think marriage is out of the question for you. Maybe for me, though. You haven't heard the secret I carried all the way from Georgia, praying it wouldn't follow, so afraid people would find out."

He shook his head. "Nothing can be worse than mine."

Taking her arm, he urged her to take a seat on the bed. When she did, he sat next to her.

"I can't," she whispered. "I just can't."

"Nothing you can say would make me turn away in disgust." He smoothed back her hair.

Delta was far from reassured. "Why is it our parents can hurt us the most? They're supposed to love and protect us."

"Wish I had the answer." His sensual mouth was so near as he drew little circles in the palm of her hand.

"My mother was never married," she blurted out before she lost her nerve. "I'm a bastard child."

From there, she spilled the story about the worthless father who refused to claim her, about how he came from a wealthy family, and about how he passed her on the street with not a flicker of recognition. "I might as well have been a stranger for all the notice he took of me."

The muscles in Cooper's jaw bunched. "I can't imagine your pain. Few people have more courage and determination than you do."

"I wish that were so. No one accepted me. The other children called me names—some don't bear repeating. The adults were no better. I've always stood outside, looking in. Each time the people in Cedartown threw a dance, I'd go and watch from the shadows, dreaming that one brave man would ask me to waltz with him. No one ever did. I began going out in the woods, twirling around, pretending to be in the arms of someone who loved me."

Cooper lifted her hand and pressed a kiss on her palm. "They were fools."

"My mother was never strong, though she did *try* to love me. I represented her fall from grace and the reason for all her problems. She died a broken, scarlet woman, and I'm still a bastard child. I belong to no one."

When a tear slipped out and ran down her cheek, Cooper wiped it away with his thumb.

"In a desperate attempt to escape all that, I jumped at the chance to come West. I've heard that out here a woman can start over, become anyone she wants."

His breath fluttered the hair at her temple as he whispered, "Who do you want to be, Delta?"

She thought long and hard. "Someone with a big heart that everyone loves and respects."

"You're already that and more. You're a survivor and you're made of stern stuff."

He lowered his head and kissed her hard with a passion that seemed to come all the way from his toes. Delta closed her eyes and let it seep into every crevice of her heart, past the pain, the open wounds, and the scorn that sought to destroy her.

Though the baring of her soul had been excruciating, she felt free now and very grateful to be alive.

Getting to his feet, Cooper pulled her up. "Come here, you."

"Why? What are you going to do?"

"Dance with me." His hand slid to her waist and he tugged her tightly against him. They were so near, she could feel his warm breath caressing her skin.

"But there's no music."

"There's not? Surely if I can hear it, you can."

Delta sighed happily, relaxing in his arms. He rested his chin on the top of her head and they moved around the room, Cooper in his boots and she in her nightgown and bare feet.

How long they danced, she didn't know. Being so close to this magnificent man, his hardness pressing into her stomach, breathing his scent, made her heart race like a herd of stampeding horses.

Then somehow the band must've stopped playing. She found herself lying on the bed. Cooper lay beside her, his hands magic on her body. He ran them over her breasts, to her stomach, and down her legs.

Tingles followed wherever he went. The smoldering desire she'd felt that night in the moonlight returned tenfold. She was surprised she didn't burst into flames.

When exactly he removed her wrapper, she couldn't have said.

He unbuttoned her gown and ran the pads of his thumbs across the sensitive tips of her bared breasts.

Delta sucked in her breath. Sensations rolled over her in hot, steamy waves, each one stronger than the one before.

But nothing prepared her for the pleasure that lit a fiery path inside her as he took her nipple into his mouth. Her thoughts scattered like dandelion seeds in the wind.

She barely noticed when he removed her gown, untied her drawers, and tossed them aside. He stroked the soft folds between her thighs.

Delicious spirals of heat sent her heavenward, and she found herself in the clouds looking down. She was on the brink of some kind of desire for which she had no name, something very erotic and wanton.

Love for this man who'd carried the weight of the world on his shoulders far too long washed over her.

Twenty-nine

COOPER UNDRESSED AND STRETCHED HIS HARD BODY on top of her. He didn't know how much longer he could wait. He was ready to explode with need. Every nerve cried out for release.

He stared down at the woman who made him desire things he'd long denied himself, made him see that the future bore no resemblance to the past, made him crazy with want. Darkness and shame no longer shrouded the path before him.

Delta arched her back, straining for completion. Albeit new to this, she was an earth child, a passionate lover.

Intense hunger for what she gave so willingly made him tremble. Lord knew he wasn't good enough for her. Never would be. She saw the man he'd always wanted to be, and that humbled him.

Drawing in a ragged breath, he entered her and let her tight warmth envelop him.

No longer would he always take. From now on, he would give. Delta Dandridge would have all the things that she'd missed out on.

As release came to both of them, he swept his mouth across hers and took her cries into him, cherishing the woman who'd looked past all his faults and found a spark of good.

Afterward, they lay spent, their skin covered with a thin sheen of perspiration. Lying next to her, Cooper reached for her hand and entwined her fingers through his. It worried him that she had yet to speak. Maybe she had second thoughts about giving herself to a man like him.

"Are you all right, Delta?"

Rising up, she laid her head on his chest. "I never knew it would be like that. It was more than I ever dreamed. I guess this makes me a fallen woman in society's eyes. But I'd do it all over again. I don't regret a thing. Do you?"

"Just that I wasted so much time getting to this point."

"I'm glad you appeared at my window tonight. Thank you for watching over me and not letting Early hurt me."

He kissed her fingers. "Thank you for opening the window. I'll admit I wouldn't have placed any bets. The odds of losing were too great. You were quite angry."

"With good reason," she said firmly. "But you more than made up for your mistakes."

"Thank heavens. For such a little thing, you can sure be a regular spitfire. Of course, that's one of the things I lo—like about you," he quickly amended.

When she rolled away, presenting her back to him, he reached for her and pulled her flush against him.

They lay on their sides, his body curled protectively around hers, and like a pair of spoons, they fit together perfectly. Cooper cupped her breast and exhaled a soft breath, wondering at this new turn in his life. He didn't want to ever lose her. She was his now.

But what did this mean?

Was he prepared to do the right thing?

He'd been a bachelor all his life with no plans for his status to change. Making love to her would inevitably bring changes. Could he accept that?

The sky began to lighten a bit. It would be dawn soon and people would begin to stir. He kissed her smooth shoulder. "I've got to get dressed and get out of here. I won't give people a chance to talk. You've endured more than your share."

Delta rolled over. She looked a sight, with her tousled golden hair and thoroughly kissed lips. "I suppose you're right, but I wish you could stay for breakfast. I'm not ready to say good-bye."

The bed shifted when he stood and reached for his trousers. "I don't know when I'll see you again. Might not be until I finish this business with Early."

༺ঌ৺

Despondency enveloped Delta. Would things return to the way they had been, with her going one way and him another? Maybe he'd throw her back in, now that he'd caught her again. "What's going to happen to us, Cooper?"

"I don't know." His low voice sounded unsure.

When she shifted her gaze to his broad back, she gave a little cry. "Your scars. You said you have

Tolbert Early to thank for the ones on your belly, but your back. What happened?"

Razor-thin scars crisscrossed his back in a painful pattern. Tears welled up in her eyes. He'd suffered so much.

"My father had a nasty temper. Thought he could whip the devil out of my soul."

"If they hanged him when you were only seven, you had to have been even younger when this took place. Oh, Cooper, I'm so sorry." How could she not have noticed during the night? She pulled on her gown. Going to him, she pressed her lips to his scarred flesh.

Cooper shrugged his shoulders, his coldness returning. "The nature of the beast. It's over and done with. That's another reason why I will never have children."

Nothing was fair. Life wasn't fair. Some people had everything, and others like Cooper had only nightmares and pain. Her complaints seemed inconsequential in comparison to what he'd suffered, and she was ashamed she'd even mentioned them. Now it all made sense why he felt such a connection to Ben. Her heart ached for all the unwanted and abused children of the world.

She'd always heard people talk about how we draw our strength and our character from those who came before. But Cooper had gotten none of that from his father. And his mother had died before she got a chance to teach her son much. Maybe it was Isaac Daffern who had not only given Cooper a sense of direction but taught him the ways of an honorable man.

And where had Delta gotten her fierce determination to never give up, to keep trying when all seemed lost? It wasn't from her father, because he had given up on her before she was even born. Nor her mother either. Phoebe Dandridge had been a weak woman who cried all the time. Delta must owe it to her Irish grandmother. Seemed logical.

Cooper lost no time in pulling his shirt over his head as though embarrassed she'd seen his scars. Seconds later, he drew his boots on, strapped on his holster, and settled his hat on his head. Delta handed him his jacket.

"Thanks," he said. "When all this is over, we'll figure out where we go from here."

She nodded. Swallowing the lump clogging her throat, she tilted her head for his kiss. "Be safe."

"Always. Watch out for Early. If you need me—"

"I'll find a way to get word to you."

The door swung open silently into the dark hallway. He disappeared down the staircase. She didn't know what lay in wait for him. Or for her either. All she knew was that he'd shown her a path to a beautiful world beyond the stars and she didn't want to return to her lonely existence.

"Please, God, if you've a mind to grant wishes, watch over him," she whispered.

She curled up on the bed, clasping to her chest the pillow that had cradled his head. It still carried his scent. If only she could turn back the clock and relive the last few hours.

But that wasn't possible. She stared at the ceiling until daybreak, then forced herself to get up and wash away the signs of their lovemaking.

The day was half-over when Jenny Barclay walked into the mercantile. Delta gave a happy cry and hugged her friend. "I'm so glad to see you. And you're in time for the first meeting of our women's club. We're having it at the boardinghouse."

"I prayed I wouldn't miss it. Rand brought me back to town. I couldn't pry Ben away from the ranch, so I let him stay for a few more days." The glow in Jenny's eyes was a welcome thing to see. "I heard about your scare with Tolbert Early. I can't imagine how frightened you must've been."

"Thank goodness Cooper interrupted the diabolical man before he could carry out his plans. Why don't you go unpack your things and rest? I'll see you in two hours."

"I'm too excited to rest. I'll probably help Mabel."

As her dear friend started to turn, Delta stopped her. "Have you seen Cooper?"

"No. If he comes to the ranch at all, it's long after dark and he's gone when I get up. I'm so worried about him. He can't keep going like this."

"I'm worried too." Delta watched Jenny leave. She was afraid of Cooper's obsession with Early. Understanding why didn't make it any easier. She'd hoped Cooper had returned to the ranch after he left her this morning.

Getting her troubled thoughts off Cooper wasn't easy, but she managed by recalling the bloom in Jenny's cheeks. Delta's heart filled with pride for the woman who'd refused to be a victim. Jenny had so much courage and a love of helping others. Like Delta, she simply wanted to make a difference in one part of the world.

When three o'clock came, Delta told John that she was off and headed to the boardinghouse. Twenty-five women of all ages came. Since it was far too many for the house, they held their first meeting under a big hickory tree in the backyard. They elected Delta their president.

"This club will be open to everyone, with no restrictions," she began. "We welcome each woman. Now, what will our official title be? Any suggestions?"

Jenny raised her hand. "How about Women of Vision?"

"I like that. Any other ideas?"

"Visionary Women's Garden Club?" Mabel said.

Delta asked for other possible names but got no response. She called for a vote on Women of Vision and almost every hand rose. She was glad because the name was very fitting.

After electing Mabel as secretary, they discussed their projects and made a list.

The first order of business was getting a school-teacher. "We need to form a committee to talk to the mayor about how to pay for his or her salary," Delta said.

Jenny, Violet, and Naomi Ratliff volunteered. Naomi had dark circles under her eyes from apparent lack of sleep and wore a harried expression. Delta supposed her appearance and zeal in getting a teacher was due to the fact she had ten children at home all under the age of eleven. A teacher might very well save the woman's sanity.

"Very good. Please give us a report on Friday, when we meet again," Delta said. "I want to get busy on this matter as soon as possible."

They discussed which buildings posed the greatest need, which they should focus their efforts on first. They all agreed on the hotel, the mercantile, the saloon, and the stage lines office. She didn't voice her concerns about where they would get the paint and lumber. Lord, what if she gave these women false hope?

"I have a pet project I wish us to consider," Delta said. "I want us to start a seed lending library."

Mabel raised her hand. "What is that?"

"It's a place where seeds of all manner of plants are stored. A person can borrow five seeds to start a flower or vegetable garden, then after their growing season, they return five to the library for the next person."

"It's an excellent idea," Jenny said, clapping her hands.

"Then is it something we want to do?" Delta asked.

They took a vote and she was pleased to see it carry with a majority.

"Who do we want to put in charge of our seed library?" Delta pointed to a woman who stood on the fringe of the group and had clearly seen better times. "What is your name?"

The newcomer cleared her throat. "Gladys, ma'am."

"Gladys, you appear to have an opinion on who should head up the seed library."

"Abner Winchell, ma'am. He's a friend of mine and he desperately needs a purpose to live."

As did they all, but Delta didn't say as much. Abner Winchell had been heavy on her mind lately, though. The sight of his empty pant leg broke her heart.

"I'm glad you suggested him," Delta said. "I confess I had him in mind for this from the beginning."

After the show of hands that had all in favor, she

asked Gladys if she would speak to Abner about accepting the job and told her to report at the next meeting.

By the time they adjourned, Delta was exhausted but beaming. They'd made a lot of progress, these mismatched women of vision.

She couldn't wait to tell Cooper about it.

Sudden memories of his sensual mouth and lean, muscled body swept across her mind.

A heated flurry raced through her veins. Her body felt achy and hot and needing Cooper's magical touch.

Thirty

BUT SHE DIDN'T SEE COOPER THE NEXT DAY OR THE next. Delta suspected she likely wouldn't see him again until he'd finished this nasty business with Early.

Dear God! She sucked in a breath and prayed that Cooper's beloved face wasn't still and bloodless inside a coffin the next time she gazed upon him. She'd waited all her life for love to come along. Surely God wouldn't take him from her now.

On the fourth day following their lovemaking, Delta walked toward the mercantile to begin work. As was her custom of late, she kept a sharp eye out for Early. He wouldn't catch her unawares.

A crowd had gathered outside the mercantile and they were yelling at someone. Curious, she increased the length of her stride. Pushing through, she noticed a stranger trying to fend off Mr. Abercrombie with a leather satchel.

"What's going on?" she asked.

John Abercrombie put down the broom he was wielding as a weapon. "This man is asking questions about you. Do you know him?"

The short, stocky stranger pulled himself up, jerking his silk vest in place. "Of course she doesn't know me. I told you that." He turned to Delta. "I'm Mr. Parmer of Parmer, Hutchinson, and Mansfield. May I have a word with you?"

Before Delta could reply, Nat Rollins jumped in. "You ain't going anywhere with Miss Dandridge."

"Not unless we all go with you," said John in a firm voice, rearing back with the broom. "And if that's the case, then you might as well speak to her right here."

Sheriff Strayhorn glared. "Mr. Parmer, I have half a mind to arrest you for starting a ruckus in our town."

"She's ours and we ain't gonna let you hurt her," Nat yelled.

Delta tried to swallow the lump in her throat but found it impossible. They liked her and had become very protective. When she could trust herself to speak, she held up her hand. "Please, everyone. I appreciate your concerns on my behalf but let's hear Mr. Parmer out first. Then you can hang him."

"I assure you, you'll have no reason for a hanging," Mr. Parmer quickly said.

"Proceed then." Sheriff Strayhorn took out his knife and opened it. Parmer's eyes grew wide.

"Miss Dandridge, I have covered a lot of ground looking for you," Parmer said.

When Abercrombie raised his broom to swing, Mr. Parmer shrank behind the sheriff's large form.

"Why were you looking for me?" Curiosity and anxiety battled inside Delta.

Mr. Parmer peeked out from behind the sheriff and handed her an envelope. "I sent you two letters explaining it all. Since you didn't reply, I was charged with bringing you this bank draft."

Delta's hand shook as she closed her fingers around it. "If this is from Langston Graham, you can keep it. I don't want anything to do with that man."

She'd starve and live under a bush before she accepted a single penny from her father.

"You heard the lady—now get back on the stage and get out of our town," Sheriff Strayhorn ordered.

Parmer frowned. "I assure you this is not from him."

Then who? She opened the envelope. "Morris Merriweather? Who in blue blazes is that?"

Evidently seeing he wasn't about to be strung up for harassing Delta, Mr. Parmer stepped out. "You're a very wealthy lady, Miss Dandridge. After your man of business located an underground spring on your mother's property, a gentleman by the name of Merriweather snapped it up. Morris Merriweather owns a rather large resort company. He has plunked down an exclusive hotel on it that caters to the rich and famous. He's going to put the town on the map and have folks coming from far and wide."

Glancing at the figures on the check, Delta gasped. "Fifty thousand dollars? Oh, my dear Lord."

She needed to sit down. Her mind couldn't fathom that amount. She'd never seen that many zeroes before. It was more than most people would make in twenty or thirty lifetimes, if even then. Buying paint and lumber and whatever else was needed for the women's projects would not be a problem. She said a quick prayer of thanks.

"This is wonderful." Mabel gave her a big hug.

"I guess this means you'll be moving from the boardinghouse."

Suddenly everyone pressed around, offering congratulations and pats on the back.

"What will you do with it?" Nat Rollins asked.

"For God's sake, Nat, let the poor woman catch her breath," said John Abercrombie. "Besides, it's none of our dadgum business. This is a private matter."

"Please, my head is whirling," Delta said. "I have so many opportunities now."

"Well, I hope you're not thinking of moving away." John laid a hand on her shoulder. "If you are, we won't hear of it, and that's final. You're a part of the fabric of this town and we've grown very fond of you."

Delta fought back a sob and threw her arms around her employer. "You don't know what that means to me. I've never had a place where I felt I truly belonged…until now. This is my home and I'm afraid you're stuck with me. Thank you. Thank you all."

A few minutes later, Delta remarked that she guessed the first thing to do was put the money in the bank. Every single person, even Mr. Parmer, formed a line behind her and marched in her parade. The small bank couldn't accommodate everyone inside, so the ones left out pressed against the window. Delta never imagined in her wildest dreams that they would not only take her into their town, but into their hearts as well. Her chest swelled and her eyes brimmed with tears.

She couldn't wait to start giving back and repaying the kindness. With the money safely in the bank's hands, she asked the teller if she could speak privately to Mr. Jenkins, the owner.

The dapper, balding man leaped from behind his desk when the teller ushered her into the office and grasped her hands. "So you're the young lady who raised such a ruckus outside."

"Yes, sir, I'm afraid I'm guilty as charged."

"Whatever is on your mind, I'm all ears. Let me say you're certainly a breath of fresh air. Even lovelier than one of my prized roses."

"I do declare, Mr. Jenkins." She felt her cheeks coloring. "You're making me blush."

Jenkins held out a chair for her. "How may I help you this fine day?"

"I'm inquiring about the empty house just outside of town."

"Yes, ma'am. The Zachary place. That's a prime piece of property."

"I'm interested in buying it, if we can reach an agreement."

"Oh, I'm sure we can. The owners packed up, turned it over to the bank, and went back East. The asking price is three hundred. That's a steal."

"How many acres does it have?"

"Three hundred and sixty."

Excited by the prospect of being a real landowner, Delta gave him a wide smile. "I'll take it."

"Then I reckon it's yours, young lady." Jenkins took his spectacles off and wiped them with his handkerchief. "You do know that Cooper Thorne has had his eye on it for quite some time. He's going to have a conniption. Yes indeed. A real conniption."

Delta chewed her lip and frowned. Oh dear. It didn't set well to cross Cooper, but maybe he'd see what a great opportunity it was for her. Despite what this security meant to her, she wouldn't lose his trust over it.

"I don't think it'll be a problem, Mr. Jenkins. Cooper and I have settled our differences."

And in a most satisfying way, she might add. Which she didn't, of course. It would probably scandalize poor Mr. Jenkins.

It didn't take long to complete her business with Jenkins. She left with a deed and keys in her hand. Much to her chagrin, the crowd that had gathered around the bank followed her back to the mercantile, going on their way after she firmly told them that she had to put in a day's work. Everything was normal.

Or as much as it would ever be.

John opened the door for her. "I suppose you'll be making lots of changes over the weeks ahead."

Delta lifted her apron from the nail. "It seems to be inevitable. I'm afraid too much change makes me nervous, though."

"I've been thinking… What do you think about becoming a partner? Abercrombie and Dandridge Emporium."

"Why? This is your store, John," she said softly.

He wearily rubbed a hand over his eyes. "Frankly, I can use the help. The business was in bad shape when you came. With your hard work, it's slowly beginning to turn around. But I made some really bad financial decisions."

"Of course, you know I'll be happy to do whatever

it takes. You gave me a job when I was at my wit's end. All right, but I'll be a silent partner only and I insist that you make no changes to the sign out front."

Relief rippled over his face. "Thank you. Now, about something else…"

"Yes?"

"I want to hire a woman to fill in. You're going to be busier than a windmill in a hurricane, what with your women's club projects and getting your new place up and running."

"I can see your point. Do you have someone in mind?"

"Emmylou. She's a bright girl. Just needs a chance."

Delta recalled the day Emmylou had come into the mercantile and how upset it made the persnickety Mrs. Hatfield to see a working girl from Miss Sybil's brothel breathing the same air. "I wholeheartedly agree. Are you afraid of the repercussions, though? It could make things very difficult for you."

John's jaw tightened. "No one will tell me how to run my store. If they want to ride over to Corsicana to shop, they're welcome do so. I won't be blackmailed."

"Good for you. There's something to be said about taking a stand for what's right."

"Then it's agreed?"

"Absolutely."

"Good. I'll go talk to the girl this afternoon."

With that settled, Delta got to work. Keeping her thoughts on her job proved harder than trying to herd a bunch of cats, though. In between customers, she found herself daydreaming and making plans. The sudden windfall had changed everything.

Except her love for Cooper. Nothing changed that.

She wished she could talk to him about all this. Each time the bell jangled over the door, she prayed it'd be him.

But the day passed without the rumble of his voice.

Four o'clock came and Delta removed her apron, hanging it on the nail. It was time for the Women of Vision to gather at the boardinghouse. She was anxious to see what had developed since their last meeting.

Again, the yard overflowed. It looked like they'd increased their size by ten. Each woman in attendance seemed hungry to help in whatever way they could.

Delta clapped her hands. "Okay, ladies, let's get started. Will the newcomers say your names so Mabel King can add you to the roster?"

Once that was done, Delta welcomed them and announced, "As of this morning, we no longer have to worry about where the money will come from to fund our projects. I was greatly fortunate to come into a sizable sum and I'll be happy to donate whatever we need. I just want us to be successful in our endeavors."

Enthusiastic applause erupted.

"Now, ladies, let's get down to business. Do we have a report from the schoolteacher committee?"

Jenny wore a huge smile. "The mayor grumbled but said that the city can only afford to pay ten dollars a month and not a cent more. He made it clear that we'll have to come up with books and a place to teach."

"Thank you, Jenny. I think we can manage that if we put our heads together." Even if she had to shoulder all the cost out of her pocket, the school would happen. "Back where I came from, each student brought one egg to school every day. The teacher sold them and used the money for books. We could implement something like that here."

A murmur of agreement rose up.

"Would you like to speak to Mr. Quigley and get an advertisement in the newspaper right away? We want to strike while the iron is hot." Delta turned to Gladys. "Did you speak to Abner Winchell in regard to the seed library?"

Gladys fidgeted and Delta's hopes fled. "I asked him right out an' he said he might could be talked into it. He'll only speak to you, though."

"At least he didn't say no. That's good. Yes, I'll talk to him. Thank you, Gladys."

Delta beamed at her little army. "I think we're moving along quite well. Can everyone meet in front of the mercantile at nine o'clock tomorrow morning? We'll begin our town renovations."

Then everyone would either fight their efforts or join in. She prayed they'd drop their weapons and pick up a paintbrush. She'd had enough animosity to last a lifetime.

Thirty-one

HIDDEN IN THE BUSHES NEARBY, TOLBERT EARLY watched Thorne's woman. Taking the twit would be easy. And his revenge on Thorne would be even more satisfying. He just needed to throw the bloodhound off his trail. His old enemy had run him from all his hiding places.

Except one.

Thorne would never think to look there.

Not in a million years.

Time to make a plan and set the rancher on a false trail.

～

Over the last few days, Cooper had stayed hot on Early's trail. Rand and Brett rode by his side. The fact that they kept Early from holing up anywhere made the chilly nights a tad warmer. Early had to be exhausted, just as they intended.

As long as the devil's spawn focused on putting distance between him and his brothers, he would leave Delta alone.

This wouldn't be over soon enough for Cooper. Delta had a permanent spot in his thoughts and in his heart.

In the quiet darkness when everyone slept, Cooper took out his recollections of their time together. He recalled every detail, the way her bare skin reacted to his touch, the fragrance of her hair, the taste of her lips.

Now in the twilight, as they let the horses drink from a creek, he listened to the swirling water and murmured low, "I miss you so much, darlin'. I wish…"

What exactly did he wish?

That he was a different man?

That Delta Dandridge hadn't ridden into town and made him yearn for impossible things?

Or that he could spend all his nights in her arms?

Cooper realized with clarity that all except one of those wishes were true. If he only had the power.

"Mount up. Let's find this rotten cayuse." Cooper put his foot in the stirrup and threw his leg over.

"We could do with a little more rest, Coop," Brett said quietly. "I'm itching to find Early and be done with this, but we're dead tired. Exhausted men make mistakes. You know that."

"Do you share Brett's feelings, Rand?"

"I do. We have to be smart. Smart men don't push themselves and their horses past what is possible. But if you want to keep riding, I'm right beside you."

Cooper sighed. "You're probably right. Let's call it a night and meet at the Long Odds at daybreak."

They crawled back in the saddle and headed their separate ways.

After catching up on ranch business with Zeke,

Cooper filled his belly with two plates of hot food. By the time he finished, the mottled sky had faded and darkness cloaked the hills and valleys. Instead of finding his bed, Cooper saddled a fresh horse. There was only one place he wanted to be.

Was it wise? Probably not.

Did it offer peace and contentment to his soul? Hell, yes.

Though he wanted to ride like a madman, he took it slower out of care for Rebel. He was desperate to see the one woman who'd accepted him as he was, wanting nothing in return but simply to matter to someone. She sure as hell mattered to him. Delta Dandridge had given his life meaning.

When he rode up to the boardinghouse, a light glowed in her partially raised window. He looped the reins over a low limb of a spindly tree, then stood a minute to assess the lay of things. He'd about decided that climbing the trellis again was out, but if it was the only way, he'd do it in a heartbeat.

The old boardinghouse looked different. He walked closer. Someone had begun whitewashing it and left a ladder lying against the side.

Wasting not a second, Cooper lifted it. Once it was in place at her window, he climbed up and rapped on the glass.

Unlike last time, he didn't have to sweet talk Delta into raising the shade.

"Cooper. I was so afraid." She raised the window higher.

Once inside her room, Cooper had doubts about his visit. Maybe he shouldn't have come. He took off his hat and laid it aside. "I had some time to kill and wanted to see you. If you object, tell me and I'll leave."

For answer, she threw her arms around his neck and clung to him. "I was hoping you'd come. I've missed you so much. Did you capture Early?"

"First, I have to kiss you. I can't tell you how many times I've dreamed of tasting your lips since I left here."

∼✺∼

Love for this man who refused to break shook Delta to the depths of her being. She lifted her face and he crushed his mouth to hers with a savage intensity. Heat rushed to her nerve endings like a fuse to dynamite.

Clutching his shirt tightly, she took all that he wanted to give, while giving back in return. She couldn't get enough. She didn't want to talk. She wanted to take him inside her and feel his flesh caressing hers. Savoring. Riding the stars.

But evidently Cooper had other ideas.

When the kiss ended, he sat down on the end of the bed and pulled her on his lap. "You, darlin', are addictive. I couldn't wait to see you again."

"I have so much to tell you, Cooper. But I'm dying to know about Tolbert Early."

"He's still on the loose. We get close and about to slip a noose around his neck and he slithers away."

"I can see how weary you are of all this." Delta caressed his stubbled jaw, taking in the deep lines at the corners of his strong, full mouth, the exhaustion in his gray eyes. "When have you last slept?"

"Been so long, I can't remember what a bed feels like. Catch an hour here and an hour there when I can. Rand, Brett, and I have covered every inch of this countryside."

"I'm so sorry. I wish I could help."

"You help by staying safe. Promise me you'll take no chances."

"That may be difficult. I've bought the Zachary place."

He suddenly got to his feet, spilling her from his lap. She fought to keep from falling. Without a word, he strode to the window and stood looking out. Delta chewed her lip. He stood so straight, almost as though he had a steel rod running up his spine. She didn't know what to do or say.

"I was saving money to buy it. Almost had enough," he said in a flat voice. "That land was all I needed to reach my dream.

Tears welled in her eyes. She wished he'd turn around. She wouldn't truly know how he felt until she saw his eyes. Those grays turned cold and icy when he was boiling mad.

"Then it's yours," she whispered. "I'll sign over the deed tomorrow. All my life I never had two cents to rub together or anything much of value. I always yearned to own a piece of land, become a woman of substance. It's not important, though. Nothing's as important as the thought of losing you."

"Where did you get the money?" He finally turned.

Relief at the absence of anger bolstered her. "Mr. Parmer of Parmer, Hutchinson, and Mansfield appeared a few days ago with a bank draft. Seems a Mr. Merriweather paid quite handsomely for my mother's property in Cedartown. He plans to build a fancy resort there. Parmer sent letters, but I tore them up. Thought they were from my father. When I didn't reply, he came in person. Do you know what I can do with fifty thousand dollars, Cooper?"

His eyes widened as he grinned. "You're a rich woman, Miss Dandridge."

"I still can't believe it. I've pinched myself until I'm black and blue. Are you mad?"

"I'm happy for you. So you've bought yourself a ranch, and no, I don't want you to sign over the deed to me. It's yours, darlin'. The house looks in pretty good shape also. What are you planning to do with all that land?"

"I want to buy some cattle and learn how to be a rancher."

"Do tell." His grin widened as his eyes danced. "Anytime you want some lessons, I'll be happy to show you a few things."

"Mr. Thorne!" She gasped and narrowed her eyes. "I have a feeling you're not talking about cows and ranchland."

"However did you guess?" He sauntered toward her with that lazy walk of his. Picking up his hat, he plunked it on her head. Then he proceeded to show her a few "things."

Her breath hitched when he unbuttoned the bodice of her dress and peeled it off. Then he focused on the ribbons and lace, stripping away everything until she wore nothing but a smile and his hat. It didn't take any urging to move her to the bed, relieving her of the hat on the way.

Delta was all thumbs as she tried to unbutton his shirt. Finally he pushed her hands aside and yanked it over his head. Boots, gun belt, and pants hit the floor.

No slow, tender caresses this time. They'd been apart too many hours and days to waste one second. He plunged inside her.

This was about satisfying the burning passion inside.

About taking and giving without fear or worry.

They made love in a fiery frenzy, their breath mingling in the sultry air as their bodies joined.

She climbed on the shuddering waves and rode them as they crested. Release came quickly and with all the power and force as before.

Limp and spent, she turned to Cooper. "Thank you."

He kissed her palm. "So you liked the things I showed you?"

"I did. Anytime you want to show me more, say the word." She rose on an elbow and brushed back his dark hair. "Never in my wildest dreams did I think I'd ever meet anyone like you. Or that you'd…we'd be doing this. I don't know anything about love. Lord knows, I've never had occasion to see it between a man and a woman. But you've stolen my heart. I've found the man who can finally *see* me."

His brow furrowed and she wished she'd held her tongue. She'd clearly made him uncomfortable. And worse, she didn't know how to make it better. While she tried to think of how to take back her declaration, he frowned, then pursed his lips. Why, oh why, hadn't she kept silent?

"Cooper, I'm…"

"Don't fret about it." He nibbled on her ear and

kissed the hollow of her throat. "Now, tell me the rest of your news, Miss Dream Squasher."

"What did you call me?"

"Dream Squasher. Because you stomped mine under your pretty little foot. Now, let's get to your news."

"I'm part owner of the mercantile. John approached me about it and said he was having some financial difficulty. So I said yes and made the first executive decision. We hired Emmylou to take my place running the store."

"Of all things." His grin was back, which dispelled the pall. "I'm away for a few days and you've become a business owner in addition to rancher. What else have you been up to?"

"The women's club has taken off and we have almost forty members. Everyone is so excited and wants to take part." She paused to fully absorb the impact of Cooper's mouth nuzzling her breast. If she'd been standing, her legs would have gone out from under her. "We're… calling…ourselves…Women of Vision. Please don't stop. I don't think I could stand it."

Cooper raised his head and growled when her hand, boldly exploring lower and lower, brushed his erection. "You're playing with fire, pretty lady."

"I do hope so."

They made love again. Achingly slow, smoldering love. All the sizzling urgency from before settled into slow hot touches and passionate kisses. Then he eased inside her again. She quickly adapted to his rhythm.

Each shuddering wave arched higher and higher, carrying her along a raging stream with nothing to cling to except Cooper's scarred back.

They reached a shuddering climax simultaneously. A long minute later, Cooper rolled off and wrapped her in his arms. His ragged breath ruffled the loose hair at her temple.

As Delta's breathing returned to normal, she traced each scar.

"Penny for your thoughts," Cooper murmured, voice low.

"I'm a most fortunate woman. I left Georgia with an empty purse and a few letters. Now I have everything I could hope for." Except marriage. But maybe it would just take time for Cooper to sort things out.

And if he didn't?

Lord help her, she didn't want to consider that. How could she live as a fallen woman like her mother, shunned by society? She'd seen firsthand the difficulties of that type of life.

Yet did she have the strength to let go of the love she'd found?

Why did her choices always have to be all or nothing?

For once, why couldn't she just accept the things that were offered and not want more?

Thirty-two

COOPER LAY ON HIS SIDE WITH ONE HAND PROPPED under his head, studying Delta's face. To what did he owe the impact she'd made, not only in his life, but in those of Battle Creek's citizens?

This woman of vision, who'd grown up with so little, had given selflessly to everyone who touched her life. She'd endeared herself to this town in a huge way.

He couldn't answer for the rest, only for himself. He didn't deserve her. If he tried for the next fifty or a hundred years, he could never repay the trust and faith and love she'd shown.

Damn. He wished he could tell her he loved her.

He truly did love her. No question about that. But what good did it do to say the words if he couldn't offer the lifetime commitment that went with it? It wasn't fair to her.

Dear God! It would destroy his soul if he had to walk away from her or she from him.

He rose and leaned to kiss her closed eyelids that hid her thoughts. "You are indeed a woman of vision, you know. What an accurate name for your women's club. I'm so very proud of you and all you've accomplished. And in such a short time, no less. You took this town by storm and we haven't been the same."

Delta opened her eyes and cupped his jaw. "I asked for nothing except a chance."

"Darlin', your dream became everyone's."

They talked more about her plans: the seed lending library and putting Abner Winchell in charge of it, the people who might apply for the school teaching position, and her desire to do something with the hotel.

"I've spoken with Mr. Lexington, but he's shown no inclination to fix up the Lexington Arms. That man frustrates me to no end," Delta spewed.

"Where there's a will, there's a way. Have you thought about asking to become a partner? If you were part owner, he'd be less likely to turn down money for renovations. Two things I know about Lexington: he's miserly and he has his pride."

"I've thought about that. I need to take it slow, though, like you suggested. If I go waving my money around and trying to buy up all the businesses in town, it'll only anger folks. I want them to be involved and feel pride of ownership in Battle Creek as a whole."

Cooper tweaked her nose. "When did you get to be so smart?"

"Since you showed me the error of my ways?" Delta grinned.

It seemed ages ago since they'd argued over the women's club and shared that hug at Jenny's insistence. It had changed his life.

"And here I thought you weren't listening. You'll

figure something out. I have faith in you." Cooper lay back and wrapped his arms around Delta's soft curves. She laid her head on his chest. His heart swelled with contentment. "I could get spoiled very easily."

"Me too."

"Although the urge is strong to rush out to your new ranch, promise me you'll stay away. At least for now. It's too dangerous with Early running loose."

"You don't know how hard it will be."

"Promise," he insisted.

"All right. I won't go out there."

They slept at last. The predawn hours came much too soon. Cooper woke, remembering he'd told Rand and Brett to meet him at daybreak. He lifted Delta's hand from where it was splayed across his chest and eased out of bed. The respite hadn't been near long enough. As he dressed and buckled his gun belt, he resolved to try harder to find Early.

This would end. One way or another.

Delta opened her eyes and looked for Cooper. But he was gone. In fact, there was nothing except a few wrinkled bed sheets to indicate he'd even been there.

More stolen moments.

More sidestepping any talk of the future.

And more lonely days and nights ahead.

Throwing back the quilt, she rose and got ready to face the challenges that would come. She had several things on her agenda before lunch.

Four hours later, she located Abner Winchell sitting on his usual bench outside the hotel.

Smiling, she sat down beside him. "How are you today, Mr. Winchell?"

"Right smart, I reckon. Been waitin' to see if'n you changed your mind 'bout things."

"If you're talking about the seed library, no, I haven't. You would be the perfect one for the job. We need someone with your knowledge. I hear you had a farm before the war and kept your acres in cotton and tobacco. I hope you'll accept my offer."

Abner squinted. "Does it pay?"

"I'm afraid it doesn't. But you'd do this town a great service. In addition, you'd get to spend your days talking to all sorts of folks. The seed library could become the hub this town revolves around. Please say yes."

"Where would we put it? I'll need some space so I can organize the seeds. In the war, they put me in charge of the bullets and food."

"Oh, Mr. Winchell, I didn't know you were experienced."

His big, toothless grin stretched from ear to ear. "I won't tell if'n you won't. And call me Abner."

Delta shook Abner's hand. "Deal. I was thinking we might set the library up in the abandoned feed store. It will be perfect. When we decide to stock the store, the seeds will fit right in."

"That place is a wreck. Rats in it as big as my crutch." He shuddered. "I hate rats."

"I assure you, we'll get rid of them when we fix it up." Along with all the other buildings. All of a sudden, the enormity of what she'd tackled settled like a ton of bricks on her shoulders. Whatever had she thought?

That it would be easy? That she'd need no time for eating and sleeping? Or making love to Cooper?

"Then I reckon you got yourself a seed man."

"Thank you, Abner. I'm glad you agreed to do it."

Leaving Abner to his daily routine of watching the town, Delta paid a visit to Mr. Lexington. She found him at the Three Roses Café eating lunch. She recognized the same three-piece suit he always wore and his thick head of brown hair that stuck out in all directions like the quills of a porcupine. The thought crossed her mind that he might not own a comb. He frowned when he saw her headed his way.

"Hello, sir, may I join you?" She pulled out a chair at his table before he could reply. "I'd love to have a word with you."

"I've already told you the answer is no."

"I was hoping you'd reconsider." Delta put her napkin in her lap and asked the waiter for a cup of bean soup.

"Well, I haven't, and I would appreciate it if you'd let me eat my lunch in peace." He speared a bite of ham. "You women think you can railroad a man into doing what you want. Well, I've dug in my heels. Stay clear of my hotel."

"Would you consider selling it?"

"It's not for sale," he snapped. "If you want a hotel, build your own. You can afford it, I hear."

Sudden sadness washed over her. If she followed his suggestion, it would only put him out of business. She didn't want that. Besides, then they'd have a bigger problem. The Lexington Arms would be vacant and a bigger eyesore than when it'd been operational.

"Are you married, by chance, Mr. Lexington?"

"Not anymore. She up and ran off with a traveling medicine show and I said good riddance."

"Then you're still married, in my way of thinking."

"Got one of those divorces, if it's any of your business," he snapped.

"I'm so sorry." Her soup came and she dipped her spoon into it. "Mr. Lexington, did you know your face has high color when you're upset? You really should watch that. It's bad for your health to get your temper up."

"Oh…oh…don't you worry about that," he spluttered.

Delta's brain whirled as an idea took root. It might be just the thing. Hurrying to finish her soup, she paid and left.

The next stop was Granny Ketchum's. The old lady was all smiles when she opened the door to see Delta.

"Oh, you're a sight for these poor eyes. Just this very morning when I was talking to my cat I told him that I sure would like to see you." Granny moved aside to let Delta enter.

She kissed Granny's cheek and hugged her. "I've missed you. How have you been?"

"Feeling pretty puny these days, but I ain't one to complain." Granny dropped into a chair and Delta took the one beside her.

"I feared you might be sick. Anything I can do?"

"Naw, I'm able to sit up and take nourishment."

A grin curved Delta's lips. Though she was in Texas now, that saying was pretty universal. "I'm glad to hear it. Granny, I need your help."

The woman leaned over to pat Delta's hand. "Jus' tell me what you need."

"First, I should tell you that I figured out that you and Mr. Quigley wrote the letters to me pretending to be Cooper."

"Oh dear." Color rose to Granny's face. "You mad?"

"No. In fact, I should thank you. Those letters changed my life in so many ways. I owe you a debt of thanks. But that's not exactly why I'm here. I need help with George Lexington."

She told Granny about how stubborn he was and at cross-purposes with Delta and her vision for the hotel. "I have this idea. I want to get him married. A wife could do wonders in helping us solve our problem."

Granny chuckled. "You, my dear, are devious. Almost as much as me an' Quigley. A wife could be just the solution. Let her work her charms on ol' Lexington to get him to bend."

"Absolutely. Would you know of a likely candidate?"

"We got a handful of replies from the newspaper ad for Cooper. One of them might travel here for the chance to marry up with the owner of a hotel."

"I'm afraid we don't have time for a lot of letter writing. Perhaps you know of someone locally."

"Well, the women 'round here have been picked over pretty good. But…Widow Sharp. Now there's a possibility. Not a blessed soul knows what she looks like, though, hiding behind that black veil like she does. Wore it when she got here an' it's still coverin' her face. She could have a big wart on the end of her nose, be missing her teeth, and cross-eyed for all we know."

"She's a mystery, all right." Delta's mind whirled. Could she talk the woman somehow into removing it?

"Those apple and cherry hand pies she sells to the Lily and Three Roses make your mouth water, so we know she can cook. A man likes a woman who can find her way around a kitchen."

"When exactly did she move to town?"

"Let me see. Must've been about three years ago. It was along about the time I fell and busted my leg. Fact of the matter, I was laid up and missed all the excitement."

"Oh my goodness. That sounds really painful. I'm sorry."

Granny shrugged. "Things happen. It was an early wintry mornin' an' I stepped on a patch of ice. Went down like a sack of rocks."

"Do you think that's what happened to cause Miss Winehouse to fall and break her heel?"

"Wouldn't be a bit surprised. Ice sure is slick."

"Can you remember Widow Sharp's given name?"

Granny's forehead wrinkled in thought. "Cain't rightly recollect. Agatha? Agnes? Shoot, plumb forgot, ain't used it in so long. You might ask John Abercrombie. He might know."

"Bless you, Granny." Delta jumped up and hugged her. "I'll go ask him right now." She had a good feeling about this, if only she could talk the widow into giving up her veil.

John glanced up and grinned when Delta entered the store. "About time you paid me a visit. Have good news. Emmylou has agreed to work for us. She starts tomorrow."

"I'm so glad. Do you need me to help out today?"

"Nope, I can handle it. You need something?"

"Widow Sharp's given name. By chance, would you know it?"

"Sure do. She was my wife's best friend. Name's Clara."

"How pretty. I'm just curious... Do you know why she wears that veil?"

"Nell swore me to secrecy. I promised not to breathe a word."

Delta frowned. "It'll stay strictly between us. The answer will help me out with a problem."

"I'm not one to betray a trust. I'm sorry."

Resting her hand on his arm, Delta said quietly, "I understand. Could you tell me where Clara lives?"

"That's no secret." He told her and she left.

The neat house had a white picket fence around it. Delicious smells wafting from inside told Delta the widow was making pies. She rapped on the door.

Clara Sharp answered the knock, wiping her hands on her apron. "Miss Dandridge, what a surprise."

"Mrs. Sharp, I realize we barely know each other but I have something to discuss, if you can spare a moment of your time."

"I hear congratulations are in order. The whole gossip mill is buzzing about your sudden windfall."

"Thank you. I'm still getting used to it. May I come in? That is, if I'm not interrupting you."

"I just finished taking the last of my pies out of the vat of grease. Please come in. I apologize for my lack of manners. And please...the name is Clara."

The small parlor was handsomely furnished. The rich blues, golds, and browns blended together perfectly. A painting of a country garden added to the pleasant, warm atmosphere. Clara Sharp had the eye of an artist. And frankly it surprised Delta. She'd expected darkness from a woman who wore a veil even indoors.

Delta took a seat in a comfortable chair. "I came hoping you might accept an invitation to dine with me. I'd like to get better acquainted. All I know about you is that you make mouthwatering hand pies. They're out of this world."

"Thank you for the compliment. You're too kind."

When Clara's veil fluttered, Delta knew the woman had smiled.

"Tell me how you got started making them."

"My mother told me about them. She got the idea to make them when President Franklin Pierce was in office. He called them fried pies and ate them very often."

"We had something very similar in Georgia, only we called them crab lanterns. So your mother taught you to make them?"

"Yes. I'm most grateful I showed aptitude, since it's the only talent I seem to have."

"Oh, Clara, don't you believe that for a second. Judging from this room, you have a most interesting gift. I've never felt so at home. The colors you chose are outstanding." She gazed at Clara, trying to guess her age. Dark brown hair with hints of gold. No wrinkles or age spots on her hands. A striking voice that didn't tremble. Putting all that together, the pie maker was probably in her early or mid forties.

"Again, I thank you. We never seem to view ourselves as others see us."

"About that invitation... Will you take supper with me this evening?"

"I've never eaten away from home. The stares, you know."

"We won't pay them any mind. Please say yes."

"You're very convincing." Clara hesitated a moment, then answered, "Yes, I suppose I will."

"Wonderful. I'll see you at six o'clock."

Delta left with hope in her heart. Clara Sharp would be perfect for George Lexington. All Delta had to do was find out the reason for the veil and get Clara to trust her.

It didn't sound so hard when she said it real fast.

Thirty-three

COOPER'S HEART POUNDED IN HIS CHEST. HE SCRAM-
bled over a downed tree and made a flying leap at the
fleeing figure of Tolbert Early.

The men went down in a flurry of arms and legs.

"I got you now, you rotten piece of filth." Cooper
slammed a fist into Early's jaw and enjoyed the pleasure he felt. This had been a long time coming and he
meant to take his time.

He kicked Early's gun into some thick undergrowth. Grabbing his adversary's shirt, he yanked
him to a sitting position. "It's time for you to pay
the piper."

"Go to hell," Tolbert spat.

"Don't have to go. I'm already there." Cooper
looked around for Rebel. No sign of the horse nor
Early's either. Where Rand and Brett went, he
couldn't say. They'd gotten separated when they rode
upon Early and his scraggly group.

They were about fifteen miles from town. Too far
to walk. Breathing hard, he sat down, keeping his gun
pointed at Early. Any sudden move and he'd blast the

man to kingdom come. He'd rest a bit, then see if he could locate the horses.

With a smirk on his face, Early started to reach inside the dirty jacket he wore.

"Keep your hands where I can see them," Cooper ordered.

"Cain't a man have a smoke?"

"Not until I get you to the jailhouse." He didn't trust this wily devil as far as he could throw him.

Early laughed. "Like that'll happen."

"You've always underestimated me. You did when I was fourteen, and nothing's changed."

"You had no call to shoot me!" Hate glittered in Early's black eyes.

"That so? My memory isn't that fuzzy."

"I was just trying to teach that boy a lesson. He had it coming. He stole my gold watch."

"That *boy* is my brother, and he didn't steal a damn thing." A lad Brett had developed a friendship with had lifted the watch, intending to trade it for food. Brett had taken the boy's beating rather than snitch on him. "You're a sorry piece of scum that's not fit to live. So why did you come back now, anyway?"

"To kill you. All three of you. You put me in a living hell. I got this crazy itch and cain't scratch it. I aim to make you know what it's like 'fore I put a bullet in you."

"That a fact? Seems things are working out better than I thought. You'd have gotten off too easy, had you died back then."

"I hope you're keeping an eye on your lady friend," Early said softly.

Ice filled Cooper's veins. Though it was a struggle, he kept calm. "I don't know where you get your information, but I don't have a lady friend."

"I watched you climb into her window. Are you right sure pretty Miss Dandridge is safe?"

Cooper jumped to his feet. Towering over Tolbert Early, he held his Colt to the man's forehead. "One hair gets out of place and there won't be a hole deep enough for your men to hide in."

"You might want to rethink that."

Early's words echoed in Cooper's brain before pain exploded in the back of his head and everything went black.

~

"What kept you?" Early snapped, jumping to his feet.

"We was busy tryin' to outrun Thorne's brothers. Finally shook 'em," a man who answered by the name of Too Tall said.

"What happened to the other four of our band?"

"Don't know. Maybe those fellers captured 'em. What are we gonna do with this one?" He waved his gun toward the man on the ground.

"Well, don't just stand there, shoot him."

Too Tall backed away. "I don't mind shootin' a man in a fair fight. But in cold blood goes against my principles. You can't pay me enough to hang for you."

"You little coward. Hand me your gun and *I'll* kill him."

"Use your own. You ain't gettin' mine."

Livid, Tolbert knelt in the brush where Thorne had kicked his weapon and began pawing the ground.

Pounding horses' hooves interrupted the search. He stood as Thorne's two brothers galloped into the clearing. Leaping onto the back of Too Tall's horse, Early and his cohort lit out.

◦❦◦

Six o'clock found Delta sitting across the table from Clara Sharp. She'd half expected the widow to have second thoughts. But she hadn't, and that thrilled Delta.

"Thank you for coming, Clara. This is wonderful."

Clara placed her napkin in her lap. Her fingers were long and elegant. "I confess, I almost changed my mind. But you're a very intriguing woman, and I wanted to get to know you."

"There's nothing unusual about me. I'm boring."

"I beg to differ. You're very lovely and you've managed to light a fire under this town. How you did it I'll never know."

The waiter came and took their orders.

"I simply fell in love with Battle Creek, and it broke my heart to see the disrepair of the buildings." Delta thought she glimpsed a smile through the widow's black veil.

"But you won the citizens over and made them see your vision. That's quite a feat. You've made a difference in so many lives, my dear."

"It makes me happy to help." Delta's gaze swept the small café. She smiled and nodded to George Lexington, sulking at a corner table. If anyone could get the unhappy man smiling, it would be Clara Sharp. "Do you by chance know Mr. Lexington?"

"We've met. He complimented me on my baking skills. What a lonely, lonely man. I feel sorry for him."

"Me too. But he frustrates me to no end with his refusal to do anything to the hotel. I simply don't know what to do next. I've tried everything."

"Don't be too impatient. Sometimes it takes a while for men to come around." Clara had a beautiful, melodious voice.

"I sure hope so." But Delta was no longer thinking about George Lexington. As usual she found herself wondering where Cooper was and what he was doing. She yearned to see him. Maybe he'd climb up to her bedroom tonight. Her breath quickened. "How long has it been, Clara?"

"Been?"

"Since you've been widowed. Isn't that why you wear the veil?"

"My husband has been gone for a good many years, but that's not why I'm dressing this way. This veil shields me from pitiful stares. You see, I have a hideous scar and can't bear to see the shock on people's faces."

"I'm so sorry. I apologize for prying. Maybe one day you'll have enough confidence to lay it aside."

"I doubt that."

"The people here are very accepting. It wouldn't make any difference to them." They'd certainly accepted Delta.

"Perhaps I might try it one day. You inspire me."

Their food came and Clara satisfied Delta's curiosity about how she would eat. The woman simply slipped her fork under the veil and into her mouth. Same with the glass of milk. Much to Delta's dismay, she didn't get as much as a glimpse of Clara's features. Scar or no scar, something told her Widow Sharp was a beautiful lady.

They finished their meal and stood outside the café. The brilliant sunset cast a purple glow. On impulse, Delta hugged her new friend. "Thank you for spending this time with me."

"It was my pleasure. We'll have to do it again."

Rand rode into town just then, leading another horse with a bound man in the saddle.

"Oh my goodness." Fear wound around Delta's heart. There had evidently been a fight. Where was Cooper?

Clara grasped her arm tightly. "What on earth happened?"

"I don't know, but I'm going to find out."

Both women hurried after Rand, almost beating him to the jail. They pounced on him when he dismounted.

"Where's Cooper?" Delta demanded. "Is he hurt?"

"Are you all right, Mr. Sinclair?" Clara's voice trembled.

"Ladies, let me get this prisoner inside first, and then I'll answer your questions."

Delta gently took Clara's arm and they moved to the side to watch Rand hustle his man into the stone jail. Why the widow trembled so seemed a bit odd, but given how closely she worked with Rand it made sense. After all, Clara made hand pies for the saloon and even did Rand's laundry, Delta had heard. They stood there silently waiting.

At last Rand came out. "Delta, Coop is all right. Early's man bashed him on the head with the butt of his gun and made him see stars. But last I saw, he was his old stubborn self. It'll take more than that to do him in."

"Thank you for the report, Rand. I worry about him out there."

Clara touched his shoulder. "You look tired. Are you all right? They didn't hurt you?"

Rand shook his head. "No, Mrs. Sharp, they didn't hurt me. Wasn't for lack of trying, though. This time we almost had 'em. Next time we will for sure and end this mess. Now, if you'll excuse me, I need to grab a bite of supper and get back out there."

"Be safe and don't take any chances," Clara said softly.

They stood a second watching him head to the café, then hugged and parted ways, with Delta returning to the boardinghouse.

Though she knew most likely Cooper wouldn't visit her room after dark, hope persisted. If only she could see those gray eyes and feel his body next to hers. She'd like to talk to him about Clara Sharp. The mysterious widow had captured her curiosity. And what was the connection with Rand?

She stared out over the town. Her heart sang. Change was already apparent. And no one had killed her over it. Truly a miracle.

Slowly she undressed and slipped into her soft cotton gown with a row of lace around the neck and bottom of the sleeves. Smoothing the folds, she marveled at such luxury. She'd spied it in the mercantile and snatched it up. That she could afford such things now had begun to sink in, though she suspected she'd always be frugal. Fear that her fortune would all go away in a heartbeat made it impossible to get too comfortable.

She'd just turned down the bedcovers when someone frantically pounded on her door. Her blood froze.

Thirty-four

"DELTA, HELP ME!" THE WOMAN'S DESPERATE VOICE sent chills up Delta's spine.

Jerking the door open, Delta gasped. Jenny clutched her stomach. Blood had soaked her clothes and the floor. So much blood. "Oh, dear Lord!"

"The baby." Tears streamed down Jenny's face, almost healed from the beating. "Hogue…"

"Let's get you to bed. It's going to be all right." Delta helped Jenny to her room and noticed the over-turned chair and the quilts on the floor. It appeared a fight of some kind had taken place. But who? Hogue was still in jail. Or was he?

Evidently hearing the door slam back against the wall in her attempt to get Jenny through it, Mabel came running. They tucked her sister, Delta's best friend, into bed. There was no need for words. Words couldn't help now. So they silently went about the business of doing what they could.

"I'll find the doc," Delta said, praying it wasn't too late.

Mabel nodded. "I'll stay with her."

Throwing on the dress and shoes she'd just pulled off, Delta hurried down the street as fast as she could. Luckily Doc Yates was in. She quickly explained the situation and they lost no time returning to the boardinghouse.

After gathering more clean cloths and towels to help stanch the blood flow, the two women waited outside Jenny's door, anxious for the results of the doctor's examination.

Jenny's ashen face and the image of her lying so still and quiet dug into Delta's mind and refused to leave. Her chest ached for the woman who'd been through so much. It wasn't fair. Life had kicked Jenny in the teeth and now it sought to steal her baby also. When would her friend receive peace and live her life free from violence?

At last the door opened. Doc Yates removed his stethoscope and sadly shook his head. "There's no saving it."

"And Jenny?" asked Mabel, wringing her hands.

"I'll do my best. She's hemorrhaging badly and is unconscious." He rifled around in his black bag and took out a jar. "Will you make some tea with this goldenseal? It might help. Then come back inside. Jenny needs both of you."

Mabel took the jar of herbs and disappeared down the stairs. Upon her return, Delta followed her into Jenny's room.

"What else can we do?" A thick lump formed in Delta's throat. She stood by the bed, gripping the iron bedstead tightly. If he told her jumping over the moon would help, that's what she'd try to do.

Doc Yates gathered a small bundle wrapped in a towel. "This little thing needs burying. Jenny would want that. It was a girl."

Tears welled up. This wasn't right. Nothing about this was right. Jenny would never hold her daughter in her arms. Never kiss her cheek. Never sing the child a lullaby.

"I can't," Mabel sobbed. "I just can't."

"I'll take her and arrange for burial." Delta held out her hands and accepted the tiny life that would never be. "I'll make sure everything is proper. May I borrow your kitchen, Mabel?"

Mabel wiped her eyes. "Yes, whatever you need."

Downstairs, Delta unwrapped the babe. Her chest heaved with unshed sobs as she tore off a clean piece of cotton sheet and tenderly folded it around the fragile body. Thank goodness Ben was still at Cooper's ranch and wouldn't have to see this.

After laying the infant in a wicker basket that she lined with soft downy cloth, she put it out of sight should anyone enter while she was gone. Then she hurried to the mercantile to find a box of some sort.

A spring storm blew in, bringing thunder and lightning. Rain soaked her before she reached the darkened store. She pounded on the door until John came to unlock it.

Quickly explaining the situation, she added, "Preferably a box that has a pretty design on it."

"I have just the thing. My heart breaks for Jenny." John went to the back and emerged with a small box that had gold ornate lettering that read God's Child on the top. "I think this will do."

"It's perfect." Delta hugged him tightly. "Thank you. But wherever did you get this?"

"I made the tiny casket for Granny Ketchum, only the baby lived. When yellow fever claimed the boy five years later, the box no longer fit."

"How tragic. The poor dear. She's seen a lot of heartache in her years on earth." Delta glanced at the box. "Will you come to the burial?"

"Absolutely."

Midmorning on the following day, she cradled the box that held the baby inside, standing in the pouring rain over a small hole someone had dug. Seemed the entire town had turned out, even Clara Sharp. Rand and Brett stood stone-faced with heads bowed. Like the rest of the citizens, the two waited quietly until someone started an old hymn.

The biggest surprise of all was seeing Cooper striding toward her, his leather chaps slapping against his long legs. Of course, she knew he'd come if at all possible. Wild horses couldn't have kept him away.

As Delta wept, she felt his arm slide around her waist. Leaning into him, she found the strength she needed.

"Give baby girl to the parson, darlin'," Cooper said.

His words barely registered. Silently she handed the small box to the circuit-riding parson who had ridden into Battle Creek only that morning. The God-fearing man offered up a prayer for the baby girl and for her mother who was so gravely ill. Then he lowered the ornate box into the ground.

"We commit this babe to the ground: earth to earth, ashes to ashes, dust to dust. The Lord bless her and keep her."

One by one all the mourners drifted away, leaving only Delta and Cooper.

"Are you all right?" Cooper's rough voice cut through her grief.

She met his steady gray eyes. "It'll take time. Why, Cooper? Why did this happen? Before Jenny lost consciousness, she murmured Hogue's name. Did he cause it? Isn't he still in jail?"

"Should be. I'll definitely find out. Darlin', I have no answers. I just know that justice will be done." His rumble was as cold and brittle as the stormy day. "Come on, let me get you back to Mabel's. We need to check on Jenny."

"Just a moment." She took some pretty spring flowers from a basket at her feet. Squatting, she placed them on the tiny soggy grave.

～

Cooper helped her to her feet. He'd never been very good at knowing what to say at a time like this, and it was even worse now. Clearly, Delta's heart was breaking. She didn't need him spewing the fury that bubbled inside his chest like a poisonous gas eating away at all that was decent and good.

He ignored the rain dripping off the brim of his hat and drew her close to him. He paused to collect his horse where he'd left the animal at the cemetery gate, then arm in arm they walked to the boardinghouse.

Mabel had stayed behind with Jenny instead of attending the hasty service. Delta bustled about the kitchen, helping to prepare a quick meal. Cooper was glad she had something to occupy her. He climbed the stairs to Jenny's room.

She lay motionless, the rise and fall of her chest barely registering. He sat down and took her hand in his. Somehow, someway, he had to make this up to her.

There was only one way he knew.

He should've done this a long time ago.

Clenching his jaw, he smoothed her hair. "I can't bring back the life you lost, but I swear on all that's holy, I'll exact retribution. I'll make someone pay."

Thirty-five

THE RAIN HAD STOPPED, BUT A CHILL WIND BLEW when Cooper slammed the door to the jail. No sign of Sheriff Strayhorn. All the better. No one to stop him.

He lifted the brass key ring from its usual nail on the wall and opened the door to the row of cells. The hired men Cooper and his brothers had captured from Tolbert Early wore wary expressions.

But his business wasn't with them.

Pausing at Hogue Barclay's cell, Cooper slid the key into the lock and swung the door open. Barefoot and half-dressed, Hogue backed into a corner, his eyes wide with fear.

Cooper didn't say a word. He marched into the stone cell. Grabbing Hogue by his shirt front, he slung him into the narrow walkway.

"You cain't do this. I have rights. Strayhorn will have your hide," Hogue yelled, desperately looking for someone to save him.

"I'll gladly pay the cost, whatever it is, to rid the world of you." Cooper shoved him through the front

door and into a good-sized mud puddle in the street.
He landed face-first.

"Help!" Hogue hollered when he got the mud out
of his mouth.

A crowd of men and women gathered to watch,
but no one interfered. Cooper didn't think they stayed
back because of the ring of men—Rand and Brett and
John Abercrombie—positioned between him and the
group. Public sentiment ran with Jenny. In fact, when
Cooper threw Hogue onto the back of a horse, the
onlookers began to clap.

Cooper and his prisoner rode until dusk cloaked
the hills and valleys. Finally Cooper stopped and
dismounted. He yanked Hogue off the horse and
slammed a fist into his midsection and delivered several to his jaw. Bone crunched under his fist.

"You're going to leave the territory and never
come back."

"Who's gonna make me?" Hogue wiped blood
from his mouth.

"I think you know the answer to that," Cooper
spat back.

"You cain't keep a man from his wife, his family.
I got a right to see 'em. This is all her fault. She's a
willful woman. Wouldn't listen to a damn word I said.
I warned her about bringing another whelp into this
world for me to feed. Had to do something."

"Tell me who you hired to do your dirty work."

"He already left town. Came by the jail after he
finished to let me know."

"I said a name." Cooper drew back his fist again.

"Ezra. Ezra Olden."

"How do you know him?"

"Hitched up with him down in Sonora and we became drinkin' buddies."

"Where can I find him? I'm sure you know."

Hogue shrugged. "You ain't gonna find him. Said he was goin' down to Mexico someplace, where the liquor's cheap and the señoritas free. Said he wouldn't be back."

Cooper pulled his Colt from his holster and pointed it at the man he wanted to send to hell. Before Delta came, he would have. "Start walking. If you ever come back, you'll be taking your life in your hands. I won't be responsible for what I do."

"You won't shoot. You ain't got it in you. An' I ain't walking anyplace. I'm barefoot." The man sidled toward the horse.

Cooper's finger tightened on the trigger and orange flame spat from the barrel.

Hogue grabbed what remained of his bloody ear. "You shot me!"

"I'll put a bullet between your eyes next. Try me if you think I won't. Get away from the horse. Start walking." Hate and anger blazed a hot path through Cooper. It didn't set well that he could do no more for Jenny and her baby girl. But he was hell-bent on stopping the killing that had destroyed his life. At least he could try.

When Hogue had limped no more than a few yards, he turned around.

But Cooper would have none of his stalling. He placed several shots around the man's toes, watching the dirt kick up. "I catch you back here, my brothers and I will use you for target practice. Forget you ever knew Jenny and Ben. You're dead to them."

Once Hogue disappeared from sight, Cooper slid his gun into the holster and climbed into the saddle. Weariness washed over him in waves. He yearned for Delta. Only she could make his soul whole again.

Pounding hooves came from behind. Cooper turned in time to see Sheriff Strayhorn galloping toward him. The lawman didn't appear in the frame of mind to pass the time of day about the weather.

"Where is he?" Strayhorn demanded. "I know you busted Hogue Barclay out of jail."

Cooper thought about denying it, but he didn't want to insult the lawman's intelligence. He had too much respect for him.

"If you're asking if the son of a packsaddle is six feet under, I'll relieve your mind, though I came within a hair of putting him there. You can't tell me he doesn't deserve to be."

Strayhorn relaxed his grip on the reins. "Not saying that at all. After burying Jenny's baby today and knowing the beating most likely contributed to the death, I have no love for Hogue Barclay." The sheriff jerked his hat off and raked his fingers through his hair. "But damn it, Coop, you can't go around busting people out of my jail. You're not the law."

"You going to arrest me?"

"Nope. You didn't kill Hogue, at least. More than half the town would give you a medal for what you did. When I heard the gunshots, I wondered if I'd find Hogue dead."

"He's only minus half of an ear. I think I showed

uncommon restraint." The memory of Hogue holding his bloody ear brought a half smile. "I think he got the message he's not to return to this part of Texas."

"I wouldn't want anyone to know this, but I do like your style, Coop." The hefty sheriff grinned. "Now, what are you gonna do about Tolbert Early?"

"Most of his gang is in your jail. It's only a matter of time until he messes up. I'll be there when he does."

"Folks are jittery, seeing as how he marched right into town and threatened Miss Dandridge."

"Don't think the jackal will try that again. Rand, Brett, and I have kept him on the run. Doubt he's had a decent night's sleep in weeks. And we know he's carrying around one of our bullets in his leg."

"Good strategy. You'd make a good lawman, Coop."

After saying good-bye, Cooper turned toward the Long Odds. He'd get some food in his belly and check on the ranch. Zeke appeared to have things under control, though.

But the main thing on Cooper's mind was Ben. He needed to see how the boy fared without his mama. If homesickness had hit, Cooper didn't know what he'd do. Jenny was too sick to have her energetic son underfoot.

❦

Her body totally exhausted, Delta stretched out on the bed. Though it neared midnight, sleep refused to come. Her battered spirit would not let her rest. She worried for Jenny. The woman had such an uphill battle.

"Jenny needs plenty of rest and lots of love," Doc Yates had said before he finally left a few hours earlier.

Doc hadn't mentioned prayers in his list of helpful things to do, but Delta had certainly been doing a lot of that.

Never far from the surface, tears leaked from the corners of her eyes. She swallowed hard and whispered, "God, please take baby girl in your arms and hold her close. If you've a mind, sing her a lullaby. Tell her what a wonderful, loving woman her mother is. And if it's not too much trouble, tell her how much I wanted to know her. Oh, and if she cries, you might try rocking her. Babies love that."

After her talk with the man upstairs, Delta felt better. She rose and checked in on Jenny. Surprise rippled through her to see Cooper sitting quietly beside the bed. He looked up when she entered. Seeing tears in his eyes brought panic.

"Is Jenny…?" The words barely squeezed past the fear.

"She's sleeping. Woke up when I got here and drifted right back to her dreams." He rose and dragged her to him. "God, how I've missed you."

Delta ran her fingers through his dark hair, drawing comfort from his strength. "We didn't get much of a chance to talk, and you disappeared after baby girl's service."

"Had to take care of something."

"I heard about you busting Hogue out of jail. You didn't…?"

"Nope, he's alive, though I guarantee he'll not be back. I made sure of that. He'll pose no more danger to Jenny."

Mabel opened the door and entered. If she noticed

Delta in Cooper's embrace, she didn't say anything. She had an armload of fresh towels and another cup of the healing tea that they had to spoon slowly into Jenny's mouth. It was painstaking work, but they'd started to see results.

"I need to change my sister's packing," Mabel said. "Why don't you try to get some sleep? I'll stay with her until morning."

❧

They turned to leave when Mabel spoke again. "Cooper, I'll not say a word if you go to Delta's room. She needs you."

Cooper nodded and closed the door. Once inside the room next door, he took Delta's face between his large hands and gently kissed her. His chest swelled with a different kind of need. This was a need to take her pain, to let her know that she wasn't alone.

Taking his time, he undressed her. Only after he'd tucked her naked body between the covers did he remove his clothes. Lying down beside her, he pulled her soft curves against the hard planes of his body and kissed her hair. She began to sob quietly.

"It's all right, darlin', I'm here. Cry your heart out."

"I'm sorry. I can't help it."

"You're exhausted. You've carried a big load on those shoulders of yours." Cooper tenderly wiped her tears.

"This is such a harsh, untamed land. I don't know if I'm cut out for this. What if I move out to my ranch and find it's too much for me? What then?"

"Darlin', it's perfectly all right to have doubts.

Nothing in life is a sure thing. Shoot, uncertainty riddles every day of my life. You simply have to have faith that things will work out for the best and keep plugging along."

"So what chance do I have if you—who happen to be the strongest, most capable man I know—face such struggles?"

He rose up on an elbow. "Here's what I know. You're a deeply determined woman. You're no more able to sit down and give up than to stop breathing."

The smile that formed lightened his worry. "You're right."

Tucking her hair behind her ear, he kissed her temple. "I make you these four promises. You'll never have to walk alone. You'll never be invisible to me. You'll always be my forever woman. And finally, I'll help you blaze the trail only you were meant to travel."

Delta brought his hand to her mouth and kissed each finger. "You're a wise man, Cooper Thorne. I've been trying to think of a name for my ranch and now I have the perfect thing."

"Pray tell, Miss Dandridge."

"The Four Promises."

"I like that."

"Me too." She snuggled against his chest, laying her head on his shoulder. Soon her soft breathing indicated she was asleep.

Cooper smiled and tightened his arm around her, marveling at her boundless spirit. He hadn't known what a special woman she was when he first laid eyes on her that morning here at the boardinghouse. It seemed so long ago. In fact, he couldn't remember not knowing her.

Resting his chin on the top of her head, he murmured, "Sleep well, darlin'. I'll watch over you."

A few hours later, he eased out of the bed and dressed. Being with Delta had renewed his soul and smoothed away the anger that ate away at him after dealing with Hogue.

Now it was time to get back to the business of tracking and capturing Tolbert Early. He needed his life back and it wouldn't be too soon.

Cooper gently kissed her cheek. "One day things will be different," he murmured softly. "That's another promise to you."

She rolled over in her sleep as he tiptoed out the door.

Thirty-six

OVER THE NEXT FEW DAYS, JENNY SLOWLY CAME BACK from the brink of death, though she had yet to get out of bed. Delta spent a lot of time with her. She'd told her about Cooper marching into the jail, throwing Hogue onto the back of a horse and running him out of town. Jenny seemed relieved that she no longer had to live in fear of the man she'd made the mistake of marrying.

On this day, Delta brought a savory bowl of soup and some yarrow tea Doc Yates prescribed.

"You don't have to keep waiting on me," Jenny protested weakly. "I'm sure you must get tired of all this."

"Nonsense." Delta put the tray on Jenny's lap. "I can't think of anything more rewarding than helping a dear friend. You'd do the same for me, if the circumstances were reversed."

"Yes, I would." Jenny lifted the spoon, then laid it down. Big tears swam in her eyes. "I understand you gave my daughter a proper burial. I can't thank you enough."

"She was like my child in a way. Very precious."

"I loved her, you know, even though I never held her in my arms. I wish…"

"I know," Delta said softly. "I do too."

While Jenny ate, Delta updated her on the Women of Vision. "We're getting lots of applications for the school teaching job. Would you feel up to looking them over?"

"I'd love to. It'll make me feel like I'm contributing."

"I'll bring them this afternoon after you take a nap. Doc Yates said lots of naps will aid in your recovery."

She waited for Jenny to finish the soup and took the tray to the kitchen. Then she tackled her chore of finding a place to hold school. She knew eventually she'd build a new schoolhouse and turn it over to the town. But they needed something in the meantime.

As usual, she found herself in the mercantile. John had become like a father, and when she needed someone to talk to, she sought him out.

"If worse comes to worst, you can always hold school in a tent," he said.

"I suppose."

"Then there's the barn at the Richardson place at the edge of town."

"A barn? Would they let us use it?"

"The Richardsons sold their animals and went to visit their son in New England. Expect to be gone for six months."

"That would work," Delta said as excitement grew. "Who would I see to ask about it?"

"Their daughter, Polly Strayhorn."

"The sheriff's wife?"

"One and the same."

"Thank you." Delta kissed his cheek. "You always save the day somehow."

"I'm glad to help. I think if me and Nell had had a daughter, she'd have been exactly like you."

"That's very sweet. By the way, how is Emmylou working out?" Her searching gaze found the young woman working away in the dry goods section of the store. She barely resembled the woman who'd plied her trade inside Miss Sybil's brothel.

"She's a jewel. Smart head on her shoulders."

"I'm glad. I knew there was more to her than what appeared at first glance."

"Emmylou has written her folks. They're coming to visit. She hasn't seen them for five years."

"That's wonderful." Delta said good-bye and went to look at the Richardsons' barn.

It was strong and sturdy, but needed cleaning up. After determining that it would fit the bill nicely, she paid Polly Strayhorn a visit. Though the big sheriff had to be at least fifty, his petite wife was quite a bit younger. Delta put her in her thirties. She was such a warm, inviting woman who had to stretch to reach five feet, with rich reddish-brown hair. The couple made an odd-looking pair.

After discussing the matter of the barn, Polly said she'd love to have the school there and didn't expect any payment.

"Consider it my contribution to the town," Polly insisted. "We've needed a school for a long time. It took you and your Women of Vision to make it happen. Do you have room for one more in your club?"

"Absolutely. You'd be most welcome."

Delta found herself humming as she left. She went
to the boardinghouse, left the schoolteacher applications with Jenny, and donned an old dress. Needing to
do something with her hands, she joined the women
who were painting the newspaper office. With a
paintbrush in hand and determination in her heart, she
busied herself in something constructive that would
benefit everyone who lived in Battle Creek.

While she worked, she thought about her Four
Promises Ranch. She couldn't wait to get out there
and begin living on her land. She'd need lots of help
at first, though. It occurred to her that she could begin
assembling a foreman and ranch hands. She'd only
vowed that she wouldn't go out there until they'd
caught Early.

Where did someone begin to look for qualified
people to run a ranch?

John Abercrombie came from the mercantile to
join her. "Need someone to help paint? Emmylou can
run the store for a few hours."

"I'd love to have you." She handed him a paintbrush.

Thundering hooves pounded behind her. She
turned to see two galloping horses, barely missing
the graves in the middle of the street. Her heart froze
when she saw Rand. Brett rode the other horse.

Blood had stained Rand's shirt a bright crimson.
He slid off his horse, landing in the dirt, as the animal
came to a stop.

A scream rent the air and Delta realized it came
from Widow Sharp. Delta ran to help and she and
Clara arrived at Rand's side at the same time.

Clara lifted his head. "Son, how bad are you injured?"

Son? What was the woman babbling about? Delta tore her petticoat and pressed it tightly to the bullet wound in Rand's chest. He moaned from the pressure she applied.

"I'll never forgive myself if you die," Clara sobbed. In her distress, her veil slipped off.

Delta stared at the woman's perfect features that bore no scars or blemishes. Recognition swept through her.

Clara was *Abigail Winehouse*, the famed opera singer. But what was she to Rand? Nothing made sense. Rand was orphaned, same as Cooper and Brett.

Brett moved the two women aside. Putting Rand over his shoulder, he carried his brother to the doctor's office and pounded the door until Doc opened it.

Clara tried to push inside but Doc Yates stopped her. "Wait out here until I—"

"I'm his mother. I need to be with him."

"You'll only be in the way, ma'am. I'll let you in as soon as I treat his wound," the doctor said kindly.

Rushing forward, Delta took Clara's arm. "He'll be all right. Doc knows his business. Rand is in good hands."

Having heard the part about Clara being Rand's mother, the townsfolk besieged her, everyone shooting questions.

"Where have you been all these years?"

"Rand is an orphan. Did you just leave him in the orphanage and take off?"

"She's Abigail Winehouse," exclaimed another.

With that, the questions flew fast and furious. Delta led the poor woman away from the crush to the quiet parlor at the boardinghouse. They sat on the worn velvet settee.

"You'll be safe here. Can I get you something?"

Clara appeared to be in shock. "No, thank you. I'm sure you have a lot of questions."

"I respect your privacy. If you don't want to talk about it, you don't have to."

"I've made so many mistakes." With a shaky breath, she began. "I was young and foolish. I was determined to do anything to better myself. Such a fierce yearning to become famous, to have people flock to see me, consumed every waking moment. When Rand was five years old, I left to go on a tour of the West. My husband, Jack, stayed behind with our son. Somehow, Jack fell through a patch of ice in the river in a town forty miles away and drowned. I assumed Rand had been with him and died also. It was a year before I got back and people who could've told me what happened had disappeared. I didn't know until I passed through here three years ago that my son was alive. Rand was the one who helped me up when I fell and broke the heel of my shoe. He bore such a striking resemblance to Jack, so I asked his name." Clara paused.

"You knew it was indeed your son," Delta said. "But why didn't you tell him?"

"I didn't want to ruin his life. I got back in the coach and traveled to the next town, where I bought a black veil and came back as Widow Sharp."

"I still don't understand."

"At first I just wanted to watch him and be close by, nothing more. I saw what a good life he'd made. He'd moved on. He didn't need a mother. I saw how close he was to Cooper and Brett. It was too late for me to come back into his life."

"It's never too late for a mother to reunite with her son," Delta said softly.

"I hope he sees it the same way you do."

"Why the veil?"

Clara shrugged. "I knew the citizens of Battle Creek would recognize me and interfere with my plans. It would've created a big problem. So I kept my anonymity."

"Yes, I can see that." Delta studied her beautiful face. "What do I call you now?"

"That depends on Rand. If he turns away from me, I'll leave and it won't make any difference."

"And if he doesn't?"

"I'll simply be Abigail Sinclair. Winehouse was my stage name. Rather fanciful, don't you think?"

Delta leaned to hug her. "I know he'll be proud to claim you."

❧

"You're *who*?" Rand exploded.

Delta watched Abigail shrink inside. She felt sorry for her friend. Nothing hurt worse than rejection. She should know. She took Abigail's hand and squeezed.

"I'm your mother, Abigail Sinclair."

"Exactly what proof do you have?" He slung his words like arrows.

Abigail reached into her reticule and handed him a child's bracelet with the word *Rand* engraved on it.

He studied it for a long minute, then he glanced up. "Why didn't you come after me at the orphanage? Just tell me that."

Through tears and a trembling voice, she told him the reasons why as she'd explained to Delta.

"But why didn't you come to me sooner, after you moved here? For three years, you let me think you were a widow woman who made a living making and selling pies. You could've told me the truth. I'm a reasonable man."

"What right did I have coming into your life at this late stage?"

"Why now? Why not keep quiet?"

"I let it slip out. When I saw you bleeding and barely conscious, the words flew from my mouth. Too many people heard for me to deny it."

Rand lay back and closed his eyes. "This is going to take some getting used to. I'm not sure... It may be too late."

"That's fine. Take your time. If you'd rather I moved on, I won't give you any argument. I'm only asking for a chance."

"We'll see how it goes. Just don't expect too much."

"I love you, Son."

His blue eyes flew open. "I've waited a long time to hear those words."

Delta's lip quivered as she tried to hold her emotions in check. A child would give anything to know they were loved and valued. Dear God, she'd have done anything to hear her father tell her that.

Thirty-seven

BRETT ROSE FROM A CORNER CHAIR. DELTA HADN'T noticed him sitting there. When he left the room, she followed him.

"Wait a minute, Brett. Who shot Rand?"

"Don't know exactly, but I can guess. Shot came from a high ridge." His dark eyes met hers. She admired his quiet strength. The woman who caught him would be a fortunate lady.

"And Cooper? Where is he? Why isn't he with you?"

The youngest brother laid a warm hand on her shoulder. "Don't worry, he's fine. He rode up to that ridge to try to intercept the shooter. I volunteered to bring Rand into town."

"It's dangerous out there. This is the sheriff's job. Cooper is no lawman."

Brett chuckled softly. "Try convincing him of that. I gave up a long time ago."

"He invented the word *stubborn*, all right. We've been dancing around several issues ever since I stepped off the stage. I swear, finding out what he's thinking will take an act of Congress. Lord knows, he's sure not saying."

"Coop has deep feelings for you. I can see it in his words, his body, and especially his heart." Brett's soft words came as a surprise.

"I love him," she whispered. "I can't stop it. But I know he'll never give up his bachelor ways."

"Don't be too sure. One thing I learned a long time ago is to never give up on anything or anyone."

"You're a good man, Brett Liberty. I wish you well."

Delta watched him stroll toward the café, his carriage tall and proud. His wisdom and the way he had of looking into a person's heart were rare gifts. She prayed he'd find someone to love and share his life with.

≈

Daylight faded fast. Cooper squatted next to a stream and filled his canteen while his horse drank his fill.

A bad feeling sat in his gut like a jagged knife.

What it meant, he didn't know. Guessing Early's next move was like trying to rope the wind.

He was bone weary. What he wouldn't give to see Delta. Lying next to her was heaven. If only he could spend the rest of his days waking up in her bed. He couldn't imagine anything he'd rather do, if it were possible.

She was surely ingrained into the fabric of his soul.

It had taken every ounce of strength to keep from saying the words she longed to hear. But giving empty promises wasn't in his nature. If the day ever came where he let himself say the words, they would come directly from his heart.

He went about the task of gathering wood for a fire.

Rand was on his mind. He prayed the wound wasn't too serious. At least Doc would fix him up and he and Brett would rejoin him as soon as they could.

After getting the fire going, he rummaged around for his coffeepot. Camping next to a stream had advantages and soon he had coffee, a fresh fish, and a can of beans. Not too bad.

Lying on the cold ground a little later, his thoughts again turned to Delta.

She'd given the people of Battle Creek something they'd never had—hope. She made them see that anything was possible, that they could achieve so much if they all pulled together. And where on earth had she gotten the idea for a seed library? He'd never even heard of such a thing. He burst with pride. He had one smart lady.

Yes, Delta Dandridge had shown him a good many things.

Made him eat his words too.

He smiled into the darkness, feeling her lips on his, feeling himself slipping into the warmth of her tight sweetness.

And feeling her love wrapping around him.

Delta pushed open the Richardsons' barn door and moved everything they'd need inside. Mabel, Naomi Ratliff, and Violet were among the Women of Vision who accompanied her. Violet's hat, a creation of long drooping plumes and big flowers, made Delta smile. Certainly not the thing to wear to a barn cleaning, but she would take all the help she could get.

Readying the structure enough to hold school in it would be a chore. But the more they worked and raked and swept, what they needed became clear to Delta.

Fresh hay. Lots of it.

Excited, she turned to Violet. "We'll spread a thick layer of fresh hay on this dirt floor. It'll mask the animal odors and make everything smell good. Mr. Fletcher just cut his hay. Maybe he'll donate what we need."

Violet beamed. "Of course, that's just the thing. I'll ride over there and ask him right now."

One by one the women left to go take care of their children and husbands. When Delta looked up, she was alone.

Deep shadows drifted across the structure, bathing it in smoky grays and piercing blacks. Why hadn't she brought a match to light the lantern she found hanging on a nail? Walking to the door, she peered out into the purple haze of growing darkness.

Then she froze.

The wagon she'd borrowed from Rand was gone.

Fear tiptoed up her spine, along with Cooper's warning to stay in town and keep an eye out for Early.

She'd been so wrapped up in making the barn into a school she'd forgotten to take heed. Recalling Early's late visit to the mercantile and how he'd caught her alone increased the icy fear that chilled her through and through.

"Stop that this instant," she admonished herself. She was only a half mile outside of town. She could walk easily.

It would just take a second to go back into the gloomy interior for her shawl, then she'd be on her way.

But things didn't always go according to plan, she found.

Just as she retrieved her shawl from a nail where she'd hung it, a man stepped from a far back corner.

"So we meet again," he said.

The gravelly voice paralyzed her. She wanted to run but her feet wouldn't move. A scream froze in her throat.

Only a handful of people knew where she was.

"I'm not afraid of you, Early," she bluffed. "Cooper will be here any second."

"Nice try. I know he's nowhere near this place."

When he stepped closer, she saw the rope in his hand. In the other, he held that bowie knife.

Run!

Fighting rising panic, Delta sprinted for the open door.

Early threw the rope and caught her around the neck. He pulled the rough hemp tight, choking her.

Struggling to breathe, she sagged to the dirt floor.

Thirty-eight

WHEN DELTA CAME TO, SHE FOUND HERSELF BOUNCING around the bed of a wagon as it moved down the ruts of a road. A wooden crate shared the space with her. Sharp pain tore through her.

Early had bound her ankles to her neck from behind using the length of rope, tightened so that it drew her legs up. He'd also tied her wrists and had crammed a gag soaked with some sort of vile liquid into her mouth. As the wagon came to a stop, she feigned unconsciousness and readied to make her move. She might only have one chance to escape.

From beneath lowered lids, she watched Early remove the crate. The rope cut into her wrists in the struggle to free herself. But no matter that she used all her strength, the knots refused to loosen.

Footsteps crunched on the ground as Early returned. He uttered a loud curse and removed something from beneath the seat.

Delta's stomach tightened with fear so overpowering she could taste it. She didn't know what Early planned, but she knew him capable of anything, even torture and murder.

Please, Cooper, find me.

But he wouldn't know where to start. No one knew.

She rose as far as the ropes allowed and looked around. Early strode into a ramshackle structure.

Who knew what the sinister man had in mind? Whatever it was, it wouldn't be good.

Desperate, Delta began to think. She found that by twisting and turning she could push herself toward the end of the wagon. Once there, she could fall off onto the ground. Hopefully Early wouldn't hear the sound of the thump from inside the old structure. And with any luck it would help loosen the ropes.

Inch by inch she worked herself toward her goal.

Her heart echoed in her ears like pounding hooves.

Then came the falling part. She stilled her fear and braced herself for impact. With one last twist, she propelled herself over the edge. The blow knocked the wind out of her. Bruised and battered, she lay there for a moment, struggling to fill her lungs.

Stifling her whimpers, she assessed her situation. She'd landed in a clump of low vegetation.

But as she tried to regain her momentum, her skirt snagged on a jagged branch of the brush.

Stuck.

Unable to move, she contorted her body this way and that.

The noise couldn't be avoided. She just prayed Early wouldn't hear and come out of the barn.

Please, God, just give me one chance.

Precious seconds ticked by. Knowing she had only a few moments before he detected her, she used all her remaining strength and slung her body sideways. She rolled, ripping the fabric free.

Quickly, she maneuvered herself into a nearby thicket and wriggled into the shielding greenery. Then she set to work on the bindings at her wrists. But without her teeth or an implement of some sort, it seemed hopeless.

Yet she couldn't give up.

Straining and pulling against the rough hemp, she made a bloody mess of her hands.

Still the bindings held fast. Hopelessness washed over her.

Before she could do more, Early stalked to the back of the wagon.

Delta lay perfectly still and held her breath.

The man cursed loudly, kicking the ground. He looked beneath the wagon and then searched the surrounding growth.

"Come out, girlie," he called. "I know you can hear me. I'll find you, make no mistake about that."

Silent tears ran down Delta's face. Prayers that someone would find her before it was too late formed in her heart. She didn't want to die this way.

Please, God, she needed to tell Cooper how much she loved him before the light went out in her eyes.

Early stomped through the dense thicket where Delta hid. Suddenly he reached down and grabbed the rope that cut into her throat. Only she, and God, could hear her silent scream.

"You know better than to hide from me." He yanked her up and dragged her toward the barn. "A little birdie told me you came into some money. Too bad you won't live to spend it."

Delta fought, jerking and thrashing about as much as the rope allowed. If only she could free her feet. Or a hand. Or her mouth. Anything.

But in the end, she could only succumb to his strength and watch in horror as her hell unfolded from Early's evil, twisted mind.

"Won't anyone think to look for you here, girlie." He dropped her to the dirt floor and laughed. "Not Thorne. Not his meddling brothers. Not anybody."

She looked around, trying to discover where she was. Some abandoned farm, judging by the decaying wood.

Every bone cried out.

Beads of sweat formed on her forehead and ran down her face.

Praying she'd meet a swift end, she closed her eyes, accepting her fate.

Moments later, new fear lodged in her throat as she watched him sling a long rope over a rafter. Whimpers of despair penetrated the gag. Her eyes widened when she watched him set the wooden crate on end beneath it.

Oh God, he meant to hang her.

Unable to speak, she resorted to loud grunts of protest. If only he'd remove her gag so she could bargain. She'd give every bit of money she had to her name in exchange for her freedom. She'd gladly part with the windfall.

Everything that money had represented—independence, finally being a woman of substance, doing good for so many people—it meant nothing now.

Early cut the rope binding her legs to her neck and yanked her up onto the narrow box.

Only the arches of her feet found purchase, leaving

her toes and heels hanging off. The whole thing wobbled, threatening to tip over.

"Don't panic an' you'll be all right," Early said. "It's up to Thorne how long you have before your legs give out or you topple the box over."

Delta took a deep breath and forced a calm she didn't feel.

But when Early knotted the noose around her neck and hoisted her up so only the tips of her toes touched the crate, she trembled violently from one end of her body to the other.

Dear God, how would she live through this?

❧

Sleep wouldn't come. Cooper rose. Dousing the fire, he pulled up camp and rode to the only place that gave him peace.

The boardinghouse was dark. He climbed to Delta's window, but she didn't answer the tap on the pane.

Odd that her curtains were open and the shade up. Clearly she wasn't in the room, even though it was after midnight.

Had Jenny's condition worsened?

Panic gripped his throat, blocking the air he needed.

Climbing down, he went around to the back door. Luckily Mabel had forgotten to lock it. Darkness bathed the kitchen.

As quietly as he could, he found the stairs and went up. He opened Jenny's door and looked in. She was asleep in her bed. Tiptoeing down the hall, he rested his hand on the knob of Delta's room and steeled himself for what he might find.

But everything was neat and tidy, not in disarray as he'd pictured in his mind.

It felt as though someone had drenched him with a bucket of icy water. Fear raced along his spine. No time for quiet now. He needed answers and he wasn't going to wait until morning.

Cooper strode down to Mabel's room and knocked.

Mabel opened it and glared. "What are you doing, trying to wake the dead?"

"Delta's missing," he barked.

"What do you mean?"

"Gone. Bed hasn't been slept in. When did you last see her?"

Mabel scratched her forehead. "This afternoon, I guess. I thought it odd that she didn't show up for supper but figured she must've lost track of the time."

"Where was she?"

"At the Richardson place. We worked in the barn, getting it fixed up to hold school for when we get a teacher."

"You didn't leave together?"

"No. I had to come back and fix supper for my boarders."

"Thanks, Mabel." He whirled and thundered down the stairs.

Vaulting into the saddle, he turned the horse toward the Richardson place, riding full-out.

The moonlight cast a pall over the barn, which sat eerily quiet. The door stood wide open. He leaped from Rebel before the animal stopped, and raced inside.

Quickly, he located the lantern and lit it. Bloodstains on a wooden railing brought crushing pain.

Then he saw drag marks in the dirt. His hands curled into a tight fist.

Someone had hurt her.

Delta only wanted to make things better for people and the town she'd adopted.

Now she was at the mercy of a madman.

Thirty-nine

DELTA FOUND OUT HOW UTTERLY TERRIFYING EARLY could be. Though a sliver of moonlight sifted through a crack between one of the boards, it couldn't drive back the demons that pressed so close. She shivered from the cold, and mind-numbing fear gripping her. The deafening silence would surely drive her mad.

The overpowering smell of death suffocated her. Funny that she'd never considered death and fear had a smell. Now she knew with certainty.

And then she heard them.

Rats.

Each time they bumped against the crate, she had to struggle to keep her toes from slipping off. One slip was all it would take.

Desperate for something to take her mind off her impending death, she focused on Cooper, recalling his touch along her bare skin, his kisses, and the sound of the deep timbre of his voice.

She loved him with all her heart and soul, and she believed he loved her too. No one would risk what he

had to be with her if love didn't figure into the equation
somehow. He simply couldn't say the words. And maybe
it was wishful thinking to hold on to hope that he would.

But she wouldn't give up on him.

Everyone except Isaac Daffern had. That rancher
had gazed into the future and had seen what a vital
man Cooper would become.

She pictured herself back in her room lying in his
arms, their legs entangled in the sheets. He'd leave a
trail of kisses down her neck to her breasts, caress her
body, and gently lower himself on top of her when she
could bear no more sweet torment.

What were the four promises he'd made?

Oh yes. *You'll never have to walk alone. You'll never
be invisible to me. You'll always be my forever woman. And
finally, I'll help you blaze the trail only you were meant to travel.*

All of a sudden, she understood clearly that last
promise. She couldn't will him, or anyone, to do
something they weren't supposed to. She had to live
her life and let everyone else live theirs. It all made
sense. What a fool she'd been.

He was a bachelor and she had no right to try to
change him, to bend him to her will.

Like a soft lambswool blanket, she tucked those
promises around her. She wasn't alone. She had
Cooper and his promises. Somehow she felt a little
warmer and less afraid.

❧

Cooper pounded on Strayhorn's door. He didn't care
if it woke everyone in town. Delta needed help and
she needed it now.

Wearing a holster hastily buckled around a night-shirt, the sheriff glared. "What in blue blazes are you doing? Have you gone loco?"

"Sorry to wake you, but this couldn't wait until morning."

Forcing calmness he didn't feel, Cooper explained the situation. "We need everyone we can get to round up and start searching for her."

"Give me five minutes to dress."

"I'm going to roust Rand and Brett. We'll meet you at the jail." He didn't know if Rand would be up to helping or not, but he hoped so.

Few patrons occupied the saloon. Cooper strode to the living quarters above and barged in.

Rand struggled to rise from a chair. A thick bandage encircled his chest. He didn't waste any time with formalities. "What's wrong? How can I help?"

"Depends on your wound."

"Let me worry about that part. Nothing will stop me when there's a life on the line. Want to tell me what happened?"

"Someone has taken Delta. I'm guessing Early." Cooper gave what details he knew. "We need Brett's tracking skill."

"Try down the hall. Decided to spend the night here instead of riding out to his place. Frankly, I think he harbors this secret desire to play nursemaid. Like I need that."

"I'll get him."

"I'll throw on some clothes. I'm coming."

"No, you're staying. You're not up to it."

"Like hell. I'd like to see you keep me from it." Rand stood there with his arms crossed and glared.

"We'll talk about this in a minute." Seething over his brother's stubbornness, Cooper whirled and went down the hall.

Still fully dressed, Brett grabbed his hat, buckled on a gun belt, then the sheath that held the longest-looking knife Cooper had ever seen.

"We'll find her," Brett assured him.

Minutes later, they stood with Rand in the hallway. "Don't have time to argue with you, Rand. Just don't hold us up. We're going to ride hard and fast."

"You won't have to worry about that." Rand glared. "You've never left my ass in the dust before. Won't this time."

After meeting up with the sheriff and his deputy, the men rode back to the Richardsons' barn and searched every inch of it. They discovered Delta's shawl lying on the dirt floor.

"She fought like the dickens," Strayhorn said.

Cooper beamed with pride. His woman was a fighter. She didn't lie down for anyone.

Brett examined the drag marks. "It was one man. Strange how he dragged Delta. Her legs aren't stretched out. The way he pulled them upward, they just about have to be attached to a rope tied around her chest or…"

"Or what?" Cooper snapped.

"Her neck."

Cooper's legs went out from under him and he sank to the ground.

"Don't worry, we'll find her." Brett knelt and rested a hand on Cooper's shoulder. "The wagon ruts are deep."

"Lead the way." He jumped up and strode to his

horse. One thing was clear—Early was a dead man. Didn't matter how long it took. He'd rain fiery hell down on anyone who harmed Delta.

Sheriff Strayhorn and his deputy took turns riding beside Cooper as though they could read his black thoughts and intentions.

Brett dismounted at Fire Creek and walked up and down the bank, scowling at the ground.

Cooper got down and joined him. "What are you thinking?"

"Doesn't make sense for him to cross the creek. And I don't think he did. He's only wanting us to think he did. See how he drove right down to the water?"

"But the ruts on the other side aren't as deep."

"No."

Strayhorn scratched his head. "What's going on?"

"Early had two wagons."

"Or he could've dumped Miss Dandridge in the creek, thereby lightening his load," Strayhorn pointed out.

Cooper stared at the fast-moving water. "No, I can't see that. Knowing Early, he'd want me to watch and not be able to do anything to stop him. Part of this revenge thing."

"I agree," Rand spoke up. "He's all about making us pay. Throwing Delta over without anyone to see would steal his thunder. Brett is right about the two wagons."

"So where did he go from here?" Strayhorn asked.

Brett knelt to brush away some branches. "He turned around here."

The wily devil. Cooper shook his head. Thought

he could trick them by covering his tracks. Many a man used that old ruse.

Through the night, the group painstakingly followed the marks until losing them on a rocky patch of ground. No matter how many times they retraced their steps, they were unable to pick up the trail. At last dawn came. A group of men and women from town caught up to them. Mabel brought warm biscuits and sausages for everyone, which was a welcome sight.

But the fixings to make coffee were even more well received. They promptly built a campfire and soon had hot coffee in hand while Cooper and the men outlined a search plan.

"Thank you all for coming," Cooper said. "With your help, we can cover more ground."

"Delta belongs to us," Mabel said firmly. "Anyone threatens her messes with all of us."

"That's right," John Abercrombie said. "She's like a daughter to me. I won't rest until she's back safe and sound. Just tell me how I can help."

"I figure if we each take a certain section, we can find her a lot sooner. Time is of the essence. I know she's hurt and bleeding." Cooper didn't add that it was cold during the night and she had nothing to keep her warm. He didn't like to think about how scared and cold and hungry she must be.

God help him, if he ever got her back, he'd make some changes.

Holding a cup of coffee in his hand, Rand stood beside him. "She's tough, Coop. Plus, she's one of the smartest women I know."

Cooper met his gaze. "We have to find her before..."

"We will. Have faith."

"I love her, you know. Never told her that." And now he might not ever get another chance.

"She knows. Some things a person just knows."

"I've been too afraid that I wouldn't be a good husband, that I'd be like my father, to tell her the things I need to say from my heart."

"We can't grasp the future while we're still mired down in the past. Turn loose of old hurts and grievances and grab hold of the future with both hands."

"When did you start sounding like a preacher, Rand?"

"Maybe since I found my mother. Or rather, since she found me."

"Where?"

"Battle Creek. Been under my nose the last three years. Widow Sharp is Abigail Winehouse...uh, Sinclair."

"I'm happy for you, brother." Cooper wearily ran a hand across his eyes.

"Not sure how I feel about it yet. The idea will have to grow on me some."

A few minutes later, everyone got back in the saddle and wagons and began scouring the countryside for the woman who meant so much to them all.

If anyone stumbled across her, they were to fire three shots in the air.

Cooper took the section around his ranch that extended all the way to Delta's new property, the Four Promises Ranch. It made sense to him that Early would stay close. The man couldn't torment him if he didn't. He'd want to see the pain in Cooper's face. That would be part of the pleasure Early would take in his dastardly deed.

Not finding anything around the Long Odds, Cooper rode down the lane of the old Zachary place that now belonged to Delta. He took in the thick copse of trees and the rose bushes running the width of the house.

Red. The roses were a beautiful red.

He could picture Delta here. Of course she'd put her own stamp on the place. That went without saying.

And maybe he could see himself here also.

With a lump in his throat, he dismounted. The soft, gentle wind sighed through the tall trees like pure silk caressing a lover's body.

Then came a distinct rustle of leaves.

The hair on his neck rose.

Eyes watched him. Eyes that had no soul. Cold, dead eyes.

Forty

Spinning into action, Cooper drew his Colt and scanned the area. "Come out and show yourself."

Someone tore through the brush; then he heard a galloping horse racing down the road.

He quickly holstered his Colt and leaped into the saddle. It took precious wasted seconds getting the skittish horse to stop crow-hopping and dancing around. By the time he gave chase, the man was a good distance in front of him.

But Rebel was the better animal and began gaining ground.

Faster and faster they flew.

At last he got alongside. Cooper jumped and pulled the rider off. Landing with a jolt on the packed road, he slammed his fist into the other's jaw.

Over and over they rolled, each fighting to get the upper hand. Somewhere in the scuffle, his quarry lost his revolver.

Finally, breathing hard, Cooper sat on the man's chest and stared into familiar features.

Tolbert Early.

"Where is she? Where's Delta Dandridge, you piece of filth?"

His enemy sneered, "You'll never find her."

Drawing his Colt, Cooper fired three shots into the air to let the others know he had Early.

"Why? She did nothing to you."

"I took you for a smarter man than that, Thorne." Early wiped the blood from his mouth. "You care for the sweet Miss Dandridge. Sometimes a man knows greater pain when the one he loves is in danger and he can't help them. I want you to suffer. I want you to know loss like I've known it. I want you to hurt, to slowly die inside. And then when that happens, I want to put you in a grave."

"Keep talking. You might say more than you intend to." Lord knew, he certainly hoped so. When Early squirmed trying to get Cooper off him, Cooper made himself comfortable, pushing his adversary's head farther into the dirt. With the searchers being so scattered, it would take a while for them to get there. Meanwhile, he wasn't going to give Early a chance to escape again.

Minutes ticked by as the sun climbed higher. Buzzards circled overhead as though sensing a feast soon. Finally, galloping riders converged on them from all directions.

Sheriff Strayhorn quickly dismounted. "See you caught the miserable rotten lowlife. Tell you anything?"

"Not yet." Cooper got off Early and yanked him to his feet.

"He will," Brett said softly, easing his knife from its sheath.

Cooper nodded at his youngest brother. "I wouldn't bet against you. You're the best at what you do."

"What have you done with Miss Dandridge?" Strayhorn demanded, jerking the prisoner to him. "Tell me or I'll let the Indian work you over with his knife."

"Ain't scared of no Injun. I worked him over real good years ago."

Rand lunged, sinking his doubled fist into Early's gut. "I wish to God we'd killed you. We meant to. Just sorry it didn't take the first time."

"I have news for you, Early," Brett said in his quiet way. "You didn't break me then, and you never will. You see, I'm stronger than you. Others tried and they also failed."

"Where did you find him, Coop?" Strayhorn asked.

"The old Zachary place that Delta purchased."

"Had to be a reason for him being there." The sheriff tossed Early onto the back of a horse and lashed him to the saddle.

Hope filled Cooper's heart as the group returned to the place where he'd found his hated enemy. Strayhorn yanked Early off the horse and slung him to the ground. While he and Brett questioned the prisoner, Cooper and Rand searched the root cellar, well, house, and barn but came up empty.

Cooper shouted Delta's name over and over, hoping she'd answer.

The voice he longed to hear didn't reply.

"Wild horses cain't drag it out of me, Thorne," Early screamed. "Better be on your toes or she'll die a horrible death. She's waiting for you and you'll never come." His demonic laugh echoed through the valley.

Though anger raged inside, Cooper tamped it down. He couldn't afford to lose his temper. Delta's life depended on it. He stalked to the spawn of Satan, who lounged there on the ground with his stringy gray hair and hate-filled eyes that glittered like lumps of black coal.

The urge to put a bullet in the man's brain almost overpowered Cooper. He'd only felt this level of violence three times in his life, and twice had been with the same man.

"Let her go. Take me. I'm the one you want, not her."

Early raised his shackled hands. "As you can see, I ain't exactly free to do what I want."

"I'll talk to Strayhorn, get him to release you. Just tell us where to find Delta and I'll go with you anywhere, let you take your vengeance out on me."

"You'd do that for her? You know I'll kill you."

The answer required no thought. "I'll gladly give my life for her. Anytime, anywhere."

"Very touching," came Early's surly reply.

"What's your answer?"

"No, I think I like you squirming and wriggling on this hot skillet too much. It's very…enjoyable."

Everything turned red and got very quiet. Cooper drew back and slammed his fist into Early's face. Blood and spittle flew. Strayhorn came to see about his prisoner.

Early spit out a tooth. "You gonna let him do this to a shackled man?"

"I didn't see anything. For all I know, you could've tried to get away and tripped," the barrel-chested sheriff said. "I have as much sympathy for you as you got for Delta Dandridge."

Tolbert Early got to his feet. "She don't hafta die."

"You're the only one who can do something about that," Strayhorn spat back. "Tell us where she is and maybe you won't hang."

With one quick lunge, Early grabbed Strayhorn's gun. Aiming it at Cooper, he fought to get his finger on the trigger.

Cooper raised his hands. "Better kill me now. Or God have mercy on your soul."

A soft whirring sound split the air as Brett's knife pierced the wall of Early's chest and imbedded itself to the hilt.

"No!" Cooper felt all hope ebb from his body. "He's the only one who could've told us where she is. We may never find her in time."

"He would've shot you, Coop," Brett said. Standing next to Cooper, he clasped his shoulder. "I did the only thing I could. We'll keep looking everywhere we can think of. We'll find her. I give my word."

Cooper stared at his brother. Though Early's death made the odds of finding Delta slim to none, it was fitting that Brett should end the man's life. He'd often wondered if Brett had it in him to take a life, and now he knew. The situation had forced the answer.

"I know. Thank you for saving my life."

The rest of the townspeople arrived and everyone fanned out, desperate to find the woman who'd given them a dream and pride and helped them see how much more they could be.

Cooper seemed drawn to the woods at the edge of

the property that bordered the Four Promises. One patch seemed odd. It was covered with a thick layer of tree limbs that someone appeared to have broken off. The leaves had just started to die, so they hadn't been there long.

Cooper gave a strangled cry and knelt. He and Rand frantically tossed limbs this way and that.

Maybe Delta lay below ground somehow.

It fit that Early's twisted mind might devise this sort of torture.

Oh God, would he find her alive or...?

Rand shouted for someone to bring a shovel. Cooper didn't wait. He began clawing the soft ground with his hands, all the while praying that he'd have another chance to tell her he loved her.

Brett raced to them. "No one has a shovel."

He yanked the long knife out that he'd pulled from Early's body and began digging with it. Abercrombie ran with some boards he'd found in the barn.

Cooper dug like a madman. His beloved, the woman who brought peace to his tormented soul, needed him.

He blinked away the tears. He had to save her just as she'd saved him.

At last a wooden box came into view. Opening it, Cooper found nothing more than a length of rope and a sprig of leaves from a wild plum tree.

What the hell? Was it a message of some sort, a clue of what he'd done with her?

He stared at the rope, willing it to speak. Yet the braided hemp offered no answers.

Sagging into the loose dirt, Cooper's despair settled into the depths of his soul like a dark, musty tomb.

He'd lost her.

Dear God, he'd lost the woman he loved.

⁓⁓

Exhaustion and the darkness played havoc with Delta's mind and body.

Then the rats' constant sharp squeaks and their whirring, whispering movements instilled even more terror into her heart. She'd heard of their razor teeth and how they could gnaw off a person's arm.

Each passing minute, the rope tightened around her neck a little more as she began to tire from the prolonged forced position.

Maybe she should end this unending torture.

She had only to step off the crate and it would all be over.

One simple move. That was all.

⁓⁓

Cooper had lost the only person who gave his life meaning. Then strong hands rested on his back and shoulders. He realized his brothers huddled close around him as they had in the orphanage so long ago after Mr. Huxley struck him repeatedly with a rod for standing up for Rand.

"We can't give up. We won't let Early win," Rand said, grim faced. "Let's go back to the start and rethink this."

"I agree." Brett sat cross-legged in the midst of the dead leaves and moist earth. "Tolbert Early never did anything without a reason. The man loved to taunt. To me, this rope says he has Delta tied up somewhere."

"And not too far away." Rand's eyes lit up with hope.

"You might have something," Cooper said slowly. "Early always thought he had more brains than us. Learning his habits over these weeks like we have, we know he would put her right under our very noses."

Brett picked up the rope they'd unearthed. "We've got to find her fast. But where do we look?"

"The ultimate insult would be to stash her somewhere on either the Long Odds or the Wild Horse. Someplace we'd never think to look."

Brett jumped to his feet in a bound. "The Wild Horse. Early said that wild horses couldn't drag it out of him. He left a clue. You have the Long Odds land too difficult to get onto. But I've been out helping you chase the devil for weeks and left my ranch wide open."

"What about the wild plum cutting that was in the box? You don't have any on Wild Horse land as far as I know," Rand pointed out.

"That's true, but there's a whole thicket just off the northeast boundary in a little canyon. I pick wild plums there every season. And, Coop"—Brett got excited—"there's an old structure of some sort that's half-hidden by the thick undergrowth on that section of land. Or there was the last time I rode out that way."

"That's it." They had some direction to go in, some hope. Heavy weight lifted from Cooper's shoulders. He strode to his horse, with his brothers on his heels.

◈

Tears streamed down Delta's face. She never imagined her life would end this way. She had so much left to do. In fact, she'd only begun to find herself and her place in the world.

In just a few short weeks, she'd learned what truly loving someone with all her heart and soul meant.

Cooper's face suddenly swam before her.

His deep voice that never failed to weaken her knees told her not to give up. He was coming. All she had to do was hold on just a bit longer.

New hope brought the strength she needed.

Cooper *would* find her.

He *would* hold her in his arms again.

Riding as though a pack of hungry coyotes chased him, Cooper led the way to Brett's ranch.

It felt right.

He could sense Delta's presence.

When they crossed onto Wild Horse land, Cooper pulled up and let Brett take the lead. Cooper's horse danced around in a circle, wanting to run.

Brett yelled as he went by, "I can't believe I didn't think of this before."

"I'm just glad you did now."

The horses were lathered by the time they reached the canyon. They got off and walked the horses down a faint trail to the bottom. Cooper couldn't see any kind of building and was about to tell Brett he was all wet when he spied a weathered structure through a tangle of vines.

Cooper began running, yelling Delta's name. He ripped away the door and rushed inside, sending huge rats scurrying in every direction.

His breath came out harsh when he saw her suspended.

Better be on your toes or she'll die a horrible death beat like a death drum in his ears.

Bound and gagged, Delta stared down at him, blinking in the dim light. Tears left tracks through the dirt on her face.

He rushed forward. Cooper held her while Brett quickly cut the rope. The minute his brothers had freed her, he swept her up into his arms, hugging her against his chest.

After a moment, he put her down and gently removed the gag from her mouth. Rand threw his jacket around her shoulders. They all had wetness glistening in their eyes.

Not caring who saw, he pressed his lips to her swollen mouth.

She was his lady, his life, his future, and he'd shout it to the world.

"You came," she whispered.

"As soon as I could." The words came out husky as they squeezed past his narrowed throat.

"I prayed that I wouldn't die here alone without your arms around me. I was scared."

"I know, darlin'. I wish I could've made things different. If only I could go back and do everything over."

She pressed her fingers to his mouth. "Hush. We all have things to go through. It's life."

"You're exhausted and need food and a bed, but I have something to say first." Cooper cradled her against him, daring anything or anyone to take her from him.

She feebly stroked his jaw. "You don't have to say it."

"Oh, but I do." He kissed her fingers. "I love you, pretty lady. I think I did from that first moment—just took me a while to know it."

Fresh tears sprang into Delta's eyes and trickled down her cheeks. Cooper knew she hadn't held out much hope for a miracle, and yet she was willing to take him anyway. She was truly a special woman. He wouldn't find another like her if he searched the world over.

Finally he raised the question he thought he'd never get another chance to ask. "Will you have me, Delta Dandridge? Do you think… Will you be my wife?"

"*Always.*"

He tightened his arms around her and tenderly lowered his lips to hers for a long kiss that promised a lifetime of tangled sheets and hot caresses.

Forty-one

A MONTH PASSED, BRINGING GREAT CHANGE AS DELTA slowly recovered from her ordeal. Doc Yates explained that her throat and wrists would forever carry scars from the rope, but no matter. Each morning she woke with thankfulness in her heart.

She'd thrown herself into making the Four Promises her home, determined to put Early and his deranged scheme from her mind.

Her dream of being Cooper's bride would soon come true.

He loved her.

Smoothing her dress, she pushed aside the curtains of her new home and gazed out at the land she'd never thought it possible to see again. She couldn't get enough sunlight. For her, the darkness held suffocation, rats, and nightmares. That first week, Cooper had never left her side.

Though they hadn't made love since his marriage proposal, he'd slept with her fully clothed and held her as though she was the most precious thing to him. He'd wiped her eyes when she cried and murmured soothing words in her ear when the night pressed around, strangling her, trying to pull her back into her hell.

Delta saw the ache that came in Cooper's gray eyes each time he glanced at the red scars that were still raw, especially the one around her neck. She knew he blamed himself and wished she could take his pain. But she couldn't. Time would have to heal both of them.

The month had also brought healing in other areas. Cooper finally told Jenny about her real father and how very much Isaac Daffern had loved her. Jenny cried, then smiled and said she wished she could've known him. Delta was happy for the peace it gave her friend.

Now, she gazed with pride at the ranch that seemed so vital and energized and new. Her Women of Vision and a slew of men from town had dived in and worked like a hive of bees to help her get it fixed up.

Change also came to Battle Creek. In the last week alone, two new businesses had arrived, a gunsmith and a cobbler. Then a real honest-to-goodness man of the cloth had ridden into town and started to build a church. The new schoolteacher, Mr. Peter Callahan, seemed well suited to the community. As Delta looked from her window, counting her blessings, pinching herself at her great fortune, Cooper rode up on Rebel. His gaze met hers. When he grinned, showing his white teeth, her heart fluttered.

My, my, her handsome husband-to-be stole her breath.

She ran out to meet him and flew into his arms the second he reached the porch.

"You're a mighty lucky woman, Miss Dandridge," he growled, holding her tight against him.

"How's that, Mr. Thorne?"

"If it weren't for my deep sense of honor, I'd throw you onto the back of my horse, take you somewhere far, far away, and have my way with you."

Happiness spilled from her heart. She buried her hands in his hair. "Oh, you would, would you?"

"Yes, ma'am." He slanted a kiss on her mouth.

They'd say their *I do*'s in five more days when Judge Hawthorne passed through. Delta had already bought yards of satin and silk, lace, and delicate seed pearls. Mabel, Abigail Sinclair, and Violet had worked night and day sewing the lovely creation. Delta could hardly wait.

"I love you, Cooper. Are you sure you can give up your bachelor ways?"

He tucked an errant lock of hair behind her ear. "I'll do anything to have you, pretty lady. Thank you for not giving up on me even though I'd pretty much given up on myself."

"I knew you'd come around eventually. Took your own sweet time, however."

"No one better knows how to show me the error of my ways, darlin'."

"Just remember that when you bow up your back and dig in your heels like a government mule, dear. Lord in heaven, I do have my hands full. But I wouldn't have it any other way." Delta burrowed into his embrace, reveling in the strength of his arms around her.

"We make a good pair. All I know is the future will be interesting. And exciting. I can't wait to get started."

She tipped her face up to meet his gray stare that

melted her. He began with her eyes, kissing them with reverence before moving to her cheeks and throat and finally her mouth. His kiss seemed to come from somewhere deep inside where the ability to love that he'd locked away all those long years ago lived.

He seemed to be coming alive by degrees, allowing himself to feel things again.

When he let her up for air, she took a step back. She'd put this off too long. "We have things to decide, Cooper."

He sighed. "Such as?"

"Where will we live? Here or the Long Odds?"

"I won't ask you give up this ranch, darlin'. I know how much this land means to you, my Texas mail-order bride."

Outside, busy workers were erecting her crossbar. It had taken two wagons to haul the massive timbers.

"And I don't expect you to live here, away from the Long Odds. You've worried and sweated and given a good deal of blood to keep it. It's a part of you; it's your heart and soul."

"Then what do you propose?"

"Compromise?"

"I love it when you wrinkle your cute nose like that and raise your lovely eyebrows." He tried to pull her to him again, but she took another step back, not wanting to be sweet-talked—that would come later. Her cowboy knew exactly how to put a sleepy, contented smile on her face.

First they had to get some things ironed out. "One day we'll give this to our son or daughter. But for now... What if we split our time between the two ranches? Would that work?"

"Darlin', anything will work if we put our minds to it. I think it's an excellent solution." His eyes sparkled with devilment. "This way, if we have a spat we can go to our separate houses until you come to your senses."

Delta playfully hit him. "Me? So that's already decided? And we absolutely will *not*! We'll work our spats out like any other married couple. By talking and spending lots and lots of time making up."

"I like the making-up part. Are we having a spat now? I want to try out your theory."

She let him tug her against him. Kissing came so easy, and each time his sensual mouth touched hers, her knees lost the ability to hold her up.

As the kiss ended, they stood arm in arm, gazing at the newly raised crossbar that proclaimed the land the Four Promises Ranch.

Cooper's four promises had saved her from the pits of hell. She'd always remember and hold dear each one.

And remind him daily that he needed to add a few more...

Kisses every morning, noon, and night.

And that he'd always call her darlin'.

Please enjoy this excerpt from the forthcoming

TWICE
A TEXAS *Bride*

North Central Texas
Winter 1879

UNDER A GRAY SKY, RAND SINCLAIR'S SWEEPING
glance took in his newly purchased Last Hope Ranch.
The outbuildings, the barn...shoot, even the fences
had a permanent lean like drunken sailors after a year
at sea. He pulled up the collar of his coat against the
biting January wind.

What had he been thinking? What did a former
saloon owner know about ranching anyway?

The only thing he could rightly claim to understand
were the drunks he'd served whiskey to at the Lily of
the West in Battle Creek, Texas, three miles away. A
drunk wanted his whiskey straight from the bottle, his
woman warm and willing, and a soft place to lay his
head. Rand had no idea how to care for the cows he'd
buy come spring. All the beasts seemed to do was eat,
drink, and moo.

Come to think of it...maybe cows and drunks were
more alike than he thought.

Yet despite his reservations, he wanted this ranch more than anything else in the world.

This was his dream.

His chance to prove to himself that he could be the kind of man Isaac Daffern, the rancher who'd raised him and his brothers, had wanted him to be. He *needed* to prove that he measured up, not only in his brothers' eyes, but his own.

If he failed, he would lose everything that mattered.

A door banged. He glanced down the ramshackle porch in the direction of the sound. Must be the wind. Every door on the place needed work, refusing to stay fastened. Tall weeds littered the yard, and the sucker rod of the old windmill groaned and complained with each rise and fall, the sound amplifying the stark emptiness around him. He was unprepared for the overwhelming loneliness of this new life he'd chosen.

Maybe diving into work would help. But not today. Making the ranch fit for living would have to wait for a warmer day.

He swung to go back inside by the fire when he caught a flash of blue disappearing into what must've been an old bunkhouse.

What in God's name?

The tall grasses whispered in the stiff breeze and he heard the unmistakable sound of a door closing. The deliberate softness of that sound raised the hair on the back of his neck. Maybe he wasn't so alone out here after all. He reached for his Colt and stole forward. Between the building's slatted wood, he glimpsed movement.

Rand took a deep breath and yanked open the door. "Whoever's in here had best come out."

Soft scurrying provided no clue.

Maybe he was mistaken and it was a small animal after all.

But no animals he ever knew wore blue.

A poacher? A thief? Most likely someone up to no good.

Cautious, he stepped inside. Thick gloom closed around him and the dank air clogged his throat. Spiderwebs hung from the ceiling like torn gossamer fabric from a dance-hall girl's dress.

And then he caught the faint whiff of some sort of scent. Flowers?

"Anybody here?" Eyes were watching him. He renewed his grip on the Colt, readying for anything. "You're trespassing on private property. Come out. I won't hurt you."

Three more steps, then four. As his eyes adjusted to the dim, he saw two forms huddling in a far corner. When he got closer, a woman leaped to her feet, brandishing a stick that came within a hair of whacking his leg. Surprise rippled through him as he jumped back. He never expected a *woman*. She was shivering either from fear or the icy wind.

"Please, I don't mean you any harm, ma'am. My name's Rand Sinclair and I'm the new owner here." His gaze flicked to the second person, a young boy.

The boy gave a sudden lunge, positioning himself in front of the woman with his arms extended. "Get back, mister. Leave us be. We ain't hurtin' nuthin'."

Rand finally remembered the Colt and slid it back into the holster. "I know, son, but it's dangerous out here. Let's get inside out of this weather.

From the looks of you, I reckon you're cold and tired and hungry."

"We don't need you," the slip of a boy flung at him.

"Maybe not. But seeing as this is my land, like it or not, right now you have me. I have a fire going, and food. I'll share it. You don't have to be afraid."

"We always have to be afraid." The woman lowered the stick, though. "It's the only way to stay alive."

That said it all. Clearly, she had trouble trailing her. He knew all too well what that was like.

"Ma'am, *can* we eat?" the boy asked, his teeth chattering. He seemed to be relaxing his guard too.

Rand said softly, "Think of your son if nothing else. He needs a warm fire and food. He'll get sick. You wouldn't want that. I won't hurt you. Please, I just want to help. I think you'd do the same for me if I were in your shoes. Out here we take care of each other."

She took his measure with a hard stare. After several long seconds, she dropped the makeshift weapon and reached for her son's hand. Rand removed his coat and put it around her shoulders. He held the door, then led them toward the two-story frame house.

As they walked, he viewed their condition out of the corner of his eye. The woman's torn, dirty blue dress. The youngster's grimy face and clothes. Yet the mysterious trespasser carried herself straight and tall like someone who was accustomed to a better life and who took pride in herself.

Inside the warm kitchen, he put three sticks of wood into the cookstove and moved the skillet onto the fire. "I take it you've been traveling a ways. Where are you from?"

"That's not important," the woman replied absently, taking off his coat. She stood, looking around the room several minutes, taking everything in.

With his attention split between trying to watch her and cracking eggs, Rand discovered some had missed the bowl entirely and landed on the counter. He scooped them in with the others then fished out several pieces of broken shell that were swimming amid the whites and yolks.

When he glanced her way again, he found her running her fingers across the faded wallpaper.

The boy sat at the table sniffling, and when he coughed, it came from deep inside. "We didn't steal nuthin', mister."

"No one's saying you did, son. I can see you're not that kind. You have kin around here?" Rand asked the woman.

She didn't answer. She stood lost in thought, staring at two sets of horizontal marks beside the door. Her spine straightened and she sucked in a breath as she touched the penciled-in measurements.

Rand guessed she was remembering something that meant a lot to her. Unexpected memories could certainly jar a person. He wished he could say something to offer comfort, but nothing came to mind.

"I'm not much of a cook," he rambled on. "This is only my second day at it. Surely I'll get better." He gave her an apologetic grin. "How long have you been in that old bunkhouse?"

Her head snapped up. "You're full of questions, mister."

"Sorry. A bad habit. My brothers always say that

I should've been a census taker. I get on their nerves sometime, especially my oldest brother's."

With a sudden swoosh, flames erupted in the skillet.

Before thinking, he grabbed the handle. The minute his hand came in contact with the heated metal, he pulled back with a yell. Searing pain radiated through his hand, every curse word he knew poised on his tongue, wanting to come out.

Only a day and a half and he was already burning down his house.

Quick as a flash, his mystery woman grabbed a flour sack as a mitt and carried the skillet of burning grease to the door where she set it on the ground. Then she came and gently took his hand, dipping it into the pail of cold water he'd carried in that morning. The relief was welcome.

"Thank you. Like I said, I'm a stranger to this." He met her stare and saw compassion in their depths, a far cry from the brittle anger that had been there just minutes ago. She wasn't as hard as she wanted him to believe.

Her dark brown hair shot through with strands of scarlet was warm in the lamplight. But her soft amber eyes, the exact color of whiskey, revealed a deep-seated distrust and a whole lot of grit.

"Do you have some salve by chance?"

"On the shelf above the stove. I never thought I'd need it this quick."

"Sit at the table and I'll doctor your hand."

"You don't have to do that, but I appreciate your offer." He took a chair next to the boy, who had laid his head on his arms. The lad was clearly ill.

Before she went for the salve, she felt the boy's forehead. Her frown told Rand his suspicions were true.

"It would be best if he lies down," he said quietly. "At least until I get you something to eat. You'll find some quilts in front of the fireplace in the parlor."

A gentle shake roused her son. "Come, Toby."

Rand's gaze followed them to the parlor, which was visible through the doorway. Great love for her son shone in the way she tucked a quilt around him, then kissed his cheek. Rand was glad he'd persuaded them to come inside.

Returning, the mother found the ointment and carefully spread it across the red whelp on Rand's palm. He'd never known such a soothing, tender touch. As the owner of a saloon, he'd been touched by lots of women, but this was different. It almost felt like the feathery caress of a whisper. He closed his eyes for a moment, savoring the sensation.

Finally, she put the lid on the salve, tore a strip off the flour sack, and wrapped it around his hand. "There, that should do it."

"I owe you." He gave her a wry smile. "But I'm afraid it'll take me awhile to get you that breakfast I promised."

"You sit here. I'll fix it." She rose and took another skillet from a shelf under the counter.

He watched, amazed at her competence as she put a dollop of butter into the skillet, beat the eggs, cut thick slices of toast, and had it all ready before he knew what was happening. It astounded him how she seemed to know her way around the kitchen. Where he kept the skillets, the butter, the eggs. But he decided that most kitchens were pretty much laid out the same and women instinctively knew where everything was.

"I don't have milk for the boy. Haven't had time to get a milk cow."

Her amber stare met his. "No need to apologize. I can't let him have it anyway. Fever will curdle milk."

"I believe I might've heard that somewhere. Sorry." His gaze drifted to the mound of scrambled eggs on their plates. They sure looked fluffy and light, just like the café in Battle Creek made them. His mouth began to water even though he'd already eaten.

It became even more apparent that she had good breeding a few minutes later. She went to get the boy from the pile of quilts but wouldn't let him eat until they'd both bowed their heads and given thanks.

Toby she'd called him. The lad's fevered eyes lifted to Rand's. "Thank you, sir."

"You're welcome, son." Rand swallowed a hard lump in his throat. The scrappy child reminded him of himself and his two brothers seventeen years ago. They'd had nothing and no one except for each other, were on the run for their lives, forced to trust strangers for survival.

He poured himself a cup of coffee. "I would've made biscuits, only I don't know how. Me and cooking are like two snarling strangers and I'm pretty sure I'm not going to win."

She spoke low. "This is fine. It's filling. More than we had outside. You have no woman?"

"No." And that's the way Rand wanted it. He would live alone the rest of his life. "What's your name, ma'am?"

"It's not important. I deeply appreciate your kindness, but we won't be here long enough to socialize, mister."

"Like I told you, I'm Rand Sinclair, not mister. And a name is always important…to someone."

"Not anyone I know." She sighed. "It's Callie. That's all. Just Callie."

"Glad to meet you, Callie."

"I didn't know anyone lived here." She forked a bite of food into her mouth. "I'm not a poacher."

"I guessed that," Rand said quietly. "You're welcome to stay as long as you want. But it's too cold out there. I can't in good conscience let you go back to that bunkhouse."

Callie's chin raised a notch. "Then we'll move on."

He couldn't let this woman and child risk it out there in the unforgiving Texas winter. His conscience would never forgive him. And he suspected he needed them as much as they needed him. This morning had already proved he might well starve if left on his own.

An idea took root. "Wait a minute and hear me out first. I'm looking to hire a cook for me and a few ranch hands when I bring them on in a few months. I'd love for you to fill the job. If you're willing, I'll furnish room and board in exchange. You'd live off this kitchen." He walked to a door and opened it to show her the small bedroom that had not one single stick of furniture in it. "I know it isn't much, but it's warm."

She lifted an eyebrow. "And you? Where would you sleep?"

"Upstairs. You have nothing to fear from me. This kitchen would be your domain. You alone would rule it. I have some furniture ordered that will be here in a week or so. As I told you outside, I recently bought the place. It'll take time to fix it up and get it looking decent. Frankly, I could use the help."

The boy coughed, the sound rattling from deep inside his thin chest. Concern darkened Callie's eyes. She tenderly smoothed back his hair.

"Winter is supposed to be a bad one," Rand pressed.

"I make no promises about how long Toby and I will stay."

"Agreed."

"And no one can know about us being here."

"Can't promise that. I have two brothers and they'll both be here helping me. The oldest, Cooper Thorne, is now the sheriff in Battle Creek. Brett Liberty is the youngest. I won't lie to them. But I can agree to not tell anyone else."

"You swear?"

"Yes. My word is my bond."

"You're not to ask any questions."

"Understood. Do we have a bargain, Miss Callie?"

The lines in her face relaxed a bit. "Toby and I will stay. Just for a while."

Why it meant so much to help them, Rand couldn't say. Maybe he simply wanted to pay forward Daffern's kindness to him. Yet when he and Callie struck the deal, it seemed to lift the dreariness of the gray gloom that had closed around him.

What had seemed overwhelming before now appeared manageable. He would succeed. He had a strong back and hands that itched to carve out something he could be proud for others to see, even if those "others" were just the pair of strays he'd found.

Rand allowed himself a slight smile for the first time that day. "Excellent. I'll go into town to round up a bed for you and anything else you think we might need."

Though God only knew where he'd get the money. The thought of accepting help from the mother who'd recently come back into his life after twentysome-odd years stuck in his craw. His relationship with her was...well, complicated. He didn't know yet if he could forgive her for leaving him in an orphanage.

Still, the simple fact was, except for putting some money by for repairs and to buy cattle in the spring, he'd thrown everything he'd gotten from the sale of the saloon into this piece of ground. That left his brothers. Cooper and Brett would give him anything he needed. They'd always been there for each other and always would.

Whatever help he had to ask for, he'd make it crystal clear it was only temporary. A loan, not charity.

"We're not used to much," Callie insisted. "Like you, some blankets on the floor will do just fine."

"All the same, I planned to buy more furniture and a cow anyway, so I'm not doing anything special." Or was he? Rand only knew he saw their need and related to their plight. Didn't mean anything. "Meanwhile, look over the supplies I brought. Whatever's missing, I'll get from the mercantile. I'll bring in more wood before I go. Enough to keep you until I get back."

Her curt nod indicated the discussion was over. She

rose, picked up their plates, and carried them to the wash pan.

Rand buttoned his coat and put on his hat and gloves. He intended to bring in some water so she wouldn't have to go out.

The north wind sent a chill through his bones when he stalked to the woodpile he'd cut only yesterday. He'd done that first thing, knowing how fast a person could die during a norther. After he carried in several armloads, he filled a couple of pails with water.

Once he had his new cook and her son taken care of, and her list in his pocket, he hitched his horses to the wagon. It would be a miserable ride into town, but he didn't have much choice. Callie and Toby would have a bed before nightfall.

He didn't know from what or whom they were running. Memories of a woman—a friend from town, Jenny Barclay, whose husband had beaten her within an inch of her life a year ago—swept through his mind. He recalled her dark bruises and the injuries that had laid her up for weeks. He had vowed then that he'd never let that happen to any woman again.

The next bottom-feeder who thought he could thrash his wife and get away with it had better run, because Rand would kill him.

Was Callie married? Seemed likely, since she had a son.

Despite the absence of any visible sign of abuse, he didn't discount that often scars lay buried deep inside where no one could see. He knew more than a little about scars, how they puckered and left whelps long after the wound closed. He sighed, shoving the painful darkness of that particular part of his life back into its hole. With some effort, he corralled his thoughts, bringing them back to Callie.

For sure, something had happened to send her and Toby out in the cold. Though he'd promised not to ask any questions, he cursed his damnable need to know. She aroused a strong curiosity and he probably wouldn't rest until he figured out her story.

Besides, he couldn't effectively protect her if he didn't have any idea what had caused her life to intersect with his on this cold wintry morning.

Rand set his jaw.

No matter what he had to do.

No matter the secret Callie kept.

No matter the circumstances that led her to his door, he'd keep her safe.

He'd stake his life on keeping that promise.

❧

Though Callie Quinn appreciated Rand's kindness more than he knew, she didn't trust him. She couldn't. Too often generosity had invisible strings attached.

He'd show his true colors eventually.

All men did.

They all betrayed. They wounded. They lied.

But for now, she'd take the shelter and food he offered. She had little choice. Toby was sick. Still, she intended to keep her eyes open. At the first sign of Sinclair going back on his word, she'd run. She would never forget the crucial mistake she'd once made. She could never make up for that, but she could make sure she didn't repeat the lack of judgment that had cost her everything.

She swallowed hard, forcing back a sob. Though seven years had passed, the gaping hole was still in her heart. Her hands shook when she smoothed back her hair and forced her thoughts away from that horrible night when her world ended.

As soon as he set out for town, Callie gathered the ingredients to make a mustard plaster. Toby's cough worried her. The boy was sicker than she'd let on to the rancher. But she wouldn't let sickness or disease, not even a thief in the night, take the only good thing in her life.

And God help her, she'd protect him from the man who vowed to snatch him out of her arms and see her dead.

She mixed together the flour, mustard, and water, her glance going to the pile of blankets where he lay in front of the fire. His forehead was burning up as fever raged in his small body.

When she had the concoction ready, she spread it on a clean flour sack and applied the poultice to Toby's chest. Remembering her mother's admonition from too many years ago to count, she watched closely for signs of blistering. After fifteen minutes, she removed the plaster and applied the same to his back. She planned to reapply it through the day.

After covering him with a blanket, she put a hearty soup on to cook, made with a few potatoes, carrots, and onions she found in a little root cellar below the kitchen. Once that was done, she strolled through the house.

Each room brought back memories of the time she'd lived there with her family. The bedrooms upstairs that had belonged to her, her twin sister, and older stepbrother were in great need of care with their peeling wallpaper and warped floors. She moved where a window seat had stood and glanced out the window at the tall tree they'd scaled one night to dance in the moonlight.

They'd felt loved and happy here, giggling and planning for when they grew up.

Turning away, she went down the hall.

The room where her mother died was filled with ghosts. Sadness and gloom hung on to her like gray, clinging spiderwebs, resisting all her efforts to brush them off.

She didn't tarry there. The pain was too great. Returning to the first floor, Callie went around to a hidden closet under the stairs and opened the door. She and Claire had played in there on rainy days. The room had been their own private sanctuary where they could tell each other secrets and promise to spend the rest of their lives together as best friends.

Pulling a gold locket from beneath her bodice, she opened it and gazed at Claire's likeness. This was the only prized possession she'd been able to grab in her hurry to leave.

A sob rose up, strangling her.

Why hadn't she stayed away? She'd known it would be hard.

But she had things to do here before she moved on.

She mustn't forget she had secrets to dig up.

❧

The sky had turned pitch black by the time Rand Sinclair returned. Callie was at the stove sliding a

pan of corn bread into the oven when the back
door opened.

The tall rancher filled the small kitchen even
before he stepped inside. His windburned cheeks
told of his misery. Guilt washed over her. If not for
her and Toby, he wouldn't have faced that long ride
to town.

When he removed his hat, his startling eyes—so clear
and bluer than a wild Texas sky—stole her breath.

"You must be frozen," she said, hurriedly pouring
a cup of hot coffee she'd made earlier.

"Smells good in here." He removed his coat and
gloves and hung his hat on a hook by the door. He
took the cup she handed him and curled his fingers
around it as though desperate for the warmth.

"I made soup. Let it simmer all day. Nothing fancy."

"It'll hit the spot." He sniffed the air. "Was that
corn bread you just put in the oven?"

"Yes, I hope you don't mind."

"What a crazy question. I'd kill for a slice of hot
corn bread." He sat down at the table. "Like I told
you, I don't know how to do much more than boil
water. Do you know how to make biscuits?"

Callie allowed a slight smile. He sounded like a
wistful little boy, afraid to ask for too many favors. "I
do. We'll have some for breakfast."

A wide grin covered his face. "You don't know
how much I'm looking forward to morning."

"It'll come soon enough."

He took a sip of coffee. "How long until supper?
I need to unload the wagon and put my horses in the
barn as soon as possible."

"Probably twenty minutes or so. I'll help you and it'll go faster."

"I appreciate the offer, but it's too cold for you out there." He emptied his cup and set it down, then got his coat, hat, and gloves. "Better get to it. The prospect of hot corn bread will make me hurry."

She watched him go back outside, shivering from a sudden onslaught of frigid air that swept in through the open door. No one had cared about her in such a long time. Maybe, just maybe, he was an honorable man and truly what he seemed.

Was it possible?

He came back a few minutes later with packages and bundles teetering precariously in his arms. She flew to take some from him.

"I may need a little help getting the mattress inside if you don't mind." He laid the packages down on the floor.

"I'll be happy to."

"You stay inside. Keep the door shut until I bang on it. Don't want to lose all this wonderful heat."

Over the next twenty minutes, she assisted, taking some of the load after he got the bedstead and mattress to the door. By then, the corn bread was done, golden and delicious. She set it in the warming oven while he took the horse to the barn.

Checking on Toby, she was relieved to find his fever had broken.

"I'm hungry, ma'am."

"I have some nice hot soup for supper. Do you think you can wait for Mr. Sinclair to come back in?"

He nodded. She smoothed back his sweat-drenched

hair, giving thanks for the improvement. Overcome with emotion, she kissed his cheek. "I love you, little man. We're going to be all right. I'll make sure of it. I'm going to keep you safe."

"Love you too," he said quietly.

When Rand returned from the barn, she had the table set and the pot of soup and the corn bread sitting in the middle.

"Horses are cared for, and now I can hardly wait for supper." He removed his outerwear and blew on his hands to warm them, taking the fresh cup of coffee she offered.

"We can spare a few minutes for you to thaw out by the fire. We don't have to eat right this instant."

"Oh no you don't, lady," he growled. "I'll not take a chance on eating cold corn bread. I'll warm up when that home cooking hits my belly. Won't talk me out of that pleasure."

Callie called Toby and they all took their places. She'd barely said "Amen" before Rand dove in. She watched in amusement, wondering at his enormous appetite. You'd think he hadn't eaten in a month of Sundays.

With the rancher occupied, her gaze wandered over his hair, which was the color of worn saddle leather. The light brought out golden glints that danced amongst the brown strands touching his collar. Dark stubble on his jaw lent toughness to his handsome face. The long fingers lifting a slice of corn bread to his generous mouth appeared far more suited to a banker or lawyer.

Like it or not, she was curious about him.

As though sensing the direction of her thoughts, he leveled his vivid blue eyes on her. Her mouth dried. To hide her discomfort, she quickly turned to Toby. "Do you like the soup?"

"Yes, ma'am. It's good."

"More corn bread, young man?" Rand asked.

"No, sir."

"You're still looking kinda peaked."

"He's better," Callie said. "I kept a mustard plaster on him all day. It helped break his fever. He's not coughing as much. I'm sure tomorrow will see more improvement."

"Thank goodness I found you when I did, even though you were ready to break both my legs with that big stick."

"You scared me." She felt heat creeping into her face. "You looked eight feet tall standing there with your gun drawn. What did you expect?"

"Thought it was poachers. The Colt was a precaution. Never thought I'd find you and Toby in the shadows."

Callie laid down her spoon. "I'm grateful for this warm house and hot food. I'll try not to make you regret taking us in. Toby and I will stay out of your way."

"Now hold on a minute. My house is yours and you'll consider it that way. You're doing this old bachelor a huge favor. Most likely I'd have died from starvation if you hadn't taken pity on me."

The sincerity of his words wrapped around her. She could almost let hope into her heart. But that would be dangerous. Nibbling on her corn bread, she turned to the question she'd been dying to ask.

"What did you do before you bought this parcel of land, Mr. Sinclair?"

"Owned a saloon in Battle Creek. The Lily of the West."

Laughter quickly rose, refusing to let her squash it. "You were a saloon owner? You never operated a ranch before, have you?"

A wry grin flirted along the corners of his mouth. "Sounds ridiculous, doesn't it?"

"Pretty strange. So you don't know anything about cows?"

"Not much, although I used to live on a ranch when I was a boy." He slathered butter on another piece of corn bread and took a big bite. "Figure my brothers can teach me what I don't know." Rand explained that his brothers Cooper and Brett were in the ranching business and that the best rancher ever born raised them. "What about you? Where did you live?"

Icy panic brought a chill to the warm room. Callie drew herself up. "You agreed that you wouldn't ask any questions. Not even a day has passed and you're going back on your word."

"Let me get this straight. You can ask me anything you want, but I'm not allowed to find out even the most basic things about my new cook?"

"It'll be this way, or we'll head out the door."

Rand gave a heavy sigh. "All right, I apologize, Callie. Didn't mean to pry. Just wanted to get to know you a little. I promise to watch it from now on."

Toby pushed back his bowl and asked to be excused. Callie's gaze followed him as he headed back to the pile of blankets.

"I accept your apology. This time. But I meant what I said." She rose and collected her and Toby's bowls. Then to dispel the tension, she said, "If you brought apples from the mercantile, I'll make a pie tomorrow."

"I certainly did. A pie would be most welcome."

Refusing to let her take his bowl, Rand rose and carried it to the wash pan himself. Callie watched him refill his coffee cup and return to his seat, stretching out his long legs in front of him. It was clear that this bachelor was accustomed to doing things himself. He didn't expect her to wait on him. She found that a relief as she set about washing the dishes.

"I'll finish this coffee then set up the bed, but first— I brought you and the boy some things from town. Open the packages, Callie."

When she turned, she found herself staring into his blue eyes. "We don't need—"

"You darn well do, and I won't hear you arguing about it. Now, let those dishes go and find out what's in these packages. I'll help you with them later."

The man was awful bossy. She was about to tell him what he could do with those packages when the sight of Toby lying listless in front of the stone fireplace stopped her. To survive the winter, the child needed a coat and warm clothes. Maybe that's what Rand had brought from town. She couldn't refuse those no matter how much she wanted to.

Drying her hands on the flour sack that she'd made into a dish towel, she sat on the floor and tore off the brown paper wrapping on one of the packages. The fleece-lined coat for Toby made her breath catch in her throat. An answered prayer.

Sudden memories of her mother popped into her head. Before her death, Nora Quinn regularly bought and took things to the needy in town. One year in particular, she purchased the most beautiful coat for a little girl who had next to nothing. It had a white fur collar and a muff. Callie, eight at the time, desperately wanted that coat. She'd caught her mother not looking and hid it in her room. A day or two later, she overheard her mother talking about how the sheriff had found the girl half-frozen. She never forgot the painful stillness that came over her. She'd raced upstairs and retrieved the coat, and from then on, she never begrudged anyone the help they needed. For years she always added the girl to her nightly prayers and asked for forgiveness.

Now as she clutched the new coat, she thanked her mother's ghost and the saloon-owner-turned-rancher for looking out for Toby when she couldn't.

Rand had also bought a soft wool dress in a pretty shade of nutmeg for her, and a coat as well. She unwrapped a woman's warm flannel nightgown, then shirts, pants, gloves, and a knit cap for Toby. Rand had even thought to add two bars of fragrant soap. The last package held a comb, brush, and mirror.

A pile of quilts, sheets, and pillows lay in a neat stack. Rand's generosity brought tears to her eyes. She thought of the miserable nights she and Toby had spent in the elements, too cold to sleep. This was a far cry from that.

Maybe, for such generosity of spirit, she could possibly endure a very bossy man with beautiful eyes.

"Thank you," she whispered.

"Just glad to help. Probably didn't get everything you needed. Never bought things for a lady before." A curious light came into his eyes as he shifted his feet and crossed them at the ankles. "But hopefully I got enough to get you by for now."

"That and more, Mr. Sinclair."

He quickly held up his hand to stop her. "My name is not mister. Thought we cleared that up at the start. My rule. I'm Rand. Got it?"

"Yes. This must've cost a fortune. I'll repay what you spent as soon as I'm able."

"Don't want paid back," he growled. "Your thanks are more than enough."

"Very well. You have my thanks." But no matter what he said, she wasn't through with the subject. She would find a way to repay him. One way or another.

"You're welcome."

"I need to put more salve on your burn."

"My hand is fine. Not much pain."

Callie took his good hand and led him to the table. "All the same, I'm putting more ointment on the burn," she said firmly.

"I know better than argue with a determined woman."

"Good." She got the tin of thick balm and dabbed it onto the palm of his hand. It had already taken away much of the redness, though she knew it had to hurt.

Afterward, he tried to help her in the kitchen, but his fumbling presence only lengthened the task. Finally, she nudged him toward the bed he still had to set up in the room off the kitchen where she and Toby would sleep. He took the hint at last and disappeared.

In the midst of the quiet that followed came a

horrendous crash. Looking in, she saw the iron bedstead laying over on the floor and Rand struggling to
right it. He stood in the middle of a tangle of metal,
muttering a string of cuss words and trying his best to
keep her and Toby from hearing the colorful language.
Callie covered her mouth to smother the laughter.

His care to keep from being heard touched her.
His show of respect raised her opinion of him several notches.

Quickly she moved to offer her services. She
held the headboard while he attached the rails, then
switched to the foot and did the same. With that
secure, she handed him lengths of rope and watched
him knot them back and forth across the open space.
This would serve as a base for the unwieldy feather
mattress. At last, she took one end and he the other
and lifted the thick mattress into place.

A little later, surprise rippled over her when he
threw a rag rug onto the floor beside the made-up bed
onto which they'd spread quilts. "To keep your feet
from getting too cold. Keep this door open to draw
heat from the stove. I'll make sure it stays lit."

"Rand, you're a good man." Gathering tears that
she refused to let fall blurred his face. "Keep your
bed where it is by the fireplace in the parlor. It's too
frigid upstairs."

His breathtaking blue eyes widened with surprise.
He was silent for the space of a heartbeat, then cleared
his throat. When he spoke, his voice was raspy. "As
you wish."

Outlaw Hearts

The beloved classic, marvelously reissued

by Rosanne Bittner

USA Today bestselling author

~~~

At twenty, Miranda Hayes has been widowed by the Civil War and orphaned by a vicious band of rebel raiders. Alone on the harsh, unyielding frontier, Miranda is surprised to run into the notorious gunslinger Jake Harkner, a hard-hearted loner with a price on his head. Suddenly Miranda finds within herself a deep well of courage…and powerful feelings of desire she's never known.

Hunted by lawmen and haunted by his brutal past, Jake has spent a lifetime on the dusty trail and on the run…until he meets a vibrant, honey-haired beauty who is determined to change his violent ways. But does she love him enough to risk her life to be his woman—an outlaw's woman?

~~~

Praise for Rosanne Bittner:

"Bittner has a knack for writing strong, believable characters who truly seem to jump off the pages." —*Historical Novel Review*

"Fans of such authors as Jodi Thomas and Georgina Gentry will enjoy Bittner's thrilling tale." —*Booklist Online*

For more Rosanne Bittner, visit:

www.sourcebooks.com

Do Not Forsake Me

The much-anticipated sequel to *Outlaw Hearts*

by Rosanne Bittner

USA Today bestselling author

~~~

1890, Oklahoma Territory

Jake Harkner spent the first thirty years of his life as a notorious outlaw, until the love of Miranda changed his ways. Now Jake's grown son, Lloyd, rides with his father as a Deputy U.S. Marshal.

Still reeling from the death of his wife, Lloyd seeks fulfillment in work and doesn't pay enough attention to his young son until tragedy strikes again in the form of vengeful outlaws. Now it's up to Jake and Lloyd to scour the West for the missing boy, with the help of a young Cheyenne woman, Dancing Wind, whose unexpected kindness promises to make Lloyd's heart whole once more.

~~~

Praise for Rosanne Bittner:

"Bittner sweeps readers away to the days of early Western romance." —*RT Book Reviews*

"Ms. Bittner has a way of bringing the pages and characters to life..." —*Romancing the Book*

For more Rosanne Bittner, visit:

www.sourcebooks.com

To Love and to Cherish

A Cactus Creek Cowboys Novel

by Leigh Greenwood

USA Today bestselling author

━◆◆◆━

Torn between a desire to be free…

When Laurie Spencer said "I do," she just traded one pair of shackles for another—until her husband's death leaves her with an opportunity to escape her controlling family. Determined to be independent, Laurie approaches sexy rancher Jared Smith with an offer she hopes he can't refuse…

Jared's determined to make it in Texas, but with the local banker turned against him, his dream may be slipping through his fingers. When Laurie offers a partnership, it looks like his luck may be changing…but when she throws herself in the deal, Jared's not sure he'll be able to respect the terms of their agreement and keep his hands to himself.

There's something about Laurie that awakens every protective instinct Jared has…and when all hell breaks loose, there's nothing and no one who'll be able to keep this cowboy from her side.

━◆◆◆━

"Greenwood is a master at Westerns!" —*RT Book Reviews*

For more Leigh Greenwood, visit:

www.sourcebooks.com

About the Author

Linda Broday resides in the panhandle of Texas on the Llano Estacado. At a young age, she discovered a love for storytelling, history, and anything pertaining to the Old West. There's something about Stetsons, boots, and tall rugged cowboys that get her fired up! A *New York Times* and *USA Today* bestselling author, Linda has won many awards, including the prestigious National Readers' Choice Award. Visit her at www.LindaBroday.com and on Facebook and Twitter. She loves to hear from readers.